What the critics are saying:

American Beauty

American Beauty is a funny, off the wall romp. Brad is hilarious as a masculine super stud dressed in drag and totally over the top. Kirsty was determined to help him discover his inner-male. I laughed out loud throughout this story. Ms. Ladd has written a great first book. - *Carolyn, A Romance Review*

This story has likable characters, and a great supporting cast that will have you laughing out loud, and some sexy scenes that will have you lowering the air conditioner. - *Dee Gentle, GWN Online Book Reviewer*

Better Than Ice Cream

"Better Than Ice Cream is a side-splitting romance that will make you laugh until you cry. It's also a very erotic tale that will make you wish you had some ice cream just to cool you down..." – *Jennifer Ray, The Road to Romance*

"Better Than Ice Cream is an amusing and refreshing contemporary erotic romance. In this story, Ms. Sparks brings us a delectable and lusty Cajun hero who certainly knows all about seduction..." - *Mireya Orsini, Just Erotic Romance Reveiws*

SWEET & STICKY
An Ellora's Cave Publication, October 2004

Ellora's Cave Publishing, Inc.
PO Box 787
Hudson, OH 44236-0787

ISBN #1-4199-5067-3

ISBN MS Reader (LIT) ISBN # 1-84360-640-2
Other available formats (no ISBNs are assigned):
Adobe (PDF), Rocketbook (RB), Mobipocket (PRC) & HTML

ISBN MS Reader (LIT) ISBN # 1-84360-787-5
Other available formats (no ISBNs are assigned):
Adobe (PDF), Rocketbook (RB), Mobipocket (PRC) & HTML

Edited by *BRIANA ST. JAMES*
Cover art by Syneca

SWEET & STICKY

AMERICAN BEAUTY
ASHLEY LADD

BETTER THAN ICE CREAM
ALICIA SPARKS

AMERICAN BEAUTY

Ashley Ladd

Chapter One

Police Lieutenant Brad Mueller paused outside his Captain's door wondering why he was being summoned this time. Captain Crowe was still pissed about how blind he and his partner, Cole Fischer, had been and about how they'd blown the stakeout when they'd *let* a mere wisp of a girl jump a motorcycle over their police car and escape. Because of that, the entire department had been made into a laughing stock by the local media.

"Stop flirting with my secretary, and get your butt in here, Mueller. Leave the poor woman some clothes on." Crowe sounded too cheerful, too devious. He wasn't to be trusted when he sounded so giddy. He wasn't happy unless he was making someone miserable.

That someone was probably him.

Brad winked at the pretty redhead stationed outside Crowe's office and wondered what Machiavellian plan the Captain had in store for him this time and why his partner had been excluded. *Odd.* He and Cole had been a team for several years, and this was the first time they'd been split up.

"Good luck, stud." Crowe's assistant tossed him a saucy grin. She straightened her silky hose showing a long expanse of curvy, seductive leg.

"Today, *stud.*" Crowe hovered in his doorway. A mixture of amusement and annoyance flickered across his black devil eyes.

Brad entered the lair, waiting for the proverbial dragon to strike. He stopped in front of the Captain's cluttered desk and stood at attention.

"I'm sending you on an undercover stakeout, Mueller. You'll start today. You don't have plans for the next month or three, do you?"

Brad thought about the big softball tournament coming up and grimaced. Stakeouts had seemed so exciting in the movies when he was a kid. Now he had to stifle the groan that rose in his throat. But he did an important job that he loved, so he had to take the good with the bad. "What is the mission, sir?"

"We want you to break up a chop shop operation. You can act gay, can't you? You'll need to dress in drag."

"You want me to dress *how*?" Brad shook his head to get the cobwebs out. Maybe he should get his hearing tested. The Ft. Lauderdale criminal element had been using him as target practice a lot lately. Perhaps the ear-shattering gunfire had affected his eardrums more than he'd realized. He certainly couldn't have heard what he thought he'd just heard.

Captain Crowe leaned forward, his hands clasped together, his onyx gaze squinty but unwavering. Early afternoon sun glinted off the shiny, bald spot at the top of his head. He had dressed in another cheap suit that looked as if he had slept in it again, and he loosened his tie as he stretched his squat neck. "You're going undercover and that's final. Get used to it. So you'll dress a little...*flamboyantly* for a few weeks. How hard can it be to pretend to be a gay in Ft. Lauderdale?"

Brad gazed steadily at his captain, refusing to let the man's gaze squirm away. *How hard could it be? If it was so easy, why didn't the captain do it himself?* "Why me?"

The captain dropped his gaze, denoting his power position in this conversation. "Why not you? You're a mechanical whiz, you speak several languages, and you're single. You know every make and model of car ever made. We're trying to break up this car ring and we need someone with your knowledge and expertise." The captain tossed a report at him, the pages fluttering as the report flew through the air.

Brad caught the folder and scanned the small print, his brows pinching together as he read that more than two hundred cars had been stolen in the past year. He whistled under his breath. "We certainly got a problem on our hands." He lifted his gaze and pinned it on his captain. "So why do I have to go that far undercover?"

"Because there's a place for rent next door, but the woman won't rent to a straight guy, and we don't have any female grease monkeys in the precinct." Crowe rubbed his head, polishing it, and rocked back in his squeaky swivel chair.

"Fischer knows more about cars than me. Why not him?" Brad dropped the report on the captain's mahogany desk, scattering papers to the floor. He stuck his hands deep into his pockets, his fingers flexing and unflexing in agitation. He knew his partner wouldn't thank him for the recommendation but he had to know why he was the only one up for the job.

"You kidding? His wife would kill me if I sent him to live with a young single woman." Crowe released a long sigh, his gaze narrowing up at Brad. "Besides, Fischer can't speak a lick of Spanish and your talent with languages just might save your neck on this case. Besides, with your reputation as a lady's man, I need some reassurance you won't blow the case sweet talking your pretty landlady."

"Does this mean I can't have any babes till the case is over?" He didn't know if he could make it more than a couple of weeks without a woman. He hoped the shower at his temporary digs had a plentiful supply of ice-cold water and that it wouldn't give him a heart attack.

"Not till the case is sewn up tight. The sooner you wrap it up, the sooner you can get back to your lady friends." The smug smile on the captain's face told Brad that might just be his main motive in putting this little *condition* on this case.

Brad stared at the window at the shimmering sunshiny day where a particularly tempting duo of breathtaking young ladies strolled by in bikini tops and short shorts on their way to the beach. He wasn't surprised when his slacks suddenly stretched uncomfortably tight across his hips.

The captain followed his gaze and shook his head, a knowing smile playing around his lips. His mustache twitched. "Down boy."

Brad tore his gaze from the luscious view with much effort. It swept across Crowe's trophy cased baseball on its way back to his boss. At least he could play ball. *Couldn't he?* "I can still play softball, can't I?"

Crowe looked away, cleared his throat, and loosened his tie. An unhealthy purplish-red color stole up his neck and into his pudgy cheeks. "Well, uh, that's out, too. At least not on the police league or anywhere near it. But you're pretty well known at the ball fields so you'd best stay away from the game totally. We can't have anyone recognizing you and blowing your cover."

No baseball! This was inhumane! Brad swore under his breath, feeling as if his world had just screeched to an explosive stop. "*No baseball?* I won't do it, sir. Find someone else."

Crowe drummed his fingers on the arm of his chair, and narrowed his eyes at Brad. "I'm not going to argue this with you, Mueller. Do it or hand in your resignation."

Brad swore silently, his gaze dead ahead on his superior. The captain knew he was bucking for a promotion and was a career man. "That's blackmail."

"What am I supposed to do on my off-duty hours?" No women? No baseball? No life?

"I don't know. I'm not your mama. Try reading a book. Go work out at the gym." Crowe hitched up his slacks, crossed to the door, and wagged his finger to someone on the outside. "We're ready."

Ready for what? Brad gazed at the Captain and the open door beside him suspiciously.

A man decked in a royal purple silk leisure suit adorned with epaulets that widened his narrow shoulders waltzed into the office. Long blonde hair flowed down to his waist. None of Brad's lady friends possessed such gorgeous hair or eyelashes.

Brad stood stoic at parade rest, unsure what to make of the man who entered, winked, and blew a kiss his way. "I'm here to save the day, sweetie." The longhaired man tweaked Brad's chin and puckered his lips. "You have such a cute baby face. No wonder all the girls swoon over you, Cupcake, myself included." He pinched Brad on the thigh without warning.

"Don't do that again." Brad backed up and narrowed his gaze at the man, assessing him.

"Mueller meet Mario Sabotini. He and his crew are going to outfit you and give you some tips to help you on your assignment. Give him your total cooperation, hear?" Crowe picked up his baseball and tossed it absently in the air a few times, torturing Brad.

"This is unnecessary, sir, and you know it." Seething, mesmerized by the forbidden ball and all it represented, Brad couldn't take his eyes from the image.

"Lucky boy. I'm going to teach you to strut on the wild side. You just may find you like it." Mario opened the door and clapped his hands. "Chop chop. We don't have all day girlfriends," he said in a singsong voice as he flounced up to Brad again. The tassels on his epaulets danced and twirled in rhythm with his gait. His flaxen locks captured the sun's rays, glistening almost silver.

A troupe of fashion experts paraded into the office wheeling in trunks of clothes, make-up and hair dryers. They turned and examined Brad, shaking their heads. "Our work's cut out for us," Mario said with a hint of annoyance as he approached with a measuring tape that dangled from his fingers.

"Hurry up and get this over with," Brad said, holding out his arms so he could be measured for his new wardrobe. With all this poking, prodding, and fluffing, he felt like a damn mannequin.

Mario ignored him and tossed a dazzling smile at the captain. Pulling up a piece of Brad's hair, he said, "This will look very in if we spike it and dye it white. Of course we'll have to lose the sideburns and shave around the ears." He tapped his chin with French tipped manicured nails. "We'll tweeze those thick brows and pierce his ear, too."

"The only holes I want in my body come from bonafide criminals. No body piercing." That hadn't come out right, but the captain ought to know what he meant. Brad looked down on the much shorter, thinner man. It was a shame all that hair was wasted on a man. He knew women that would kill for such a glorious head of hair.

Unabashed, Mario tossed him a kiss and flipped his hair over his shoulder, still advancing with the needle. "You don't mean that, Cupcake."

"This is the last warning I'm giving you. Get with the program or hand in that resignation. Hear me?" Crowe roared so loudly the windows rattled.

Brad called upon his courage and every thespian cell in his body. Scowling, his Adam's apple worked overtime, and his pulse raced. "I'd better get a dandy review for this, sir."

Crowe marched to the door and paused. "Make him gorgeous." He laughed heartily, shaking his head.

Mario snorted and jutted his chin out. "It'll take more than clothes and make-up to transform him." He shook his head as if that were a crime and he turned to his assistants. "This is going to take some serious overtime."

A snort rose in Brad's throat too fast to bite back. What if he didn't want to be transformed? That was supposed to be an insult?

Mario tsk-tsked and stuck his head out the door. Dust mites danced like magical fairies around the silvery locks that fanned out. "Captain, dearest! He's growling at us again. Are his rabies shots up to date?"

Snickers erupted in the outer room and Brad couldn't wait for this day to end.

Lieutenant Cole Fischer stuck his head around the door and grinned from ear to ear at Brad. "I just heard you're deserting me for a few weeks, pardner."

"Not by my choice." Brad grimaced. "Can you take over as team captain while I'm gone?"

"You're backing out of baseball? They must be sending you to Siberia." Cole shook his head and rubbed his chin as he backed out. "Will do, Buddy. By the way, Haley sends a dinner invite. Let us know when you get back."

Mario's crew advanced on Brad as a mob, combs, hair spray, curling irons, and blow dryers held high in their hands. Mischief danced in Mario's eyes as a boyish dimple popped out on his left cheek.

"If I survive," Brad muttered under his breath, submitting to his sworn duty with as much aplomb as he could muster.

* * * * *

Kirsten Engel frowned when her doorbell chimed the National Anthem. She wasn't expecting anybody. No one had made an appointment to see the room for rent. Her best friends, Gigi and Marshall always barged in the back door. They never rang the bell. Her ex-fiancé Frank hadn't relinquished his key yet and wouldn't ring the bell at a place he still considered half his.

The bell chimed again before she could reach it. "Coming!"

Maybe Frank had sent a moving company to get his things. *Good.* She was about to throw his things in the canal out back if he didn't hurry and get his stuff out of her house. The alligators seemed to be particularly hungry this year. Or maybe she'd have a yard sale and sell his stuff for the money he owed her. He hadn't paid a penny toward the mortgage in months.

Or maybe Alvarez, her spooky neighbor, wanted to borrow something again.

She opened the door cautiously, the chain still attached and straining. Shocked, she almost swallowed her tongue. *Bizarre. What was it?*

A tall muscular man wearing satin, lace, and high heels posed on her doorstep. White blonde hair spiked up and a beauty mark decorated his upper lip. A large golden hoop earring that almost touched his shoulder and a macramé handbag that swung at his side accentuated the outrageous outfit. "I've come to rent the room advertised in the Sun Sentinel."

"Y-you want to rent my spare room?" She unlatched the chain and opened the door wider. Her mind spun dizzily as she let her gaze sweep over the apparition. Her boss was gay, but he'd never worn anything like this costume. At least, not in front of her.

He didn't wait for an invitation, just sashayed in, his heels clicking on her hard wood entryway.

Staggered, she almost choked on her words. "My ad said *strictly females.*"

The blond man, if that's what he was, stuck out his hip and anchored his free, manicured hand on it, chuckling. "Honey, I'm as feminine as a female can get."

If he was feminine, mankind was in danger of extinction. She mourned the future of her race. He was the best physical specimen she'd ever seen. Discounting his clothes and make-up.

"I-I don't know." Her temples throbbed but she resisted the urge to massage them. She didn't have an answer prepared for this possibility. *Why was he trying to complicate her already abysmal life?*

When he fished in his bag and pulled out a baby pink change purse sprayed with seed pearls, she tried not to gape. "I'm prepared to pay cash up front." He withdrew ten crisp, shiny hundred-dollar bills and waved them under her nose.

But then, maybe it wouldn't be so terrible after all?

Intoxicating, newly minted currency mingled with White Shoulders perfume and overpowered her. Or maybe it was the sight of all the lovely green currency that she needed so desperately to save her home. Her mouth watered, her fingers itched to touch it, and her resolve wavered.

Salivating, she tore her gaze away from the money and assessed him again, chewing her lower lip. Polite and pleasant, he didn't act like Jack the Ripper. He was more a mixture of Arnold Schwarzenegger and Boy George, with Boy George tipping the scales. *What a waste. Why couldn't the straight guys she met be half so gorgeous?* "Are you sure you're gay?"

Yikes! Talk about being politically incorrect. She wished she had swallowed her tongue. It'd be better than slow death from embarrassment. "I-I'm so sorry. That didn't come out right. I only meant, I don't have to worry about you coming onto me?" Grimacing, she glanced down at her large body with the curves in all the wrong places. She crossed her arms over her stomach in a delayed attempt to hide her barrel waist. She didn't have to worry about straight men coming onto an elephant like herself so why was she worried about her prospective tenant?

Mischief danced in the sky blue eyes made bluer yet by creamy turquoise eye shadow. He waved the feather boa draped around his neck, at her. "Gayer than a three dollar bill, sweetie. You have absolutely no worries from me. We'll be best girlfriends before the night is out and gossip about men all night."

If there were any straight, available men over twenty-five left. Wasn't the breed extinct? Except for that awful ladies man, Brad Mueller that ordered scads of American Beauty roses from her flower shop, and he was worse, juggling at least a dozen women at any given time.

The scent of all that lovely money tickled her nose. What a gift – but was it from heaven or hell? If she accepted it, would she be selling her soul? She hoped not, but the fear niggled at her mind. Still, the bank wouldn't wait much longer for their money before foreclosing on the house.

Homeless. She shuddered, envisioning herself camping out under the I-95 overpass with killer mosquitoes and alligators. Or worse, she'd have to admit defeat, move home with her parents, and share her old room with her snoring grandmother. *No!* Mr. Feather Boa had to be far preferable to the dismal alternatives.

She stuck out her hand to seal the deal. "You've got yourself a room." Her hand fit perfectly inside, as if they matched. She mourned the loss of such male possibility.

"I'll sweeten the deal. I'll split half the cooking and housework with you." His gaze raked over the paneled walls and white carpet peeking out of the living room.

"How can I refuse such a deal? Done!" *A man willing to do domestic chores?* Frank would rather have died than help her with women's work. What a delicious offer. "We'll give it a try, then, Mr. …"

He shook her hand, his grip limp but warm. "Bradley. Bradley Miller. And you're Kirsten Engel?" His manicured fingers curled around hers sending a lightning bolt up her arm.

She snatched her hand away, hiding her ragged nails beneath her arms, vowing to clip and paint them before night's end. It wouldn't do to let her male roommate display prettier hands than her. Nor did she want to feel thrills or chills for such an off-limits person and couldn't begin to understand how she could. "My friends call me Kirsty."

He grinned, displaying perfect, glistening teeth. "Kirsty, then."

The way he uttered her name, so warm and husky sounded positively decadent and she had to shake herself again for fantasizing over the impossible. He sounded almost flirtatious and she did a doubletake, her stomach clenching. She must be losing it.

He held out the money to her forcing her to drag a hand out for it. She was careful to keep her palm up and her nails hidden. He counted the crisp bills aloud and laid them in her hand. "My things are in my car. Do you mind if I move in now?"

Her thoughts swam. "Now? This minute?" She gulped, puzzled how he could be so ready to move in. She thought she would have a little time to get used to this unexpected complication but apparently not. "You've been homeless?"

"Oh, no, no, no, dear heart." He flung the boa again, tickling her nose with the downy feathers. "I just had a monstrous fight with my ex-boyfriend, Mario. What an absolute bitch!" He sniffled, dabbing at tears with a lacy handkerchief. "He said I have fat thighs." He thrust out his hip and pinched non-existent cellulite. If only her thighs were half so thin she could die happy. "I challenge you to find an ounce of fat on these thighs. He says I binge day and night and night and day and drop disgusting donut crumbs in the bed." He punctuated his plight with a huge pout. "I do *not* drop donut crumbs in bed."

She didn't want to ogle the man's thighs and she definitely didn't want to think about him sharing a bed with this Mario person. She did her best to blank it from her mind and focus instead on saving her home. The money felt like security, warm and solid in her hands. "Do you need help with your stuff?"

"What a lovely offer. That spoiled princess Mario would never lift a finger to help me. He thought he was queen of the world. I don't need him or his honeyed lips. I'll show him I can make it on my own." He flounced through the front door, leaving her to follow.

Her heart ached for Bradley. That Mario person should be horse whipped. A strong urge to bake cookies for him washed over her but then she remembered he was in this mess because of his fat thighs so she put food on the taboo list. What else would lift a gay man's spirits? Shopping? Barbara Streisand music? A new love interest?

Bingo! Marshall would know what to do. Maybe Marshall could even take him out and show him a good time and introduce Bradley to his friends. She'd call him as soon as she returned to the house.

The incessant revving of the engine and tinkering sounds from the adjoining yard made her wince as she made her way down her cobblestone path to her driveway where Bradley's car sat. Alvarez, her next-door neighbor, was in love with his car. With all cars it seemed. He spent all his time fixing his friend's vehicles. What a blessing her house was soundproof or the noise would drive her insane.

"Noisy neighbors?" Bradley turned and stared unabashedly at the semi-open garage door next door.

Kirsty scrunched her nose, shrugged her shoulders, and tucked her hair behind her ear. She prayed it wouldn't scare away her new paying tenant. "He's the neighborhood grease monkey. He's always tinkering with someone's car. Don't worry. He's usually much quieter than this." She squelched an urge to glare at her neighbor and prayed he wouldn't make a liar out of her by being grossly loud today.

Bradley chuckled. "I'll have to introduce myself and see if he'll take a look at my engine. Betty Lou's making a horrid, rattling noise."

She thought he meant someday, maybe even later that evening, but he sashayed across the front lawn between their houses.

"You hoo! Mr. Mechanic. I need a word with you." Bradley flounced across the thin strip of yard that the townhouses shared waving his feather boa around.

A greasy, grimy face peered out from under the garage door. A string of unfriendly rapid-fire Spanish ensued.

The door opened all the way and her burly, swarthy neighbor ventured into the sunlight, grinning, showing off two chipped front teeth and a gold tooth. Sunlight glinted off the ratchet he clutched. Grease streaked his face and hairy arms.

From where she stood, Kirsty noticed that a pegboard filled with hanging tools covered one wall of the garage. Enough car parts to fill an auto shop littered the garage and there were large filing cabinets and a computer tucked in the far corner. Oil stained the concrete floor.

When a Lexus drove into his driveway, her neighbor's expression tightened. Alvarez waved Bradley away and rushed off.

"Nice guy," Bradley said sarcastically, as he fell into step beside her and opened his trunk to reveal two large suitcases and one shoulder bag. He handed her the shoulder bag and carried the larger cases himself.

"So what do you do?" Heat rose in her cheeks and she cleared her throat uneasily looking quickly away from him, pretending to study her other neighbor's new flower bed. "I mean, what is your line of work?"

"I style hair. Have you heard of Chalet Noir?" He warmed to his subject. "I do all the celebrity hair in Miami and all the visiting royalty. Don't tell the press but I did Fergie's hair last time she visited."

"Upstairs and to the right," she directed, following him when he reached the stairwell. The straggly ends of her hair fell across her eyes so she blew at them. She was definitely no Fergie – not even the *before* version. Stubborn locks fell straight down the middle of her face. "*Great!* I could use a good haircut. I'm sick to death of looking like the shaggy dog. Maybe you can make me look human again." If he had his shears with him, maybe he would cut it for her tonight. "Once you get settled in, I'd consider it a huge favor if you'd..."

"Oh, my, my, my. Home, sweet home." Bradley cut her off as he tossed his luggage on the queen size bed in his new room and clapped his hands together in front of his face. "It's absolutely darling." He twirled around, and then opened the closet and dresser drawers. "This will do perfectly." He began stuffing lingerie and frilly feminine things into the drawers.

Embarrassed, Kirsty backed out of his room, averting her gaze. Her hand hovered over the doorknob and she couldn't wait to escape. "I - uh - I need to call my boss and start dinner. Do you like fish?"

Bradley pivoted on his heel, women's thongs in his hands. "I adore salmon and California rolls. I'm not overly fond of trout, however."

She cleared her throat and lowered her eyes, heat scorching her cheeks. "Salmon okay, then?"

He flashed a dazzling smile at her. "Absolutely divine. I'll just finish unpacking and join you in a jiff." He blew a kiss into the air and then unrolled the famous Marilyn Monroe picture where her dress blew up around her face. "You don't mind if I hang this in my boudoir, do you?"

"Not at all." She ordered her eyes not to bug out in her head and to act as if everything was normal. She tried not to stare at his furry Lucite slippers peeking out from beneath the dresser. Fluttering her fingers at him, she mumbled, "Ta ta." She rushed to her bedroom across the hall, locked her door, and rested against it for several moments.

Finally after she caught her breath and calmed her nerves, she called Marshall at home.

"Wanton sex goddess for hire," her boss crooned into the phone. Bee Gees disco music beat in the background.

Kirsty groaned, her heart beating to the disco rhythm. "Give me a break, would ya, Boss Man? It's just me, peon extraordinaire." She bowed low even though he couldn't see her through the telephone wires. Good thing she wasn't hooked up to her webcam. Marshall would strangle her for such impertinence. "Obiwan, I need your help."

"You didn't burn down my store, did you?" Suspicious panic laced Marshall's svelte tones. "All my beautiful babies gone. My life's work. My sole source of income..."

"Don't freak out on me. I'm not calling about the store. I have this new friend who's really depressed because he just broke up with his boyfriend." She wrapped the phone cord around her pinky, darting furtive glances towards Bradley's room. "I thought you might be able to give me some ideas how to cheer him up."

She crossed her fingers. "He's pretty cute and your type and I thought maybe I could fix you up with him. Maybe he's the dream man you've been looking for." Pangs of sadness washed over her but she firmly set them aside. She had absolutely no control over the situation except to keep her own feelings and thoughts in check. The man couldn't help it if he preferred men over women, could he?

"Where is he?" Marshall's voice came out breathy and anxious. "Point me in his direction."

"He's my new roommate. He's setting up his bedroom." She glanced toward Bradley's room, hoping he'd hit it off well with Marshall.

Marshall squealed in her ear. "Don't let tall, dark, and handsome escape. When can I meet him?"

"But he has blond hair..."

"I'll suffer." The phone crashed in her ear.

Chapter Two

Brad awoke with a start when music blared in his ear. He blinked several times at the feather boa draped over the bedpost and the gilt framed painting of Marilyn Monroe. God but he missed his Babe Ruth and Hank Aaron posters, and the eons of baseball card albums enshrined in his real bedroom in his own apartment.

Scratching his crotch, he yawned and then sat up, kicking his covers to the floor in a heap. The itch traveled so he scratched his bare torso as he stood. He needed a shower so he could stand himself much less venture into public. That and a cup of hot black coffee might help him to feel human again.

Raking his fingers through his sleep-mussed hair, he padded to the bathroom on bare feet, clad in a prissy, pink robe he'd found in the suitcase Mario had packed for him.

He ran smack into his landlady as she rounded the bathroom door without warning, her ample breasts spilling out of her black silk nighty. *Boy, did she boast one bodacious set of ta tas.*

Her full breasts felt soft and erotic against his suddenly heated flesh. He found her ample curves alluring. Without thinking, he whistled, long and low. "Wow." He caught her satiny scented shoulders to steady her and then set her away from him and tried to tear his gaze from the provocative vision. But it was nearly impossible; he was hypnotized. The diaphanous material teased him with shadows. Her pouty lips beckoned him to kiss her, drawing him forward. But he stopped when her amazing eyes rounded wide with shock.

His landlady was the Porterhouse Steak of babes. He could bury his face in her chest and get lost for days. His cock throbbed just thinking about anchoring itself in her harbor.

The warm hand squeezed his shoulder jolting him. Her unencumbered breasts grazed his chest, the silk of his dressing gown accentuating the erotic feel rather than masking it. He couldn't take another second of torture without erupting. His inferno was about to explode.

"You okay?" Kirsty's concern almost pushed him over the edge. She was so sweet, he wanted to gobble her up.

He wasn't a randy teen anymore, a walking hormone. He was a thirty-two year-old cop for God's sake. He could control his firearms. He just couldn't control his pistol which was loaded and ready to fire any second. He had to escape the bewitching beauty now before he got busted down to sergeant…or worse.

"Not too good, sweetie. Mrs. Migraine's visiting again. I'm in desperate need of a warm shower. They do wonders to relax me." He held his forehead dramatically, hiding his eyes to mask the passion he knew must be blazing in them.

She grabbed his arm, stretched it across her shoulder, and snaked her arm around his waist. "Maybe you should take a bath instead. You can barely stand up. Here, let me help you."

Man, would he love for her to join him in that tub. Maybe if he explained the situation, she'd keep his secret, and let him stay.

Yeah! Maybe when gators flew.

It was because she didn't want a male roommate that he was in this predicament. And what if she was in on the operation with her slimy neighbor? He couldn't take that chance even if he calculated the chances at a thousand to one.

"No! Don't touch me." *God, he sounded like a harpy.* And he hated shrews. He liked his women soft and sweet like the one driving him crazy right now.

Self-preservation propelled him away from her. He needed anti-Viagra for the rest of his sentence on this mission-from-hell.

He grimaced, hating the idea of being gelded for even a week. Crowe would rue the hour he tried to castrate him. He was created to hunt pussy, not be one.

Kirsty fell back. An adorable blush crept up her generous cleavage and stole into her cheeks. "I-I didn't mean anything sexual by it. I wasn't trying to come onto you. Truly. I mean you don't look at all masculine."

He scowled at her eulogy of his masculinity. His undead cock flexed painfully, wanting to assert and insert itself. He obviously wouldn't be holding a wake for it tonight.

"I know, sugar." The lie threatened to choke him almost as much as the saccharine endearment.

He ushered her into the hall and locked the door behind her.

The freezing water would do a lot for hard-ons. But why be so cruel to himself when some hand action and his vivid imagination could do the job a whole lot better?

Brad stripped, wadded up his shorts, and threw them at his reflection in the mirror. Instead of adjusting the spray to arctic temperatures, he set it to warm. He had two of the three ingredients to make his recipe for a faux lay work. But he hadn't found where the little minx hid the soap. Surely she used it. She smelled spring-garden fresh.

Then a bottle of shower gel jumped out at him, dangling next to a lilac loofa. This had to be a joke. Real men didn't wash with lacy puffs. But they did slam dunk them into the garbage can. *Score one!*

He squirted a blob in his hand and then stroked his burning cock.

He closed his eyes and imagined that Kirsty's hands, not his, pumped harder, frantic now. *Damn!* She wanted him bad inside her tight pussy. All of him.

And he couldn't turn down a lady. Especially not a hot, sultry mama like her. He bet her cunt was wet and hot, too.

He moaned as his dream lover seduced him, pushing him down in the tub, straddling him, and sliding down his raging shaft. She swallowed his entire length and hugged him with her vaginal walls. Not many women could take his full length. But Kirsty was a perfect fit.

Hunger glazed her eyes and she licked her lips. She writhed wantonly, riding him hard till he bucked beneath her.

Her cunt milked him. She rode him harder, faster. Her panting, her beautiful breasts swaying in front of his face, kissing close, urged him on.

His heart slammed against his ribs as his buttocks pounded the enamel. His feverish testicles swelled with his seed. They burned as never before, demanding release.

Fireworks exploded, stealing his breath. After dragging in several big gulps of air, his sanity trickled back. He'd just had some of the best sex of his life and the babe was a damn dream.

The dream banged on the door, rattling the decorative brass butterflies on the wall. "Everything all right in there? You didn't fall, did you? I thought I heard a loud thump."

Make that several loud thumps. His ass would be black and blue. There was a reason man had created soft mattresses. He swore under his breath as he scoured away all trace of his episode. At least he was lucid again, if not necessarily human. And he no longer reeked of his own body oils.

He sniffed and frowned. Instead he reeked of coconut which was only slightly better than the tutti frutti perfume Mario had slapped on him.

"I slipped, but I'll live." Then he added the modifier to protect his cover. "Sweetie."

"Okay. Call if you need me. I'll be in bed."

His cock sprung back to life. *Damn! Shower time again.* The vision of her flung across her sheets, her legs spread wide, her nipples dusky through her transparent teddy tortured him.

He turned the spray back on and enlisted his hand again. He'd have to up his rent to cover her water bill.

* * * * *

A naughty smile dallied on Kirsty's lips. She was teased and perplexed by the tantalizing glimpse of Bradley in the bathroom mirror. His robe had tented with a full-blown erection.

She was puzzled. Had she aroused him? But he didn't like women. And he'd done gymnastics to hide it from her.

Maybe he liked women more than he thought he did.

Tantalized by the wicked thought, her vagina twitched. She punched her pillow and fought it away. What chance would she have even if he started liking women? No man would be attracted to a marshmallow like her. He was the one with the hard abs and buns of steel, not her.

She kicked her covers off and the bed protested, banging against the wall.

She tossed and turned, burrowed into the bed, and dragged the pillow over her head, Bradley's image teased her mind. Finally, the AC whooshed on, cooling her, and she pulled the covers up and snuggled under them. The soft whir lulled her and her breathing slowed. Finally she drifted to sleep and began to dream.

The mattress depressed. Something wet and velvety tickled her ear and she groaned. *It was a tongue!*

It plunged into her ear and swirled around the lobe. Then it delved deeper, swirling around in smaller and smaller circles.

She squirmed against the tongue and gave better access to her breasts, the nipples so hard and pointy, they ached.

Large, warm hands crept around her waist, and tickled the underneath of her breasts.

Teeth nipped her playfully. Then burning lips kissed her neck. Soft, yet firm, they sent shivers racing through her.

She rolled back against an anxious cock. Slick with her mystery lover's juice, it was primed for fucking.

Wildfire shot through her and her cunt throbbed. She wriggled out of her restrictive panties, and kicked them off the bed, freeing her folds. She spread her legs wide.

He rubbed her button with his fingers, knowing exactly how to provide immense pleasure. The vaginal muscles spasmed and her clit hardened to a nub. He inserted one finger, then two, as she strained against his hand.

Her juices flowed like a river, down her legs. He blazed a trail of fiery kisses down her stomach and then ran his tongue along her slit, making her moan. Then he sucked her clitoris gently.

She writhed against his magical lips burrowing her fingers through his thick hair.

He inserted his finger and stroked her. A second finger prodded her, stretching her entry. He sucked her fiercely, her juices coating his lips.

Marvelous sensations rippled through her. She ground her hips harder. She needed him now. "Fuck me!"

Her lover rolled her onto her back. He growled and ripped her teddy off with savage teeth.

Thrilled, she shivered as her breasts spilled out for his heated gaze to ravage. But she wanted more than merely his gaze on her. She wanted him on her, in her, filling her.

He buried his face in her breasts then suckled her nipple, taking it deeply into his mouth. His tongue circled the tight bead, condensing into smaller and smaller circles. He climbed on top of her, and his magnificent cock pressed against her pussy, and he rubbed it up and down.

She skimmed her hand down his back, awed by the power pulsing through him. She wound her fingers around his scorching cock, gliding them along his impressive length.

He shivered and moaned against her breast. His hand kneaded the other one and he pinned her to the bed.

Squeezing his penis, she tugged on it gently, yet firmly. Horny and feverish, she guided his cock to her entrance.

Her labia swollen, her clit screaming, her core aflame, she craved their union. She thrust against his cock, leaving no room for doubt that she wanted him to take her.

He tore his mouth from her breast and dragged in air. "You're a little hellcat."

She growled back, more lioness than cat, and met him thrust for thrust. The headboard slapped the wall as his balls pounded her legs.

Their juices flowed freely, mingling. The musky scent wrapped around them, and seeped into her bed sheets.

He captured her lips and they drank deeply of each other. Starved for air, she broke the kiss, gasping. Her core went into meltdown and she exploded in orgasm.

She thrust her hips against him, wrapped her legs around his waist, and held him prisoner inside her as the dam burst.

He plunged deeply and cradled her in his arms. His heart hammered against hers erratically.

Their come overflowed her cunt and dribbled down her legs.

The rapture subsided, leaving her in bliss. She snuggled against him, his cock still nestled inside her, albeit softening.

A fountain of moonlight pierced the room and alighted her dream lover's face.

Ecstatic, she purred and burrowed more deeply into his arms. She awoke just long enough to bemoan the fact her lovely night had been just a dream. She willed herself back to sleep and tried to slip into the same dream.

* * * * *

The lady uppermost in his thoughts sauntered up behind him as he brushed blush on his cheeks the following morning. Her hands fell lightly onto his shoulders and she pressed against his back, torturing him yet again.

"You know it's fun having you here. I've really missed having someone to talk to." She watched him closely, as if she critiqued his technique, and then she delved into her vanity drawer and withdrew her make-up case. Unzipping it, she fished around in it until she pulled out a long black tube. "Voila!" she said with a smile, handing the tube to him. "You really need some mascara to make those blond lashes of yours stand out. I know. I have the same problem. It's a bitch being so blonde that our lashes are almost invisible, isn't it?"

He took it from her, careful not to touch her, trying to keep the imminent erection at bay. He twisted the make-up open, loathe to admit he had no earthly idea how to stroke his eyelashes without putting out an eye. He turned it over in his hand, examining the demonic creation. How in the devil did women put this gunk on their eyes? Cole and his other buddies at the precinct would bust a gut if they could see him now, unable to figure out how to wield this little twig.

His fingers fumbled with the wand and he stared at it cross-eyed. Why did women put themselves through such torture? He preferred the natural look over the made-up look, so he really couldn't understand it. But Kirsty watched him with a raised brow, so he had to tough it out. His fingers slipped and he smeared it on his cheek instead. He bit back a curse. *Shit, this was more dangerous than a hot pursuit.*

"Tsk tsk." Kirsty made a moue with her lips as she chuckled at his expense. "I thought a master hairstylist would be a master make-up artist, too." She snatched the mascara from his hands and leaned over him, her robe falling open.

His mouth watered. He loved her bazoombas and wished he had the right to see them naked. Was she trying to tempt him? And if so, out of curiosity or lust? Did she want him as he wanted her?

"Here, let me do it for you." She tried to bite back the smile that hovered on her cupid's lips.

Words stuck in his throat so that he couldn't reply when Kirsty played Dr. Frankenstein on him, thrusting her chest in his face, and the mascara wand at his eyes. Brad blinked praying this stuff wouldn't blind him. He wanted to drink in this view forever.

Kirsty straightened up, scowling at him, and waving the black wand in his face. "I can't apply mascara if you squeeze your eyes. If I didn't know better, I'd think this was your first time."

He had to work harder to keep his cover. He opened his eyes so wide he thought they'd pop out of his head. "I won't flinch again." He'd prop his eyes open with toothpicks if he had to or super glue them open. Make-up manufacturers should be hanged. "Make me gorgeous."

"Yoo hoo!" A tall, muscular man with dark hair and glasses waltzed into the bathroom as if he owned it, clapped his hands, and squealed in delight. He plucked the wand from Kirsty's hand and jabbed it at her. "You held out on me, sweetie. He's absolutely adorable." His gaze dropped to Brad's pants. "And what a crowning glory."

Dread filled Brad. The heat drained out of his body and his cock shriveled, trying to hide. He looked from the newcomer to Kirsty noting that she didn't seem to have a qualm about this man invading her bathroom. He wondered what her relationship was with this man and if he could be the infamous Frank. "Move out of the way and let Auntie Marshall do her stuff." Without invitation or warning, the brazen intruder sat on Brad's lap and puckered his lips. "You taken, sugar puff?"

At least he wasn't the ex-fiance, but who and what was he? Before Brad could find his voice, Kirsty spoke up for him, shaking her head vigorously. "No. He just broke up with his lover."

Marshall gazed deeply into Brad's eyes. "You poor thing. You just go ahead and cry on my shoulder. I'm the best listener in the universe, am I not, sunshine?" Marshall tilted Brad's chin up, his finger tickling the sensitive flesh of Brad's throat. "Don't flutter if you don't want a stick in your eye."

Brad cleared his throat, still in shock and mortified that a man flirted with him trying to gain sexual favors. The fighting instinct roiled up and he had to suppress a growl. "Don't you think we should be introduced before you sit on my lap and mascara my lashes?"

Marshall pouted as his eyes shot daggers at Kirsty and he shook his finger at her. "You didn't tell him I was coming, did you, you naughty girl? For that I'm not sharing my flambé with you today." Turning back to Brad, Marshall mascaraed his lashes expertly. "You're even more gorgeous. Now you have to go out and paint the town with me, tonight. There's this great party and my date dumped me, too."

Kirsty looked crestfallen and the twinkle he'd so admired disappeared from her eyes. "Tonight? I was hoping to get to know him."

Brad warmed to her idea, but feared it would be more dangerous than accompanying her friend. Crowe had given strict orders to stay away from her as much as possible. "Tonight sounds great."

"You won't regret it," Marshall said without even glancing at her. "I'll pick you up at eight." Marshall puckered up for a kiss and aimed at Brad's mouth.

This was going too far in the line of duty. Selling his soul wasn't in his contract. Brad jumped to his feet, dumping Marshall on his rear unceremoniously. Sticking out his hand, Brad helped the man up and shook his hand, remembering at the last second to keep his grip weak. "Bradley Miller. And you're Auntie Marshall?"

"Marshall Allen, Kirsty's boss. I own 'Flower Power', home of the most beautiful roses in America."

Brad's eyes widened at the revelation. His phone and email were set on speed dial to Flower Power. He sent all his lady friends roses from Flower Power. Thank God he'd not given Kirsty his real name or she'd recognize it for sure if she'd worked there any amount of time. This assignment grew more volatile by the moment. "I've heard your radio ads. Sounds like a fab place."

Marshall beamed as he rubbed his behind. "Play your cards right, sugar puff, and I'll fill your house with roses."

Kirsty sighed loudly and rolled her eyes heavenward. "Make the date already before I'm late for work. You know how grouchy my mean troll of a boss gets when I'm two seconds late."

Marshall grabbed Kirsty's hand and tugged her out of the room, reaching behind him to pinch Brad's butt when Kirsty couldn't see him. "She's so nice and respectful I don't know how I can stand it." He turned, walked backward a couple of steps and batted his lashes at Brad. "I'll pick you up at six, sweetie. Don't eat lunch-Darrin puts on a spread to die for."

"Looking forward to it, sweetie," Brad parroted his endearment, taking instruction from the master.

Marshall merely tossed a secretive grin at Brad. " I'll swing by at six and we'll light up the town."

Brad tried to figure out what Dustin Hoffman would do as Tootsie and fluttered his fingers at his new landlady's boss, smiling as widely as he could make himself. "Can't wait." If good old Dusty could do it, so could he.

Kirsty pulled Marshall out the front door, giggling. "Stop undressing the poor man with your eyes. He'll catch his death," she said loudly enough for Brad to hear.

Curious about Kirsty's chummy relationship with her boss, Brad followed. Heat crawled up his throat to his cheeks at his landlady's observation. The only person he wanted undressing him was his landlady, and not with her eyes. But she was too busy laughing her ass off at him. Regretfully, he couldn't come onto her under threat of being sacked.

He spied a pile of car doors next door, stacked up by the garage, and his temper dissipated. Strange. Reputable fix-it shops didn't stack valuable car doors as if they were rotted firewood. Crowe was onto something here. He needed a way to get a closer look without causing suspicion.

The only thing he could think of was to sabotage his car and see if the guy wanted to pick up some quick cash to fix it. Maybe he could dent his car door and ask if the guy could replace it with one in the yard. If he did all this, Crowe had better authorize the funds to restore his baby to new after this job was done.

Brad blew an exaggerated kiss back to Marshall on the wind. That's what Tootsie would do, wasn't it? Except, his logic was flawed. Dustin had been trying to pass as a woman. He racked his brain for another character to emulate, who had been in his peculiar position but couldn't think of one. He was on his own and didn't like feeling lost.

Soon as they left, he strutted back to the house, stuffed his baseball gear into his oversized tote bag, scarfed down a blueberry pop tart, and locked up the house. He licked the fruity crumbs and icing off his lips as he climbed into his car.

Soon as he drove past the neighbor's house, he patted his leather dash board. "I'm all kinds of sorry I have to do this to you, Betty Lou. You know I'd never hurt you if I had any other choice."

Once he escaped his temporary neighborhood, he pulled over into a secluded woodsy area, loosened the car's distributor cap and reset the timing belt. For good measure, he poured a little oil over the hot engine to make it smoke and almost choked when a black cloud covered him in grease.

As Betty Lou limped home, he berated himself. She coughed and spluttered all the way. He stroked her steering wheel. "I promise I'll give you a shiny new paint job and a set of Pirellis as soon as all this is over." He cringed as the oily smoke washed over his windshield making it almost impossible to drive.

Sirens blared behind him and then blinding lights flashed in his rearview mirror.

"Great!" Brad checked his mirror simultaneously hoping he knew the cop so he'd get out of the ticket and that he didn't know the cop so that he wouldn't be recognized. He pulled over to the shoulder of the road, stopped the car praying she'd start up again and pulled his wallet from his purse.

A short, rotund officer that Brad had never seen before waddled up to him. His name tag announced him to be Officer Jon Boudreaux and the badge on his sleeve pronounced him to be a member of the Margate PD. "You gotcha some engine troubles, Bubba? You're sure stinking up this stretch of road."

Brad decided not to divulge his cover by flashing his badge and passed over the fake ID Crowe had given him. He stayed in the car dutifully so as not to spook the man. The smoke could easily conceal a weapon and if he'd been in the other man's shoes, he'd be extra careful under the circumstances.

* * * * *

Betty Lou spluttered and died half a block from Kirsty's house. Scowling, huffing and puffing, covered in grease and soot, Brad pushed the car home.

More cars littered his neighbor's driveway but there wasn't a soul in sight. As the garage door was open, he took a chance and pushed his car to his neighbor's yard. He bent over and wiped his greasy hands on the sprinkler-dampened grass.

Brad poked his head around the garage door, drinking in the sight of stacks of expensive automotive parts. "Knock knock. Anybody home?"

His beady-eyed neighbor cracked the door between the kitchen and the garage a hair and stuck his nose out. His bushy mustache twitched. "Si? What you want, gringo?"

Brad flung his feather boa around his neck and struck a feminine pose, jutting out his hip. "I'm just in dire straits and I don't know what I'm going to do. I need your help."

"What, I look like Florence Nightingale?" He stuck a gun barrel out the door. "Get lost, gringo.

Brad already had a wad of money out and flashed the green stuff at the man. He sidestepped the barrel. "I'm desperate. Please help me. I'll pay you double whatever you would normally charge me for the repairs."

Greed stole across the man's face as his gaze devoured the bills. His mustache twitched and he licked his lips. "Mañana. Loco day."

Brad didn't want to wait. The man just pretended to run a legitimate business anyway. "I'll pay triple the price." He fanned the currency. Out loud, he counted hundred dollar bills, all marked with invisible ink.

"Uno momento. Tamale burn, if I no get." He lowered the gun and clicked on the safety. "Stay." His gaze raked Brad's flamboyant dress. "No touch anything."

Brad ran his fingers through his hair to spike it and winked at the man "The only thing I want to touch isn't outside in the garage...*yet, sugar.*"

The man's eyes widened as he slammed the door and dead bolted it.

Brad wandered around, soaking in the contents of the garage, letting his photographic memory catalogue everything. The garage looked like a chop shop all right, hidden in the heart of suburbia, USA. Of course, lots of Floridians weren't acquainted with their neighbors, especially not renters. Not that he stayed aloof from his real neighbors, but many other people did.

Alvarez reemerged but kept his distance from Brad.

The neighbor on the other side of Kirsty's house emerged from his garage wearing goggles and ear protectors, pushing his lawnmower as if it were a race car. His grass could only be two inches high. Tops. Brad was sure the guy gave his lawn better care than the White House grounds received.

Mr. Mechanic stared at the other neighbor and rubbed his chin. "Loco gringo's so in love with his lawn he's gonna hump it."

Brad snickered. He liked a well-groomed lawn, but didn't let it make him into a slave. Keeping in character, Brad whistled long and low and tried to put himself in Mario's mind frame. "Ooh. Sexy pecs."

The mechanic stepped backward three steps and crossed his heart. "We get one thing straight, you keep your hands off me."

Brad loved to tease and couldn't resist. He puckered his lips and threw the mechanic a kiss. "But you're so precious and adorable my fingers just itch to run through your luscious dark hair. You're so macho."

The man backed up more and tripped over a jack lying in the driveway. He scooted back even more, fear flashing across his eyes. "You go home now and wait. I come tell you when it's finished."

Brad winked, starting to have a bit of fun. "Okay, sugar pie. I'll just take a long, luxurious bubble bath. Join me if you like and I'll soap you all over." He felt safe offering because the other man had made it plain he wouldn't take him up on the offer. Pivoting on his high heel, he almost fell flat on his face but caught himself by grabbing a fat palm tree. Gritting his teeth, he ignored the man's hoots of laughter.

Brad dead bolted his door, showered instead of bathing, and then towel dried his hair and body. He wrapped the towel around his hips and checked the house to make sure his landlady hadn't returned, and then he accessed his email from her computer and ordered roses from Kirsty's flower shop to be sent to his ex-girlfriend who had seen him in drag coming out of the police station the previous evening and suggested they get together for drinks later. He had a reputation to protect.

* * * * *

When an email popped up on Kirsty's computer screen she opened it. Clucking her tongue and shaking her head in disgust, she called out to Gigi, "Lover boy's back and wants two dozen American Beauties delivered this afternoon."

Gigi ambled over to the computer and gazed at it with longing, resting her chin on her palm. "Bugger! Why can't I find a gorgeous chap to be all dotty and doting over me so that he sends me roses? Tell him I'm a singleton." She wrestled Kirsty for the mouse.

"You've got to be joking, right? He's only sent roses to the whole free world. He gives ladies' men a bad name." She wrote up an invoice for the roses and looked on the map to see where the lucky lady's address was this time. It turned out that the lady of the week lived near her out in Coral Springs.

"You under the weather, Kirst? Don't you *like* to get roses?" Gigi stared at her as if she had sprouted two more heads. "Sounds pretty groovy to me."

Kirsty turned her back on her man-hungry friend and pulled two dozen American Beauties out of the refrigerator and prepped them. Ladies' men weren't interested in women who weighed in at 181 pounds like she had that morning. She bit down hard on her lip to stop it from trembling before she turned around to her friend. "Sure, if the guy's sincere. But not from some two-bit charmer who sends roses to every pretty girl in town."

Gigi pouted, sticking out her lower lip half a mile "Not every pretty girl in town. He's not sent them to me...or you."

Kirsty grimaced down at herself as she turned around. *Right – pretty. Not.*

"Or to me." Marshall flounced in, separating them. "I don't want to hear you badmouthing our best customer. Viva la Don Juan! As long as he's romancing the Ft. Lauderdale ladies we have no worries about closing our doors. May we find a hundred more like him."

"Well, keep Lothario away from me. I'll prep his roses but if he ever shows up in person, you two can duke it out. I want nothing to do with the likes of him." Kirsty turned her nose up at the mere notion of such a nauseating thought.

Marshall walked up behind Kirsty and massaged her shoulders. "You still pining for Mr. Love 'em and leave 'em, eh, sunshine?"

Kirsty scowled, snorted, and tossed her head. "No way! I don't know what I ever saw in him. I like my men sweet and kind...and loyal. No ladies' men for me, thank you very much." Sweet men reminded her of her new roommate. They didn't come much sweeter. Too bad he didn't like women. He would be so handsome in normal men's garb. She sighed. Wishing wouldn't do her any good. She didn't have a magic wand to change his sexual orientation. She pricked her finger on a thorn and yelped. Blood oozed from the tiny cut.

"What now?" Marshall rushed to her side, his expression more concerned than his words.

She sucked her finger tasting the salty blood on her tongue. With her mouth full, her words came out garbled. "That rose bit me. I told you that Mueller man was bad news."

Marshall pulled the first aid kit out from under the counter, cleansed the wound, and bandaged her finger. "It's just a little prick..."

"He's a big prick." Kirsty scowled at the email again.

"Ooh, just the way I love 'em." Marshall's eyebrows danced jauntily.

"Give it a break, Marshall." Kirsty turned away from him, yawning deeply.

"You'll live, princess."

"That's what they told Sleeping Beauty, wasn't it? Is it five o'clock yet? I need to stop by the hairdresser." She hoped the hair salon down the road could squeeze her in tonight as Frank was due tomorrow. "Frank's going to see the new improved me when he comes by to collect his stuff " If only she could lose four or five dress sizes before then as well, she'd be perfect.

Marshall looped his arm around Kirsty's shoulders and squeezed. "Forget the do. You got to make the ex jealous with another man." He puffed out his chest. "I volunteer."

Gigi howled with laughter and almost rolled on the floor. "Have you forgotten that Frank knows what a pouf you are?"

"And loathes you?" Kirsty's mind worked furiously. Who else did she know that could make him jealous? One of her neighbors? The macho grease monkey in the attached house? Or the lawn lover on the other side of her house? What a wretched life she led – she didn't know any other men to ask. *How pathetic.*

She finished the roses and instructed the delivery boy to take them to their victim, feeling somehow guilty that she played any part in this lothario's seduction. She wished she could warn her sisterhood about his womanizing ways without bringing the wrath of Marshall down upon her head.

* * * * *

The front door slammed behind him and high heels echoed like gunfire on the tile floor. "I'm home!"

Brad waved the cloud of smoke out of his face that threatened to engulf the kitchen and tried not to cough as he hurriedly turned off the back stove burner and turned on the fan overhead. Charred, shriveled shrimp mocked him. Even the water chestnuts lay wrinkled in the wok. "Don't come out here." He dumped the spoiled stir-fry down the garbage disposal trying to destroy the evidence before she caught him.

He sucked in his breath and almost muttered under his breath, *dang it --caught.* Then he imagined how Mario would react in the same situation so he squealed like a teenage girl and clapped his hands to his mouth. "I murdered those poor beautiful shrimp for nothing."

"Too late." Kirsty peered around his arm. She sniffed and wrinkled her nose. "Yum. Burned stir-fry. My fav." She sniffled behind him as if she choked back sobs and he felt horrible for ruining the shrimp.

"It's okay to cry. I cry when I ruin shrimp, too." He turned to take her in his arms to comfort her, a reflex reaction, and stopped dead when he took in the debacle she made. Butchered, monstrous hair that stuck out in clumps in some places and bald patches in others, assaulted his vision. Bloodshot eyes stared at him helplessly and puffy mottled red flesh made her look as if she'd contracted the plague. "What happened to your beautiful hair?"

Tears dripped down her cheeks as she tried to dab them away with her fingers. "Sh-She mangled it. It'll take *years* to grow out. I can't go out in public like this."

"She who?" Had she gotten into a catfight with a friend or with someone over this Frank bastard? His protective instincts boiled up inside him and he reached for her, hugging her to him and massaging her back.

She hiccoughed against him and her tears wet his shoulder, but he didn't mind. He led her out of the kitchen and into the living room where he eased her to the couch beside him and where they wouldn't be overcome by the smoke.

Her silky hair tickled his cheek. Her perfume wound around him, mesmerizing him and it would take an act of God to move him away from her. He separated from her and held her chin high with his forefinger so he could examine her better. It only got worse upon closer inspection. "It's not that bad," he lied. "We can fix it." As soon as the words were out, he remembered he was supposed to be a master hairdresser and his words implied he would do the reparation. Maybe he should have agreed to cut her hair. Skilled or not, he wouldn't have massacred her hair like this. The hairdresser who'd done this to her should be locked away for life without parole!

A watery smile touched the corners of her lips. Nodding vehemently, she pouted. "Yes it is. Frank's going to laugh at me now. I wanted him to regret dumping me. I want his eyes to bug out of his head. Oh, his eyes are going to bug out of his head all right when he gets a load of me now. I'll never live this down." Sarcasm dripped from her lips.

Brad couldn't allow that. He wanted to know more about this jerk and what he'd done to her. "So what did this yahoo do to get on your black list?"

Her eyes narrowed and her lips thinned. "He thought he was Romeo and hit on everything in a skirt. I caught him playing around on me and found out he even came on to my best friend, Gigi. Then he told me it was my fault because I'm so – so gar-gargantuan and hideous." Her hands clenched so tightly her knuckles paled and her lips trembled. "I can't stand ladies' men who think they're God's gift to women. I never want to lay eyes on one again."

Brad's protective instinct went into overdrive and he spurted out, "He must be blind and stupid. You're not fat by any means. You're curvaceous and absolutely gorgeous." Kirsty's eyes grew huge in her pixie face as she gazed up at him. "You really think so?"

Brad back pedaled. "Well, uh, yeah - for a woman."

When she still looked at him questioningly, he added, "I have an artiste's eye. I still appreciate feminine beauty."

Kirsty's lips quivered into a tremulous smile and his heart went out to her.

She pulled back from him and wiped a tear from her face. She patted his cheek and elicited a shuddery sigh. "Why are all the nice guys unavailable?"

Brad wished he could tell her just how available he really was. *Christ! He got hard just thinking about her.* Crowe must be laughing his ass off. He either had to hold her or hit something. It was time to go to the batting cage and hit something.

She bit her lower lip and worried it with her cute teeth. "I just had an idea. Would you do me a big favor?"

He crossed his heart and gazed deeply into her eyes, drowning in her tempting gaze. "Cross my heart and hope to die, hope to get an arrow in my eye."

She chuckled as color began returning to her ghost-white cheeks. "It's a *big* favor." She examined him closely. "Tell me, have you ever kissed a woman?"

It was his turn to be taken aback by her boldness. "Once or twice. Eons ago – in my former life." It seemed like an eternity anyway. He couldn't believe he'd only been on this assignment two long, tortuous weeks. It felt like an eternity since he'd gotten laid. His cock swelled and flexed. Did she want him to kiss her now? His lips tingled and his heart soared. Crowe be damned. If this adorable woman wanted him to kiss her, he didn't think he could say no. He didn't want to say no.

"Can you pretend to be straight for one night? Probably just a couple of hours?"

"How straight?" *Kissing straight? Or fucking straight?* His cock sprung and almost burst his zipper. It would not do for her to see this unless he wanted her to know without a doubt just how hot she made him. *Time for another shower session.*

"Why?" His voice came out much huskier than he had intended it to, so thick he almost couldn't push it out.

She cleared her throat and lowered her eyes, regarding him through veiled lashes. "Could you pretend to be my boyfriend? Just for tomorrow night while Frank is here?" she rushed on, as if embarrassed to ask him this favor or afraid she'd embarrass him.

"Do I have to kiss you?" *He hoped so.* He'd take any excuse.

"Probably not, but, uh, can we play that by ear? Even if you do, you don't have to use your tongue." She looked everywhere but at him. Her thick lashes fanned her high cheekbones and despite her punk haircut, she was more alluring in this moment than any woman he had ever met. Visions of kissing her, sticking his tongue down her throat, made him impossibly hard. He wasn't engineered to hold back. He'd never had a straight, single woman reject him, and he wasn't in the practice of stopping with platonic kisses. Even in pretense.

If he kept up like this, he'd blow his cover. Soon, he'd be able to kiss her without abandon whenever and wherever he wanted to but he couldn't do it yet. All her prayers would be answered. She'd forget all about the rotten ex-fiancé of hers and not even remember the jerk's name. "Let's just play it by ear."

She tried to smooth her ruined hair with one hand. Grabbing him with the other hand, she tugged him behind her to the kitchen. "Pretend boyfriend or not, he won't drool with me looking like a Star Wars reject." She glanced over her shoulder at him and frowned. "Nor will he drool if you prance around frillier than me. We're getting me a wig and you new duds."

"If you get gorgeous in a wig, then you won't need a handsome macho man to make the fool jealous," Brad said logically. His mind warred with his libido. He knew he tread on quicksand and his woman-starved-self wanted to sink right into it. He fought his baser self, knowing his job was on the line.

"And I won't have to get dull, dull, dull just to impress him." She snorted as she detoured to the kitchen where she'd left her purse and grabbed it. It swung so violently from the sudden jerk it almost knocked him unconscious. "You got bricks in that bag?" He rubbed his forehead where the weapon had hit him amazed when his fingers traced the indentation it had left. That purse might scare the street scum he dealt with more than the revolver strapped to his ankle.

"Anchors just to put unruly men in line." Changing 180 degrees without warning, she almost made him jackknife behind her as she trudged to the front door.

"Ouch." He meant that both metaphorically as well as physically. An entire baseball game didn't give him as many aches, pains, and bruises as this exasperating woman. "You should register that thing as a lethal weapon."

"Maybe I will." She unlocked the passenger car door and commanded, "Get in."

He slid into her cramped car, his legs felt like an accordion until he adjusted the seat back as far as it would allow him. Tall men like him didn't do compact cars well. Give him a big luxury car like Betty Lou or better yet a truck.

When she backed out of the driveway, he remarked dryly, "Why do I feel as if I've been kidnapped by a space alien?" Of course if he had to be kidnapped, she was his kind of kidnapper.

"Hey!" She play punched his shoulder, shades of her normal self returning. "An alien? Where's the best place to buy a wig?"

He had no clue. Speechless, he avoided her eyes. "Walmart?" Quickly, he added to cover up his faux pas, "There must be a salon on the main strip."

She cut the car hard right, throwing him against her. "Hang on," she said too late, as the tires squealed.

Dizzy, he sat up. His focus blurry, he wasn't sure if one duck or four crossed in the road ahead. "How about if I drive?" He hadn't realized how much the near scalping had traumatized her. Or perhaps she was always a lousy driver. Either way, their lives were at risk.

"My insurance doesn't allow anyone else to drive my car." She turned right onto the four lane boulevard, cutting off a speeding mini-van barreling down on them that swerved with just a second to spare without causing a major wreck. She didn't seem to notice.

Brad held his breath. His toes clenched inside his shoes, and he wished he had control of the car's brakes. She definitely couldn't afford to give up her insurance. He'd never met anyone who needed it worse. "How about if I just throw up then?" He unwound the window and tilted his head at it. She scowled. "Funny, very funny."

He moaned, clutching his griping stomach. "Who's being funny? Pull over now." He'd felt less at risk shooting it out with armed criminals than in this out of control land rocket.

"Wigs," she muttered with vehemence, swerving the car into a crowded parking lot.

He was tossed across the seat like a rag doll, his head landing on her shoulder. He righted himself as soon as the car stopped spinning beneath him. "Cross your fingers they have something better than the Cruella Deville look."

She shook her finger at him, fire flashing in her eyes. "If I come out looking like a skunk - which is still better than this monstrosity - I'll be a more wicked villainess than she ever was."

"Why is this ex-creep of yours so important to you? Why do you care what he thinks?" It was beyond him why such a beautiful, lovely woman wasted one brain cell on a man who had treated her so poorly.

She turned a blank stare on him, her pupils dilating. "Marshall will put a bag over my head and relegate me to the dungeon if I come to work like this." She tore the clutch and ground gears as she parked in front of a wig shop.

He noticed that she sidestepped his question about her ex-fiancé. Hopefully, he'd set her straight. The guy didn't deserve a woman like Kirsty even with horrible hair. He followed her into the wig shop, his pulse quickening just watching the way she swayed seductively in front of him.

"I have a code red emergency!" she announced to the store, as she gravitated to the dark red wigs, fingering them. She turned the price tag over in her hands and winced. "Ouch!"

"So your alter ego wants to be a redhead? I thought all women dreamed of being blonde like Marilyn Monroe?" Playing around, he tried a straight black haired wig on and modeled before a floor length mirror. He looked like Elvira in drag.

"I've been the butt of blonde jokes all my life. I'm tired of people accusing me of having half a brain because my ancestors are Scandinavian." She put the red wig over her choppy hair and pivoted on her heel and posed for him. Puckering up, and batting her lashes, she crooned, "Julia Roberts and Nicole Kidman eat your heart out."

He whistled long and loud, agreeing with her assessment. When a saleslady sidled up with a hopeful, hungry glint in her eyes, Brad vowed to stay close to Kirsty lest the woman try to sell her every wig in the store.

"Oh, I was just teasing about this one." Kirsty yanked it off and put it back. "I should get something that's my natural hair color."

"They're fifty percent off today," the pencil-thin sales lady with waist-length raven locks said in a singsong voice, picking it up and holding it up to Brad. "This is quite a bargain - it's all natural human hair. Tomorrow, they return to full price and I don't know when we'll have another sale." She brushed a strand over the top of his hand. "See how soft and natural it feels? You could get two for the price of one."

Brad took it from her, bent on buying it, chills running down his spine. He could just imagine Kirsty wearing this - and nothing else - while they made hot passionate love. Just the thought turned his blood to molten lava and his breath quickened. "You did say you wanted something new and sophisticated, did you not?" he reminded his landlady.

She eyed the wig longingly, practically drooling. "I was thinking something shorter and sassier..." She fingered a short curly brunette wig with lots of bounce, one that looked like Cole's wife's style, except for the coloring.

"They're on sale today - I'll get you both. Let me see you in that. Try it on."

Crimson stole up her cheeks and she veiled her eyes as she tugged the snug fitting cap over her skull. Crooked, she looked silly and cute all at the same time. He couldn't help but chortle as he reached over and straightened it for her. Then he stood back to inspect her. Tapping his finger on his chin, he circled her. "I like the style, but that color washes you out. Your coloring is too ruddy to go with that color hair. You'd better stick with blonde and red." He spied a curly blonde wig in the next aisle and retrieved it.

Nonplused, she gaped at him, her exquisite eyes wide and brimming with shock.

"You'd do well to listen to him, dearie," the sales lady said in a conspiratorial whisper. "Gay men have impeccable fashion sense. You were smart to bring him along."

A smile tugged at Brad's lips. He had impeccable fashion sense when it came to helping a lady. He'd had a lot of experience.

"Would you like two more wigs? You could buy four for the price of two and could be a different woman almost every day of the workweek. All your friends will drool, darling." The forty-something year old diva sashayed to a coiffed and glamorous silvery blonde wig displayed in a place of honor. "With the right dress, you could look like Marilyn Monroe."

Kirsty shook her head vigorously. "No!" Embarrassment flooded her face and she softened her "no". She glanced down at her figure, embarrassment flickering in her bright blue eyes. "I'm not the Marilyn Monroe type."

"Yes you are." The tenacious woman eyed Kirsty critically as she stroked the faux hair lovingly, her long well manicured fingers twirling a strand. "Men love this look - especially in bed. We sell beauty marks at the register."

Kirsty swallowed hard and slid a glance at Brad who pretended not to notice. "Two will be fine for now. I'm ready to check out."

"Can I wear this now?" Kirsty asked, taking the red wig. "I can't stand my hair this way."

"Sure, dearie. Wear it in good health. You sure you don't want more while they're discounted? Once you wear our wigs, you'll never get enough. The men go absolutely wild over them. It fulfills their fantasies of having a different woman in their bed when you dress up for them."

Brad hadn't thought Kirsty could turn any brighter red, but he was wrong. Her face fairly burned with the infusion of color that flamed in her cheeks. The thought of Kirsty wearing a different wig for him in bed every night made his blood boil. Visions of his landlady imitating Marilyn Monroe almost undid his control.

The woman sent a sly glance to Brad as she eyed his funky hair. "You might like one too, doll. They're all the rage on South Beach."

The sales woman's words dashed unwelcome reality in his face. He pretended not to hear her, and then thought again about the fantasy of having a different Kirsty in his bed nightly. The thoughts were too much and he told her to go on out to the car and he'd join her in a minute.

"Ciao. You look absolutely gorgeous in your new hair." The woman's fingers fluttered midair behind Kirsty's back. The bell tinkled over the glass door and a balmy breeze rushed in as Kirsty exited without answering.

"I'll take the Marilyn Monroe job, and that Farrah Fawcett winged thingie behind you," he said in a low voice once Kirsty was out of earshot.

"You won't be sorry. Your boyfriend will love it." she gushed all over him, wrapping the wigs with care. "May I add you to our mailing list?"

"No, I don't think so." He shook his head, stuffed his card in his wallet and jammed the wallet in his pants pocket. "I know where you are now." No way did he want mail going to Kirsty's house in his real name. These would fuel his fantasies for now and once he was free to pursue her, he could always come back for more.

His friend had confided to him how erotic he found it when his wife donned different identities for him. The thought of Haley and her chameleon-escapades made him pause. "You don't ride motorcycles, do you?" he asked Kirsty when he climbed into the tiny car pulled up to the curb.

Her new hair swished around catching the last rays of the setting South Florida sun as she turned to look askance at him. "Once or twice, years ago as a passenger. Why?"

He breathed a sigh of relief. He'd have a heart attack if she jumped his police car on a motorcycle, the way Haley had once jumped over

Cole's black and white. He couldn't stand the thought of Kirsty getting hurt. "Oh, no real reason," he lied. "I just saw a gal riding a cycle and it made me wonder, that's all."

"I used to ride and jump horses. And parachute jump. And snow ski." Surprised, worried by her unexpected daredevil lifestyle, he gulped. *Great.* He'd prefer it if she rode motorcycles. "You're quite the athlete."

She chewed on the end of her new hair as she negotiated traffic, much more sanely now. "Don't you like sports?"

Without thinking, he responded with conviction, "Softball." He kicked himself for revealing a side of his real self. Some undercover cop he was. "

Uhm. I wouldn't have pegged you for a softball type of guy. Guess I learn something new every day."

He tapped his fingers on the armrest, wishing he were playing softball now. "We play at Mills Pond." Well, he wasn't lying. He just let her assume what she would. His stomach grumbled. "Pick a restaurant, any cuisine," he offered, famished.

Fine dining establishments, fast food joints, and middle of the road restaurants lined University Drive, vying for business, most of their parking lots crowded. This part of town had just about as much entertainment as the beach but lacked the craziness of a tourist attraction. Coral Springs was a nice family community that could fit well in the Midwest if not for its palm trees and balmy year round temperatures. Very few tourists ventured this far west bordering the Everglades. Nor were any snowbird villages closer than Tamarac. Teenagers flooded the local Barnes & Noble and Starbucks Coffee until closing time nightly. This is where Brad wanted to raise a family one day. Unless he ever won the lottery, then he'd live in Parkland in a half-million dollar estate.

"You like seafood, right?" She veered into a local seafood restaurant, running over the curb and screeched to a halt.

"You must have strong tires," he mumbled, surprised they hadn't popped with all the abuse she heaped upon her poor car. She needed serious driving lessons.

Kirsty opened and held the door for him. "After you."

"Thank you." He didn't like the role reversal. He wanted to spoil his woman, treat her like a lady, and not behave like a wimp. He fumed at his predicament.

"Two. Non-smoking," Kirsty told the hostess who greeted them, preempting him again. Next, she'd order dinner for him, also.

He hoped she didn't take charge like this with regular men. He couldn't live his life this way.

"Brad, honey," a familiar voice squealed in delight and then hands clapped, and heels clicked on the hard floor. "You've been a naughty boy, hiding from me." A pout laced Cindy's voice as she threw her arms around him and squeezed the oxygen from his lungs.

Kirsty's glance flickered over the buoyant brunette, her inscrutable gaze lingering on the other woman's slim waist.

Brad turned his head just in time to avoid Cindy's upturned lips. They grazed his cheek undoubtedly leaving her mark.

"Aren't you going to introduce me to your friend, sugar?" Cindy batted her lashes at him coquettishly. However, hurt pooled deep in her irises.

Brad felt like a cad – a trapped cad. He'd dated Cindy on and off for a couple of years, but didn't feel the slightest inclination to make their relationship permanent. He'd avoided her lips, however, more because he didn't want to anger Kirsty than blow his cover.

"Cindy, meet my landlady, Kirsten Engel. Kirsty meet my good friend, Cindy Parker." Turning to Cindy who was sizing up Kirsty, he asked with dread, "You here alone?"

Cindy flipped her hair over her shoulder, almost smacking him in the face. "Oh no! I'm here with Cole and Haley. Haley sent me over to fetch you."

Brad's stomach dropped with a thud. He looked around the lounge, spotted Cole waving at him, cracking up hysterically. "You don't say," he said through gritted teeth. "Tell the *prince* we'd rather be alone and I'll take a rain check…"

Kirsty tsk-tsked. "Don't be rude on my account, Bradley. I'd love to meet your friends." She followed Cindy before Brad could stop her.

Trudging behind the ladies, he signaled his partner over their heads, finishing with a threatening slash across his throat.

Cole stood, his eyes twinkling. Beside him, a very pregnant Haley struggled to her feet, her back bowed.

"It lives and breathes!" Cole chuckled at his own bad joke, his lips twitching.

Haley's ocean blue eyes widened in her elfin face and her jaw dropped open. Scratching her head, she asked, "Brad?" Her bulging gaze roamed from Cindy to Kirsty and back.

Brad tried to smile and failed. Goose pimples attacked Brad's arms and his hair stood on end. "You look radiant, Haley." And ready to burst with her unborn baby any moment. He couldn't wait to be a godfather to the little tyke.

"You gonna stand all night or pull up a couple of seats and join us?" Cole winked at his wife. "We're having bugs. Want some?"

Kirsty's eyes bulged out almost as far as Haley's. Her lips twisted in a grimace. "*Bugs?*"

"*Big bugs.*" Cole spread his hands wide. "About yay big. Juicy, too."

Haley hit her husband playfully on the shoulder as she waddled toward Brad in a pair of pink fuzzy slippers. She smiled at Kirsty. "Family joke. He means *lobsters*, but he's retarded so don't pay him no never mind. We don't."

"Hey! You obviously pay me a lot of attention." Cole patted her swollen belly, making Haley blush to the roots of her hair. "Besides, you started the family joke." He drew Haley down for a quick smooch.

Haley broke away and grabbed Brad's hand, tugging. "Mind if I borrow your *man*?" Haley asked Kirsty, her gaze dissecting Brad as if he were a newly discovered species.

Cindy jumped to her feet, almost knocking over her chair. "*We'll* bring *him* back shortly. Promise." Although Cindy's voice bubbled over with glee, her gaze shot daggers through Brad.

Haley pulled while Cindy shoved him back near the kitchen and restrooms. Rounding on him, Haley burst out laughing. "Spill! Are you in *drag*?"

Cindy tilted her head toward Kirsty. "Who's the broad? Is she why you've been avoiding me and not returning my calls? Or," Cindy licked her lips with the tip her tongue, "did you just come out of the closet?"

Brad couldn't believe his predicament. How much could he tell them safely? He had to tell them something as they knew something was completely amiss and he couldn't have them giving him away to Kirsty. He opened his mouth to speak, and then spied Alvarez round the corner. He ducked into the nearest door pulling his entourage with him.

Haley and Cindy faced off against him, shock etching their features. "Since when do you use the ladies room?" Haley asked, tapping her foot in a staccato rhythm.

Brad cursed his hasty retreat without looking where he was going. He was getting careless which could get him fired and killed.

Cindy sashayed up to him and touched his eyelid, and then examined her fingertip. "And since when do you wear baby blue eye shadow and mascara? Is there something you need to confess?" Cindy's voice trembled. "I never suspected. You always seemed so..."

"Macho?" Brad asked puffing out his chest.

Cindy frowned. "Horny."

"What gives?" Haley circled him, rubbing her swollen belly. "Does my husband know what all this is about?"

Brad nodded and raked his fingers through his spiked hair. He checked the stalls to ensure no one listened to them. "You swear not to breathe a word? Can I trust you?" When they nodded, he continued, "I'm undercover to bust a chop shop."

Cindy's brows tented. "A *gay* chop shop?"

Brad rolled his eyes. "No. But they won't suspect me in this get-up. Plus Kirsty wouldn't rent to a man..."

Haley slapped her thigh and broke out in laughter. "Kirsty really believes you're gay? She thinks she's safe all the while she's shacking up with the biggest Casanova in town?"

"Ironic, isn't it?" Cindy said to her friend and then heaved a huge sigh. "How long do you have to keep up this charade?"

"Until I get my man." He scowled. "I meant until I get the goods on..."

Cindy chortled and struck a decidedly feminine pose.

Kirsty sauntered in and stopped dead when she saw Brad. "B-Bradley. I knew you were gay but I never dreamed I'd find you in here." All color drained from her face. "I'll just come back later when it's a little less crowded." She backed out slowly.

"We're just leaving, aren't we girls?" Brad cupped Haley's elbow in one hand and Cindy's in the other and propelled them to the door. He couldn't believe his rotten luck.

"You bet, *girlfriend*," Cindy said in a singsong voice, her lips still quirking.

"I hope your *bug's* still hot and juicy," Brad teased, getting her back. Great pleasure filled him when Cindy wrinkled her nose and stuck her tongue out at him. "I'll get you for that."

"I dare you." He flounced out, his chin regally high, his hand on his hip. If he had to make a complete fool of himself, he might as well enjoy it.

Chapter Three

Kirsty fretted all the next day over Frank's impending visit. She should've just boxed up his stuff and sent it to him COD.

She wore her curly blonde wig to work and received raves from Marshall and Gigi. "You look lovely, sunshine." Marshall blew her a kiss and tossed her a red rose. "I get dibs on borrowing it."

She caught it and tucked it behind her ear, feeling very tropical. Then she spied the email from her *friend* the lothario, ordering two dozen American Beauties to be delivered to another one of his women. She groaned out loud, her stomach churning. "Gag me," she muttered, as she printed out the order.

"Stop defiling our best customer," Marshall ordered. "I wish I could clone the guy. Anyone who buys as many roses as he does deserves to have his statue erected in City Center."

Gigi pinched Marshall's arm. "You wish you could clone every sexy bloke."

A far away dreamy gleam entered Marshall's hazel eyes. "So true. Don't tell me you don't wish the same." He tapped Gigi's cheek with a rose petal.

Gigi blushed and giggled and nibbled on her diet cookie.

When Kirsty didn't laugh or smile, Marshall asked, "Something wrong, sweetie?"

Gigi answered for her. "The wanker's collecting his gear tonight."

"Good riddance and hallelujah!" Marshall snorted. "You can do much better than him. Don't you waste one more thought, one more tear, on that sorry excuse for a man. I'd be glad to come over and toss his stuff out the window for him."

Kirsty just wanted it to be over and move on. Bradley's face flitted across her mind. If only he weren't gay, she could really go for him in a big way. Why did she always fall for men who were not interested? Frank was a prime example, not that she could recall what she had ever seen in him. "I won't after tonight."

She rushed home, vacuumed, swept, and mopped her floors. Then, getting on hands and knees, she scrubbed the baseboards. Frank would see a spic and span house, as well as a new gorgeous Kirsty. She'd even lost a couple of pounds this week, just unfortunately not enough to move down a dress size.

"What 'pray tell' are you doing down there?" Bradley towered over her, his shadow eclipsing her, his arms crossed over his powerful chest. Scrubbed clean of make-up, dressed in macho hip-hugging blue jeans, a muscle shirt, and a Marlin's baseball cap, the vision of him stole her breath.

She stared at him like a complete idiot. If she wasn't careful, she'd start drooling and completely humiliate herself. Finally she managed to choke out, "Where's your earring?" She still crouched on the floor at his feet.

"Tell me you're not doing this to impress the sorry ex? Scraping paint off walls won't win him back." Bradley held his hand out to help her up. His scowl rebuked her.

When she placed her hand in his, lightning scorched her and she bit back a gasp. "What do you think will impress him?" She grimaced. "And I don't want him back – *ever*. I'd rather cozy up to a crocodile. I just want him to realize what he'll be missing."

Brad pulled her up and she stumbled, falling against him. His broad hands caught her around her waist, steadying her. He gazed deeply into her eyes and a grin tugged at his chiseled lips. "A little flirting maybe. Some eye contact." He lowered his head a couple of inches so that their breath mingled. "A well-placed kiss…" His thumbs caressed the small of her back, mesmerizing her.

He stared at her lips with such molten heat and obvious desire, that he had to feel something for her. When his sizzling gaze dropped to her chest, her panties began to get damp. Maybe he could be turned around and saved? Did she dare try? Would she have a prayer?

Perhaps he was a terrific actor and not the least bit attracted to her? He might laugh in her face. Or pity her. She drew back, lowering her eyes, forcing herself to breathe normally. She couldn't stand to be pitied, especially not by him. "That should make a believer of him."

* * * * *

The door slammed open without ceremony and Frank stomped inside. When he spied Kirsty in Bradley's arms, he scowled heavily. "I see you didn't waste any time. My bed's barely cold and you're in another man's arms."

Kirsty stiffened in Bradley's pseudo embrace, the smile fading. Trust it to Frank to be complimentary to her. *Not.*

Bradley cupped her cheek in his hand and then slid a finger under her chin and lifted her lips to his for a searing, languorous kiss. When his tongue delved the cavern of her mouth, she trembled in shock. No one had ever kissed her so thoroughly, so magically, or turned her on like this. Especially not Frank.

When Bradley released her lips, he leaned his forehead against hers and smiled into her eyes. To Frank, he said, "Why should she waste time on the likes of you when she can have a real man?" He stroked her bought hair as if she was the most precious person in the world.

She beamed up at him, all pretense of acting vanished. She'd never felt so feminine, so cherished, and she had to remind herself that she wasn't his type.

Frank huffed past them, stomping loudly down the hall in his cowboy boots.

Bradley's fingers caught in her hair and it pulled sideways on her head so that the middle part was parallel with her lips. His eyes widened as he fumbled to help her right it before their unwelcome guest turned around and spied the strange sight.

Kirsty gasped and paled. "Hurry! He can't see my mangled hair. I'd rather shave my head totally bald." She tugged on the hair and pulled it too far to the opposite side, completely mortified. She couldn't imagine a bigger moron.

"I bet you'd look sexy that way – like that Star Trek babe." Bradley licked his lips, mirth dancing in his eyes. "Let me." Bradley yanked the wig on both sides, studying her as if she were art deco. "You should have cemented this in place or at least used bobby pins." He turned his head in Frank's direction. "Maybe we should supervise him - make sure he doesn't steal anything."

She didn't want to look at her ex any more than she had to. Revulsion flooded her at the thought, but agreed with Bradley's wisdom. Linking her fingers through her pretend boyfriend's, she pulled him after her. If she had to go into the lion's den and make herself sick to her stomach, she refused to go alone.

They caught Frank squatting in front of the entertainment center in the living room dumping all her CD's and DVD's into his box. His grubby fingers defiled her beloved music and movies.

"Those are mine!" Furious, Kirsty ran to the box and fished through it, taking out her movies and music, cradling them in her lap. "You don't even like 'Seven Brides for Seven Brothers' or 'Pillow Talk'. You call them moldy chick flicks," she hissed, venom in her voice.

Frank adopted an innocent expression, looked heavenward, and tapped his foot. "I must've picked them up by accident."

"All of them is *not* an accident." Her blood boiled as she glared at him. How could she have ever thought she was in love with this snake? This disgrace to mankind? She wasn't going to let him out of her sight, not even to go to the bathroom lest he steal her diet pills, towels, and shampoo. Well, maybe she'd let Bradley take that duty. It'd serve Frank right.

Bradley looked at his watch pointedly and tapped it with his fingernail. "You have fifty minutes and then I'm tossing you out."

Color suffused Frank's sunken cheeks and sparks flared in his eyes. "You can't let him talk to me like that under my roof."

"*Your roof?* Last I looked, only my name was on the title and you hadn't paid your share of the mortgage in months." Kirsty stood on tiptoe to reshelve her movies and music. "You have no claim on this house." *How dare he even think such a thing!* It was her house. Her home. She'd bought it before they'd ever met. It was her blood, sweat, and tears in this house. Her elbow grease.

"I wouldn't be so sure. My attorney tells me I get half of everything…"

Flabbergasted, Kirsty's jaw opened so wide it ached. "We weren't married and we weren't even together two years. You mooched off me and you know it. You don't deserve even one square foot of *my* house."

Frank studied his buffed nails and then shined them on his polo shirt.

"The law disagrees."

He stretched to his full height, jutting out his chin, short compared to Bradley. Holding out his hands, palms flat as if to halt her from advancing on him, he backed away from her. "But don't take my word for it. My attorney will educate you soon enough."

"Get your clothing and get out." Bradley turned on Frank, backing him the rest of the way into the corner, towering over him and making the smaller man cower. His shoulders flexed, tensing, and the hair on the back of his neck bristled. Menace oozed from his every pore. Energy radiated from every sinew.

"Call Cyclops off before I sue you both for assault. I have friends in the FLPD." Frank trembled, his beady eyes narrowed in his purple face. His chin wobbled in uncontrollable quivers as he tried to lift it regally and failed.

"Can't do it. I've not touched one flea bitten hair on your mangy head." Bradley linked his hands behind his back to prove his point. The cords in his neck stretched and his pulse throbbed. Veins bulged in his muscled arms. "Don't even think about lying, scum bag. I have a witness and you don't."

"An hour's not long enough..."

"Fifty-five minutes left and counting. Whatever's left is getting packed up and put on the curb unless she gets it, then it's probably getting heaved in the canal." Bradley tilted his head at her. "For some mysterious reason, she's not too happy about your womanizing ways and trying to steal her house."

Frank's black gaze ping ponged from her tenant to her and back. "I only want what's mine..."

"Fifty-three and counting." No emotion clouded Bradley's voice. "I'd get a move on if I were you, Pal. Hell hath no fury, you know..."

"I'm goin'. I'm goin'. Move already, Conan." Frank shoved past Bradley, banging into the tall blond's shoulder with his. "A big girl like you should be grateful to get any man. Paying the rent is little price to pay for the privilege."

Bradley spun around and grabbed Frank by his collar, and lifted him off the floor, peering eye to eye with her ex. "This is the last warning you'll get. Stop harassing Kirsten or you'll have to deal with me. I don't ever want to see your sorry mug on this property or even on this street ever again. Got it?"

Frank's feet dangled a good four inches off the floor. Terror flooded his eyes and his Adam's apple swelled as if he had a goiter. He struggled but only succeeded in looking like a sick guppy. "Now I'll sue you for assault."

"I'll deny he touched you," she said. "I don't see any bruises or marks on you to support your claim."

Frank scowled and scurried upstairs when Bradley finally released him.

Bradley linked his fingers through hers and her pulse went crazy. She prayed he wouldn't notice how her hand trembled or that her fevered fingers burned into his. He was the most unsuitable man she could pick to be attracted to – even more unsuitable than her ex-fiancé. He pulled her behind him, dogging Frank's steps.

"You don't have to watch over my shoulder," Frank said sullenly, a pout in his voice. He banged stuff into his boxes and threw his clothes unceremoniously on top of his suitcase, even his expensive Italian suits. He rooted through the closet, swearing under his breath. Then he pivoted viciously, waving a dark brown leather shoe in the air maniacally. "What'd you do with my other shoe? These cost me three hundred bucks! They're imported."

His temper tantrums tired her and she mentally rolled her eyes. Sarcasm bubbled from her lips. "I ate it?" Obviously he thought she'd deliberately misplaced it or he wouldn't be screaming at her.

Bradley shot the shorter man a warning look that would make a sane man back down. His eyes narrowed, blacker than the devil's. But no one had accused Frank of being sane in a long time. Least of all her. "Lay off her," he growled, his lips tight and drawn. His muscles tensed against her.

Shock and a little thrill of pleasure darted through her. Bradley had become her protector, more wonderful and exciting than Sir Lancelot could ever hope to be. She couldn't help but grieve that he wasn't in a position to scoop her up and carry her away to a happily ever after. At best, brotherly or best friend feelings stirred inside him for her – and that wasn't what she craved.

She shot a tiny, superior smile at Frank, feeling secure that he felt intimidated by her boyfriend. His bluster had faded into a chagrin that caused him to back up a few steps. "Believe me when I tell you I haven't touched your stuff. I was too afraid of catching something." She didn't want to lay a finger on anything he'd touched.

Frank finished packing and sneered. "I don't know what you see in her big..."

Fire flashed in Bradley's eyes. "Here, let me help you with that, *friend*." Before Frank could respond, Bradley grabbed the other man's bags and box as if to tote them, but then dropped them over the railing. They hit the floor with a sickening thud and crackle of glass. "Oops. They slipped."

Frank gasped, his face purpling and his eyes bulging out as he scurried down the stairs. He kept glancing back at Bradley fearfully, his nostrils flaring and perspiration beading on his broad forehead. He shook his fist into the air, his head craned back so he could glare up at them. "I'm filing a police report! You'll hear from my attorney."

Bradley shrugged, a lazy grin spreading over his face "I'm real scared. Even if you win, I'd be surprised if I had to shell out $2.50 for all your junk put together." He chortled mirthlessly and he slid his hands up Kirsty's arms sensually. His fingers trailed the pulse to her neck, up her jaw, and then cupped her cheek, mesmerizing her. He murmured seductively, his breath fevered against the tender flesh of her neck and lips. "I'll just take the trash out and then we can finally be alone. Light the candles and put on some romantic music..."

The way he said alone made her tremble from head to foot. And the image of candles flickering erotically made her juices flow. The thought of them making slow, languorous love bathed in the soft glow of candlelight almost brought her to her knees. "You don't play fair," she whispered against his lips, tiptoeing up to him. She let her fingers run through his thick blonde hair, reveling in its silkiness. She might never get another chance.

His cheeks curved in a saucy grin. "Playing fair isn't any fun. And I live to have fun, darlin'."

She almost fainted, wondering if his words held a double entendre. His voice couldn't be so smoky velvet, so hot, if he wasn't interested in her, could it? Instead, she clung to him lest she fall at his feet. Maybe she was losing her mind - as well as her sanity.

"I'll be right back," he murmured huskily gazing deeply into her eyes. She could swear passion flickered in them, which sparked an answering flame in the pit of her stomach.

"Time's up." Bradley was down the stairs in a flash, picking up Frank by the collar and carrying him out the door. Then he tossed the bags and box outside. He slammed the door, cutting off Frank's threats and curses, and then wiped his hands down his jeans. "Problem fixed," he announced smugly. "I don't think you'll have to worry about him anymore, sorry son of a bi..."

She stared at him, trying to size him up, and remained puzzled. She didn't know anyone who acted half as macho as Bradley just had. "You don't mess around, do you? Remind me not to get on your bad side." She forced herself to laugh lightly to brighten the mood and hide the tumult of her wayward feelings.

Bradley winked at her, and a dimple cleaved his chin. Sunlight bathed him in a godlike glow. "You couldn't get on my bad side, sweetie." *Sweetie.* There was that word. Marshall called her *sweetie.* Marshall called all women sweetie. It was a hallmark phrase. Her smile faded as all joy drained out of her and she trudged up the stairs to rearrange her ransacked room.

Chapter Four

"So, did you finally lose the wanker?" Gigi sidled up to Kirsty at work the next morning, leaning against the counter.

Lost in her muddled thoughts, Kirsty, turned unfocused eyes on her friend, and then blinked. Gigi's trademark was wearing bright, outlandish clothes, but she'd outdone herself today. Blinding, sparkling red and orange sequins covered a skin-tight pantsuit. She'd tied a sequin-covered scarf around her head and the ends dangled over her shoulders. Kirsty gasped and jumped back, rubbing her eyes. "Don't scare me like that! Warn me to wear my shades."

Gigi giggled and played with the tassels on the end of her scarf. "So how'd it go last night? Did he beg you to take him back? Or did he whine like a baby about how badly you mistreated him?"

Kirsty stripped a rose of its petals and then started shredding them.

Gigi's brow arched. "That pervy, eh?"

"Lousier. He threatened to sue me for the house and file assault charges on Bradley."

"That went well." Gigi shook her head and bristled. Then she frowned. "Bradley assaulted him? How? By hitting him with his feather boa?" She plucked the new rose from Kirsty's hand before she could shred more inventory. "It's not the poor flower's fault."

Kirsty lowered her voice conspiratorially. "Not exactly. He pretended to be my boyfriend to make Frank jealous." Visions of her muscular tenant filling out his tight jeans flitted through her mind as her cheeks, and pussy, flamed. She squirmed in her chair remembering his long, slow kiss and how his tongue had invaded her mouth.

"Soooooooooooooooooo, did it work?" Curiosity blazed in Gigi's eyes.

"It steamed me up." Kirsty swallowed hard wishing her voice wasn't raw with emotion. She twisted her ring on her finger, refusing to meet her friend's gaze afraid it would be accusatory, or shocked. "I'm in big trouble, aren't I?"

"Did you steam him up, too?" Gigi couldn't sound more serious and she laid the rose down on top of the ones she was arranging. "Did he snog you? I mean did he stick his tongue down your throat?" Fluorescent light bounced off her sequined legs shooting rainbows about the room.

"Yes, yes, and…yes." Kirsty examined her nails to save her eyes as well as her dignity. She chewed her lower lip. "You should've seen the show he put on for Frank. My knees are still wobbling."

Gigi clapped loudly and jumped up and down. Glee danced in her eyes. "Maybe he's over his head for you." She pressed her fingertips to her temples and squeezed her eyes tightly shut. "I'm getting a brainstorm."

Kirsty was very familiar with her friend's brainstorms and visions. They were practically legendary. Gigi considered herself psychic, which was okay if she was in the mood to give out free tarot card readings, but not for unsolicited advice to the lovelorn. A tsunami of dread struck her square in the stomach. "Heaven help me. No!"

Gigi's eyes opened wide. She grabbed Kirsty and shook her. "You can save him! Make him drool over you."

"Oh puh-leaze. No fag hags allowed in my store." Marshall flounced by them, scowling darkly. "I wish you would stop trying to save us. I'll let you in on a little secret - we don't want to be saved. We're happy happy happy just the way we are, Sisters!" He banged his books on the table and thrust out his hip. "Stop harassing that poor fellow. Let him be. Maybe he's AC/DC."

"We're not harassing anyone. It's not as if she's going to tie up the poor man or handcuff him…" Gigi stared her boss down and straightened to her full height. "She'll just use some feminine wiles on him and if he responds, so be it."

"I will?" Dazed, she gaped at her friend. "When did I say that? I don't remember anything of the sort." Scanning her memory with all her might, she found no trace.

"Thank God." Marshall breathed a sigh of relief and plopped into his chair in front of his computer. A second later his modem chimed and a spunky voice announced, 'You've got mail!' "I should warn that poor man what you're up to." He clicked his mouse and opened his mailbox.

"You do and we'll walk." Conviction laced Gigi's sultry tones as she crossed her arms over her chest and she bobbed her head forcefully.

Kirsty gulped, her still sickly bank account plaguing her mind. "We?" Gigi turned and stood tall next to her. "Solidarity, Sister," she hissed in Kirsty's ear. "Together we stand, divided we fall."

"Stop helping me!" Kirsty hissed back. "You'll help me right into my grave."

Gigi ignored her. "I know! Let's have a contest. You both want Bradley, right?"

Horror crashed in on Kirsty. "You want me to *seduce* him?" She pointed at their boss. "And him to seduce him? Doesn't this sound a little kinky to you?"

"Kinky's good." Marshall looked up from his email. "You may be cute Kirstykins, even candy to a straight guy, but you won't even turn my Bradley's head. Don't embarrass yourself trying."

Fury engulfed Kirsty. Fuming she stomped across the room. Squaring off in front of him, she stuck out her hand. "I'll take the bet. Chicken?" Steel tones challenged him, yet she wobbled as if on a precipice. What morass was she about to dive into?

Marshall narrowed his eyes and stroked his mustache thoughtfully. Then he scraped his chair back and took her hand. He squeezed so hard it was a wonder her poor fingers didn't break. "You're on. May the best girl win." He sashayed to the refrigerator, extracted two-dozen of their best roses, and sent her a piercing gaze. "This is war. Anything goes, sweetie." He called the delivery boy and whispered into the phone, cupping his hand in front of his mouth so they couldn't read his lips.

* * * * *

The doorbell peeled the National Anthem which he had begun to hum without realizing it, as Brad stepped out of the shower. "Hold on!" he yelled, knotting the towel around his waist. He slipped on water and banged his knee against the wall. Swearing, he hopped on one foot as he clutched his aching appendage.

"Yeah? What d'you want?" Brad wrenched the door open, ready to rip off the unfortunate soul's head if they didn't have an excellent reason for disturbing him. If he couldn't play ball because of this, he'd be madder than a hornet.

A red haired, pimple-faced, lanky young man with ears too large for his head, smiled shyly, and held out an eloquent box with a huge red bow to him. "Bradley Miller?"

When Brad narrowed his eyes and nodded his head, the kid thrust the box against his chest. "Roses from a special admirer."

"Who sent roses to Kirsty?" Jealousy tripped through him, making him surlier. Could it be that scum Frank? Was this his way of apologizing for being a total jerk? Or maybe the guy had been jealous of him?

Crimson crept up the boy's neck to his cheeks and he cleared his throat. "They're - uh - not for Kirsten." He read the gold embossed card, breathing heavily. "To Bradley with all my love. Marshall." The kid squinted at him through his long, scraggly bangs "You Bradley?"

Brad had to bite back a humorless chuckle. Marshall was courting him? Was he really surprised? He'd been set up for this all along. Crowe and his cronies must be laughing it up right about now. "Guilty."

"Sir?" The kid held the box out to him and a receipt to sign. "Please sign for me."

Brad scribbled his name and took the box. It wasn't the kid's fault he was Marshall's messenger. Opening it, déjà vu assailed him when he spotted two dozen roses - American Beauties if he wasn't mistaken. A note topped the cards that threatened, "Tonight, Dearest, I'll make you mine." Hadn't he used similar words for one or more of his many girlfriends when he sent them roses? Was this Marshall guy stealing his best lines?

The kid hung around, shuffling his feet, staring him boldly in the eye.

"What d'ya want? A tip?" He didn't have his wallet on him obviously. He'd give him the tip of his life - don't become an undercover cop. With his almost neon carrot top that was highly unlikely, however, so he settled for a scowl.

Emotions shifted over the boy's ruddy face. "Did you have a message to send back to my boss?"

A million retorts popped into Brad's mind, but none he could say aloud to anyone under thirty and this kid looked as if he had virgin ears. He wrinkled his nose and shook his head. "I'll give it to him in person." Feeling bad, he said, "Wait," and ran upstairs to get a couple of bucks out of his pants pocket to give the kid. "Here you go," he mumbled. "Thanks."

"They match your complexion perfectly," the little wise acre threw behind him as he loped down the path jauntily. He stuffed the wadded up greenbacks in his torn jeans pocket and whistled as he climbed into a car held together haphazardly.

Brad slammed the door wishing he'd given the smart aleck the first tip that came to mind instead of cold cash. As soon as the freckle-faced messenger left, he flung on the first wrap he found – one of Kirsty's frilly robes hanging on the back of the bathroom door – and trudged outside. He buried the roses deep in the garbage so his landlady wouldn't see them. He was supposed to give roses, not receive them.

"You're looking lovely this morning." His neighbor burst into heavy laughter as he weeded his flower bed on hands and knees. He snipped a blade of grass off with a pair of scissors, and then lay down on the grass to check the height of the rest of his yard.

The only grass Brad cared about was the Astroturf on the Mills Pond baseball fields. As long as they stayed properly maintained, he had no gripes – not in that arena at least. He paid a lawn service to do his grass. Life was too short to waste when he could be at the ball fields.

"Your grass is a quarter inch too high, you know. You need to maintain it better. "

Brad regarded the grass cross-eyed. Nightmares of military housing regulations taunted him and he felt like spitting at the guy's feet. "I'm just renting. I'll be sure to pass your message on to the landlady."

The man scrambled to his feet and started pruning his bushes, "Don't let her forget. We should have an association here to monitor these things." He pointed at the cars and car parts in the next yard. "An association wouldn't stand for that eyesore de-escalating our property values."

Brad backed away, hoping the man's insanity wasn't catching. Last time he checked, this was America and people could use their yards as they wanted within reason. If he didn't have inside information, he wouldn't give a second thought to that yard. He liked a nice looking neighborhood as much as the next normal guy – but he wasn't anal like this dude either.

Kirsty called and asked him what his favorite food and color was, sounding very secretive. Then she made him promise to be there when she got home.

Visions of a sexy, diaphanous teddy tortured him as he showered, shaved, and cleansed his face of all the hated make-up in preparation for her mysterious arrival. Then he cleaned house and waited for his blonde sprite of a landlady to show.

He must've dozed off, for he awoke with a start when silky hair caressed his cheek and a lace-covered breast grazed his arm. "Wake up, Sleeping Beauty," a very sultry, husky voice crooned. "I brought home your favorite – Prime Rib and chocolate covered strawberries." She perched on the couch beside him, leaning over him, her creamy breasts almost falling out of a slinky, frilly creation he was sure was illegal throughout the First World.

Had he thought of her as a sprite? Temptress was more like it. No, *siren* was the apt description. Those dusky aureoles peaked out at him again and his blood pressure shot sky high.

He swallowed hard, his pulse hammering and his breathing uneven. His cock sprung to full attention. He knew he should move away, make a joke, or do something to diffuse the dangerous situation, but he couldn't. Not when she scooted back and rubbed against him, torturing him inhumanely.

She smelled of lilacs, vanilla, and strawberries. Then he realized it was an oddly smoky vanilla scent, and fresh juicy strawberries. He pried his gaze from her tight nipples and noticed for the first time how the dim lights flickered from candles on every surface. "Is it my birthday?" His voice crackled, sultrier than hers. His cock ached to get out of his palace and play. *Down boy!* It had only suffered a female drought for a few days, not the eon it felt like.

Kirsty licked her shiny lips, slow and languorously, her pink tongue just peeking out those luscious lips, promising pleasure beyond compare to any man brave enough to take up her invitation. And she undoubtedly invited him. But why? Until tonight, she'd been sweet and teetered on the shy side. Why had she morphed into this voluptuous seductress who knew all the moves, and flaunted her voluptuous body in sucking distance, to drive him so wild to forget himself and his mission?

Stars twinkled in her eyes and she ran a fingernail down his chest, which she let hover just below his navel, at the snap of his jeans. Her nipples strained against the see-through lace, taut little buds teasing him unmercifully.

He longed to touch the outer rim of her dusky areole, and his mouth went dry. He could taste it deep inside his mouth.

"What do you want for your birthday?" She leaned over him, and her bodice gaped open to give him a nearly full view of the gorgeous breast.

He sucked in his breath unable to tear his gaze from the perfect view. When she sat down again, rubbing against him, his shaft strained to be free. He didn't know how much more torture he could stand. Never had he restrained himself before and he could barely remember why he needed to now. The female was not only willing, she was begging him to fuck her.

"Hungry?"

He almost fell off the couch, but rolled into her instead, increasing his pain to even more excruciating levels. "Starved," he admitted, hoping she didn't plan to tease and torture him all night like this. If she seduced him, as she surely seemed to be doing, he could succumb. Even Crowe couldn't fault a red-blooded man for being unable to resist the lures of a nearly naked seductress.

"In that case," a slow smile dawned over her face making her glow, "Open your mouth wide. I have something special for you." Her gaze burned with passion, her eyes nearly midnight blue, mesmerized him. Unable to resist what he wanted with such a burning intensity, he closed his eyes, opened his mouth and sought what she so freely offered. He wanted to taste her breast, or better yet, be treated to her luscious cunt.. Crowe would never have to know. Since when was his love life the department's business?

When she rubbed a plump round object against his lips, and pushed gently, seeking admission, he expected to feel satiny, heated flesh, and taste her warm lilac scent. Instead, rich, hard chocolate tantalized and prodded a smile to his lips. He parted his mouth, letting her slide the candy inside. Then cool, succulent fruity flesh exploded in his mouth, and tiny seeds tasted sour on his tongue. Delicious as it was, it wasn't his favorite taste in the entire world – pussy.

"Do you like that?" Her voice ravished him, pushing coherent thought further and further from his mind.

He gazed at her, his vision unfocused as her chest hovered only an inch away at most. Swallowing hard, he caught her wrists and dragged her down to him. His cock demanded some action and it wasn't listening to logic. "Why are you doing this? You're playing with fire, you know."

"Am I?" A flirtatious grin flitted on her lips. "Does that mean you're attracted to me?"

"Yes." *Little did she know just how explosively hot he was, how his cock burned to bury itself inside her tight vagina.*

"So you're attracted to women, too? Have you ever made love to a woman before?"

If she only knew... "I'm a sexual creature, if that's what you're asking." He answered her as vaguely and specifically as he could, and he nuzzled her long, sexy throat. It was a monumental effort just to speak, to breathe with her so close. Every time he inhaled, her flowery fragrance wrapped around him and sent his senses spinning. If he weren't already lying down, his knees wouldn't have held him. "And yes, I've made love to a woman before." He flipped her over, so that she lay beneath him, and he pressed against her, leaving no doubt about his attraction to her, or his intention to take her.

She lowered her eyes, her lashes dark crescents against her high cheekbones. Small, perfect teeth caught her lower lip. Then, her eyes flew open and she pierced him with a smoky, sultry gaze that stole his breath. "Fuck me."

His cock lurched, and molten lava boiled in his veins as he stared down at this exquisite woman who had captivated him from the first moment he'd laid eyes on her. His thumbs caressed her shoulders as he searched the depths of her amazing eyes. "Are you sure? I don't think I can stop once I start kissing you."

"Then hurry up and kiss me." She linked her hands behind his head, wound her fingers in his hair, and pulled his mouth down to hers. Her lips parted wide and her tongue reached out to mate with his in a primitive dance he couldn't resist. She moaned – or was that him? Or maybe it was both of them in chorus.

His hands roamed her searing flesh, so silky and satiny, so hypnotizing. He wanted to bury himself in her and never crawl out. He plundered her lips with his as his hands pushed her lacy seductress outfit to her hips, baring perfect breasts.

She wriggled against him, burrowing closer, pushing his robe off. She licked his lips, savoring them. "Uhm. I love chocolate. Maybe I should get out the chocolate syrup so we can lick it off each other."

He remembered hot, erotic stories Cole related about Haley's cookie dough. But chocolate syrup sounded equally erotic. "Do you have any?" Not that he wanted to let her go even to walk to the kitchen to get it. Maybe next time – he'd be ready.

She licked his chest, her tongue soft yet sandpapery, making him jump out of his skin. "Chocolate. Butterscotch. Strawberry. Pineapple… you name it." She started to rise, but he clamped his arms around her waist, holding her tight.

"Uh uh. You're not escaping me that easily." He nibbled her lips then worked his way down her neck to the swell of her breasts. He couldn't tell if it was her heart or his pounding arrhythmically. He only knew he'd spontaneously combust if he didn't take her now.

"Don't worry. I'll be right back."

He rubbed against her, barely able to restrain himself. "Now." Urgency and passion vibrated in his voice, in his every muscle. His hands explored every inch of her, learning the tactile feel of her, leaving his imprint on her.

She reached into his pants and touched him, tentatively at first, then grew more bold, winding her fingers around his thick rod. Her hands felt cool yet stimulating on his fevered flesh as she stroked the throbbing length of him.

He groaned into her mouth, dueling with her tongue. He bucked against her magical palm as she stroked him and rubbed the tip of his leaking shaft with petal-soft fingers. She played with liquid fire, a fire completely out of control. If she didn't watch out, the backdraft would consume both of them. He returned the favor, sliding his hand under the rim of her lacy panties only to realize it had no crotch. His juices flowed wetter and faster with the knowledge. He tested her with a finger, sliding it into her pussy. He stroked in and out of her and then slipped a second finger inside, stretching her.

He quivered, feeling closer to this woman than to any other. His heart swelled, beating fast against his ribs. His cock burned, but more than his own pleasure, he wanted to ensure hers.

She squirmed, ready for him to fuck her, but he wanted to taste her first, to give her immense satisfaction unlike any other man had ever given her. He lowered himself to the floor and buried his face between her legs. He licked her swollen labia, then sucked her hard clit, drinking in her luscious juices. He loved how she squirmed and wiggled against him, how her breath caught in her throat.

Wanting to give her more pleasure, he dipped his finger back into her well, loving the feel of her smooth vaginal walls, and how they squeezed him.

She bucked harder, arched her head back, and moaned. The sweet sounds wrapped him in such exquisite warmth, he never wanted them to stop.

But she became more demanding, greedier, and drew him up with her on the couch. She opened her legs wider to him, shivering. Her strong thighs squeezed him, velvety soft.

Her eyelids half closed lazily, flooded with smoldering dreams and promises.

He wanted to drown in those eyes, almost as much as he wanted to bury himself in her supple tightness. He needed to fill her with his cock more than he needed to breathe. Unable to wait another moment, he pushed his pants down to his ankles and thrust into her cunt as deeply as he could.

She gasped, or maybe it was him – he couldn't tell. Their moans and groans sounded amazingly similar.

He captured her lips again and his tongue delved into that cavern, exploring her, branding her his, even if he couldn't officially tell her yet. He drank of her deeply, knowing he could never drink his fill of this sweet wench.

She met him thrust for thrust, her breasts crushed against his chest, the tight buds of her nipples deliciously erotic. Her body molded to his perfectly. Their hearts chimed in rhythm.

His cock slammed into her and then his balls smacked her buttocks. His testicles pained him they were so swollen and tight. The only sound louder than their slurping juices was the sound of the couch banging mercilessly against the wall.

His pulse pounded in his head and he lost all sense of time and place. Blood thrummed through his veins, and he throbbed deep inside her, luxuriating in her wet, hot, folds. Reality narrowed to the woman in his arms.

Their moans grew louder, and their breath came out in short bursts as he shuddered on the precipice of bliss in her arms. Orgasm mounted inside him. And then his seed spewed into her like a tidal wave.

He cradled her against him gently, drinking deeply of her chocolate covered lips. The scent of their lovemaking permeated the room, mixing with the smoky vanilla, and her flowery essence. Her full breasts pillowed against him as she strained closer and wriggled uncontrollably in his arms, an undeniable sign that she too had found heaven. Stroking her hair, he murmured against her ear, "You're incredible." He dipped the tip of his tongue in her ear, delighting how she shivered delightfully against him again.

Her lips caressed the heated flesh on his chest, trailing fire down to his nipple. She swirled her tongue around it in wide sweeps. Against his feverish flesh, she murmured, "So are you. I knew you were attracted to me in spite of your sexuality . We proved Marshall wrong."

"What?" His universe spun dizzily, his sun eclipsed by meteors of dread. Horrible thoughts obscured his happiness and he suspected the worst, an occupational hazard. He pushed himself up and off her and grabbed the ruffled robe on his way across the room. "What do you mean you *proved Marshall wrong*?"

She sat up, swiveling her legs over the couch as she attempted to cover her breasts with the see-through lacy teddy. Goosebumps popped out on her arms, and her toes curled and uncurled. "I didn't mean to say that..." Her gaze skittered away from his and she tilted her head pretending to look at something else.

"But you did say it. You can't take it back." He crossed his arms over his chest, shielding his heart with armor. *So this had all been a bet to see if he was gay or not?* "Exactly what did you mean by that?"

Telltale pink stole up her pretty cheeks as she rubbed her calf with her bare foot. "Gigi suggested you might really be interested in me, deep down. Marshall said it was impossible. So he suggested a bet to see which one of us could win you over..."

He wasn't anyone's fool. He swore vehemently under his breath as he shoveled unsteady fingers through his disheveled hair. "You think this," he poked his finger at the scene of the crime, "proves I'm not gay? Maybe I swing both ways?" He felt awful when she cringed, but he had wanted to make a point to make her think, and had blundered in without thinking in his blinding fury. "Hell!" Now she'd think him a total loser, and he wasn't so sure he wasn't. He couldn't keep up this charade and Crowe was going to hear it now.

Furious beyond thinking, he stomped out of the house, to confront his captain and stopped short when a horrible sight met his eyes. Betty Lou was missing in action. He kicked the dirt, swearing even louder. "Damn! Son of a bitch stole my car." He felt like dragging the lousy neighbor out of his house and making him cough up the vehicle. Of course he knew he couldn't blunder in and blow the case, even if it had suddenly become personal. So he stomped inside, ignored the she-devil, and took the stairs three at a time to his bedroom where he locked the door and called Fischer to come and rescue him.

Chapter Five

"Well, we both lost the lousy bet." Kirsty slammed her purse onto her desk the next morning, glaring at her boss. Fury raged through her as she glowered at him. The look of pain in Bradley's eyes still broke her heart.

"How could we both lose?" Marshall's brows tented. When Gigi walked in unaware of the tension in the air, Marshall poked a finger at her, "Did the itty bitty titty brigade win on the independent ballot?"

"What?" Gigi and Kirsty echoed simultaneously, looking at each other, then at their boss in consternation. *What in the world was he talking about now?* He went off on a lot of strange tangents without warning. Sometimes he seemed to speak a second language.

"Who are you accusing of having itty bitty titties?" Gigi thrust her chin out regally, danger signals flashing in her murky eyes. She tried to thrust out her chest, but there wasn't much to thrust out unfortunately. Opposite of Kirsty, she was flat on top and perfectly rounded on the bottom.

"Not me," Kirsty said, brusque. That was at least one benefit of being big.

"Brag brag brag." Gigi scowled at her, tapping her foot. "So why is he attacking me? Is he PMSing about going over the hill this weekend?"

"Watch it," Marshall warned, his voice humorless. Anyone who knew Marshall knew he was sensitive about his meteoric advance into old age. He thought turning forty was paramount to death. "Any over the hill jokes and you're fired."

"Like this is a *good* job?" Gigi heaved a huge sigh. To Kristy, she said sotto voce. "He's only saying this because he wants a big surprise party."

Kirsty kicked her friend in the shins. Gigi knew darned well that they had a huge surprise party planned for Marshall's big four-zero, and she had no business spilling her guts. She'd worked too hard on his party to spoil it now.

Marshall wadded up a sheet of printer paper and rocketed it at Gigi, hitting her in the shoulder. "Leave my sight, ungrateful woman, if you think it's that bad here. Like I can't replace you like that?" He chuckled mirthlessly and snapped his fingers loudly in the air above his head. He waved a batch of papers at her. "Tons of people have begged me to work here."

Gigi whispered in an aside to Kirsty, "He's menopausal, poor dear." She giggled. "Absolutely delusional."

"That's it!" Marshall stomped to the door and wrenched it open, denting the wall. Thrusting his chin into the air, he announced, "I'm leaving for the day before I fire the both of you. Don't burn the place down"

Gigi fluttered her fingers in the air. "Ta ta." She took Marshall's spot at his computer and checked his email. "He just wanted an excuse to escape early. "

Kirsty agreed, smiling. "Now we can plan his party. Did you invite all his friends and family?"

"Check. Did you arrange for tea and biscuits?" Gigi tucked her short hair behind her ears so that her Zircon ear studs sparkled.

"Yep. Party platters and drinks." Mentally, Kirsty ticked off the astronomical price on her fingers. "So what if it only took one month's salary? Marshall's worth it." Good thing Bradley had paid her up front for two months rent. "I also got his birthday gifts. Did you?"

A devilish smile lit up Gigi's face. "He's gonna love my gift. I went to the naughty chocolate shop at the mall and bought him an edible penis. A big long, schlong with the biggest balls you ever saw, just the way he likes them."

Kirsty almost choked and covered her mouth with her hand. "You didn't!" Of course her friend had. The more outrageous the better. Leaves fluttered to the floor around her feet as she busied herself arranging flowers for a large funeral. She couldn't erase the thought of the cock from her mind. It made her think of Bradley and his mouth-watering cock.

Bells tinkled above the door and Kirsty looked up to meet Bradley's scowl. It felt as if big winged dragons fluttered in her chest and her knees almost gave way. Heat stole up her cheeks and she hoped he wasn't a mind reader.

"You could get him a dildo. They had electric and battery powered..."

"Hi, Bradley," Kirsty said coolly, cutting off her loud-mouthed friend as fast as she could, appalled at the furnace burning in her cheeks.

Gigi whirled around in her chair and had the grace to look embarrassed. "Hi, Bradley." She turned back to Kirsty and mouthed, "Oh my God. How much did he hear?"

A tight smile twitched over Kirsty's lips. "You didn't hear a thing, did you, Bradley?" He'd heard the most damaging part of course. He might as well have read her mind after Gigi's big mouth.

Bradley leaned over the counter, mirth dancing in his eyes. He plucked an American Beauty from a bouquet, strolled over to her and tucked it behind her ear. "Not a thing. Do I get an invite to this bash?"

Gigi hid her face in her hands and groaned. "I did not say what you think I said. That was my evil, kinky twin, Ginger."

His fingers burned her skin and she jumped back. She couldn't take this exquisite torture, couldn't believe how she had seduced him just yesterday. This was the first time they'd talked since then, if you could call this talking. She'd been mortified by her boldness, especially when he reverted to alternative ways.

"Of course you're invited - but only if you sign in blood that you'll wear all black." Kirsty avoided looking into his eyes.

"And you bring an absolutely outrageous gift." Gigi circled him, looking him up and down, tapping her chin with her forefinger. "Or you could be the entertainment?"

Kirsty nearly hit the floor. *She couldn't stand to watch a lot of horny men and women ogling Bradley.* "Entertainment?" she choked out, croaking like a frog. All of Marshall's friends snatching at his magnificent cock was not her idea of entertainment. Jealousy hot and fierce blindsided her. "No!"

Bradley turned his questioning gaze on her. "You don't think I can do it? First, tell me what it is, and let me decide." He puffed out his chest and favored her with a haughty glare.

She pulled him off to the side, away from Gigi's prying eyes even if she couldn't get far enough away from her friend's laughter for her liking. Once she found a private corner, she couldn't voice the words

"Well?" He towered over her, so tall she had to crane her neck to look at him.

Incorrigible, Gigi followed them and asked, "Ever jump out of a cake? Naked?"

Kirsty glared at her friend till she backed away. She couldn't look him in the eye so she stared at her feet. Marshall's friends didn't know the meaning of quiet or sedate thus she prayed they wouldn't get too rowdy and get hauled off to jail. "It's a crazy idea, so don't even give it a second thought."

"Why don't you jump out of the cake?" His stare made her sizzle from the inside out. "You're his best friend."

Her lips contorted as she looked down at herself. She shook her head. *No way.* "Naked? I don't have the right equipment for that crowd. Besides, I'm practically his little sister."

A thoughtful expression flitted across his face. "It might be fun to jump out of a cake and surprise old Marshall. What's the special occasion? Did he finally find his soul mate?"

So he was thinking about taking Gigi up on her outrageous offer? She snorted at the thought of love 'em and leave 'em Marshall settling down ever. It'd be a miracle if just one man stole his heart. "Hardly. He's turning forty – poor guy thinks he's dying - and this is our chance to get him back for all the jokes he's pulled on us." She slid him a surreptitious glance, hoping his presence here today meant he forgave her. "Did you have a reason for stopping by? Or were you just hoping we'd ask you to jump out of a cake in your birthday suit?" She prayed that he just couldn't stay away from her and a little thrill shot through her at the thought.

Shadows haunted his face as his features shifted into a scowl. "Not quite. Did you see anything suspicious yesterday? I mean, anybody hanging around our house or my car?"

Shocked, she stared at him open mouthed for several moments. Finally, she found her voice. "Someone stole your car from my driveway?"

His lips twisted wryly. "Unless she drove away by herself. I just filed a police report and someone's probably going to stop by and ask you some questions, see if you saw anything out of the ordinary. I didn't want you to be alarmed when they showed up asking for you."

She wracked her brain but hadn't noticed anyone except the neighbors outside. Shaking her head, she frowned. "I didn't see anything unusual. But you know, why don't you ask the neighbor who's in love with his lawn if he saw anything suspicious. He spies on everyone in the neighborhood all the time. Rumor has it he watches us with binoculars. It's hard to believe someone could steal anything with him on the prowl all the time."

"Yeah, the guy isn't very shy, is he?"

She had to smile at that. Her neighbor had no problems expressing himself. "So you're stranded?" Worry settled on her. "How're you getting to work?"

"Rental car - so long as they leave their grubby mitts off that until they track down my Betty Lou. Which reminds me, don't leave your car unlocked."

"Thanks for letting me know. I'd better tell Gigi before she has a heart attack."

He saluted, pivoted sharply on his heel, and headed to the front door. "Don't wait up for me tonight. I'll be late."

Her smile fell and she tried to tack it back in place lest he see. "Can you take Marshall out and keep him busy till everyone arrives? If you dare let it slip, I enjoy *slow torture*."

"Moi let anything slip? I'm the soul of discretion, sweetie. Marshall won't have a clue - leastways not from me." He flicked her chin as if he didn't have carnal knowledge of her, as if she were his little sister.

"Does this mean you'll do it? I'm forgiven?" she ventured, holding her breath.

"I'll do it. But forgiven for making me the object of your childish bet?" He screwed up his face and thought hard, while holding his chin. "No. Not that easily. You'll have to do some heavy groveling to get back on my good side."

Could she play with his heart? To what extent did she want to? "You're a strange man, Mr. Miller."

"You don't know the half of it." He dug his car keys out of his pocket and jangled them by his side. "You need some groveling lessons, 'cause that wasn't it."

"Kirsten, Dear!" Gigi called in a singsong saccharine voice. "You have visitors."

"That's them. I'm gone." Bradley sprinted out the door before Kirsty could spit out another word. He disappeared around the corner so fast she wondered if she'd imagined his visit. His bizarre behavior was beginning to worry her.

She trudged back into the store front, wondering why Bradley had high-tailed it away so fast. Didn't he want to get his car back? Or was he hiding something from the cops?

* * * * *

Brad didn't trust Cole not to show up. His best friend lived to give him a hard time. Yet again, maybe he should have stuck around to make sure that his buddy didn't put Kirsty through an inquisition. Now that Cole had found his perfect woman and was about to descend into daddyhood, he'd become an obnoxious match-maker.

He was going to get the scum who stole his car and it better not be stripped or a fish motel at the bottom of some canal. It didn't make sense to him that a chop shop next door would steal a car and put it in their own driveway, but he'd start his investigation there nevertheless. Did that mean that this chop shop had franchises around the city? Maybe up and down the East Coast? Or maybe they hauled it over to Naples on the West Coast. If they stole a car in one neighborhood, did they transport it to their buddy in a different neighborhood?

Or maybe there was a rival car thief ring who either didn't know there was a chop shop next door or they were aiming at stealing the stolen cars? Brad's thoughts ricocheted around in his brain, trying to figure out the mystery. Theory was fine, but proved nothing. He needed cold, hard facts.

So he snooped around his neighbor's yard when the guy went out. He copied down the etched bin numbers. Then he set up a wire tap. Then he asked Haley to run a computer query of all the stolen cars in the three county vicinity of Dade, Broward, and Palm Beach, including all the suspected and known chop shops.

Not content to sit and wait for information to come to him, he contacted his secret source, a scraggly but scrappy con artist named Lenny, who could be coerced to divulge such information in exchange for either immunity or a few hundred bucks. He drove down to Lenny's hideout and snuck into the old motel /filthy rat-trap by the beach, and waited in the dark hoping Lenny wasn't pulling an all nighter or out of town. He pushed aside old newspapers, girlie magazines, and beer bottles and made himself at home on the couch. When his eyes adjusted to the dim room, he noted cigarette butts swimming in stale liquor next to a plateful of chicken bones and congealed mashed potatoes.

What seemed like hours later when Brad was stifling a yawn, Lenny banged into the room, his arm around a cute young thing, his lips taking liberty with her throat. "Just you and me, Baby," Lenny crooned, pushing her tank top off her shoulder

Brad stood, clearing his throat. "And me. How you doin', Lenny, old pal?"

Lenny jumped nearly three feet in the air and squealed. Holding his hand to his throat, he gulped. "That you, Mueller, you dirty rotten scoundrel?"

Light flooded the room, blinding Brad for the first few seconds so that he had to squint to see Lenny's face. The stench of stale beer had intensified ten-fold since the man had ambled into the room and Brad tried not to breathe too deeply lest he get drunk on the fumes.

"What's goin' on, Len?" Shiny black curls bounced around the woman's waist. Miles of curvy leg protruded from a mini skirt that barely covered her womanly treasures. Manicured fingers that had seen better days wrapped around Lenny's bony wrist. "You in trouble again?"

Lenny scowled deeply and shushed her. "Wait for me outside, doll, would ya? I'll get rid of him," Lenny's squinty eyes narrowed and he did a double take, "or her, in a few." When she still clung to him, he pushed her toward the door. "Go on. Give us men some privacy."

When she'd left, pouting prettily, her ample curves jiggling, Brad focused on his old friend. "You don't look too happy to see me, Leonard. I wonder why? You guilty of somethin' again?"

Bright color suffused Lenny's face and his Adam's apple protruded. His pulse raced as if it were in the Indy 500. "I'm clean, man." He held his hands out, palms flat, and backed up a step. "I don't need no trouble. I don't know nothin'."

Brad advanced on the squirrelly thief, clapping him on the back, and then rested his arm around his thin shoulders. "Who do you think you're kiddin' here? I know you. You know all the dirt in this town."

Lenny sniffed him and snickered. "What is that pretty feminine perfume you bathed in? You smell so sweet, today." His glance slid over Brad deliberately as well. "And you look so pretty in pink."

Brad glared at him and moved away. "Well, yeah, I'm undercover. I'll send you an invitation to the bon fire when I burn these things. I need your help so I can hurry up and get back to normal." He chafed in his black nylon slacks and hot pink blouse.

Lenny eyed him fearfully, grimacing. "I'd rather go back to the pokey than look like you. No offense. You're not really...funny...are you, dude?"

Brad snarled, baring his teeth, and punched his open hand with his fist. "Want I beat you up to prove I'm not funny?"

Lenny gulped. "No. No. I believe ya, man. No need to get physical. But I don't know anything..."

"How do you know you don't know?" Brad growled from deep within his gut, frustration gnawing at him. "I haven't even told you what I need."

Lenny's shifty gaze roamed his shack but refused to settle on Brad, a sure sign he wasn't as innocent as he pretended to be. "Really man. I just want to live my life. Live and let be - that's my new motto. I don't meddle in other people's business and they stay out of mine."

He'd had enough. Crossing the room in three giant steps, he backed his informant against the wall, towering over him. "I'll believe that when pigs fly. I need any and all information you have on any chop shops in Dade, Broward, and Palm Beach. Especially about a twerp named Alvarez." Brad grabbed him by his collar and lifted him high. "I really want to know. *Now*. No more games."

Lenny's feet dangled midair. His cheeks paled and his breathing quickened. He swiped at the perspiration beading on his brow as he hung limply.

"Why you so hot to get these guys? It could be very dangerous." His voice shook and rose a good octave. "Very dangerous."

"Let's just say they lifted my wheels, so now it's personal. And I'm tired of competing for Miss America." His legs itched inside the nylon torture tubes and the shirt gave him the heebie jeebies.

"Good reasons." Lenny nodded profusely, his beady eyes mere black specks over his gaunt cheekbones. "Do you think you could put me down now?"

"Sure thing." Brad opened his hand and let Lenny drop as he smiled wickedly at him. "That better?"

Lenny sprawled at Brad's feet, his knobby knees and elbows scrambling to push himself up. "You treat me with such kid gloves." He rubbed his backside, groaning. "I gonna get protection if I rat on the mob?"

"The mob? Organized crime is behind all these car thefts?"

"Naaa, my granny's card club up at Century Village got bored and decided to nab vehicles in their spare time," he drawled in his harsh New York accent. "You should see those old broads strip a car."

"Ha ha. Everyone's a comedian." Brad advanced a step and made as if he were going to grab Lenny's collar again.

The man sidestepped him, his eyes widening with fear. He rubbed the balding spot on his head. "All right, all right already. Just makin' sure you'se serious."

"Any more serious and I'll let you chill in the lock up all night. I'm not in a good mood," Brad ground out between clenched teeth. If that wasn't the understatement of the year. Much longer in this disguise, and he'd go postal.

"What do I get outta this?" Lenny held out his hand, fingers twitching.

Brad sighed and dragged his wallet out of his pocket. He pulled a hundred off his bank wad and placed it on Lenny's outstretched palm. When Lenny left his hand dangling mid air, Brad scowled. "More?" He mumbled under his breath, "You greedy little son of a bi..."

"My memory's not what it used to be. Must be catchin' Alzheimer's." Lenny's lips twitched. "You know that medicine is outrageous - cain't remember 'xactly how much."

Brad slammed a second hundred on top of the first. "You're only thirty one, a year younger than me, so don't give me that, sonny. I checked your records." All in all he had to hand over five big smackers before Lenny remembered enough to help him out.

"Carlos Becerra and his gang are headquartered at South Beach. They have a coupla shops up here in Broward, too." He scratched his chin and swatted at an imaginary mosquito.

"Addresses. Names. I need exact information." He flipped open the mini notepad in his hand and poised his pen. His fingers itched to write. "Come on, Lenny. The sun's set twice since I got here," he growled.

"What's the hurry?" Lenny's lips smirked. "Got a hot date with your boyfriend?"

"He he he," Brad laughed without mirth and then punched the wall, making a picture fall to the floor and smash. "Spill. Now. I doubt you'd be such a joker behind bars." He glanced at the time, scowling. "My ball game starts across town in twenty minutes. It'll take me thirty in rush hour traffic. I get mean when I'm late for my ball games." A rumble started in his throat as he imagined his team having to forfeit because he didn't make it on time. Worse, he wouldn't have time to change before getting to the field. He'd be later than a mad hare.

"Okay, okay, already!" Lenny snatched up the picture, dusted it off carefully, and then held it to his chest. "That's my dear departed mom." He kicked the broken glass under the couch with the toe of his shoe. He rattled off names and addresses without having to look at a paper.

Brad's brows tented but he wisely kept his counsel. When his informant finished, he patted him on the back hard, knocking him forward half a foot. "You did good, Len. I'll be seein' you soon." He flipped him another fifty dollar bill over his shoulder. "Buy yourself a gold frame for your mama."

"No need to hurry back. I'm thinkin' of movin' to a swankier joint uptown, so don't be surprised if you can't find me. I won't be tellin' my landlady where I'm goin'."

"I'll find you," Brad said jovially with a smile in his voice. He had informants to tell him where his informants hid. "I found you this time, didn't I?" He let the screen door slam behind him. "Be keeping your ear to the ground for me. Call me if you hear even a rumor of anything about Alvarez and his hijackers. You got my cell number."

Lenny waved him off. "Yeah. Yeah. Sure. I'll tattle everythin' I hear and see to you. But it'll cost you pretty."

Brad took a long last look at Lenny's dump and decided the city trash heap would be a preferable place to crash over this tumble down motel. "You've certainly got expensive tastes, don't you, Lenny? Catch ya later."

He stripped off his shirt as he sped across town, his foot smashing the accelerator deep into the floorboard. Then he spit on his hand and used it to rub the make-up off best as he could. Ruby lipstick smeared on his hand and he wiped it on his slacks, grimacing.

A carload of teenage girls whistled at him, whooping it up when they passed him as he drove shirtless. "Whoo, baby! Wanna join us for a hot time?"

"Maybe when you grow up in ten years." Even if he couldn't get the thought of Kirsty out of his mind, or the feel of her off his skin, he wouldn't mess with that jailbait, cute as they were. He smiled at them and waved, then accelerated around the corner to their disappointed ahhs and giggling. He shrugged into his bumble bee-like jersey as quickly as he could and still steer the car.

He copied the names and addresses as he drove so he could give a copy to Haley to check out on her computer for him first thing in the morning. The note pad bounced on his knee and his lines were so squiggly he could barely read his own hen scratching. When the car swerved beneath him, other drivers honked behind him and furious motorists shouted obscenities at him. "Good old Ft. Lauderdale. Gotta love it," he grumbled under his breath as he smiled and waved at his non-fans. He scribbled down the license plate number of one particularly obnoxious driver, promising himself to see if the guy had any outstanding warrants or tickets.

Cole hustled to Brad's car when he hit the brakes. "It's about time, man. What kept you?"

Brad scrambled out of the car, his cap already on his head, his glove on his hand. He kicked off his high heels and grabbed his cleats. "What field we on tonight? Who we up against?"

"Field Three and we're playing Hollywood PD. Hansen's pitching." Cole snarled.

"You still jealous of that bozo? You know Haley adores you." He sprinted toward Field Three, his socks scrunched up in his fist.

"You gonna parade out there like that?" Disbelief quarreled with laughter in Cole's voice. He whistled long and slow. "You sure got perty legs, Bradley," he drawled. Then he burst out in a loud belly laugh, holding his stomach.

Brad glanced down at his legs just now remembering he'd left his softball shorts in the car, and then shot a deadly glare at his partner and soon to be ex-best friend. "Shoot! Don't call me that sissy name." He hated being called his full name and couldn't wait to rectify the matter with Kirsty. He whirled around and marched for his car.

Cole caught him and spun him around. "No time. It won't kill you to play in those tight lycras. Maybe you'll do better."

Brad simmered as he dreaded how his teammates would heckle him. He didn't have long to find out.

"Brad! I was so worried you'd skipped out on us tonight." Cindy ran out to him, hugged him fiercely, and gave him heavy liplock, trying to stick her tongue down his throat.

He kept his lips tightly closed. Not that Cindy wasn't a knock-out. She was gorgeous and she knew it. But the most feeling he could drum up for her was friendship. The only tongue he wanted down his throat was Kirsten's.

Haley waddled through the dug out, her back arched, her stomach jutting out. The last of the evening's rays glinted on her bouncy blonde curls. She grimaced and waved, fluttering her fingers. "About time the team captain shows up," she griped. "We almost had to forfeit. Of course, my feet are bigger than watermelons so I'd rather not play anyway."

"Your wife always this cranky?" Brad whispered to Cole. "You not giving her any?"

Cole rolled his eyes. "Her back hurts. Get your mind out of the gutter, Romeo. Just because you've been transfigured into a eunuch doesn't mean I have been."

"Ouch! Your wife's not the only cranky one." They stepped onto the field and made their way to the dugout where Cole kissed Haley.

Cindy still clung to Brad. She traced his jaw with her fingers. "I could help you with your problem. Old Crowe and your roommate would never know."

"Old Crowe wouldn't ever know what?" The Captain himself boomed behind them. "What the devil are you doin' here against orders, Mueller?"

Cursing under his breath, Brad whirled around nearly knocking Cindy over in his haste.

His bloodshot eyes scanned the fields. He lowered his voice but he had one of those bass voices that still rumbled. His pudgy hands waved frantically in the air, sunlight flashing off his rings. "What if someone recognizes you?"

Cindy squealed, turned beet red, and jumped behind Brad. Her hands squeezed his arms so tightly his flesh tingled. She trembled against him and in a muffled whisper, she warned, "He's been in a mood all day. Beware - he's looking to crucify someone."

Brad kept his expression stoic, straightened to his full height and squared his shoulders. He tried to quell the frogs leaping in his stomach. He didn't wish to be a human sacrifice today. "With all due respect, sir." He swallowed hard and ordered his tongue to cooperate and he lowered his voice, while keeping it as respectful as he could. "Do you think car thieves would hang out with an entire league of policemen?"

"You directly disobeyed my orders, Mueller. What am I supposed to do with you?" Crowe glared at him, the tick by his right eye spastic, rage echoing in his voice.

Cole cleared his throat and stepped forward. "Pardon me, Captain sir, but whatever you do to my brain dead buddy here, could it wait till after the game? He is the team captain and without him we'd be one man short and have to forfeit." Hope flared in his black eyes.

Haley and Cindy chimed in chorus, their eyes big and pleading in puppy dog fashion. "Please, sir. We need him."

Cole's words sank into Brad's brain. "Hey! Who's brain dead, moron?" He swiped at Cole's head with his glove, knocking his baseball cap to the dusty floor.

Cole knocked Brad's cap to the floor, too. "Who do you think I mean, dude?"

When Brad bristled and bunched his shoulders, Haley stepped between them, placing her palms flat on their chests and pushing them away from each other. She clucked her tongue. "Tsk tsk. Children, you must learn to play nicely. No name calling on my watch." Haley groaned and slumped at their feet, her azure eyes glazing over. She reached up to grab her husband's hand. "Help," she pleaded in a weak voice.

Alarm flashed through Brad as he crouched beside her, a few seconds behind her husband. Her flesh felt chilled when he squeezed her hand.

"What's wrong, baby?" Cole cradled his wife in his arms, rocking her back and forth. "Is it the baby?"

"Oh, God. Is she in labor? Is the baby going to come *here?*" Cindy knelt beside Haley as well, stroking her hair away from her face. "Anyone got a cell phone? Somebody call an ambulance!"

"I-I think so." Haley struggled to sit up, her breath spurting out in punctuated gasps. Then she clutched her stomach and screamed. "Something's wrong, Cole."

Cole's wild-eyed gaze sought Brad's. He mouthed, "Call 9-1-1. Get help." He whipped out a handkerchief and dabbed perspiration off his wife's brow and then his own. "If anything happens to my wife or our baby…" Fright reverberated in his husky voice. Louder, he murmured in his wife's ear, "You'll be okay. We're getting help."

Brad almost yelled into his cell phone, "Send an ambulance to Mills Pond, Field Three. Woman's having a baby. There are complications. Something's wrong." He paced in front of his friends, his chest tight with worry. He planned on being Godfather to this little tyke, so he or she had better come out healthy. Nor did he want anything bad to happen to Haley. She'd become very important to him, too. And if anything happened to her, his brother would be devastated.

Within moments, the paramedics arrived and whisked Haley and Cole away to Broward General. Haley huddled on the stretcher in a fetal position, her pallor completely white.

"We'll meet you there," Brad promised as Cole climbed into the back of the ambulance. To Cindy, he ordered, "Let's go."

Cindy looked almost as pale as Haley, her eyes round and bright green against her ashen face. She nodded silently, and then swiped a renegade tear off her cheek. Her lips trembled when she spoke, her voice raspy and barely a whisper. "Will she be okay, Brad?" She linked her fingers through his and gazed up at him.

He opened the car door for her and helped her in. "I hope so, Cin. I pray so." He buckled her seat belt for her as she looked to be in shock, and then he sprinted to his side of the car.

Chapter Six

Kirsty couldn't sleep worrying about the surprise party the next day. She hummed to distract herself and so she wouldn't feel so lonely. She missed Bradley more than she cared to admit and she was more than a little worried that he was out so late without checking in. She knew that he was officially her tenant and at best, a friend. She also knew that he was an adult. Still, her watch read ten P.M. and she hadn't seen him since he'd rushed out of her store earlier that day.

An extremely wicked, delicious idea occurred to Kirsty. Everyone, especially Marshall, teased her about her horrible cooking, so she was going to get them back and good. She found a long, thick rectangular foam form she used for flower arranging and carved it into the shape of a gravestone, just like the real cake she'd made earlier in the evening.

She iced the fake cake carefully. Then she decorated it with care, adding icing roses and leaves around the rim. For the finishing touch, she wrote in cursive writing *Happy Birthday Over-the-Hill Marshall*.

She stood back to admire her handiwork, and grinned. She couldn't wait for Marshall to cut his cake – at least to try to cut his cake. She'd hide the real cake until after the joke played itself out.

"You're up late, sweetie," Bradley murmured in her ear, his hot breath tickling the sensitive curve of her throat.

She jumped as she hadn't heard him enter, and whirled around. Icing squirted from her hands, all over the front of Bradley's jersey. Horrified, she tossed the icing in the sink. "Oh no! I didn't mean to decorate you. You just startled me sneaking up on me like that." She glared at him as she tried to wipe the icing off his shirt, smearing it into a bigger mess instead.

"Maybe it'd work better if you licked it off," he crooned suggestively, staring at her intently.

"Wh-what?" Had she heard him right? Had he just flirted with her? Hope flared in her heart and made her knees go weak.

He cupped her chin with his warm palm, sending shivers through her. "You heard me, Kirsten."

"Like this?" Brazenly she closed the gap between them, unbuttoned three buttons and spread his shirt wide and then her fingertips grazed his firm, heated chest, smearing icing all over him.

"Hmm." Bradley closed his eyes in ecstasy and shivered. "You're a siren.

She pressed her lips to his chest so that his heartbeat pulsed into her mouth erratically. His thick curly blonde chest hair tickled her cheeks and chin. "You like sirens?" she murmured, blazing heat down his chest, pausing to unbutton another button.

"Hmm. I adore them."

Her brow arched, but she didn't move away. She enjoyed pleasuring him, making him squirm and shiver. All it took was a little flick of her tongue on his chest, and he melted against her. "So you're beginning to like women?"

He dropped angel kisses onto the top of her head and then turned her face up so that he gazed deeply into her eyes. "I like you." His eyes darkened to the shade of sapphire, and sparkled brighter than any of the gems she'd ever seen as he lowered lips to plunder hers. "You taste like birthday cake," he murmured into her mouth as his hands roamed her body, igniting flames in her belly.

It was her turn to squirm.

"You're not a siren - you're a witch." He nuzzled her neck with warm, oh so soft and luscious lips. All the while, he pulled her shirt out of her waistband and tugged it up and over her head, revealing her ugly industrial bra.

She pulled back to read his expression and shivered at the passion clouding his midnight blue eyes. "Why do you say that?

He pulled her back into his arms and plundered her lips with a masterful kiss that left her weak-kneed and nearly incoherent. Against her lips, he mumbled, "Because you bewitch me. Because you weave your magic around me so that I can't think straight. So that I want you so badly, I can't think of anything or anybody else but you."

Stunned, deliriously happy, she pushed her niggling doubts aside. Miracles did happen. She'd helped him find the man hiding deep down inside him and drawn it out. She'd saved him. "You drive me wild, too." She pressed closer to him, wishing to be impossibly, excruciatingly, wonderfully closer.

He reached around her and unsnapped her bra, his fingers trailing fire in their wake. She moaned and arched toward him, her nipples aching to be caressed by his fingertips…and his tongue. She wanted to rub them against his chest. She wanted to feel his muscles contract and feel the pounding of his heart against them.

He removed the annoying piece of cloth tenderly as if she was made of porcelain and his gaze devoured her. Feverish already, his heat seeped into her, elevating her temperature. "You're a work of art." He molded her to him, crushing her breasts to his chest as he kissed her senseless, until they both gasped for breath.

"I can't believe I'm feeling this way - with you." When his tongue flicked the sensitized nipples, she nearly puddled at his feet and had to clutch his arms for support.

"Mmm," he murmured against her heated flesh, his tongue licking one nipple and then the other. "You taste fantastic." He pulled the nipple deep into his mouth and suckled it, driving her delirious with joy. As hot as the fire flamed from his lips, it flamed hotter in her womb where his cock strained against her belly.

Temptation gave way to an insatiable need to touch and explore this wondrous man. Boldly, she unbuttoned his jeans and slid his zipper down torturously slowly. Hot for him, she yanked his briefs down, releasing his rock-hard, throbbing cock.

His hands followed hers as he stepped back and tore off his clothing, flinging them high in the air to the symphony of her uninhibited laughter. Kneeling before her on one knee, he pulled her slacks down, his fingertips blazing fire behind them as they cascaded down her thighs to her knees, then her calves, and even to her toes. "And you called me a siren?" Did such creatures as male sirens exist? Surely he'd be the death of her. No one could feel this much pleasure and joy and not explode from sheer happiness. Much more of his touch, and she would explode.

"You want me as much as I want you." It wasn't a question. His voice had never been deeper or huskier. Slowly, reverently, he pulled her panties down as he stayed on his knees, eye level with her womanly treasures. Then he moved closer, and shocked her, when his tongue licked up the inside of her legs, and flicked over her aching clit which clenched into a tight little bud.

Excruciating pleasure rippled through her. Her pussy quivered and she opened her legs wider to give him free access to her cunt. Her bones turned to liquid, and she cradled his head against her, trembling uncontrollably as his tongue massaged her swollen labia and then delved inside her slit. Heaven couldn't feel better than the sensations whirling through her. She soared above the clouds.

When she slumped against him, he pulled himself up to his full height and scooped her into his arms. "You deserve better than the kitchen floor." He strode to the stairs and then climbed them two at a time, his power seeping into her.

He kicked open his door, then froze, grimacing, his gaze raking over the picture of Marilyn Monroe, and then his pink frilly bedspread. "No. I don't think so." Pivoting on his heel, he carried her to her bed where he laid her down gently, as if she were the most precious person in the world. Then he climbed astride her, and smiled into her eyes. "You're so very beautiful." His smoky velvet voice caressed her as he stroked stray tendrils of hair away from her eyes.

Their gazes locked, and she licked her suddenly dry lips. When he flexed against her, his erection rubbing against her stomach, she shivered again. "So are you." She hadn't been able to get his image out of her mind and her fingers couldn't help but caress his satiny, yet firm flesh. Arching against him, she gave him a silent but unmistakable signal that she was ready for him.

He slid a finger inside her moistness, and they moaned together. He kissed her full and hard on the lips, as his finger probed her, and his thumb rubbed the nub of her clit, bringing her to the brink of ecstasy. Just when she thought she could stand no more and was afraid she'd come without him, she mumbled a fervent plea in his mouth, "Take me now."

He removed his hand, shifted his weight on top of her and teased her with the tip of his long, hot cock. He poised it above her velvety lower lips, then rubbed it over the soft petals until she wanted to scream and pull him inside.

"Tease," she accused huskily as her tongue licked and nibbled his salty male nipples. More feverish than she'd ever been, unable to quench the fire rampaging through her veins another second, she thrust her hips upward eager to know his possession.

"Exquisite." Feverish, his hot gaze devoured her. He melted her heart with the sexiest, cockiest smile this side of a Brad Pitt movie.

It was a wonder he didn't have women breaking down his door and ripping off his clothes.

He slammed into her, rocking her bed, the frame banging dizzily against the wall so powerfully she expected it to cave in. Masterfully, his muscles rippling against her, he rammed his entire length into her so deeply she could swear he caressed her womb.

Perspiration slicking her body, her breasts sliding deliciously along his chest, she met him thrust for ecstasy filled thrust. When she felt the flow of lava of the hottest orgasm she'd ever had consume her pussy, she plundered his lips, her tongue mating with his, her fingernails raking his back.

Chapter Seven

Brad awoke in paradise, a naked angel snuggling up to him nuzzling his bare chest in her sleep. Fountains of sunlight kissed her luscious, voluptuous body and she glowed, all blonde and golden, as if sprinkled by fairy dust. The faint dusting of freckles across her cheeks fascinated him, so he brushed his thumb over them.

"Bradley?" She shivered and murmured sleepily, her voice thick and sultry. Her arm curled around his waist, and her nipples hardened instantly into tight buds.

He couldn't tear his gaze from the taut rosy areoles, large and round one moment, then pointy and hard in the space of a second. Did he do that to her? His own pulse rioted in response, pounding so hard it roared in his ears, and his cock grew rock hard and throbbed against the juncture of her legs.

Unable to stop himself, he tested her by probing deep inside with his finger. "Ooh, baby." Moist heat sheathed him and she shivered against him. He wouldn't mind waking up next to her like this, hot and naked, every morning. His cock in particular loved the idea.

She smiled at him, a full lusty smile on lips swollen from his kisses. Squirming against him, rubbing her awesome breasts against his chest, teasing him, she fanned his fire to fever pitch.

He wrapped his arms around her and rolled her over so that he was on top and poised to plunge his cock deep into her pussy again. He couldn't fill the reservoir of this angel.

Stars twinkled in Kirsty's eyes as she gazed at him adoringly. Her tongue trailed wet fire along his chest. Then she murmured against his heart, her lips hot and moist, "You have feelings for me, don't you?"

That stopped him cold and he froze, staring down at her hooded eyes and pouty lips. Should he admit that he was never gay and it was all a police undercover ploy? Wouldn't that make her ecstatic? Or should he let her believe she'd changed him?

He noodled the problem as she traced his nipple with a long fingernail and crooned in a sultry voice, "Do you want children?"

His blood froze in his veins, his mouth went dry, and he lost his erection. Children? As in marriage? Wife? 2.3 kids? A big dog? House payments and cutting his suburban lawn every Sunday afternoon like Mr. Lawn Lover? He gulped, not once, but twice, as mortal fear squeezed his testicles. "S-someday," he finally murmured so that he could barely even hear himself. "M-maybe. Don't make the mistake of thinking I'm a white knight in shining armor, though." Commitment phobia clawed at him. He was too young to be tied down to one woman, even one as enchanting and beguiling as this one.

She licked her lips, slowly, hypnotizingly, making his stomach clench. Her eyes rounded up at him. "Only maybe? Did I say I was looking for a white knight on a trusty steed?"

The dreamy look in her eyes refuted her words, making him nervous. In his experience, all women longed for a white knight to carry them off to some dream fantasy.

"You never wanted a Bradley Junior to play with? Or a little princess to spoil?" Her fingernail continued its path down his side, to his thigh, and then inward. "Or to wake up every morning cuddled up to a warm, willing woman who adores you?" Her breath tickled his chest in short, punctuated bursts, as her words oozed out like warm honey.

Horrified, he hoisted himself off her and catapulted off the bed. He held out his hand to stop her from coming nearer and confusing him with her pheromones or whatever it was that made him dizzy with desire for her. Had his brain cells gone on vacation? Since starting this mission, he was a puddle of hormones. He backed away slowly as he would from a dangerous animal. No way could he get trapped in her snare. Not now. Not like this. "Whoa, baby. This is going much too fast. My head's spinning." He glanced behind him, seeking the escape route. "Kids? As in marriage?"

Confusion dilated her eyes. She crouched in the middle of the rumpled bed, her hair in dazzling disarray, her full pouty lips bruised, swollen, and tempting beyond belief, and her skin glistening with a sheen of perspiration. When she thrust out her spectacular chest, he nearly lost his grip. Slowly, she bobbed her head, her wig askew and about ready to fall off. "That's the acceptable process. Man. Woman. Lovers. Marriage. Children."

"Can't we just go back to the lover phase?" This was moving way too fast for him and his head spun. Although he knew that was hopeless now. Once a woman began talking marriage, especially children, the relationship was doomed. "I can do lover." He backed up another step, unable to take his gaze off her magnificence.

Her brow quirked as she gazed steadily at him. "Exclusive lover? With any chance of more...in future?"

A door slammed downstairs, and footsteps thundered in. Not just one pair, or even two, but either a crowd or one giant centipede. Women chattered, and then a man's deep voice boomed, "Kirsten Marie! You home baby girl? Come give your papa and mama a big kiss."

"Come kiss your Grandmama, ma chere!" a sweet but wobbly voice trilled upstairs.

"Don't forget your Auntie Norma, sugar lump," a slightly deeper voice drawled.

"Or your big sister," a young woman's voice wafted up behind the others.

"No! Not now!" Kirsty bounded off the bed, draping a sheet around her haphazardly. The sheet caught on her foot and she tripped, landing in a heap at Brad's feet. Her face turned purple, and her eyes were wild, almost feral. "They can't find us like this. Dad'll kill you and Grandma'd have a heart attack."

"Dad's on his way up, Kirst. Get decent," Jules warned, giggling.

"Yikes!" Her eyes widened in horror at him. "He can't find you in here this way. Don't just stand there." She wadded up the nearest piece of clothing she had and tossed it to him. "Hurry, put this on."

Heavy footsteps pounded the stairs, shaking the floor. "You okay, baby girl?"

Brad had no desire to get entangled in a domestic dispute, or be caught butt naked by an outraged father, so he shrugged into the garment as quickly as he could and belted it as Kirsty did likewise. Then he looked down at himself and grimaced. *Great*! Kirsty's frilly lavender robe cloaked him. He sprinted for his bedroom, hoping time hadn't run out.

"Who are you?" A Viking of a man with white blonde hair and bright red face caught Brad's collar. His lips curled back in a snarl. "What the devil are you wearing, *son*?" His gaze leapt from Brad to Kirsty's bedroom from where it was obvious that Brad had just come. "And you were in my baby girl's boudoir." It wasn't a question by any stretch of the imagination.

Kirsty spilled into the hall, her face almost as flushed as her sire's. She stumbled on the sheet, cursed under her breath, and caught herself on the railing. Her eyes shifted from Brad to her father and back helplessly. "Daddy! What a surprise? You should've warned me you were coming. I'm so glad to see you!" She enveloped him in a big bear hug, imploring Brad with her expressive eyes to escape while he could.

Her father didn't respond in kind but chose instead to glower at her, flame shooting from his eyes. "What was this fancy pants doing in there?" He yanked the collar hard without warning and Brad started choking.

"Please, sir," Brad said, spluttering. "I can't breathe." His eyes rolled back in his head and he tried to pry the man's hands off him to no avail. If it didn't stop in two seconds, he'd have to apply self defense measures, Kirsten's father or no.

"For Heaven's sake, Daddy. This is the new millennium and we're both consenting adults. Let him go before he suffocates." She reached up and uncurled her father's pudgy fingers from Brad's neck.

"Th-thank you," Brad choked in deep breaths. He stood tall and squared his aching shoulders. Using his most authoritative detective's voice, he stuck out his hand to shake. "Bradley Miller. I'm pleased to meet you, sir."

"Hmph! Bradley, huh? Sissified name if ever I heard one." Kirsty's father declined to take Brad's hand, instead, linking his hands behind his back. His gaze roamed over Brad's attire. "Matches your girlie outfit." He leaned forward, peering hard at Brad's face. "You ain't one of those sissy boys, are you?"

Stumped, Brad stared at the man for several seconds, paralyzed. Look like he had to come clean, if anyone would believe him in such a get up. "I'm..."

"Hey, gringo!" Their neighbor and his suspect called in a gruff voice. "Gotta car to show you."

Car? Brad's ears perked up. Hope and frustration warred in him. Maybe he could end this charade and get his life back.

"We're busy right now," Kirsty said in a melodious singsong voice, a frozen smile plastered on her face as she put her arms around her dad and tried to lead him downstairs. "Bradley will have to come over later."

"This can't wait. I need to know if you want this car now, or I sell to somebody else. Many buyers want this car. But I do you favor as I know some lowlife stole your wheels."

Damnit! Who was going to show up next?

"Who's Bradley?" An old lady asked in a twitter. "I thought she was betrothed to that gopher face Frank?" A heavy cane rapped the tile floor and feet shuffled.

Bradley skirted Kirsty and her father carefully and then took the stairs two at a time, holding his robe closed instead of letting it flap around his legs as it tried to do. "On my way. I need to see that car." His toes itched in trepidation. What if it was stolen? If he could buy it, and trace it, then they could nab the guy. Why hadn't he thought of this before? Maybe because he hadn't been thinking exactly clearly. Maybe he hadn't been using his head at all.

"This yours?" a flirtatious, smirky voice taunted him. In a blur, he noted a twentyish woman with a similarity to his landlady but with white-blonde hair like Kirsty's father's. She was dressed very stylishly and her hair curtained a gaunt version of Kirsty's rosy face. Then he focused on the piece of clothing that dangled from her finger, and he almost tripped over his feet. She held out his hot pink shirt with attached boa.

Brad barely donated a scathing glance at the hated clothing. "Never saw it before in my life." He brushed past her, eager to escape. He counted four women, all with a strong family resemblance to Kirsty.

Kirsty gasped loudly and snatched the clothing. "That's mine," she lied, balling it up and stuffing it in her pocket. "Costume party," she muttered.

"They're all yours? You wear two sets of clothing at a time including men's briefs?"

Brad winced, braking to a halt for a second, and then continued out the door. *Ouch.*

"Stuff it, Jules," Kirsty said, gritting her teeth.

"That must be Bradley," one of the older ladies said in awe, shaking her head. "Pretty robe but ghastly with his coloring. Tsk tsk."

"That's him all right," Kirsty's father said, snarling, his ears and nose changing from crimson to fuchsia.

"Hunky," one of the women said, whistling.

Brad slipped through the hedge, glad to escape. "This the car?" He eyed a white Mercedes, sizing it up.

Meanwhile, the thief sized him up. "You gonna get arrested cha cha'ing around in your frou frou like that, gringo." The man's beady eyes scoured Brad and his mustache twitched.

Brad ignored his taunt as best he could. By now he should have alligator-thick skin. He circled the vehicle noting its pristine condition and Pirelli tires. "Fine looking vehicle," he said, trying to peer in the tinted windows. He shaded his eyes from the glaring sun to see better. "Does she drive well?"

"Can I take her out for a spin?" He pretended to drive a car with exaggerated movements. "I'm desperate for a car, you know." In a conspiratorial voice, he confided to Jose, "My lousy insurance company's just sitting on their butts while I suffer this horrible fate. If she drives well, and the price is right, can I steal her from you today?" He petted the hood gently, wishing he could really afford a vehicle like this. He could just dream on with his salary. He couldn't even afford a used Mercedes in this buff condition.

Cautious joy flooded the man's face. "You like test drive? You try out her? I got the keys."

Jose scratched his dark stubbled chin as he stared at the car. "Well, I cannot part with her for less than three thousand American dollar...cash."

"Is that all?" Brad snatched the keys and slid into the driver's seat. He leaned over, patted the passenger seat and then winked broadly. "Come on, Sweet Pea. I'm just itching to see how much power she has under the hood." He revved the engine, the car's awesome power seeping into him.

"You go like that? Feet bare? No pants?"

"I won't tell anyone if you won't." Brad blew a kiss to him and shimmied his shoulders. When the man hesitated, Brad said in honeyed tones, "Something the matter with this baby? Is she really a heap o'junk? Are you afraid I won't want to buy her?"

The man dove in the car. "No no no, senor. Little Pepe's perfecto. Splendid." The thief kissed his fingers. "Fabuloso! You drive. You see."

"Hang on, sugar." Brad squealed the tires backing up, then rammed the stick into drive and shot forward.

"You see? She got grande pick up. She go fast, no?" Jose stroked the dash board reverently. "Muy benito, no?

Brad drove around the neighborhood, past the Episcopal church and the private school, not taking a chance he'd get picked up on University or Sample, the main drags. Since he didn't really care how well the car ran, he returned home shortly and parked. "I'll pay you three-thousand dollars today and you turn over the title?"

Jose shifted uneasily and deceit flickered across his eyes. "I no have title here. You give me two-thousand American dollars now and take car. I give you title soon."

Excitement flowed through Brad. This moron had to be a crook. *No title?* Who was the jerk kidding? He reached over to squeeze the man's thigh to keep in character and was relieved the guy slid over out of his reach. "Deal, sugar pie. I'll just run upstairs and bring down your cash." Brad flounced away. "I'll be right back."

"I was scared Daddy ran you off," Kirsty hissed in a stage whisper. She ran up to Brad and hissed through gritted teeth, "Marshall's waiting for you to take him on his date. Scoot upstairs and for God's sake, take off my robe."

He couldn't resist. He pinched her cheek and winked. "You gave it to me, sweetie."

"Well, yeah, hurry and get him out of my living room and away from my father. I need to decorate or there won't be a party." She shooed him upstairs. "I'll try to get rid of the family." She didn't sound very hopeful.

"Aren't you going to introduce me to the parents? Invite them to the party?"

"Heavens no! Not...not today. Daddy's already in a snit finding you in my bedroom and Jules is her obnoxious self." She waved him up. "Skeedaddle before they hear us and come to investigate. Please!"

Brad wore his black silk shirt with the iridescent buttons that Mario had raved over, matching black jeans, and black leather ankle boots with a silver chain across the ankle in preparation for the party. He took out twenty crisp hundred dollar bills and then stuffed his wallet in his back pocket. Then he snuck downstairs as quietly as he could and almost made it to the door when someone tapped him on the shoulder and made him jump.

"You're supposed to take Marshall with you." She glared at him. "You're going to ruin the surprise wearing that now."

"Chill. He won't suspect a thing. Just don't mention his birthday and he'll think you forgot all about him." He glanced at the door. "I'll be back in a sec. Stay here." Kirsty followed him to his chagrin.

Brad counted out twenty one hundred dollar bills in Jose's gritty outstretched palm. "That should do it."

"Your keys, senor." The man started to drop them in Brad's hand when Kirsty burst in the middle of them, wild-eyed, a hand on each of the man's chests.

"Wait! Where's the title? You can't sell a car without a title."

"Kirsten," Brad hissed, trying to pull her away from the treacherous mechanic. He prayed Jose didn't carry a loaded gun. The guy looked edgy enough to use it. "It's cool. We've got a deal."

Bristling, she yanked out of Brad's grip and faced off against him. "You can't seriously be thinking of buying a car without a title from this clown, can you?" She jabbed a finger at the Mercedes. "It's probably hot. You'll go to jail for dealing in stolen property."

"Go inside, Kirsty. I'll handle this." God, she was blowing the deal and he'd been so close to nabbing this scum.

Kirsty fisted her hands on her hips and stuck out her lower lip. Her freckles popped out across the bridge of her nose as her cheeks reddened. "I'm not going to let you buy stolen merchandise nor park it in…"

"It's not stolen," Brad lied, willing her to take the hint. "Let me handle this."

She crossed her arms over her heaving chest and dug in. "I'll believe that when he produces a legal title and signs it over – in front of a notary."

Scowling darkly, Jose plucked the keys from her hand and thrust the money at Brad. "No one questions Jose's integrity. I no need these. Other buyer take car – pay me more." Jose jumped in the car, locked it, and sped away, spewing red dust and sand from the tires. He pounded the steering wheel, waved his arms about, and yelled to himself.

Kirsty turned to Bradley. "What were you thinking? I can't believe you're so naïve. That guy's a crook who has no qualms taking advantage of people like you." She clucked her tongue and arched her neck. "Didn't you question him at all?"

Marshall burst out of the house in a huff, light glinting off his dangly earring. "So there you are bad boy. I thought you stood me up on my birthday. I would never have forgiven you." He strutted down the garden path and then daintily pecked Brad's checks. "Well, you're here now so let's be on our way." He turned to Kirsty. "You sure you don't want to tag along, sunshine? Bradley can ride bitch."

She shook her head, her eyes dark azure with jealousy, her icy gaze affixed on Marshall's hand that lay on Bradley's arm proprietarily. "No can do. Family's inside waiting on me."

Marshall frowned and rolled his eyes. "Ditch mommy and daddy. Send them to Disney World for the day to play with Mickey and friends."

"They just arrived. That would be rude." Kirsty fluttered her fingers at them. "Have fun for me, but not too much fun. You land in jail, I won't bail you out." She spun on her heel and sashayed off, the curls of her wig bouncing around her shoulders.

Marshall pouted at the door Kirsty disappeared into. "No happy birthday? No bad taste over the hill jokes?" His shoulders slumped and he trudged to his car. "Nobody loves me anymore. Everybody forgot me." He heaved a huge sigh and crawled into the car. Then he brightened and turned a dazzling smile on Brad. "Except you. You love me, don't you?"

Oh oh. What a loaded question. He couldn't bring himself to say *I love you* to another man. Crowe could fire, hang and quarter him, but he wouldn't say it. He couldn't even say it to Kirsty when a price tag of 2.3 kids and a dog came with the deal. He mumbled, "Yeah. Right."

"Pucker up." Marshall leaned toward him, batting his lashes. "Don't I get a big birthday kiss?"

Brad thought fast and hard. "I – uh – have cold sores all over my mouth. Nasty things. You wouldn't want to catch them." He pushed his cheek out with his tongue and then winced for effect.

"Give me a rain check, then, sweetie." Marshall snapped his fingers and grinned. "Come on. I'm atrophying while you're standing around lollygagging."

Brad gave himself up to fate and climbed into Marshall's pink Cadillac and slid onto the mink covered seat. He'd never dreamed pink mink when he'd joined the force. Shoot outs with gangsters, maybe. Wild motorcycle chases, hopefully. Saving damsels in distress, definitely. But never pink mink.

Chapter Eight

"You trying to get rid of us, Kirsty?" her mother, Peg, asked, hurt welling in her violet watery eyes. "If we interrupted other plans, just tell us. I told your father we shouldn't barge in unannounced." Her mother sniffled and dabbed her nose with an embroidered hankie. "I'll understand if you're not up to seeing us, if you're too embarrassed by us to introduce your own mother to your new boyfriend. You always felt stifled being a preacher's daughter."

Kirsty's head pounded and she checked her watch again. Time was running out. Her birthday party guests would arrive in under three hours and she hadn't changed, blown up the balloons, decorated the house, or picked up the party trays and ice. She massaged her forehead to relieve her tension. Under normal circumstances she'd invite them to the party without a second thought, but this wasn't a normal party by any means.

"What is it, dear? You can tell me. Are you pregnant?" Her mother's gaze lowered to her non-existent waistline lovingly, perhaps longingly.

Kirsty's head snapped up. Appalled that her mother could think such a thing, she stared open mouthed for several moments. "God, no!" She fidgeted as she unloaded her dishwasher and straightened the kitchen counters. "Nothing so major as that." She expelled a long sigh. "It's just that I'm throwing a surprise 40th birthday party for my boss, and well, I'm not ready and the guests are due to arrive in less than three hours. I'm doomed."

"Is that all?" Peg clapped her hands in glee, delight twinkling in her eyes. "I adore a good party. We'll help you prepare, don't worry." She rolled up her sleeves and tucked her strawberry blonde hair behind her ears. Even though it was liberally sprinkled with silver now, fire still burnished it. "Just tell me what to do."

Kirsty leaned against the counter, her pulse fluttering weakly, and her heart racing. "Well, uh, it's not that simple." She pinched her thumb and forefinger together in the air for her mother's benefit. "There's a *teensy weensy* problem."

"Whatever could it be, dear heart?" Concern masked her mother's exquisite features. "You can tell me anything. If you're not pregnant, what else could it be?"

Kirsty rubbed her forehead again, holding a headache at bay. "I just don't think you'll mix very well with my friends."

She rushed to assure her mother that she wasn't embarrassed of her before she crumpled again. "At least Daddy won't. My boss is gay. So are a lot of his friends. I can't promise they'll behave very well, and well, you know how Daddy is." She winced, waiting for her mom's shock.

"Your father's an adult and it's time he learns that. He'll just have to deal with it for a few hours. Now tell me, how can we help?" Peg scoured the sink as she spoke.

Kirsty knew it was useless to try to stop her mother from cleaning. She began to feel better and perked up. "Well, I need someone to blow up all these black balloons. I want them to cover the ceiling. And the downstairs still has to be decorated with gravestones, skeletons, and crepe paper. If someone could whip up some punch and veggie dip while I run up the road to get the party platters, that would be a huge help. Gigi was supposed to be here to help me set up, but she's MIA as usual."

"Consider it done, darling. I'll put your father to work blowing up balloons. He has a lot of hot air to get rid of."

Kirsty spluttered out the water she'd been sipping and almost choked. She set her cup in the sink and covered her mouth when she coughed. "Stupendous!" She didn't deign to comment further on her mother's astounding comment as she took sour cream, salsa, and vegetables out of the fridge and set them out on the counter for her mother. "Can you make the old standby? I'll run to Sam's Club and be back before you know it." She kissed her mother on the cheek, grabbed her purse off the hall table, and scrammed.

Speaking of Gigi, where was she? Kirsty dialed her friend's cell phone number as she strolled briskly to her car in the driveway. Geckos scattered and tried to blend into the grass and walls. The midday sun blinded her, making her squint. She pulled out her sunglasses and stuck them on her nose. She couldn't stand to be out in the bright light without them. "Answer, girlfriend," she muttered into the receiver as she shifted her purse higher on her shoulder so she could open the car door without banging the hell out of her car. "Pick up!" Her left toe tapped impatiently on the floor as she accelerated out of the drive.

"Where are you?" Kirsty asked with silky sweetness, when Gigi answered. "Zero hour's in under three hours and all I have done are the cakes. We'll be the ones surprised if we don't hurry."

"Crikey! My stupid alarm fritzed. Just let me shower, do my hair, and change, and I'll be straight over."

Kirsty deciphered her friend's British English to mean that her alarm hadn't gone off, allowing her to sleep in late on the morning she needed her help most. When a family of ducks waddled into the street without warning, she swore under her breath and swerved sharply into the left lane to avoid them. Her tires squealed and the car coming towards her swerved into a mailbox, splintering it.

"Sorry! Avoiding ducks," she called out her open window. No one looked to be hurt so she kept going. The other car had had plenty of time to stop or pull over safely so she didn't feel guilty that he'd crashed his vehicle. Some people just didn't know how to drive.

"Stop foolin' around on the cell phone and drive!"

"Duckie? What's duckie, pet?"

Kirsty shifted the phone under her chin, her shoulder getting a crick. Grimacing, she enunciated carefully into the phone, "Ducks - D - U - C - K - S. Not duckie." She glanced in her rear view mirror and winced when the man kicked his tire and then stomped his feet. "Definitely not duckie." She turned south onto University towards Sam's and the mall. There was a lot of traffic for Saturday at noon and she chafed waiting through two lights at Royal Palm, clicking her fingernails on the receiver. "Look, I'm picking up the party platters and ice, so if I'm not home, just go in and transform the place into a crypt."

"They won't play spin the bottle, will they?" Trepidation warbled in Gigi's voice. "I don't know that I could take that."

"Don't go there." Kirsty pulled a long face, and then ran the car over the curb as she pulled into Sam's busy parking lot. Everybody and their brother must be here today. She should've picked it up last night and stuck it in the refrigerator.

"Tell them, not me." A loud crash sounded in the background and Gigi squealed. "Gotta run. The cat just knocked over the garbage bin again, naughty, naughty creature."

"Don't forget to wear all black." Kirsty had to be very stern as Gigi loved bright, flowery clothing and hated dark, drab colors. Especially black. She'd been grumbling all week about having to dress out in black.

"Yes, Morticia, even if I feel like the freakin' bride of Dracula. I'm ringing off now. Cheers."

"Back atcha," Kirsty mumbled into the dead connection and then stuffed the phone into her purse and dug out her membership card to show at the check point, wishing she didn't have to show this horrid picture with her pudgy cheeks. Every piece of ID she owned looked like mug shots of the undead...blurry, blotchy, and washed out. Her blonde hair usually faded into the background making her look bald.

Almost four hours later, black balloons covered the ceiling, grave stones popped out of the floor, and skeletons danced from the ceiling. All of Marshall's friends hid in the kitchen so they could jump out and surprise the birthday victim when he walked in, before he saw the decorations.

"What's keepin' Marshall and Bradley so long?" Gigi complained, twirling the onyx earring in her lobe, her impatient gaze on the front door as if she could will their presence. "Think they're shaggin' somewhere and Bradley forgot the time?"

Jealousy wound around Kirsty and she swallowed hard as chuckles erupted throughout the room. "Bradley promised they were on the way," she said in a tightly controlled voice. "Come on," she whispered to herself.

"I knew it!" her father announced. "I knew that Bradley was a sissy the first time I laid eyes on him. It's unnatural." Paul snorted and sent her an accusing glare. "I'm gonna strangle him if he laid a hand on you."

Everyone else turned around to pinpoint her father with sharp gazes but no one said anything.

Kirsty wanted to sink into the wall and become part of it.

"You certainly know how to kill a party, don't you Paul?" Peg rolled her eyes at him and shook her head. "Perhaps we should leave if you're going to be a sourpuss. Kirsty's put a lot of time and planning into this and I'm not going to let you ruin it for her."

"You can mosey on along, if'n you want to, but I'm not budgin'," Aunt Norma announced, shaking her walking stick at Paul. "I'm a stayin' right here and I'm a gonna boogie down the night, with or without you." Her coiffed, tinted hair gleamed cotton candy pink under the florescent lights and clashed horribly with her red suit.

"All right, Auntie!" Jules cheered and snickered, and then playfully punched Kirsty in the shoulder. The black t-shirt she had borrowed from Kirsty hung on her in folds to Kirsty's chagrin.

"Me, too!" Kirsty's grandmother said loudly. "No one's dragging these old bones out of here till I'm good and ready and I won't be ready till I've had a slice of that birthday cake and kissed the birthday boy. You learn to appreciate birthdays when you've lived as long as I have."

"Which is, Ma?" Peg said sweetly, tilting her head.

"Older than Methusaleh," Aunt Norma supplied, cackling.

"I'll be eighty-seven this March and proud of it. I gave birth to you Missy, when I was thirty..." Mirth danced in her grandmother's thin voice.

"Ma..." Peg warned, straightening to her full impressive height which dwarfed her tiny mother who stood smaller still as her shoulders were hunched with age. Those shoulders were covered with a lovely hand-knitted white shawl with pearlescent beads woven through that Kirsty admired greatly.

"Shush! They're here! Everybody hide!" Dennis, one of Marshall's friends hissed in a stage whisper. "They'll hear you." The man's tall stick-thin frame was topped with a mop of bleached blonde hair that hung over his eyes. He was sorely in need of another dye job as his roots had grown out a good inch. Kirsty wasn't sure what to make of him, or for that matter, several of Marshall's friends. Of course, she'd seen all of them in the shop at one time or another, but never all together like this. It was rather overwhelming.

All thirty-something guests scrambled to take cover, yet tried to peek into the hallway. Anticipation twinkled in their eyes. Silly grins split their faces. Kirsty's father hadn't killed the party spirit after all, even if she still wanted to throttle him. Was it a sin to murder a pastor who spoke his mind too freely? *Debatable.*

The door opened and Marshall stepped in first while Bradley hung behind. "You home, sunshine?" Marshall called, walking in slowly, peering down the hall.

"Surprise!" Everyone jumped out. Some blew New Year's Eve horns that curled in and out. Others shook tin ornaments. Some just screamed so loudly Kirsty thought her eardrums would certainly burst.

Dennis reached the surprised but happy looking Marshall first, and gave him a big mushy kiss.

"I can't watch this," Gigi whispered into Kirsty's ear, as she shielded her downcast eyes with her hand and shifted her weight uncomfortably. "Why can't a gorgeous bloke ever stick his tongue down my throat like that?"

"Got any stiff drinks?" Paul bellowed from the living room.

Kirsty looked up at that as her father never drank, in fact sermonized about the evils of alcohol and evil spirits. "In the wet bar, Daddy. In the far corner."

Marshall broke free of the well-meaning but suffocating crowd, and twirled Kirsty off her feet, squeezing the breath out of her.

"Thank you, sweetie." A tear slipped from his eye and he sniffed. "This is the nicest thing anybody's ever done for me. You're the best, cupcake."

Someone turned up Conga music loud and Marshall grabbed her and demanded, "Conga!" He pushed her ahead of him and kicked out his legs. They picked up people as they congaed through the house. Her Aunt Norma grabbed Bradley and pulled him into the line. Her mother pulled her father into the line.

When Kirsty panted for air, she pulled away. "Anyone hungry for birthday cake?"

A chorus of "me" and "me too" rang throughout the room.

Kirsty tried to kill the secretive smile playing about her lips without much success. She pulled the fake cake out of the oven, and carried it to the dining room table where Marshall's gifts were piled high.

"Spread out. Give the woman some space so she doesn't drop my cake." Marshall clapped his hands sharply, sounding like a drill sergeant. When he spied the tombstone shaped cake, his jaw dropped open. Then he pinned her with an evil glare. "You wicked, wicked woman. Payback'll be a bitch."

"Happy birthday" broke out tunelessly, but fervently. Then Marshall huffed and puffed, trying to blow out the sizzling trick candles and couldn't. "I must be losing my touch," Marshall said, sounding peeved and winded.

Bradley finally took pity on him and plucked a candle out of the cake and doused it in a glass of water. "You've been set up."

Dennis stepped forward, a wicked gleam in his amber eyes. "I get to spank the birthday boy."

Marshall jumped back, holding his backside protectively. "I'd never survive forty-one spankings!"

Unconcerned by her boss's threat as she wouldn't turn forty for over a decade, she smiled sweetly at him. "It's your special day. Will you do the honors?" She handed a long handled sharp knife to him.

"I'd be delighted to." He eyed the cake for several minutes and then finally asked, "Is it bad luck to cut a tombstone?"

Kirsty's lips quirked. "Superstitious? It's just a cake in the shape of a tombstone. Go on. I'm starving. I've not eaten all day." To back up her statement, her stomach growled, embarrassing her. "See?"

Bradley laughed aloud and rubbed his hands together next to her. "Me, too. You cut and I'll help you pass it out."

His elbow bumped her arm and memories flooded back to her of the previous night. It seemed so long ago, but in actuality, had only been a few hours. Last night seemed unreal and she wondered if she had dreamed it.

Marshall tried to slice the cake but the knife didn't slide into it. His forehead puckered and his brows drew together. "Um, looks delicious, Kirstykins. You baked this yourself?"

Kirsty smiled at him. "All by my lonesome." She snuck a glance at Bradley. She didn't have to divulge that her tenant had helped to clean up the mess, did she? No, she thought not. "I toiled and slaved over your very special birthday cake. I hope you love it. It's carrot, your favorite." It took all her willpower not to break down giggling or confessing her practical joke. "Go on, cut it. Don't make your guests wait."

Marshall's lips twisted as he stared at the cake. Then he tried to cut it again. Finally, using both hands, he tried to saw it. He sawed so hard that he backed up into her maple China cabinet and almost tipped it over on himself. "I give up. This thing's hard as a brick." He set the knife on the table and took her in his arms. "I appreciate the thought."

Kirsty lost it and laughed so hard she cried. She swiped at the errant tears that kept flowing. When she finally took control of herself, she looked around the room at everyone staring at her.

"You okay, Kirst?" Gigi asked, trying to pull her into the kitchen. "What's wrong?"

"Nothing's wrong. It's a practical joke." Kirsty pointed at the phony cake and shook with more mirth. "That's iced foam. The real cake's still in the oven."

Marshall sighed and pursed his lips. "Ha ha. Very funny."

"Blimey. I'll go get the real thing," Gigi said escaping, pushing her way through the crowd. "Be back in a tick." She carried it high over her head as if she'd waitressed all her life.

Marshall picked up the knife and poised it over the real cake, eyeing it suspiciously. "This is a real cake, isn't it?"

Kirsty nodded, still smiling.

Again, Marshall tried to slice the cake and the knife didn't go in. "Are you sure?" he asked, frowning. He sawed at it to no avail.

Worry consumed Kirsty, and she joined him, staring at her poor cake. "Guess I can't make anything edible." She tried to smile. "You'll all be very happy to know that my mother, who is an excellent cook, made the punch and veggie dip and that Sam's made the party platters. You won't starve to death because I'm a flop in the kitchen."

"I'm just joking. I had to get you back, didn't I?" Marshall tugged her hair, and pulled off her wig, revealing her chopped hair.

Kirsty's eyes widened and she flung her arms over her awful head. "Oh, no! This can't be happening. Today's one long nightmare. Tell me I'm still sleeping." Dropping to her knees, she scrambled for the wig, wishing she could disappear. Just as she reached for it, a piece of cake plopped on it, smearing it. "The fates hate me," she mumbled.

She scooped up the wig, and carried it to the sink, where she dumped the cake into the garbage disposal. Her movements were sharp and jerky. Water didn't begin to rinse all the cake out of the wig and it splotched the hair orange. *Great! She'd look like a scoop of orange sherbet.*

Marshall squeezed her shoulders. "I'm so sorry." He circled her, tapping his finger against his lips. So many lines puckered his forehead it could be mistaken for the Grand Canyon. "You know, this is you. This is cute. It'll be all the rage on South Beach in no time."

"Really?" She peered into his eyes closely, not believing a word he uttered. "Are you wearing your contacts today?"

"No. Not really. It's quite the most awful mess I've ever seen. Do you have a bag to put over it?" He touched it gingerly, as if it would bite him.

She swatted his hand away, scowling darkly. "I look like a sci-fi reject."

Bradley joined them, her red wig in his hand. "Turn around and let me put this on for you." When she did as he bade, he fit the cap to her head and tenderly tucked stray hairs under the silky mass. "Voila. You're gorgeous again."

Something in his voice made her believe he meant it and shivers scraped down her spine. His fingers lingered on her cheeks and she trembled, her gaze locked with his. "Thank you."

"Do you know why the tombstones are appropriate for this party?" Marshall asked in a joking tone.

Expecting a riddle, Kirsty asked innocently, "Why?"

"Because it's *dying*. Nothing against you, but man is it ever dullsville in here. My secret weapon's in my trunk. If that can't resurrect this shindig, nothing will." He pushed off the cabinet with his foot and trotted to the door and let himself out.

"Oh, oh. What's his *secret weapon*?" Kirsty took the vegetable trays out of the fridge and unwrapped the cellophane covering.

Bradley shrugged, holding out his hands. "Beats me."

Marshall burst in carrying a karaoke machine. "Ta da! Guaranteed to liven up any gathering in five minutes."

Kirsty groaned in chorus with Bradley. She hung her head and massaged her forehead. "Anything but that."

Marshall grabbed her wrist and pulled her into the living room. "You can be first then, to break the ice."

Terror paralyzed her as she stared wide-eyed at the demon machine. Shaking her head furiously, she tried to back away. "I can't sing. Believe me, I'm doing you a favor by not singing. You don't want me to burst your eardrums."

Marshall ignored her, hooked up the machine, and then whistled shrilly. When everyone gathered around staring expectantly, Marshall turned on the karaoke machine and turned up the microphone. "Attention. Attention everyone. That means Dennis and Lance trying to make out on the couch, too." He clucked his tongue and stroked his goatee. "Our lovely hostess Kirsty is going to start us out with some karaoke." He thrust the list of songs in her hand. "Which one, sweetie?"

"How about Tequila?" Something without lyrics.

"No cheating. You can't sing without lyrics." Marshall snatched the list from her and punched in a number.

"That's the point." She flipped her bought hair behind her shoulder, and tried to slip behind Bradley and escape to the kitchen.

Bradley stepped back, blocking her, grinning devilishly. "Go on. No one's going to throw stones or boo. If they do, they'll have to deal with me." His warm hand fit perfectly into the small of her back, teasing her spine, and he gave her a tiny push toward the limelight.

Although she felt slightly better, it was Bradley that worried her. She couldn't bear to make a fool of herself in front of him. "Doesn't a dying woman at least get a stiff drink? Give me a glass of that brandy, straight up." After she swallowed a finger in one gulp, fire blazed down her esophagus, blurring her senses. Everything and everyone looked fuzzy around the edges. "That's better. I'm ready now."

Marshall handed over the microphone and turned on the switch. Almost immediately, the sweet, romantic, heartbreaking strains of Olivia Newton-John's 'I Honestly Love You' filled her ears.

Kirsty gulped. Why this one? Bradley's intense gaze drew hers, and they locked for infinitesimal moments. When he nodded slowly, his eyes dark and inscrutable, she clutched the microphone tightly and closed her eyes, trying to convince herself she was alone in the room. Then Bradley's beloved face flashed before her, and she sang along with the words she knew by heart. Something stronger than her made her open her eyes, and she gazed right into Bradley's passion-filled gaze.

He stole her breath, and the words stuck in her throat while she lip-synched the words.

Marshall leaned over and shut off the words, and then joined her, curling his arm around her waist. "I'll help you out," he whispered in her ear. "But you have to sing."

She groaned, but sang a duet with him, her gaze never leaving Bradley's chiseled features and intense eyes.

When the song finally finished, what felt like a few centuries later, Marshall linked his hand with hers, lifted it high, and then bowed low, forcing her to follow his movements while the crowd cheered. Winking at their fandom Marshall announced huskily, "Give a round of applause for the stunning Kirsten! We'll talk her into another duet later, but for now, the amazing Marshall will sing a classic for you."

Kirsty clapped as she hurried away from the spotlight. Stopping by Bradley's side, she turned to watch her boss.

"Yeow!" Marshall squealed, shaking the tension from his body. "I have a special dedication, from moi, to someone I hope feels as special about me as I do about him." Marshall blew a kiss to Bradley, and then burst out in Rod Stewart's 'Do You Think I'm Sexy', shaking his booty. He strutted to Bradley, thrusting out his hip and puckering up not more than an inch from Bradley's lips. Then he leapt into Bradley's arms without warning, and sat on his lap.

Kirsty wanted to drag Bradley out of the room away from her flirtatious boss. Instead, she watched in a mixture of fascinated horror and side-splitting merriment as Marshall flaunted himself in front of her tenant.

When Marshall tried to hand the microphone to Bradley, her grandmother snatched it from his hands. "My turn. I've always wanted to try this nifty thing." She belted out a Back Street Boys rendition and everyone's jaw dropped several inches.

Next, Dennis stepped up to the mike, and sang a Barbra Streisand hit, sidling up to Bruce. Then he kept the mike and performed a Motown melody, twirling and spinning like the Four Tops. He finished with a cartwheel come split to everyone's amazement.

When he forced the microphone into Bradley's hands, Bradley scrunched up his nose, much as Kirsty had. "It's time to watch Marshall open his gifts." He strolled to the table and handed Marshall a gift wrapped in matte black finish. "This is from Gigi."

"Coward," Kirsty mouthed to him, grinning.

"Brilliant," he mouthed back as he tapped his temple.

"No! Not mine first," Gigi pleaded, cowering behind Kirsty, clutching her upper arm so tightly the blood didn't circulate in Kirsty's lower arm and her fingers fell asleep.

Marshall favored her with a glare. "Why not? You afraid I won't like your gift?"

"Something like that." Gigi murmured miserably. "I think he'll *hate* it."

"It can't be any worse than mine," Kirsty whispered back, dreading the moment Marshall held up the sexy teddy she'd bought him – before she knew her pastor father and grandmother would be in attendance. Maybe she could steal it away without anyone noticing and hide it till she could get Marshall alone later.

"Oh no! He's going to *murder* and dismember me for the bonus gift I got him." Gigi moved further behind Kirsty and Brad. "Protect me, will you?"

Marshall tore the wrapping off as fast as he could, eagerness in his expression. Then abruptly, his wide grin faded as he held up a giant bottle of Geritol to a cacophony of chortling.

Kirsty spit out the drink she'd just sipped, almost choking on an ice cube that slid down her windpipe, and wetting the shirt of the man in front of her. "Sorry. Sorry. I didn't mean to get you wet. Really I didn't." She dabbed ineffectually at his silk shirt, feeling like an idiot and mortified that Bradley had seen her at her worst. When the man turned around with a cocked brow, she shrugged. "Sorry. At least it's a warm day."

Shaking the huge bottle, Marshall smiled good-naturedly. "Revenge will be mine, Gigi. And I have a *long* memory."

"Think it might be time for me to return to my bedsitter in London. Or maybe I'll move up to Toronto."

"Open mine next," Dennis crooned in a sultry voice, handing a tiny gold box to Marshall. "I know you'll just absolutely adore it."

Marshall pulled out a twinkling diamond ear stud and held it up to the light for everybody to see. "You shouldn't have!" He sniffed back more tears and then opened his arms wide and ran over to Dennis and hugged him. "It's so beautiful, I'm going to cry."

Kirsty inched over to the table, and nonchalantly as she could, she pulled her present off the table and hid it behind her back, and backed up toward the kitchen, intent on escaping with it.

When Marshall pulled back, he put it on and strutted back to the table. "I'm so beautiful, I know." He turned suddenly and crooked his finger at Kirsty. "Come back here with my present and hand it over. That's an order."

"What present?" She favored him with her most innocent wide-eyed look as she tried to slip it behind her microwave out of sight.

Marshall strode to her purposefully and looked over her shoulder. He spied the gift and plucked it from her hands. "What is it you're trying to hide?" He gave her a stern look. "More Geritol?"

"No. No. Nothing of the sort." She tiptoed up to him and whispered, "Just something private. *Intimate* if you get my drift. I didn't want Daddy to see it."

Her grandmother led a chant in rhythm to her clapping. "Open, open, open."

"My public has spoken. I can't disappoint them."

"Sure." Kirsty started to back away, her gaze seeking out her father, trying to gauge his mood. "Who cares if my father kills me? No biggie. One less blonde with a bad haircut in the world."

"Stop being so melodramatic." Marshall tore off the paper and held up the sexy filmy teddy, practically drooling. "Is this for me to wear? Or for my intended?"

Bradley? Bile bubbled in her throat as her gaze vaulted from Bradley to the teddy to Marshall and back. It had never crossed her mind that Bradley might wear this. The thought tormented her and made her want to rip the garment to shreds and burn it. "It's just a joke. I thought you'd get a kick out of it."

He wiggled his eyebrows at it as it shimmered in the light. He pivoted on his heel and gave her a big smack on her cheek. "Thanks, sweetie. I like. It's much better than the Geritol."

Marshall finished opening his gifts, saving Bradley's till last. A Barbra Streisand and a Carpenter's CD, two of Marshall's favorites, fell onto the table with a clatter. He held them high over his head and did a jig. "My Bradley read my heart. It's just what I wanted." He folded Bradley into his embrace, snuggled his head onto the other man's shoulder, and then announced dreamily, "Slow dancing time. Turn the lights down low."

Kirsty escaped from the room, dodging several couples, her heart breaking. Two awful truths suddenly became clear. Bradley was bisexual. And she was helplessly, hopelessly in love with him. Marshall had won the bet, not that she cared about any silly, ridiculous game.

Chapter Nine

Brad kept busy tracking down his suspiciously absentee neighbor who had never returned after he sped away in the presumably hot Mercedes. Thus, a few days had passed before Brad realized that Kirsty was in turn avoiding him. And when he did happen to pass her in the hall or a common room, she was remote and curt, and scurried away as quickly as she could.

He couldn't take it any more. Since the neighbor had fled, there was no reason to keep up the pretense, was there? It was long past time he came clean and confessed his true sexuality and his deception.

Hunting her down, he found her curled up in front of the television watching the Bridget Jones movie for the thousandth time. Pausing, staring at the television cross-eyed, he asked perplexed, "What do you see in that movie? Don't you know it by heart now?" He certainly did.

She mouthed along to the words, heartache in her eyes as she gazed at the screen. Bundled in her fluffy but scruffy white robe, sipping a glass of diet soda and eating dry fiber cereal out of a box, she resembled the heroine in the movie. "I can relate to her," she finally mumbled. "I feel like an idiot most of the time."

He sat down on the loveseat across from her, his knees almost touching hers. He wanted to take her hands in his and massage them. "Why would you feel like that?"

She chuckled without humor and her eyes were dull and flat when she turned her gaze on him.

This wasn't the Kirsty he knew and loved. *Loved?* Till death do us part kind of love? The 2.3 kids, a dog, and a lawn in suburbia type of love? He searched his heart and soul for the whole sordid truth, unhappily concluding that he'd finally fallen in love. Fallen was right. He didn't want to be in love. He didn't want to commit to one woman. And yet, she was the only woman he wanted to be with and he didn't just want her a little, he wanted her desperately.

"Oh, I don't know."

He waited for the rest of her revelation, peering at her closely, his gaze adoring her exquisite heart-shaped face, even with dark shadows under her eyes. Hadn't she been sleeping well? Concern swelled in his heart. "You can tell me."

She put her finger to her mouth and hissed, her gaze snapping at him, "Shush. This is the best part. He comes back for her and sweeps her into his arms." She leaned forward, crushing the forgotten cereal box to her chest, rocking back and forth, sighing. "No one ever came back for me."

Alarm flooded him. "You want that jerk Frank to come back for you?" *No!* Frank couldn't have her. He'd fight for her if need be.

She turned questioning eyes on him. "No. But Frank's not the only boyfriend I had. There were others or maybe you think no one else would want me? One or two I might have wanted to come back for me, once upon a time."

He sucked in his breath and held it. How could she begin to think he would feel that way? "Do you still want them to ride up on their trusty steeds and ride off into the sunset with you?"

She studied him for several silent moments, and then stared into the drink she was swishing as if she could see something interesting. She took a long swig, and swiped the soda rim off her lips. She caught his gaze and held it. "Maybe. Probably. I'm not sure."

He shoveled unsteady fingers through his hair, unsure how to proceed, wondering what he did wrong that she was giving him the cold shoulder. He wanted his warm, loving, fun Kirsty back in his arms, kissing him. "Are you mad at me because I didn't roll over and propose the other morning and agree to have 2.3 kids and a dog?"

"For your information, I like cats," she said cryptically thrusting out her chin. "And I never said I wanted a point three child." She unfolded her legs from their Indian-like crossing, and stood quickly. Her shadow eclipsed him in the dim room, and she stared down at him dispassionately. "If you'll excuse me." She plodded over to the television in big floppy bunny slippers, and jabbed the stop button on the VCR, and then the power button on the console television.

Brad jumped up, blocking her way when she tried to leave the room. He dropped his hand on her shoulder, halting her forward motion. "Look, I have a confession to make."

"You don't owe me anything except your monthly rent and you're paid up for another two weeks."

When his cell phone blared 'Camptown Races', he dragged it out of his pocket and punched the talk button. "Mue – Miller here."

She ducked, breaking his hold on her, and then raced up the stairs.

"Damn! Look, this is really lousy timing."

"You hang up, you're fired Mueller," Captain Crowe barked into the phone so loudly it sounded as if he stood behind Brad. "Get your sorry butt down to the station pronto. We think we caught your man. Can you ID him?"

Brad's blood quickened, and he perked up. He glanced upstairs towards Kirsty's bedroom regretfully and slammed the wall with the flat of his hand. "I'll be right over." He strode out the door, and squealed out of the driveway. This late at night when the roads were practically a ghost town, he made good time to the station.

"Where's the scumbag?" he asked as he barged into Crowe's office without knocking, slamming the door against the wall.

"Come right in. Don't be so quiet about it, Mueller. Let all of Ft. Lauderdale know our business, why don't you?" Crowe beckoned him in and pointed at the chair in front of his desk. "Just give me a sec and I'll be with you." He undid his tie and flung it on his desk. His aim off, the silk tie slinked off the edge and coiled onto the floor like a cobra.

Brad picked up the tie, folded it, and laid it on the desk. He leaned forward, elbows on his knees, hands steepled between his knees, and his head bowed.

Crowe scraped his chair back and stood. "Come on," he said as he rounded the desk and headed out the door, not pausing for Brad to catch up. "Let's nail this sucker and put this case to bed. It's giving me a hell of a case of indigestion."

Brad agreed silently and trotted to catch up, anxious to close this case and get back to normal. One more day in drag would drive him over the edge. Their footsteps echoed in the hall until they reached the detention area.

Crowe stopped in front of a two-way mirror and jabbed his thumb at a sleazy, dark character sitting inside at the end of a long table. "This the guy? I need you to be sure." He lit a cigarette and took a long drag, his eyes small and squinty.

Brad's hopes crashed about his feet. He wasn't out of this ordeal yet. "No." He itched to find the guy and his gang so they could round them up and he could get back to normal and start his life with Kirsty.

He was convinced Kirsten would be ecstatic when he finally confessed he wasn't gay, and that everything would be perfect in their world.

"The rocket scientist tried to sell a hot car to an FBI agent earlier tonight. "So he arrested him and hauled him in. Seems he's been holing up over on Atlantic Beach."

Hope flared in Brad's chest. Maybe this scum was connected to the other one. "What're we waiting for?" Brad rubbed his hands together in anticipation and then wiped them down his slacks. "Maybe there are more rats to scare out of that nest. I'd like to get on with my life."

"What you waiting for? Get going!" Crowe flung the door wide and jerked his head for Brad to proceed him.

* * * * *

After several grueling hours at the station questioning the Mexican, and then rounding up his cronies, Brad was exhausted. Even though he was free to go home and be himself, he headed to Kirsty's house, eager to see her. But first, he needed a warm shower and some sleep before he bared his heart to her. Besides, she might not appreciate being awakened in the middle of the night and he wanted her in a good mood.

But something seemed amiss when he neared her house. His cop's instincts taking over, he slowed, put the car in reverse, and hid it down the street. Then he approached silently on foot.

He knew what was out of place now – the damned Mercedes was back, parked in the open garage next door, and there was an air of danger permeating the place.

He debated calling for back up and blowing his cover on a hunch or sneaking into Kirsty's house to scope things out and possibly walk into the barrel of a loaded gun. He decided to peak in the windows first in the hopes of seeing something.

But the lights were out downstairs in both houses so that all he could see were shadowy shapes outlined by the moonlight cascading over his shoulder. Frustrated, he decided to enter the house, but the doors were all locked. When he searched his pockets for the key, he couldn't find it and swore under his breath. The blasted thing must've fallen off the chain. Instead of putting the big ring though it, he'd just clipped it on. Not one of his brighter moves.

What now? Maybe a window was open. Early morning fog hung heavily in the air, coating the grass with dew, making it slick so that he slipped, ramming into the tin garbage cans on the side of the house, making a loud commotion.

Lights flickered on next door and Brad muttered under his breath as he slipped into the shadows and skirted the house. Then he tried the kitchen window, but it didn't move a centimeter, either. Kirsty had locked the house up tightly.

Then he spied a trellis thick with morning glories climbing up to his second story bedroom. The window swung partially open as the night breeze rustled the curtain. He tested the trellis to see if it would hold his weight and when it didn't move or even creak, he grinned without mirth and muttered, "Perfect." *Finally.*

He'd climbed to the top and then realized the screen still blocked his entry. Punching the screen in, he tore through it and then ripped it the rest of the way, his stomach lurching when the trellis swayed warningly. He ripped it out and squeezed his bulk through the window. He was going to have to replace the glass, and rip down the trellis as soon as he found a spare moment, so that no one else could gain entry as easily.

He huddled against the wall, crouched in case someone had heard him, and listened intently. So far, he still had no indication anyone was in this house. At this hour of the night, however, Kirsty should be here, sound asleep in her bed.

He made his way stealthily toward her bedroom, unsure whether to be happy the bedroom door was secure or to curse the fact. It had helped conceal his entry, but it also prevented him from viewing the outer hallway. Holding his breath, he opened the door carefully and peeked out the crack. Nothing. Everything lay in dark shadows. The moon must be hiding behind clouds and dawn wasn't due to break for at least another couple of hours. Starlight barely illuminated the room.

Creeping against the wall, his weapon drawn, his sense of dread increased with each breath he drew. Although Kirsty's bedroom door lay a mere four feet from his room, it seemed more like a mile. Of course her door was closed also so he couldn't see inside. If someone was in there, he would alert them to his presence by opening it.

He pressed his ear to the door and listened. Nothing. What did he expect? If Kirsty was sleeping, it would be silent. Unless someone was in there with her.

After listening intently for several moments, he drew himself to his full height, raised his weapon, took in a deep breath and flung the door wide, wincing when it crashed against the wall announcing his presence to all and sundry in the house. His gaze fell immediately on Kirsty's bed and his eyes narrowed when he took in the fact that she was missing. There wasn't a wrinkle from someone sleeping in it. Where was she? It wasn't like her to stay out all night.

He expected to hear footsteps, voices, anything if someone were in the house – unless they were hunting him down now that he'd made his presence known. Withdrawing from the room, he quickly checked out the rest of the upstairs till he assured himself it was empty. When he found Kirsty's purse with her keys and ID inside, worry rose like bile in his throat. Now he was sure something was wrong.

His radio vibrated against his hip as he made his way carefully down the step, his gun still drawn and held closely against his chest. Someone's timing was lousy. He sure as hell couldn't answer now. Staying in the shadows as best as he could, he inspected the downstairs. Still nothing. He decided she couldn't be inside. Could she be next door?

When he went to unlock the front door, he found it already unlocked. He shook his head. He was sure it had been locked when he'd tried it less than half an hour before. Did that mean Kirsty had been in the house and left? She hadn't been in bed. This was getting stranger and stranger. He didn't like it at all.

Was someone waiting for him on the other side of the door? He reversed his steps and peered out the window as unobtrusively as he could but saw nothing. Still, he couldn't be sure. He made his way to the back door and slid out. Keeping his voice low, he called the station and requested immediate backup to Kirsty's address. Then he called his partner and apprised him of his suspicions. Cole promised to come right over despite sounding groggy and ready to eat steel.

The muggy night left perspiration on Brad's brow and filled his nostrils with the cloying scent of honeysuckle and jasmine. Palm fronds brushed him as he kept his back to the house. The closer he drew to the neighbor's house, the more trepidation filled him. He cursed when he found the vertical blinds and shades tightly drawn as if someone were hiding something. Of course the dude had been hiding from the beginning as he'd never opened the blinds or curtains as far as Brad could remember.

A dog barked in the distance and Brad froze. Then he heard it – lowered voices and then a car door slam. *Shit!* Forgetting himself, he ran for the front of the house in time to see Jose shove Kirsty into the Mercedes he'd tried to sell him. He stopped dead when the moon peeked out of the clouds to glisten on the barrel of a very wicked gun.

Double shit!

Taking out his radio, he called the station again. "Mueller here. Where in the hell is my back up? I have a kidnapping in progress. I need help *now*!" When the car's engine revved and the wheels turned, he knew he couldn't wait for help. The creep would disappear with the woman – *his* woman – and he may never see her alive again.

Stepping out, he aimed and shot out the front tires on the car rendering it inoperable before the creep could see him, then he leveled it at the driver.

Kirsty's eyes were moonlike in her pale face. Wide and huge. Emotions flickered across them which he couldn't read behind the glare from the windshield but he could feel her fear, and her confusion.

Fury tore at him so that he could hardly think rationally. How dare anyone threaten his woman! When he was done with the bastard, he wouldn't have two balls left. He'd rip him apart piece by piece.

The car skid, fishtailing into a massive tree trunk. Crunching metal and feminine shrieking pierced his ears. The driver's door slammed open, groaning. Jose dragged Kirsty out by her hair, his gun barrel held to her temple. "Move, gringo. I shoot to kill."

"Bradley?" Fear flooded Kirsty's eyes now that he could see them clearly. And confusion. "What are you doing with a gun?"

Jose spat on the ground in front of his dusty boots. "He's a filthy pig."

Kirsty's eyes strained wider. "Are you?" Her voice came out breathy, raspy. She winced in pain when Jose yanked her hard, bringing the sheen of tears to her eyes.

"Yes." Turning his attention to the kidnapper, Brad glared at him. "Release her. Backup's on the way. You won't get away."

116

If possible, the man's eyes grew more feral, desperate. He nudged the barrel further into Kirsty's flesh. "No. You slide your gun here, or I shoot woman."

Trapped, Brad had no choice. Slowly, so as not to spook the man, he leaned over and slid the gun across the asphalt. "Let her go and things'll go down easier on you, man. Right now you're only up on car theft and kidnapping. If you harm her..." He couldn't choke out the words, something he'd never had trouble with before. The thought that any harm would come to her nearly paralyzed him.

Jose kicked Brad's revolver under the steaming Mercedes, not releasing the blonde.

"Me no loco, gringo. I let woman go, you shoot me. She come with me." To Kirsty, Jose commanded, "Walk!"

Kirsty shouted, "No!" and kicked Alvarez's knee fiercely.

Swearing, the gunman dropped the weapon. It hit the ground and fired wildly, breaking the stillness of the night. Then it spun around and skittered across the driveway.

Smoke veiled Brad's view and gunpowder singed his nostrils. Sickening fear roiled in his stomach at the knowledge Kirsty could be shot and hurt.

When the smoke cleared, Brad could see Jose and Kirsty struggling, their bodies a tangle of arms and legs. Intent on saving Kirsty, Brad dove for the larger, masculine form, intent on saving the woman.

"You bastard, you'll pay for..." He found his mark, grabbed his sorry neck and squeezed as hard as he could, intent on stopping this scum from hurting Kirsty or anyone else ever again.

"No, Bradley!" Kirsty yelled, tugging at him "You're going to kill him."

"What do you think he planned on doing to you?" He punched the ugly mug swimming before him, the crunch of bones perversely giving a measure of joy. The sorry excuse for a man deserved this and more.

"Break it up by order of the FLPD. Back off, Mueller." Crowe's voice came at him as if through a foggy haze.

Hands tugged at his shoulders, pulling him back and off the kidnapper. "Easy, buddy. Let the law take its course. We're here now.

We've got him." Cole's steadying, rational voice sliced through the mist clouding Brad's brain.

Brad gulped in several steadying breaths. "Where's Kirsty? Is she all right? Did that bastard hurt her?" He looked around frantically when he didn't see her immediately.

"She's safe." Cole took Brad's hand and yanked him to his feet. "She's right over here. Come with me."

Kirsty flung herself into Brad's arms when he neared his captain. "You're a cop?" Incredulity flooded her eyes and her voice as she checked him for any sign of injury, just as he checked her. Other than a few ugly, purpling bruises, she seemed fine.

He rubbed his hands up and down her arms gently, wishing he could soothe the angry bruises away. Fingerprint bruises made vile tracks up and down the precious soft flesh. "Guilty. I couldn't tell you before. I was undercover."

"So you're not really gay?" Her voice was low, unsure.

A slow smile dawned across his lips as he pulled her against him and lowered his lips to hers and brushed them lightly. Against her lips, he murmured, "Not on your life, lady."

"Marshall will be crushed," she said without any tinge of regret.

"He'll live. What about you?" Their mingled breath and the scent of her drove him crazy. He couldn't stop running his hands over her to ensure there were no broken bones or gunshots.

She shook her head slowly. "No." Drawing back a bit, she asked rather shyly, "Was everything a pretense?"

"Maybe this will answer your question," he said gruffly, unable to hold back a second longer. Plundering her lips hungrily, he feasted on her sweetness. Her breasts crushed against his chest, her body writhing against his made him forget everything but her.

"Mueller, get your butt over here." Crowe's impatient voice was followed by a discreet cough.

Brad tried to shut out the annoying voice, wasn't sure he really heard it or imagined it. Then a hard finger poked him several times in the shoulder blade. "Lieutenant Mueller," Cole spoke sotto voce, the Captain requests your presence.

Kirsty yanked back, staring at Brad as if he'd transformed into a monster. Wide, horrified eyes, stared at him. For several seconds her mouth gaped open. "Did you say *Mueller*? As in *Brad Mueller*?"

Brad gulped, unable to speak. He nodded as enlightenment dawned in his landlady's eyes.

"*Mueller?* Not *Miller?*" Kirsty grabbed her stomach and backed away. "I think I'm going to be sick."

When Brad opened his mouth to speak and took a step forward, she backed away several more steps and held her hand out. "Stay away from me. I don't know how I could be so stupid – Bradley Miller/Brad Mueller. You're the one who sends roses to a different woman every week – almost every day!"

"But that was be…"

"Leave me alone. I guess I was the only game in town while you were undercover, but now that you're free, you won't be needing a…a…" she looked down at herself disdainfully, and then glared up at him accusingly.

"A what?" Bradley took another step forward. "A beautiful, gorgeous woman?"

Kirsty snorted and stiffened. "Save it, Mueller. I'm onto you. The joke's over."

Captain Crowe cleared his throat behind Brad. "What part of my orders didn't you understand, Mueller? I told you to keep your paws off your landlady."

Brad winced and opened his mouth to reply, but the captain cut him off. "I need to ask you a few questions. " He escorted Kirsty off to the side and spoke quietly.

When Brad lifted his foot to follow her, Cole slapped a heavy hand on his shoulder. "Hold on, man. Give her time to cool off. She's been through an ordeal tonight. And you're a lucky bastard that Crowe didn't fire you on the spot for going against orders. Don't push it."

Brad wrenched free but stayed put. Whipping around to face his friend, he spat out, "I can't let her think this."

"Think what? She's right, isn't she? You're legendary, pal. It was just a matter of time before this happened. Haven't Haley and I tried to get you to settle down?"

Brad shoveled his fingers through his unruly hair. The dawn broke, uncannily beautiful, over the flat horizon, but Brad didn't give a damn if daylight never came again. "Well, the joke's on me. I'm finally ready and she won't even speak to me."

"Give her time. Maybe she'll come 'round." Cole clapped him soundly on the back, propelling him toward the captain and his team.

"Maybe's not good enough," Brad said morosely, his mind working feverishly.

"Come on. Let's wrap this up so we can go get a big breakfast. We new daddies need to keep up our strength." Cole positively glowed. He was the proud father of baby Emily, a beautiful and healthy bouncing nine-pounder, and Brad's goddaughter.

"I'm not hungry."

"You really must be lovesick. A woman's never stolen your appetite before."

"Well, this one's different." Brad climbed in Cole's shiny burgundy family van, so new it smelled strongly of leather. He pushed his hair back from his face and sighed. First he'd lost his car, then his woman. *Shit! Next he'd lose his mind.*

Chapter Ten

Much too early the next morning, a police sergeant showed up at Kirsty's door to escort her to the Ft. Lauderdale police station.

Kirsty eyed the parade of people that reminded her of the original Star Wars cantina cast. *Oh the joys of living in Ft. Lauderdale!* This was why she avoided downtown. She preferred to stay out west on the towns skirting the Everglades where life seemed saner. She glanced at her watch in alarm. Eight-thirty-five. She was due at the flower shop at ten and she feared she wouldn't make it. Marshall would fire her.

The sergeant smiled perfunctorily and nodded to her. "Have a seat and I'll let Captain Crowe know you're here."

"Will this take long?" She had to get the Lowry-Hendrickson wedding party flowers done today before Michelle Lowry threw another temper tantrum. Also, any official building like this reminded her of Bradley and made her nervous she could run into him at any moment. Perversely, she was miffed that he hadn't bothered to show up at her house or even call. Obviously he had only been playing a part. She hoped he'd had a lot of fun in his game.

The middle-aged front desk sergeant favored her with a commiserative look. "You'll have to ask Captain Crowe. I don't know."

She pursed her lips, spun around and lowered herself into a hard wooden chair with a grimace. Uneasy, she clutched her handbag to her chest.

Bored, wishing she'd brought a book to read, she studied the room full of colorful characters waiting like her. She could be here for hours. She called work on the cell phone she'd brought with her but had to settle for leaving a voice message as no one answered. Fat chance anyone had been there early. Gigi was late to everything and Marshall just didn't do mornings. If not for her, Flower Power wouldn't open till eleven or even noon most days.

Finally, Captain Crowe strolled up to her. He wore a rumpled cheap suit with a loose tie. "Thank you for coming, Miss Engel."

She craned her head back and rose to her feet all in one motion. "You're welcome." *Like she had a choice?*

The captain shook her hand professionally. "This way, please." He beckoned her to follow him down a dark, narrow corridor lined with yellowed linoleum. His strides were so long and swift she had to run alongside.

"Why am I here? Is there a problem?" She kept a tight rein on her purse and tugged at her naughty skirt that kept hitching up in back. "The trial's not for a few weeks, is it?"

He opened a door for her. "Have a seat in here and I'll brief you."

She perched on the edge of a chair, steepling and unsteepling her hands as she chafed and waited for him to explain. Stale, smoky air burned her lungs and she tried to stifle a cough.

"We need some more testimony from you. We'd like you to view a line-up. Are you up to it?" Compassion rang in Crowe's voice as he lit a cigarette and inhaled deeply on it, peering at her through a smoky haze.

She tried to quell a cough that the smoke sparked and closed her eyes to draw on her strength. Would this nightmare ever end? When she opened her eyes, she pierced the man with her gaze. "Do you mean now?"

"Was Lieutenant Mueller spying on me?" she asked pressing her palms on the table, glaring accusingly from one man to the other and back.

Crowe shook his head. "We were after the chop shop operators next door. Hopefully you can identify them in the line up. You just happened to be in the wrong place."

"Can we get this over with? I'm due at work in less than an hour and my boss doesn't like it when I'm late." She bit back a sigh and tried to get excited about doing her civic duty but in truth, she just wanted to disappear before Brad Mueller showed up. If he couldn't show up on his own at her house or bother to call her, she certainly didn't want to run into him by surprise here.

Crowe scraped his chair back and stood, massaging the back of his neck. "Sure. The sooner we can put those guys away, the better."

After she identified one of the men in the line-up, Captain Crowe thanked her. "One word of advice, young lady," he said sagely, concern pooling in his flat brown eyes. "Take that trellis down so no one else can climb up there. And do a background check on all your renters."

"Thanks," she mumbled as she strode out. Wasn't he responsible for sending a decoy into her house? Funny that he should be the one to warn her now, after the fact. It had helped her that she was naïve and foolish. *Never again!* "You'd better believe I will." Fury and frustration simmered hotly. "Ooh!" She dug her nails in her palms and sought the exit. *She was so out of here!*

Changing her mind about speaking to Brad, she stopped by the front desk on the far-fetched chance that Brad might be in the building. She'd seen a number of the cops on her case striding through the halls. Maybe all were here. "May I speak to Officer Bradley *Mueller*?" she asked through clenched teeth.

The man frowned. "We don't have an officer by that name on the list…"

"That's *Lieutenant Brad Mueller*," a beloved voice murmured in her ear, tickling her earlobe.

Bristling, startled, she whirled around. Her purse arced out and slammed into his arm. Mortified, she gasped into her hand. "Oh no! Are you okay? I'm sorry."

"I'm sorry," Brad said, pulling her to a semi-private corner. "I didn't want to deceive you, but I was under orders. I hope you believe that." He rubbed her arms. His gaze smoldered.

She narrowed her eyes up at him. "So you said. I believe you're not gay." She'd give him that much, but whether or not he cared for her was a completely separate matter he hadn't proven.

"Does that make you happy?" he asked huskily, burying his face in the hollow of her shoulder, his tongue scorching liquid fire down the column of her neck. His broad hands circled her waist, dragging her against him, sparking electricity.

Bewitched, she could hardly think, or articulate. She tried to stay strong and resist him, but his lips felt so wonderful. "Should it?"

He lifted his head and gazed deeply into her eyes. "I hope so."

Forgetting how mad she was at him, she was lifting her lips for his kiss when a perfect size three brunette wearing heavy make-up burst between them as if Kirsty was invisible, "Is that you, Brad honey? I thought you disappeared off the face of the earth."

The intruder batted her lashes at him coquettishly and pouted prettily. "I really miss all those luscious roses." She eyed Kirsty curiously. "I s'pose you're getting them all now." She whispered conspiratorially to Kirsty in an aside, "He's a slippery devil, dearie, so hold tight. He's quite a ladies man."

Kirsty frowned, backing up a step. *Roses? Ladies' man?* She should thank the woman for reminding her, although what she really wanted to do was claw her eyes out and flounce away.

"Don't tell me you didn't know what a ladies man our Brad darling is?" The brunette tossed her rich mane over her shoulder and giggled. "You haven't lost your touch, lover." She tiptoed and slashed a kiss across Brad's lips. "Call me."

"So that's one of your many conquests? It's no wonder you've not called me. You merely found someplace else to send your roses through." Mortified, she backed away, looking for the nearest escape route.

"I thought you'd be happy that I'm not gay?" His eyes smoldered as he reached for her but she ducked under his arm, slipping away.

"Congratulations!" Sarcasm dripped from her lips. "Gay. Straight. You're still a scoundrel."

Unhappiness burned the backs of her eyes and she blinked furiously to hold them back. She feared once one fell, the dam would burst. She couldn't let him see her cry, didn't want her scalp to be added to his belt. "Please just leave me alone."

Before he could respond, she turned and fled. *So much for a graceful exit.*

Why me? I'm such a jerk magnet. Maybe men thought that because she was so overweight she would take anything from them out of gratitude or desperation. She kept up a heated conversation with herself all the way to work, uncaring at all the odd stares she garnered.

Once at the shop, she slammed inside and made a beeline to her work area, ignoring both her boss and Gigi.

"What's the skinny? Are we in a tiff today?" Gigi stared at her curiously. "Your favorite customer's been ringing here like crazy," she warned in a stage whisper.

"Not *we*," Kirsty grumbled, alarmed, conversely fearing and hoping she meant Brad but hesitant to ask. "*Me*. Just stupid, idiotic me." She threw her purse on top of her desk not caring the contents spilled out and rolled onto the floor.

Marshall waltzed over and tapped his watch. "Afternoon, Kirsten. Glad you decided to join us."

"I was down at the police station. It's a long story. I'll explain it all later." *When she felt human again…if ever.*

Marshall's brows pinched together, but he honored her request. "Michelle Lowry's been calling…and wants a time estimate on her order."

Kirsty groaned and laid her head on her desk. So it wasn't Brad. *What was new?* "I can't make a wedding bouquet today. You do it."

"Excuse me?" Marshall sighed deeply. "What knight in shining armor crashed and burned this time?"

She shook her head, miserable, refusing to answer.

"You can tell us." Gigi hugged her. "I'll beat him up and Marshall will sing him to death."

Marshall scowled and shook his finger at Gigi. "Payback's a…"

"It's too embarrassing." How could she have let herself fall in love with a gay man? The fact he wasn't really gay didn't appease her. At the time, she'd believed him to be gay. In fact, it would have been better if he had been instead of the low-down lothario he really was.

"You can't be embarrassed with us, pet. We love you." Gigi stroked her hair.

Kirsty muttered a muffled, "It's Bradley. I mean *Brad*." She hiccoughed in the middle of her statement. "He's a rogue. A scamp. A 100% bonafide scoundrel."

Stunned silence followed.

Finally Marshall ventured, shock radiating over his twisted features, "*My* Bradley?"

She lifted her head a few inches. "No. Not *your* Bradley. And not *my* Brad, either. Apparently, he's *everybody's Brad*." She pounded the table with her fist. "I never want to see him or hear his name again."

"I'll get you a hot cuppa and some biscuits to cheer you up." Gigi hurried off, her short bob bouncing around her neck.

They badgered her for more details which she only gave in spurts, bitterly. Marshall looked more shocked than she.

When an email popped up on her screen, she deleted it when she saw it was from Brad. Then he flooded her box with emails. She deleted all of them, and then shut down her computer.

"Bradley's ringing for you," Gigi said softly behind her. "Do you want to take it?"

Kirsty's heart shattered. "Tell him I died." She didn't need another lothario. Frank had been more than enough to last her a lifetime. She flung her purse over her shoulder and marched to the door. "I need to be alone, okay?"

"Okay, sunshine. I'll finish the Lowry order. Be careful and get some rest." Marshall hugged her tightly before she left and he kissed her on the cheek.

"Ring us if you need anything at all." Sympathy pooled in Gigi's limpid dark eyes. And pity.

Kirsty couldn't stand the pity. She nodded and hugged Gigi and then left. She walked in circles until her feet could take no more. High heels were torture chambers men invented to punish women, she decided. When she returned to her car, she flung them in the back seat and drove home in her stocking feet.

When she rounded the corner by her house, she squealed her brakes, stunned by the sight. Rose petals filled her driveway. But that wasn't the real shocker. Brad sat astride a magnificent white steed that pranced and snorted as a beautiful reddish Golden Retriever barked at his side.

Slowly, she pulled in and parked, eyeing them. She walked over to them cautiously. She didn't like the fact that she had to look up at him, leaving her at a distinct disadvantage. "What kind of scam are you pulling now? Need more testimony from me?"

Brad cocked a bone-meltingly sexy grin at her that stole her breath. "No scam. I've brought my down payment." He stroked the horse's satiny neck. "By the way, it's illegal to drive barefoot."

She looked at her feet and shrugged, uncaring. "So arrest me, Lieutenant."

She eyed the horse. Magnificent as he was, she had never seen one in Coral Springs. This wasn't Parkland or Davie where they were common sights galloping along the roadside. "Is it legal to have a horse in Coral Springs?"

"My new car won't arrive till Saturday. Besides, he's got a badge." Brad leaned forward and pointed to a FLPD badge pinned to the bridle. He grinned widely. "I got us a big family van, like Cole bought for Haley."

She tried to hide her smile at the incorrigible man's shenanigans. But then his words teased her mind, the riddle confusing her. Despite herself, curiosity got the better of her. He had said *family van* and *down payment*. "Did you say *down payment*? And why the horse?"

"Sir Bradley – I mean *Brad* – at your service, my lady. I'm ready for the house, 2.3 kids, a dog, a couple of cats...and you in my bed every night." Before she gleaned his intentions, he reached down and swooped her up into his arms and positioned her in front of him on the horse so that she faced him. He traced his thumb down her jaw line, igniting wild fires in her veins, making it impossible for her to breathe. "The dog's a down payment. Afraid I have to take Mr. Ed back to the station before his next duty shift."

The dog barked joyfully, wagging his bushy tail. Stars twinkled in the canine's amber trusting eyes.

The horse whinnied and pranced. Sunlight winked off his badge.

Her heart skipped several beats. *He couldn't mean...* "You're proposing?"

Brad bent his head and nipped at her lips playfully. His arm tightened around her, pulling her gently but inexorably to his lips. "Uh huh. Why else would I come to you on my white steed?"

"You're really serious?" She wanted to ask if he was crazy or feverish and she prayed he was rational and well.

Against her lips he murmured, "Well, a point three kid might be a little awkward. He'd look kinda funny, too. Let's round that up."

Joy consumed her, and she wound her arms around his neck. "Brad?"

"Hmmm? What's your answer?" He traced her lips with his tongue, teasing her unmercifully.

She trembled against him, her blood boiling. "If I get another email from you ordering American Beauties, I'll have to kill you, you know." She nipped his lips, enjoying the game.

"Even if I only order them for you from now on? Kirsty?"

"Hmm?" She snuggled against him, all lingering doubts and anger dissipated. "I suppose that I can make an exception in that case. Mr. Lawn Lover's gaping at us. He must be having a coronary over having a horse in his neighborhood."

"We could ride off into the sunset," Brad murmured against her lips. "Or we could tether the horse and move this inside, Mr. Lawn Lover be damned."

She gazed upon the carpet of lush beautiful rose petals. "But I love what you did to the driveway. Who cares what the neighbors think anyway?"

Devilish mirth and passion warred in his crinkling eyes and he murmured against them, "Then you'll really love what I did to the bedroom. How about we try out that Marilyn Monroe wig?"

An evil grin curved the corners of her lips as deliciously wicked thoughts tantalized her mind. "You or me?"

A growl rumbled from deep in Brad's chest as his hands crept under her shirt and massaged her waist. His thumbs slid inside the waist of her slacks massaging her heated flesh, eliciting an answering moan from her lips. "I'm really not that kind of guy..."

"Poor Marshall will be so distraught." Just as she was when he released her, walking toward the snorting animal.

"Marshall will just have to survive without me. I'm spoken for." Deviltry lit Brad's eyes as he held up his forefinger in the just-a-minute signal. He tied the horse to the apple blossom tree in the back yard, giving it plenty of rein to graze under the ample shade. Then he marched purposefully toward her, passion blazing in his eyes. When he scooped her into his arms and hoisted her against his chest, she shivered deliciously and wound her fingers in the silky hair at the nape of his neck.

In a teasing mood, she stared at his hair and caressed his ear lobes between her fingers. "Uhm, I don't know. You'd probably look quite fetching in it."

"Not another word about the damned wig, woman!" He captured her lips, parting them with his tongue, drinking deeply of her. He kicked the front door in forcefully, slammed it shut behind them, and then climbed the stairs two at a time with her.

She thrilled to the play of his powerful muscles rippling against her chest. Rose petal perfume wafted around her before he rounded the bedroom door, and she inhaled the incensed aroma dreamily.

The sight that met her eyes made her gasp in delight. Hundreds of candles flickered enchantingly, casting shadows on the walls. Just as he'd professed, rose petals littered the bed and floor. Black satin sheets were turned down, glistening brilliantly against the silky red of the roses.

"Is this what you do with all those American Beauties you've purchased?" A twinge of jealousy skipped through her, but she reminded herself that he was hers. She was already addicted to their scent and couldn't wait to rub them all over his flesh. They would smell wonderful with his musky scent. When he laid her down atop them, it was like floating on clouds.

"No. I reserved this for you. Only you." When she held out her arms to him, he shook his head, a wicked smile curving at the ends of his sensual lips. Then he started lifting his T-shirt so excruciatingly slow she gnawed her bottom lip. The play of dancing candlelight on his hard body stole her breath as her heart hammered her ribs.

He tugged the shirt over his head and threw it across the room, draping a silk tree. When he unsnapped his jeans and kicked them off, her mouth went dry and she wet her lips with the tip of her tongue.

She couldn't tear her gaze from the evocative grind of his hips as he danced for her in just his briefs, his erection hotly evident. Unable to keep her desire in check, she rolled off the bed and knelt before him, her knees sinking into the plush carpet. He was taking entirely too long to get naked and she was wet for him. Excruciatingly so.

She drew a finger down his hard, pulsing length, electric thrills shooting through her when he moaned and buried his fingers in her hair. With her eyes level to his waist, she drew his pants down, releasing his hard cock that sprang mere inches away from her lips. Velvety and throbbing, pre-come glazed the shaft tempting her more than anything had ever tempted her in her life.

Lava smoldered in her lover's eyes and he shuddered deliciously when she wrapped her fingers around the base of his thickness. She leaned over to taste him, knowing her thirst for him could never be quenched. She swirled her tongue around the velvety head, flicking and kissing greedily. Then she licked its length, feverish against her lips, delighting as he shivered against her, fierce growls exciting her.

"Take me in your mouth." His breathing heavy, he thrust forward, rubbing his cock against her lips. He tasted so incredibly wonderful, salty and musky, that she was heady from his flavor. Opening her lips wide, she drew him inside her mouth as deeply as she could, loving the feel of his silky hardness caressing her lips. She spread her hands over his tight buttocks, running them up and down the length of his thighs.

When he began to spasm, she sucked harder, coaxing the release she knew would be incredible. Cupping his testicles in her hand, she squeezed gently, playing with them. They were heavy in her hands, matching his masterful cock. He ejaculated powerfully into her mouth, spewing his seed, filling her as deeply as she could take him, which was not even close to half his length.

She swallowed greedily, sucking faster as the warm semen pumped into her mouth, sliding down her throat. She sucked every last drop of the precious ambrosia, disappointed when no more was forthcoming.

Withdrawing from him slowly, she adored the tip, kissing it softly, reverently. She licked and nibbled her way up his chest, then stood on tiptoes to ravage his lips.

He crushed her to him, his hands roaming freely, one hand unclasping her bra, the other sliding between her legs, making her squirm. "I want to feel you against me." He freed her from her clothing, letting it pool at her feet. Pushing her back on the bed, he molded her body to his. His thumb stroked the nub of her clit, driving her insane. Wildfire flashed through her veins so that now, she was the feverish one, moaning into his mouth.

She bucked against his hand, losing herself in him. When he parted her velvety lower lips and slid his finger inside, she flexed, tightening around him. Skimming her fingers down his length, she sought his heat again, praying he was ready to go another round. She couldn't wait another moment. She needed him now. Only this time she planned on taking him deep inside her and feel his sperm shoot all the way to her womb.

"Fuck me hard." She spread her legs wide, drawing his penis to her slit. Her clit throbbed, and she lifted her hips toward him wantonly, begging him to take her.

He rose off her chest, holding his weight with his arms. He grinned wickedly and rubbed his cock along her swollen lubricated lips, driving her mad. "Be careful what you wish for." He slammed fully into her, making her scream with joy.

She met him thrust for thrust, lifting her head off the bed to watch their mating, mesmerized as she watched his beautiful cock slide in and out of her, their juices mixing. His cock pulsed, shimmering with their flowing sap. "So erotic."

He lowered his head and kissed first one nipple then the other as she arched against him and felt the beads pebble. He sucked the nub hard, elongating it inside his mouth, and she writhed, sifting her hands through his glorious hair.

She loved watching him suckle her breast as she met him thrust for thrust. An impossible ache twisted in her vagina and she thrust one last time against him, the magic of his possession sending waves of intense pleasure through her. Fire enflamed her. Her temperature soared. Her love for him swelled, wrapping her in a warmth she'd never known with another man, never dreamed existed.

He abandoned her breast to the chill brush of air and captured her mouth, moaning into it. Crushing her to him, he held her tightly, pumping harder, faster, until he shivered and pushed his entire length inside. He flexed inside her, spewing his seed as she raked his back with her fingernails.

He withdrew slowly, and then cradled her against his warm chest. His breathing grew deep and his heart rate slowed against her cheek. He'd fallen asleep!

She nestled deeper into his arms and let her own exhaustion overtake her. She could get used to this.

The next morning, she awoke in Brad's arms, purring. She slashed a kiss across his lips. "Good morning."

"Hi, sleepy head. Did you get a lot of rest?" He murmured against her lips. His cock grew hard against her.

"Why? I guess I need more energy?" *She hoped!*

"Most definitely." He drank of her lips deeply and trailed his fingers down her stomach. He cupped her pussy and rubbed her clit with his thumb, heating her up again.

"Get on your knees, doggy style," he whispered raggedly, his voice raw with emotion. His tongue delved into the crack between her buttocks, licking hungrily.

Moaning, shuddering with renewed desire, she rose on her knees, pressing her backside to his mouth, craving more of the delicious sensation. Her full breasts swung back and forth, the nipples grazing the satin sheets. "Oh!" No wonder satin was so popular. She vowed to sleep on satin sheets every night for the rest of her life.

Brad's hand cupped her pussy, and he massaged her clitoris, making her squirm against him. "Keep that up and I'll never let you out of this bed."

"Promises, promises." She wished! She wiggled her butt in front of his lips, fully intending to drive her as wildly insane as he was driving her.

"You sure you're a preacher's daughter?" He worshipped her with his tongue again, slipped two fingers into her cunt, sliding them in and out.

Joy bubbled through her and she giggled. Her voice ragged and husky, she said, "Oh yes. But just because my daddy's a preacher, doesn't mean I am. Besides, he got me somehow."

Brad rose high above her, holding her buttocks firmly before him and he thrust hard inside her making her gasp. Panting, he drove into her more powerfully than before if that was possible. His swollen cock spread her legs and she loved the feel of it gliding against her buttocks.

Her body rocked with every forceful thrust, her breasts swayed and she lowered herself onto her elbows to hold his weight. Her new position had the side benefit of making her nipples graze the bed with every back and forth swing.

He slammed into her one last time and held her against him, his hands large and warm around her waist.

She wriggled, moaning, wanting her own release.

"Did you come?"

"No." Disappointed, she shook her head, her hair swinging against her cheeks. Her nipples ached for his attention.

"Turn over." He helped her roll onto her back and then dipped his head between her legs, burrowing his face into her cunt. His tongue lapped at her, bathing her labia, caressing her clit. She watched him, holding his head, never wanting this night to end. How could she have ever thought for even a second that he didn't like women? He was ravenous! Incredible!

His sandpapery tongue seared her, ravaging her and she strained against it. He removed his finger and she whimpered, missing the wonderful sensation. She gasped when he slid it around to her anus and worked it inside. It was so tight, gloving his finger that pumped in and out, faster and faster, harder and harder.

Her fire burned brighter, hotter. Lava flowed freely through her veins, making her writhe and scream for mercy. She pounded against his hand, wave after wave of ecstasy flooding her, threatening to drown her.

His lips sucked hard until he drained every drop of her juices, refusing to let her squirm away.

Finally, when she was spent, gasping for air and holding her close, he stretched out beside her. Taking her in his arms, he cradled her lovingly, and ran the pad of his thumb over her hardening breast. "Think you can stand this every night for the rest of our lives?"

"Uhm. I hope so." Paradise. She couldn't dream of a better future than making love to her sexy cop every night.

He threw his leg over hers, nestled his cock against her warmth, and she felt it flex to life, teasing her.

Hot thrills shot through her and her nerve endings sang.

He rolled her onto her back and climbed on top, his rod hovering over her, poised at the slit of her swollen, throbbing lips. He murmured against her. "All night? Think you're up to it again?"

Her answer was to part her mouth, raise her hips, and guide him inside. She'd never get her fill of him, never stop loving him.

About the author:

Ashley Ladd lives in South Florida with her husband, five children, and beloved pets. She loves the water, animals (especially cats), and playing on the computer.

She's been told she has a wicked sense of humor and often incorporates humor and adventure into her books. She also adores very spicy romance which she also weaves into her stories.

Ashley welcomes mail from readers. You can write to her c/o Ellora's Cave Publishing at 1337 Commerce Drive, Suite 13, Stow OH 44224.

Also by Ashley Ladd:

Carbon Copy
Price Of Fame

BETTER THAN ICE CREAM

Alicia Sparks

Dedicated to Chris, Sean and Ian
And all that ice cream we eat!

Chapter One

Laura slowly ran her tongue around the tip, carefully holding her long hair out of her face. Her tongue flicked in and out before running along the sides, moving in one swift motion and then rolling around the summit before darting out to smooth across her satisfied lips. She smiled before taking the whole of it into her mouth. The pressure began to build as the liquid poured down her throat. She wasn't fast enough to lap it up as white beads dribbled out of her mouth and onto her hand. She quickly sucked the fleeing cream, as her body began to quiver a little. Her pulse raced, reminding her of a nice aerobic workout, which was all in the breathing anyway, and hers came in rapid pants.

She shifted, vying for a better position, knowing positioning was key. Well, that and a few other things. Hormones had a lot to do with it. And chemistry. Without the right mix of chemistry, all the hormones in the world wouldn't do a bit of good. She had experienced enough failures to prove that point. But not today. Today was one of those days every girl dreams about.

The discovery happened by surprise this morning, thrilling her completely. She smiled as she continued to take it into her mouth, licking, lapping, sucking a little.

She swore her insides melted as her tongue continued to work. Blaming it on the heat of the day or the heat in the room would be a lie. The orgasmic feeling had little to do with the surroundings and everything to do with the mixture of chemistry and hormones, which was about to melt around her toes and had already pooled between her thighs.

She groaned and began to work on the cone. This was damned good ice cream.

"Enjoying yourself?" Nick Martin watched, leaning against the doorframe. She knew exactly what Nick thought of her, she needed to get out more. This was evident by the half-smirk on his face.

"Tremendously," she smiled, licked her lips and then popped the rest of the cone into her mouth.

"If you get that worked up over an ice cream, I'd hate to see what you'd do to a man," he leaned against the doorframe, arms folded.

"You'd never see what I would do to a man," she snapped, a little grumpy now that her morning foreplay session with the fudge ripple had been interrupted.

"Thank God for some reprieves. Look, Amanda wanted to be sure you were still coming to dinner tonight. She is hoping to finalize the deal with…"

"With Ryan LeJeune. I know. She only left ten messages last night." This deal with Ryan had everyone on edge, especially Laura. She hadn't seen him in — how long? Too long. Not long enough. A flush spread all the way to her ears when she pictured the tall, lean cowboy. Sin on a stick. Oh yeah.

"Well, this is your deal," he reminded her, shaking her from her reverie with his scolding tone. Ever since she had been trying to perfect this one ice cream flavor, the business end of her business seemed to be falling more and more into Amanda's hands, a problem Nick constantly vocalized.

"I know, I know," she rubbed at the chocolate stain making its way down the front of her coat. Why she bothered with a lab coat and not an apron was one of those mysteries even she couldn't explain. She wanted her work to be taken seriously. As science. She was more than just a cook. "I'll be there." She finally gave up on the stain and shot Nick a look, hoping he would get lost now so she could enjoy more of this morning's delight.

"You better," he warned. "I miss my wife. When you and your sister went into this business, you swore all she'd be doing is marketing," he reminded her, ignoring the scowl on her face.

"And she is. She's helping me close the deal with Ryan. That's marketing."

"In your little world, maybe," he snickered. "But in mine, it's negotiating. And that's your area."

"Did you need something else, oh brother-in-law of mine?" She laced the question with sarcasm, hoping to send him back to work. Or make him get to the point. She had too much on her mind today to deal with her sister's husband.

"No, I didn't," he smirked. "I just wanted to remind you. And Laura," he paused before turning to leave her "lab." "You have chocolate on your chin."

She swiped at the imposing dribble and looked at her watch. She still had time to enjoy another cone — or pint — of her newest creation before changing hats and becoming Laura Reynolds, owner and CEO of *I Scream*, the only ice cream in the country guaranteed to produce an orgasm. Okay, so it didn't say that on the package, but her customers knew why it cost twenty dollars a pint. And they kept coming back for more.

She pushed away from the counter and went back to the walk-in freezer. Forcing herself to replace fudge ripple, she sighed and promised to be back tonight for an encore if she closed the deal with Ryan LeJeune in a reasonable amount of time. Until then, she needed to review the notes concerning *LeJeune's Louisiana Cane* and try to come up with a workable scheme for combining the interests of the two companies.

And try to keep Ryan's dreamy blue eyes out of her head. This was business, she reminded herself. Strictly business.

LeJeune's was going under. She knew this from the figures Jeremy sent over. And it was no wonder. Ryan had abandoned the business several years ago, leaving everything to his younger brother, Blake. Unfortunately, Blake's interest in chasing the occasional supermodel outweighed running a sugar cane processing factory, a fact that gave Laura the advantage.

She took the stack of notes from the kitchen counter and eyed her three cousins who were busy testing the new ice cream for themselves. Cate, Robin and Karen had been a part of her company since its inception.

"I'll be back later, guys," she called to them before leaving. They nodded while devouring spoonfuls of the latest creation, the satisfied smiles on their faces proving Laura hadn't been the only one to feel the rush of fudge ripple.

"See you," Karen waved her spoon in the air. Robin and Cate both just waved, too engrossed in the cool treat to say much of anything.

These were the rewards of ten years of college, she sighed. Laura learned how to manipulate the chemical make up of chocolate to produce the effects chocolate guaranteed, those of a simulated orgasm.

And the great part was that the Reynolds girls all got to test the products.

I Scream was still a small company, but if she managed to seal the deal with Ryan, she could go global because she would have a cheap local supplier for her sugar. Not to mention, she would be the first ice cream manufacturer in the country to have her hands on his new no-calorie, no-fat, no-bad-side-effects sugar substitute.

She smiled at the thought of tripling her sales, a distinct possibility if she could cut back on the fat and calories of her product without altering the taste or the orgasmic quality. Those kinds of numbers would guarantee an expansion of the company and possibly a move to a larger city, maybe New Orleans even. She could give Ben and Jerry a run for their money if she could only get out of Oak Creek.

The dinner with Ryan was a necessary evil and a thought that made her wish her ice cream were tolerance inducing rather than orgasm inducing. Ryan LeJeune's reputation as a ladies' man preceded him, making her wish anyone else owned the company.

If the South were still the land of the gentlemanly rakes, Ryan would be a charter member of the club. On the outside, he was sweet as the sugar he produced, but on the inside, he was nothing but a sticky sin-filled treat, which easily melted in the sun. At least that's what all of his conquests said. He was gone before the morning sun rose and rarely ever called back. He had even cheated notoriously on his ex-wife who, of course, said she was sure he hadn't meant to.

Some women had no backbone when it came to men. Well, Laura wasn't one of them. In fact, if her ice cream kept getting better and better, she might eliminate the need for them all together. Who needed the hassle anyway?

And in the case of men like Ryan, who had moved out of Oak Creek after the divorce—he had already slept with most of the women in town anyway—he caused more problems for her than anything else. Two months of voice mail finally convinced him to meet with her. She resented this and knew his reluctance left an awful taste in her mouth, making her wish his brother, Blake, was in charge of the company instead of sowing his own oats in Greece.

Three o'clock came without warning, forcing her to shake the Ryan brain freeze from her head. She groaned, annoyed at herself for spending so much time thinking about him. It was the ice cream, she decided.

The final negotiations hadn't been thought out yet. And the small matter of choosing a dress to wear tonight only added to her agitation. She knew how to play the game with gentlemanly rakes. Show a little skin and addle their brains to the point where they would be willing to sign on the dotted line. But could she pull it off with someone like Ryan?

* * * * *

Ryan LeJeune hitched a ride on Dusty Bayonne's crop duster. Dusty flew into New Orleans twice a week to pick up his supplies, and he agreed to bring Ryan back to Oak Creek for his meeting. What would have been a five- hour drive was only an hour ride back on the small plane.

"You gonna be in town long?" Dusty asked as he dropped Ryan off at the LeJeune factory.

"Naw. Just a couple of days," he grinned, hoping it wouldn't take longer than that to get this company to see black again. Prepared to deal with Laura Reynolds by any means necessary, he jumped down from the cab of Dusty's big 4X4 truck.

"You need a ride back, then? I head back on Thursday."

"Thanks. But my brother bought a new Porsche before he left for Europe. I'm thinking about picking it up and bringing it back." Why Blake needed a Porsche, Ryan didn't know. But he planned on giving it a spin through town and taking it into *Nawlins* for show.

Dusty laughed, "I'd race you to New Orleans, but you'd probably beat me in something like that. Don't see many of them around on I-49."

"I know. I don't know what possessed him to sink fifty thousand dollars into a hunk of metal and fiberglass, but since he did, I plan on driving it." Hot cars are chick magnets. And these days, Ryan needed one because the LeJeune well of charm seemed to have run dry.

He waved his good-bye to Dusty and then turned to head into the factory, his backpack slung over his shoulder. Blake really let things slide, he thought, eyeing the peeling paint and rotten boards lining the porch.

The front of the old factory resembled a plantation store, homage to a great–great-grandfather who managed to buy himself out of slavery by working in the plantation's store.

Granpère would roll over in his grave if he saw the state of the place. When Ryan agreed to sell his share to his younger brother a few years ago, he hoped Blake's attention to detail would serve it right. At any rate, at least his share hadn't been lost to his snake of an ex-wife, Gina. Since Blake's early departure, Ryan's negotiation skills were crucial to saving the company.

He moved his foot up and down on one of the squeaky boards. The whole porch needed replacing. But first, he had to earn the money for repairs by getting the business up to speed. And that was going to take a hell of a lot of maneuvering with Laura Reynolds. Not exactly the homecoming queen, he mused before his train of thought was interrupted.

Jeremy Bentley stepped out onto the porch, filling up the entire doorway with his broad shoulders. He crossed his arms and narrowed his eyes at Ryan. "So the prodigal son returns."

"Something like that," Ryan grinned then moved forward to shake his friend's hand.

"Long time, no see. Let's see, last I heard you were shacked up in New Orleans with a pair of redheads who worked at Big Daddy's."

"Don't believe half of what you hear," he warned, thinking it would have been nice to live with a couple of strippers.

"I guess you're here to look over the figures," Jeremy opened the door and led Ryan in.

"Yeah. I've got to get them straight in my head before the big meeting tonight." He raked a hand through his wayward hair, cursing the tangles caused by the length and the curls.

"You done your research on that company?" Jeremy shot him a grin.

"That I have," he followed Jeremy into the office and sank down into the battered leather chair in front of the desk. Nothing had changed since his father's days in this office. The calendar from the 70's still hung on the wall next to the faded poster of Marilyn Monroe.

Jeremy took his usual seat behind the desk and pushed a folder in Ryan's direction. "That tone of your voice sounds like you don't put much stock in it."

"It doesn't matter what I put in it," he shrugged. "Point is, she took in damn near three million dollars last year. All hers. Who knows what the company made? Now that she's ready to go national, I expect it to skyrocket. That's the kind of train ride I want to be on."

"Yeah, but an ice cream that can cause an orgasm?" he wrinkled his nose. "I don't even see how that's possible."

"It's a simulated orgasm," Ryan reminded him, "and I don't care how it's possible or even if it is possible. All I care is that it sells." And saves my ass.

"Well, it does. The girls that work for her swear by it, too," he winked.

Ryan looked up from the paperwork. "You don't mean they are replacing ice cream for sex?"

"Not really replacing, just enhancing, I guess."

"Humph," he mumbled. Enhancing my ass. When did sex need to be enhanced with ice cream? Never in his experience.

"You do remember Laura, don't you?"

Laura Reynolds. Yeah. He remembered her. She had been well on her way to finishing college by the time he settled down enough to start. He barely finished his business degree by the time she had gotten her Ph.D. By then, he had married and divorced. "I remember Laura."

"You think this deal with her will get us to see black anytime soon?"

"I don't know. If the price is right, I think this would be a good deal for us. We can stay afloat, but I don't know for how long." He slapped the folder shut. "My head hurts. Can you just tell me how bad things are?" Is this gonna cost me my soul?

Jeremy laughed. "You sure you want to know?"

"Yeah. And as straightforward as possible, okay?"

"Okay. Well, you know Blake ran off with a nice chunk of change. It was all his. He had been paying himself nicely for the past six years. The loan from the bank to operate for the past six months is a million. That's not bad considering, but we need to make more than that to stay afloat with the interest and all. Bottom line is we need this deal with Laura." Jeremy's smiling face straightened.

The worry there made Ryan's stomach turn. This was his business and he shouldn't have taken it upon himself to shove it off on his brother and then his best friend. He straightened. "Damn. I really didn't know we were in such a bind."

"Well, we are. And now that you're here, you can have it."

"I'm sorry I put all of this on you, buddy." For the first time since his divorce, he felt like he had really let a lot of people down. He'd fix this mess. No matter what. Laura Reynolds should be easy enough to charm—even if his skills were rusty.

"Hey," Jeremy shrugged, "it's my job. Besides, you were off trying to make your own fortune."

Ryan knew his fortune hunting landed him square in the middle of this mess. The same thing would get them out, he vowed. His grandfather's company would not fold just because he wanted to do things on his own without the family connection. He mumbled his thanks to Jeremy and then went out back to check the machinery and talk to some of the workers.

His cousin, Danny, would be here in an hour with the Porsche to give him a ride to the house. He hoped it was in better shape than the factory. Otherwise, he was going to have a hell of a mess on his hands.

Ryan knew, subconsciously, when he hopped on that plane this morning, he wouldn't be going back to New Orleans. Something about the way his tiny apartment felt combined with the loneliness in his chest made him realize then he would be returning home to stay. And, quite frankly, the thought scared him to death. His roots were in Oak Creek, but, unfortunately, the town wasn't what it used to be. And rebuilding a business in a has-been town was a task he wasn't sure he could accomplish. He had no other choice, though. He took in a frustrated breath, hoping the fates would kindly send an answer to this dilemma his way. And he hoped to God the answer wasn't Laura Reynolds.

The last thing he needed right now was a complicated woman. And if he knew anything about women, he knew this one was complicated. Stubborn to a fault, determined, and single. It wasn't right for a woman to be single and thirty. That meant one of two things in his mind. Either she was unattractive or she was hard to handle. He hoped for the first. He could deal with unattractive.

Ryan tried to pay attention to Danny's nonstop chatter on the way to the house. The high school baseball team didn't interest him, even though he knew coaching was Danny's life. Instead, he concentrated on the ulcer growing in his stomach. He should just let the whole company go under. That's what a smart man would do. Sell it while he could.

But the formula burned a hole in his shirt pocket, promising fortune beyond his wildest imagination. His company may be small time now, but the potential to make it a multi-million-dollar operation existed. Diabetics, health nuts, all those people on the various low-carb diets, they all wanted a product like the one he could offer. And orgasm-producing ice cream was a good place to start.

Danny eased the Porsche into the driveway of the white two-story house. Ryan closed his eyes and said a silent prayer. *Please let the house be okay.* The rose garden his mother planted had wilted down to almost nothing. Paint chipped in small places, but overall, the house didn't look any worse for the wear. Thank God.

"I'm just gonna pick up my truck and I'll be out of your way," Danny called from behind Ryan, who stepped out of the car to gaze at his childhood home.

"Thanks, man, for coming to get me," he turned and shook Danny's hand before taking the key ring and cringing at the "player" logo emblazoned on it, which described Blake's attitude on life. Player to the end.

"No problem. And if you need anything, let me know."

"I'll do that."

Ryan held his breath, hoping the conditions inside the house would be favorable. As he fumbled with the lock, he tried not to think about what else could go wrong today. Blake had been gone for six months. Not much could happen in six months, could it? At least Blake had the sense to lock up when he left. Stepping through the threshold, he almost tripped over the stack of mail waiting at the door.

Past due and overdue were stamped on the outside of several of them. A disconnect notice graced the top of the pile. He grabbed the mail and tossed it onto the hallway table and fumbled with the light. Great. That must have been the disconnect notice.

He tore open the envelope only to discover his correct assumption. Apparently, Blake hadn't paid the bill for quite a while. A five-hundred dollar electric bill wasn't possible for one month even in the heat of the summer. He wondered if the phone had been disconnected, too. Picking up the receiver in the hall, he had his answer. Dead as a doornail.

Glancing at his watch, he realized there were only three hours left before the dreaded meeting. His head started to pound. He took his cell phone from his belt clip and dialed the number for the electric company, hoping electricity would be enough to start things in the right direction.

"Louisiana Lectric," the voice on the other end said.

"Hi. This is Ryan LeJeune and I…"

"Ryan LeJeune! Well, I'll be. How are you, son?" the voice sounded excited to hear his name.

"Uh, fine," he didn't recognize the voice.

"This is Mabel Willis. You don't remember me, do you?"

"Mabel? Oh, yeah, sure. I remember you," he scanned his brain for a face. None came to him.

"Well, sugar, what can I do for you?"

"It seems my brother has a hefty bill with you guys here at the house and I was wondering if there was anything I could do to pay it and get the lights turned back on." Turn on the charm.

"Let me run your address and I'll tell you." She paused. "Oh, dear. Yeah, he's got quite a bill here. You gonna settle up for him?"

"How much exactly to do that?" He rubbed his temple with his free hand and vowed to kill Blake.

"Six-hundred-fifty dollars."

"The bill is for five hundred."

"That was the last month's bill."

"Well, nobody lived here for six months," he argued.

"Disconnect charge."

"Oh. Is there any way I can pay this out or something? I don't really have that kind of cash right now." The flashy sports car caught his attention through the window. He wondered how far behind it was and how much it would take to catch up payments on a Porsche.

"Well, you don't owe his money, you know. You could have them reconnected in your name. You can give us a forwarding address on Blake and come up with a two-hundred-dollar deposit to get them turned back on."

Two hundred was easier than six. "I don't have a forwarding address," he said, cursing Blake's untimely supermodel chase.

"I'll have to check it out then. I'll ask. Can you hold on?" She put him on hold before he could answer.

"Okay, hon. You bring us your deposit and we'll work on it."

He let out an exasperated breath. "How soon are we talking?"

"Two days max," she said.

"Mabel, honey," he sweetened his voice a little more, "is there anything you can do? You know, help a guy out a little."

"I'm sorry, honey. I don't own the light company."

"Okay. Thanks."

Well, he could at least have the phone hooked up. Making the call to the local phone company ensured a two-day hook up. Just to set his mind at ease about the house, Ryan called the bank before taking a shower. Mr. Webber assured him both the house and the car were free and clear. He could sell the car. As for the house, it was part of the reason he came here. He cared about it and the factory. So much so that he handed it over to his brother rather than risk losing part of it to his ex-wife. So much for doing the right thing. He should have known better than to pass his problems on to Blake. The family business should have been Ryan's responsibility. Instead of taking it, he set off to build his own fortune, free of Oak Creek, the place where several generations of his family had put in thousands of man hours building a future. Well, he was back now and he refused to let his past negligence ruin things for future generations — if there were any.

Ryan undressed and stepped into the cold water. His body froze in reaction to it. He longed for a hot shower but was thankful that the old well was still hooked up to the house. Otherwise, he figured he'd be out of water as well as everything else.

He quickly washed and rinsed his hair and then stepped out of the shower. Blake left behind most of his clothing, so he knew he'd be able to find something to wear. He'd never figure out that brother of his.

He towel dried his hair, hoping the curls wouldn't frizz in the heat. What did one wear to impress the ice cream goddess? He rifled through Blake's closet and finally came up with a blue silk shirt and a pair of gray slacks. He'd like to wear his trademark cowboy hat, but dust still clung to it from traipsing around the factory this afternoon. Instead, he opted for Blake's black boots, staying in his comfort zone in spite of the silky shirt.

He dug through his bag to find the small decanter of his prized sugar, which he planned to use to seal the deal later tonight. Grabbing the keys to the Porsche, he headed out the door. And hoped Laura Reynolds was easily impressed.

Chapter Two

"Laura?" the voice on her cell phone asked.

"Where the hell are you?" she hissed into the phone, annoyed with her sister.

"I, uhm, you're on your own tonight, okay?" Laura heard noise in the background.

"No, it's not all right. I need you tonight." Panic gripped her. She never expected to have to meet with Ryan alone.

"Well, I can't come. You see, Nick and I... God, Laura, this new flavor is incredible."

"What are you doing?" Laura hoped her voice wasn't loud enough to carry across the restaurant. What were they doing, testing the product?

"Nick saw you today, uh, testing the ice cream and...well, he brought some home."

Laura let out a sigh as her stomach twisted into a knot. Newlyweds were useless. "Fine. I'll handle LeJeune myself. You better hope this deal doesn't fall through."

"Thanks, Laura."

"Sure, whatever," she said to the dial tone. She pressed the phone against her forehead, hoping the splitting headache she developed would go away soon. She really needed a clear head to deal with Ryan LeJeune.

God, she hoped he wasn't as good looking as he had been in high school. She'd never forget that smile of his, more of a smirk than anything else. And the way he teased her relentlessly. He was older and out of her league. The fact that their houses were divided by a fence was the only thing she had ever shared with him. If it hadn't been for the three acres on either side of the fence, maybe she would have had the nerve to walk over today and see if he was home.

She wouldn't have. Real nerve was not her strong point. She may be a semi-successful CEO right now, but she was still jelly on the inside.

Especially when it came to men. Well, some men. LeJeune men in particular.

Laura signaled to the waiter as he passed. "I'll only need two," she indicated the menus. She gave a quick smile as he took away the extras. She eyed the place chosen for Amanda to sit and decided she'd much rather sit with her back to the wall, facing the door.

As soon as she stood, she saw the tall cowboy standing with the hostess. You couldn't easily miss one of the LeJeune boys. They both combined all of the wonderful elements of their Cajun and Creole heritage. While Blake's coloring was softer and highlighted with a head full of long, blonde hair, Ryan was golden brown with long dark hair. Both had to-die-for blue eyes.

Ryan looked as much at ease in the upscale restaurant as he did working in the fields. He moved with an easy grace from years of doing backbreaking labor. Laura let her eyes glide up and down his body, remembering why he always got all the girls' attention in school. In a word, he was hot.

She watched through her lashes as he strode toward her, his shirt hugging his chest with his every movement. His pants clinging to his thighs in all the right places. She bet his butt looked just as good. From the looks on the faces of the women as he walked by, she was right.

"Your table." Laura straightened, trying to ignore the obvious flutter of false eyelashes as the hostess led Ryan to the table.

"Thank you," he said lowly before turning to Laura. "Laura Reynolds." The sound of her name on his lips did nothing to calm her nerves. He said it with a challenge, making her wonder how it would sound vibrating against her throat as his lips…

"It's good to see you again." She reached out to shake his hand as formally and quickly as possible before sinking back into her chair. Nice, soft hands. She remembered hearing about Ryan LeJeune's velvet hands.

"You remember me?" He sank into the chair opposite her and then in one motion pulled it in a little closer.

"Of course I remember you," she smiled. Who could forget eyes like those?

"I always wonder. I've been gone so long."

"But not before you could leave your mark on Oak Creek." She hoped her teasing was appropriate. She very rarely ever came close to being speechless. Right now was one of those times. He was more gorgeous up close today than she remembered from high school.

"Yeah, that," he laughed. "I'm afraid not everything you hear about me is true."

"Oh, now, don't destroy my fantasies." And what fantasies they could be... Her non-existent sex drive decided to kick itself into high gear. Twisting her fingers around a napkin, she resisted the urge to fan her face and give Ryan the satisfaction of knowing he still had it.

She noticed the spark instantly flare in his eyes at the mention of fantasies. Oh, what she could do to him! She bit her lip as he reached for the goblet of water, seemingly oblivious to her once more, the spark covered with a mask of indifference. "Are you ready to order?"

"Not yet." She picked up her menu, only halfway looking at it. She was still awestruck by his cover model appearance. Man, they sure could grow 'em here in Oak Creek.

"I haven't been here in a while," he managed. "Do you have any suggestions?"

"Don't eat the ice cream," she let out a snort, feeling bold and daring and downright sexy in his presence. Everything about him made her wonder how he would feel moving above her, inside her. And all she could think of was how wild and dangerous this whole affair could be. God, she was already thinking in terms of affair. She needed another drink.

"It's not to your liking?"

"Not hardly. The eggplant parmesan is good, but you look more like a steak man." She teased, running her fingers along the top edge of her menu. If he were anything like most men, he would notice the candy apple red nail color and lose all train of thought. She had carefully chosen her outfit, wagering on Ryan's appreciation of low cut red dresses with slits up to her hips. So far, he seemed unaffected.

Ryan licked his lips, making her wonder how they would taste when they dipped down to brush against hers. Or rather when she pulled them into hers. "Actually, I'm more of a burger and fries kind of guy. But a steak sounds nice. Especially since we're on your tab," he reminded her.

"Then have a steak," she shrugged, imagining his hands slowly, carefully caressing the knife as it skillfully sliced the meat.

"I think I will."

153

Laura watched him signal for the waiter, something she would have done had she been trying not to stare at those long fingers of his. She imagined them doing all kinds of things to her that ice cream could never do. Five minutes in the guy's company and she was already prepared to write off her entire business as a grand hoax.

"So, Laura," her eyes lit up at the soft mention of her name, "tell me about your company."

"I thought we'd eat first and then talk shop later."

"Uh-uh," he shook his head. "I need to know what you've got in store for me before I eat."

What I've got in store for you... She forced herself to pay attention, to sit up a little straighter. "Well, you've heard of my company, right?"

"Who hasn't?"

"We make ice cream. And what I need is your sugar to be able to go nationwide with it." God, that came out wrong. You may as well say, honey, put it on a plate for me. She felt the redness creep down to her exposed cleavage.

He splayed his hands on the white tablecloth, then looked up at her, meeting her eyes. "My, uh, sugar?"

She fully blushed now. That twinkling in his blue eyes sent all kinds of wicked thoughts through her head. New flavor names sprang forth all at once. *Ryan Mocha Melt. LeJeune Banana Split. Laura with Ryan on top...* Before she could recover, he spoke again.

"So, tell me about your product."

She shook the carnal thoughts from her head. "It's the best ice cream in the country, no matter what *Blue Bell* says."

"I know they claim to be the best ice cream around, but even they haven't broken through the market like I hear you plan to do. And I hear there's more to it than taste."

"I see you know your ice cream. And of course there's more to it than taste. How else could I sell it at the price I get for it?" She ran her finger along the edge of her water glass.

"Of course," he smiled, watching her never-still fingers move across the water glass.

"The point is, we can offer a mutually beneficial contract. Are you interested?" So much for working the deal. Amanda would kill her if she knew all the cards were on the table and dinner hadn't even been served yet. *Serves her right for playing with my ice cream.*

"And what if your company goes belly up?" He folded his arms, but she knew he was putting up a good front. If he weren't interested in this deal, he wouldn't be here.

"It won't. I can guarantee it."

"Your dinner," the waiter interrupted. "Can I get you anything else?"

"A bottle of your best champagne," Laura smiled. "You do drink, don't you?"

"Yeah. But I had something else in mind," he smiled before looking up at the waiter. "Two unsweetened teas." He took the small decanter from his pocket as the waiter walked away and slowly placed the silver container on the table. "I thought you might want to taste it first."

"Mmmm," she licked her lips, intentionally, fully, this time. "I was wondering what that was in your pants."

* * * * *

Ryan would have spilled his water had he been holding it. Instead, he breathed in small gasps, trying to calm himself as she flipped open the container and licked her finger before sticking it into the white substance. He sat on the edge of his seat as he watched her insert the finger between her full, red lips. Jaw clenched, he wondered how it would feel to insert something else there, wondered if it would light the fire in her eyes the way his sugar just had. His body reacted to the thought, and his jeans tightened. So much for unattractive. This meant one thing. Laura Reynolds was going to be one of those difficult girls he avoided at all costs. Funny, avoiding her didn't seem to be in his vocabulary right now.

"Oh, yeah," she sighed. "This is just what I needed."

Ryan had a flashback from *When Harry Met Sally* and hoped the sugar hadn't been *that* good. He'd hate to be outdone by a sweetener.

"This is incredible. You got any other surprises there?" she teased.

He leaned forward, meeting her challenge. When her eyes widened, he realized he'd caught her off guard. "Why don't you come over here and see?"

Breathing in relief when panic flashed across her face, he knew she was teasing him. Still, she fascinated him. Had Laura Reynolds been this cute in high school? Cute. He suppressed an inward laugh. There wasn't a damn thing cute about her. She was sin incarnate. No wonder she could create an ice cream that caused orgasms. She could cause them from across the room. He wished he carried a pencil with him to drop under the table so he could get a glance at those legs. The cleavage he caught before she hid it behind the menu. He hoped the lump in his throat went away soon.

"Your tea," the waiter interrupted.

"Allow me." Ryan took the sugar and spooned it into her tea and then his, imagining how he would much rather dip her finger into his glass.

"Thanks." She smiled and then took a big sip. "Wow. It's even better like this." She drank another big sip of the tea. "This is really good."

"So do we have a deal?"

"I don't know. We haven't really discussed the deal yet. What are your terms?"

"Well, first, I need to know more about your product. To be sure mine will remain stable." He tried to ignore the stirring in his pants. Damn, he'd been without a woman for too long, and Laura looked just like the kind of sin he needed to end the dry spell.

"I'm sure I can make yours remain firm," she sipped at the tea again, apparently ignoring her own sexual comment.

Firm. He shifted in his seat. Damn it. This was supposed to be a harmless business dinner. Not an outrageous flirtation with Laura Reynolds. "I'm sure you can. I don't suppose you have any of that orgasm producing ice cream up your dress, do you?"

The smile disappeared from her lips. He won the banter, sending her a look that let her know he wouldn't be afraid to go looking for said ice cream.

"No. But I do have some back at my place." She bit her lip, making him wonder if she regretted the invitation. "Excuse me for a minute." She stood, grabbing her bag, and pushed past him as he stood.

Ten minutes and she had run for the hills. *Welcome home, Ryan.* He watched her disappear behind the wall dividing the bar from the restaurant. He sank back into his chair, mulling over her invitation and reaction to it.

He was a LeJeune. A sex machine. That's what the women in his life had always expected from him. And he had produced. Millions of satisfied customers. Well, not exactly millions. And it *had* been a long time.

He hadn't been with a woman in over a year. The town's gossip mill wouldn't buy that. A LeJeune without a woman was like summer in Louisiana without thunderstorms. It was a rare occurrence.

Hell, he was thirty-three years old. Past time to settle down. He picked up the decanter of sugar and closed it, concentrating on the click to indicate the top was back in place.

Laura Reynolds.

He could play, couldn't he? Tease. See what she was all about. It would be harmless. Right?

* * * * *

Laura ran for the restroom, dialing her sister with every step.

"Amanda. Come on, answer." She counted six rings before the machine picked up. "Amanda," she spoke to the machine. "I know you're home. Please pick up. This is an emergency." Her heart raced, threatening to beat out of her chest when she heard her sister fumbling on the other end of the phone. She hoped Amanda wouldn't hang up on her, like she had several times in the past. If she ever needed sisterly advice, it was tonight.

"Laura? You okay?"

"No, I'm not okay. Geez, have you *seen* Ryan LeJeune?" Her heart raced.

"No, why? Did you lose him?" Laura heard Nick moving around in the background. "It's Laura, honey. Go back to sleep. Sorry," she directed her attention back to the phone.

"It's okay. I'm just… I don't know what to do." But she certainly knew who she'd like to do. In fact, the thought of having Ryan LeJeune naked in her bed was the only one circling around in her mind.

"What's happening?"

"I think I just invited him back to my place for dessert," she sagged against the faux marble wall in the women's restroom. And, oh how she wanted him to come!

"This is a good thing. He's got to taste the product first, don't you think?"

"No, Amanda. I invited him back for *dessert*."

"Oh," her voice was filled with realization a half second before she erupted into laughter.

"This is so not funny."

"Yes it is. Beat you at your own game, huh? Did you wear the low cut red dress? The one with the slit up to your neck?"

Laura cursed her reflection in the long mirror. "Yes."

"Then what did you expect? He's a man, Laura. And you're a pretty hot package."

"I didn't expect this. What do I do?"

"Is he cute?"

"Come on, be serious." He was a LeJeune, after all.

"I am. Is he cute?"

"I don't know. If you cross Johnny Depp with Brad Pitt and throw in a touch of Cajun charm do you get cute?" Cute didn't even begin to cover what Ryan was. More like sexy, sinful, oh God, what had she gotten herself into?

"I'm fanning myself right now. Oh my God. Cuter than Blake?"

"Blake who?" Blake was known as the better looking of the two.

"Damn. That's pretty cute."

"So? What do I do?"

"Well, first of all, you either have to let him taste the ice cream or, uh, let him taste the ice cream." Her meaning on the last was clear. And it had nothing to do with what was in her freezer at home.

"You're no help."

"What did you expect? Nail him. Don't nail him. Whatever. Just remember to get the sweet stuff."

"Amanda? Amanda?" Damn. Laura folded the phone back up and put it in her bag. *Breathe. He's just a man.*

Laura knew she wasn't exactly an expert on the topic of men. Sure, she'd had her share of lovers, but none who even came close to her fantasy about Ryan. And none who seemed able to tolerate her or her company for very long. In the end, all of them had been disappointments, which was, no pun intended, how the ice cream came about in the first place. Oh, she may look like sin itself if she tried hard enough, but she wasn't as confident when it came to men as she liked to let on. And in the past few years, too many men had been intimidated once they found out about the ice cream. They didn't want to be one-upped by fudge ripple.

Ryan didn't seem intimidated by this little game. In fact, he played right into it. Which could lead to all sorts of fun if she would just let herself go and have a good time with this. There could be worse fates than going into business with someone who looked like that.

She noticed he sat up a little straighter when she returned. *Well, that makes one of us*, she thought. "Sorry about that."

"No problem. Are you done here?"

"Sure. If you are, I mean." If he kept looking at her like she was now a menu item, she would…well, she wasn't sure what she would do. But she sure as hell knew what she wanted to do. And it was sitting right across from her.

"I think I am. I'm actually quite ready to go back to your place and taste this ice cream I've heard so much about."

Laura moved a few steps ahead of him, hoping the distance would clear her mind. Hoping a reason why he shouldn't go home with her came to mind. "I think I'm fresh out of ice cream," she finally managed as he led her to the restaurant door.

"I find that hard to believe," he pushed the door open for her. "Where's your car? I'll be sure you get settled in."

Laura ignored the twinge of disappointment washing over her when he didn't press the ice cream issue. "It's up here. Nice Porsche," she indicated as she walked by his car.

"It's mine," he beamed.

"Figures," she said under her breath. As fast as the driver. "Well, this is me."

"Volvo. How practical. Not what I'd expect from someone who makes orgasm ice cream."

"This is going to be a problem for you, isn't it?" she folded her arms.

Ryan moved toward her and pinned her against the car. "Now why would I care?" he said softly. "You're gonna make us both rich."

"Most men don't like to compete with dairy products." She avoided his eyes, feeling his fingers burn into her bare skin, knowing he had the power to melt her with just one touch. Her ice cream didn't stand a chance. Neither did her body. "I'm not most men," he pressed in closer, spreading his legs to keep his balance as he dipped his head in to hers. He barely brushed her lips, but she felt the sizzle all the way to her toes. Damn him; he ended the kiss just as she leaned into him. "You taste like sugar," he teased.

Laura splayed her hands across his chest, hoping to push him away, but instead found herself just resting them there. His chest was rock hard beneath the silk of the shirt. She fought the urge to push the fabric to the side and dive in for a taste of bare flesh. "I didn't come here for this," she managed.

"I think you did. A girl doesn't dress like that and throw out sexual comments unless she intends to seduce. So, are you going to admit it or not?" He ran his finger along her bottom lip.

"Admit what?" That she wanted him? Right here, right now in the parking lot? To hell with the business deal. She bit her lip.

"Admit that you are trying to tease the sugar out of me."

She nodded slowly. He didn't know the half of it. And the worst part was, in spite of the kiss, he was probably just teasing.

"Good. Then tomorrow night. Your place. No teasing. No seduction. Strictly business." He tipped her nose with his finger before releasing her. "We'll settle the contract after I taste the product," he said in his best strictly business voice.

"Fine. We'll do it your way." Maybe.

All he wanted was to hear that he controlled the situation. For the first time tonight, he thought he might. Hell, since the first time today. As he watched Laura's light gray Volvo drive off, he remembered that his house was cold and dark. It would have been so much better to go home with her and snuggle up after a pint of ice cream.

* * * * *

Laura flipped through her *365 Reasons Chocolate is Better than Men* calendar. Reason number 165. Melts in your mouth, not in your hand. The Mars Company really had a winner with that logo. That, combined with the urban legends about the green M&Ms, was enough to keep people coming back for more. Plus, they made damned good chocolate.

She laughed at reason 173. Chocolate doesn't promise to call you tomorrow. How many times had she heard that line from men? Very few of them called, and the ones who did never stayed around for long. At first, she thought they were intimidated by her degrees, her intelligence. Nope, it was the ice cream. It had been ever since she created it.

Guys who drove Porsches shouldn't need to validate their manhood. Their cars did that for them. But after meeting Ryan LeJeune tonight, she knew that he would be the kind to head for the hills as soon as she challenged his manhood. And she would.

A slow smile spread across her lips as she thought of how fun it would be to bring a man like Ryan LeJeune to his knees. Women everywhere would thank her for taking him down a notch or two. And she had to admit it would be a boost for her ego, too.

She scribbled in a note on the calendar for tomorrow. Not that she'd forget her meeting with Ryan. Meeting. That was one way to put it. Something in those blue eyes warned her there was a potential for more than just shop talk. And, oh, how she wanted more!

She pulled the silver canister from her pocket. He slipped it to her before helping her into her car. As she dipped her finger into the sweet powder, she wondered about those blue eyes again. She could practically picture them smoldering over with desire, a wicked gleam shining down at her. Or up at her. Either way, she wanted him in a way she couldn't even define yet. He did something to her in their hour or so together that she hadn't expected and she really wanted to experience it again. She wanted to feel the power he gave her just by being in his presence. More than that, she wanted him to want her as badly as she lusted after him.

Of course, there was more to her fascination than just lust. Sure, he was devilishly handsome. And interested in this deal. If he hadn't been, he wouldn't have given her a sample of the product. She battled with herself over the sample. It was a sign of trust on his part to hand it over without a decision having been reached. But it could also be a ploy to drive the negotiations in another direction, one which would give him more control than she'd like.

She eyed the container again, the desire to create a new flavor overwhelming the desire to second-guess Ryan. Testing a new flavor took a week after she had the chemistry worked out. She had twenty-four flavors already. She wanted something new for this product. Something that would knock everyone's socks off. And then some.

What did her customers want? She tapped her bottom lip with her finger. She knew what they wanted. That wasn't the problem. The problem was trying to figure out a new way to package it. She needed a flavor that screamed sex. Something that tasted heavenly. Something that tasted forbidden. She could add it to the new fudge ripple, but that didn't seem right. This needed something new.

Banana split. With chocolate sauce. That would be enough to challenge Ryan's ego. She could see the package now. A nice, large banana on the front.

She wouldn't sleep tonight.

Chapter Three

Ryan rolled out of bed, frustrated by the heat. July in Louisiana was damned hot. If the electric company didn't get the air conditioning turned on soon, he'd have to start sleeping at the mill. Of course, it hadn't helped that he'd dreamed about ice cream all night. And other things.

Laura Reynolds had always been one of the smart girls. The kind the boys in his crowd knew were out of their league. He could look but couldn't touch. She hadn't dated much in high school. And when she had, the boys hadn't been from Oak Creek. He wondered why a woman so determined to get away from here had hung around. And why he had bailed.

He kept insisting to himself it was his desire to do things on his own. After the divorce, he wanted a fresh start. Part of it had to do with going somewhere where no one had heard the nasty details of his divorce. Gina had pulled out every bit of dirty laundry she could find. And when she realized there wasn't nearly enough, she began making things up. Of course, everyone believed her stories. Everyone in town knew the LeJeune boys had an eye for the ladies. And the ladies always looked back.

In the end, Ryan took what he thought was the high road and left town. He sold his share of the company to Blake, split his inheritance with Gina and booked it to New Orleans as fast as he could.

He ambled through the house and turned on the shower, thankful for the cool water. At least he could cool off here. But the water brought his mind back around to the ice cream. Which brought him back to Laura. She had green eyes like Angelina Jolie. Lips like her, too. But that hair. The hair was sinful angel hair. Buttery blond with wisps of caramel. Now there's an ice cream flavor, he thought.

Ryan was already sporting a semi-hard-on thanks to those luscious dreams about Laura's curvy body. Cold showers were meant to destroy a hard-on. Not this one. It only made him wonder how his dick would feel slipping inside of her after rubbing ice cream all over her body. That was the only way ice cream could cause an orgasm.

His cock fully sprang to life at the thought. Laura. He wanted to fuck her until she screamed his name. He wanted those candy colored fingernails digging into his back, rubbing his balls, teasing his dick. He wanted to watch them dip inside her wet warmth and then go into his mouth.

He had masturbated so many times it was second nature. But this time, his stroking was even more intense. Hazy green eyes rose up from the shower and then dipped lower, taking him into her lush mouth. As he stroked, he imagined her tongue washing over him. Cold from the ice cream. Wet. Hard.

He fell against the wall as his dick shot its load. Laura. What the fuck? He could go again. This was no damned good. And unfucking funny.

He toweled off, groaning at the beads of sweat collecting on his skin as he moved through the house. Opening a window wouldn't even help in this heat. All it would do was move the hot air around, making it hard to think. It was hard enough to do that with thoughts of tonight's meeting fresh in his mind.

He dressed casually, jeans and T-shirt and stuck his wallet into his pocket. He fingered his hands through his curly dark hair and then placed his cowboy hat on top of the still damp mess. There was one thing about having curly hair in the South. It was always unruly. He grumbled, wishing he didn't have a renewed interest in his hair. Wishing the reason for the interest would stop undressing herself in his mind. He had too much work to do today to spend it thinking about her.

* * * * *

"I want the dish. All of it." Laura looked up to see Amanda standing in the doorway of the lab, her eyes beaming.

"I see someone woke up in a good mood this morning." Laura lowered her glasses and peered at her sister, hoping she didn't look as hot and bothered as she felt. All morning the only thing on her mind had been Ryan and his sexy eyes, his deep voice, his long legs. Having him covered in ice cream and… That reminded her about the missing ice cream. "Did you at least bring the ice cream back?"

"I didn't take it all," Amanda argued. "Then where is it?" Laura had looked everywhere for Fudge Ripple #9 this morning and hadn't been able to find it.

"Maybe you should ask Cate. She was the last one here last night."

"I did. She said she hadn't seen it."

"Well, you know they didn't eat it all. They always lay waste to the first batch, but save enough for the samples. Enough about the ice cream. Tell me about Ryan." Amanda took a stool opposite Laura, who hoped she wouldn't comment about the pristine white kitchen, which was usually in disarray. A clean kitchen was usually a sign that Laura had been thinking too much. And she didn't want Amanda to know what she had been thinking about.

"Nothing to tell," Laura turned her head back to the numbers she had been looking over. Nothing except one quick kiss and a night full of wildly erotic dreams.

"Then why's the kitchen so clean? And why are you in here doing paperwork? Convenient in case you get some inspiration? Or need some?"

"There's nothing to tell," she insisted, still not meeting Amanda's eyes. Ice cream sex. Sex in the Porsche. Sex on the Porsche. Shit, she was getting hot!

"You're not even gonna try to lie, are you?"

Laura put her pen down and folded her arms. "What do you want to know?"

"Is he as sexy with his clothes off?"

"I wouldn't know." But she had thought about the image all night long, and it was enough to guarantee there was more to the man than just legend.

"Don't tell me you didn't take him home! You called me in the middle of…well, you called me and then you want me to believe you didn't take him home for the promised dessert?"

"I didn't." But she sure as hell planned to. Last night taught her one thing. Take control. Seize life. And right now, she wanted to seize a handful of Ryan LeJeune.

"But you're gonna, right?"

"I have work to do. I'm meeting Ryan tonight and…"

"Ah-ha! So you are planning on it. No, don't try to hide it." She held up a hand to quiet Laura's protest. "So, what flavor are you gonna use? You are gonna seduce him, right?"

"I think you and I both know that Ryan LeJeune can't be seduced." *It sure as hell doesn't hurt to try.*

"What do you mean can't be? He's been with half of Oak Creek."

"That's exactly what I mean. Do you think those women seduced him? Uh-uh. They probably just laid it out on the table for him. Here, have a scoop of this, big boy." She mockingly wiggled her chest and used her best Mae West impression.

"He's still good looking, huh?"

"Sin on a stick." Luscious, yummy. A thousand other descriptions came to mind.

"Hey, that's it!" Amanda snapped her fingers.

"What's it?"

"The name for the line of popsicles. *Sin on a stick.*"

Laura wrinkled her nose. "I thought we were going to keep the names clean." Even if the owner keeps thinking dirty thoughts.

"I know you didn't like *Pops Your Cherry* for the cherry fudge swirl, but I like this one."

"Well, I don't. It indicates that people will be doing perverted stuff with the ice cream." Like she had in her dreams last night. Like she wanted to do tonight.

Amanda laughed. "You think they don't?"

"What are you talking about?"

"You don't, do you? You think they just eat the stuff. Let me tell you, you're missing out." She slapped her hands on the counter.

"What are you suggesting?" Laura chewed on the end of her ink pen, this new suggestion was one she hadn't thought of before. Well, before Ryan.

"You know what I'm suggesting. These women don't use the ice cream to replace sex. They use it to enhance sex."

"Oh, God. I don't want to hear this," she covered her ears, embarrassed that she'd done the same thing last night in her sleep. And woke up from a hell of a wet dream.

"Laura," Amanda forced her hands down. "You are leading a sexual revolution here. Be proud."

"Proud that I'm contributing to lewd behavior with dairy products?" She tried to sound sarcastic, but was afraid she was going off the deep end.

"No. Proud that you're giving women the freedom to take control of their sexuality."

"They didn't need my permission."

"No, but they sure as hell need the ice cream." She winked.

"About the ice cream, where's the fudge ripple?" She hoped having Amanda on the subject of sex would convince her to tell the truth about the missing ice cream.

"I'm the marketing director, right?"

"Yes." She didn't like where this was heading.

"So let me market," she shrugged.

"What did you do?" She knew her sister's avoidance meant she was up to something.

"I sent some over to Ryan. No, I know what you're thinking," she raised her hands to quiet Laura.

"You have no idea what I'm thinking," she slapped Amanda's hands out of the way. "You sent him the test batch?"

"You've got the formula, right?"

"Of course I've got the formula. That isn't the point." Ryan had her ice cream! She wasn't ready for this yet.

"You know, poor Ryan's lights are off. It must be awfully hot in that big ol' house. I thought he could use it," she shrugged.

"I know that look in your eyes. There's something you're not telling me."

"Well, there is one thing," a wicked grin spread across her face. "You know Nick and I took some of it home last night, right?"

"Yeah."

"Well, I think you created the first his and hers ice cream flavor."

"What do you mean?" she narrowed her eyes at her sister.

"I mean, it got him hot." She winked.

"Wait a minute. You're telling me fudge ripple got Nick hot and *you sent some to Ryan*?" Holy freaking shit! She had to stop Ryan. The last thing she needed was Ryan with a hard-on. She may be forced to remedy the situation. Damn, damn, damn.

"Yeah. I did."

"Marketing my ass," Laura mumbled, grabbing her keys and purse.

"Where are you going?"

"I'm going to get the ice cream back."

* * * * *

Ryan opened the door only to be greeted by a petite blond in short denim shorts and a halter-top. *Welcome home*, he thought to himself. She held a large brown box in one hand and the other was raised, about to knock.

"Well, Ryan LeJeune. It's a good thing you're home," she smiled.

"Yeah, I'm home." He mentally ran through a list of the women in Oak Creek and came up empty. He didn't know this one. Of course, she looked to be about eighteen.

"I'm Cate Reynolds. Laura's cousin."

"Oh, Cate. Wow, you sure grew up." *Down boy. She's barely legal.*

"Well, you've been gone a while," she smiled.

"I was on my way out," he began.

"Oh, well this will only take a minute. This is for you," she held out the box. "Laura wanted it sent right over this morning. Said you should try it right away," she winked.

"She did, did she?" Ryan took the box and ran a hand along the top edge. It was a plain brown box with *I Scream Ice Cream* marked on the top. Nothing fancy there.

"Yep. I gotta get going. I have orders to fill today."

"Okay. Thanks." He watched her skip down the steps and get into a bright red Mustang. Whew, they sure could grow 'em here in Oak Creek.

Ryan's first impulse was to put the ice cream in the freezer. Of course, thanks to Blake, the freezer wasn't working right now. And if he didn't get into town soon, he wouldn't have lights any time this century. But Laura sent over the ice cream. Which meant one of two things. First, she wanted to cancel their date tonight. Or, second, this was a preview before the main event.

He laughed to himself and went inside in search of a spoon. No sense letting good orgasm ice cream go to waste.

He kicked open the screen door, deciding the front porch was cooler than the house. He practically ripped open the box containing a plain white carton of ice cream labeled *Fudge Ripple #9*. That old song *Love Potion #9* crossed his mind as he peeled off the plastic top and dug the spoon in. The cool creamy scoop had barely passed his lips when he heard the voice.

"Don't eat that!" Laura was clearly out of breath and standing on the bottom step.

"Eat what?" He took in the spoonful and smiled, thinking he'd rather take in a spoonful of her.

"Great, just great." She climbed up the steps, obviously flustered by what she had witnessed.

"Damn good ice cream," he licked his lips. "Want some?" he held the carton out to her and then snatched it away when she tried to take it. "Uh-uh. Gotta say please first," he teased, liking the idea of having her beg.

"Give me that," she reached for it again, only to have him hold it above his head. She had two options, she could leave him alone and let him eat the stuff or she could climb up his chest and take it from him. Ryan welcomed the latter.

"Is it poison or something?"

"No."

"Then it's mine. You sent it over."

"No, I didn't. My sister did."

"How is Amanda, anyway?"

"Fine. Look, give me the ice cream."

"No." He half expected her to tackle him for it, by the look in her eyes. Instead, she stood there, arms folded, as if she could talk the carton away from him. Fat chance of that. If she wanted it so badly, he was determined to eat it.

"You don't know..." she trailed off.

"I don't know what? How to handle it? I'm a big boy, Laura. I think I can manage to eat your orgasm ice cream and contain myself," he let his voice drop as he spoke, knowing his voice usually had a magical touch with the ladies. If her shiver was any indication, he still had it.

"You've been warned."

"Come join me," he headed for the porch swing. "Maybe we could share." Visions from his shower flooded his brain. A cold ice cream flavored mouth on his dick. His hard-on was back with a vengeance and threatening to blow his cool cover.

She stared after him. It only took two strides for him to reach the swing and casually sit down. He took another big spoonful into his mouth and licked the remainder off the spoon, being sure to dart his tongue out as he did. He watched her green eyes darken. Oh, yeah. She wanted him. And he wanted nothing more than to lick ice cream from her spoon.

She shook her head. "I don't want any."

"Shame. It sure is good. In fact, I think I'm gonna come right now." He threw his head back and let out a howl.

"You're funny, LeJeune. Now give me the ice cream."

He laughed, a full belly laugh. "You should see yourself. You don't get out much, do you?"

"What do you mean?"

"I mean you're all worked up over losing a carton of ice cream. I think," he pointed the spoon at her, "that it's been so long since you've had a real orgasm you don't know what to do with yourself."

"My sex life is none of your concern," she folded her arms, tried to sound tough. Ryan could see right through it. Her seduction act last night had been smoke and mirrors. The CEO of the orgasm ice cream company hadn't gotten any lately. If her customers found out, it could ruin her business.

"You've been figured out, lady." Placing the ice cream carton on the swing, he took two steps back to her and stood over her, arms folded, a challenge in waiting. To kiss her or not to kiss her? He'd only had a tiny taste last night. Now that he figured out her secret, he wanted a lot more. Inching toward her, he watched as she backed away a little with each step he took. "Two more steps and you'll fall off the porch," he warned.

She shot him a dirty look. "You're awfully full of yourself."

"Nope. Right now, I'm full of orgasm ice cream. Tell me, Laura, how does it make you feel? Is it a long orgasm? Multiple? Or just enough to take the edge off?" He watched her eyes flicker. "That's it. It just takes the edge off. So, the question is, how long have you been replacing sex with ice cream? How long have you been walking around on the edge?"

She put her hands up against his chest, holding him back. He cornered her against the porch railing. When she looked up into his eyes, he saw the answer right there. Too damned long. She didn't speak, didn't protest as he lowered his head to her. Instead, she raised up to meet his kiss. And floored him with that tiny motion.

Ryan pulled her into him the way he wanted to since he first saw her last night. Laura Reynolds. She smelled like sugar, tasted like sugar. But she wasn't a no-calorie, no-fat substitute. She was the real thing. And she was moaning into his mouth, writhing against him. And he was hard as a rock.

He lifted her against him, wanting her heat pressed up against his hardness. Her hands were in his hair now, which was damp from the heat rather than the cold shower. If he were lucky, he wouldn't need a cold shower again. To hell with his talk of nobility. To hell with his declared celibacy. Bring on the whipped cream!

He let her pull his mouth against hers harder, firmer. God, it must have been a long time for her. He felt all of her passion seep into his body from the way she clung to him to the way she welcomed him inside. Making love to her would be an experience he knew he'd never forget. If he could get her that far. Right now, that was the only thing on his mind, getting her into bed. That and the fact that the earth seemed to be spinning beneath him.

Only it wasn't the earth. They were falling. Recognition dawned on him. The porch railing had give way and they were crashing to the ground. Using his reflexes, Ryan managed to turn them so he landed on the ground, breaking her fall. She fell against him with a thud and scrambled to stand up.

"You okay?" he asked.

"Fine," she shot back.

"You sure?"

"Yes."

He laughed then. They must have been a hell of a sight, falling off his porch that way. He picked up his now dirty cowboy hat and replaced it on his head and watched as she tried to wipe the grass stains from the knees of her jeans. "That's some ice cream."

She glared down at him. "I have to go."

"You sure you don't want to take it inside? I promise not to break anything else."

She continued to glare. "See what being a pig can lead to?"

"Why don't you come on over here and show me again?" Her pert nose was turned up in distasted at his suggestion, but the whole thing was damned funny if you asked him.

Rather than retrieving the ice cream like he expected her to do, she stormed out of the yard, not looking back as she cranked up her car. Oh, well, he'd just do a little bit more experimenting later. After all, it couldn't hurt anything.

Great. She turned the key in the ignition. She just made a huge fool of herself. First, she came to reclaim her ice cream, then she ended up kissing the man. Then, as if kissing him weren't bad enough, she broke his porch. He must think she was some kind of sex-starved maniac. She cursed herself, knowing he probably thought she had used the ice cream as a front in order to come over and throw herself at him. And then break the damned porch. She really blew it this time.

She made a mental note to kill her sister and anyone else involved in today's fiasco. And she swore she'd never tell any of them about it. She broke the man's porch. She hoped to hell it was because the railing was already shot and not because of those ten extra pounds. She wouldn't be able to face Ryan LeJeune again.

She pulled out of his driveway hoping she could find another sugar supplier. This one wasn't going to work. Not now and not ever. No matter how completely tempting he was.

She couldn't help but glance back through the rear view mirror. He was dusting off his cowboy hat. And laughing. Still. Well, at least she amused him. She swallowed hard. She should have learned a long time ago that amusement was all girls like her could be to guys like him. Nothing serious. Just distraction.

Chapter Four

Something was wrong. Wrong, wrong, wrong! And it wasn't the heat. And it wasn't the fact that he was broke. And it wasn't the damned ice cream. Ice cream *could not* cause an orgasm. He didn't care how much money *I Scream* made last year, it wasn't possible.

But Ryan wasn't having an orgasm. He was having...shit, he didn't know what he was having, but it wasn't an orgasm. Okay, so he couldn't concentrate on anything. Maybe he had that ADD he'd heard so much about lately. Maybe he was a late bloomer when it came to learning disorders.

No, it was the heat. Had to be. Nothing else could account for the light-headed feeling, as if all the blood were rushing to his...oh, God. He groaned. The heat, the heat, the heat. Had to be the heat.

He stood, banging his knee on the edge of his desk. He needed to concentrate. He made it to the bathroom, thankful it was attached to the office. His jeans were too tight. He flipped on the light and shut the door. The room was too small.

He ran the cold water in the sink and splashed some on his face. Get a grip, boy. That was when he realized what was happening. Oh, God, he had a raging hard-on. RAGING. The worst ever. It would have been the best had there been a willing hard body anywhere in sight. But, no. He was closed up in his daddy's office at the mill.

He unzipped his jeans. His penis painfully sprang forth. He looked down at the swollen purple head and tried to still his racing heart. All the oxygen in his body must have gone straight to his dick because he couldn't catch his breath. Then the image came. Laura naked. Laura spread out in front of him, smiling up at him. Oh, God, he could come in 2.3 seconds. Now he was glad there wasn't a willing hard body. What a disappointment he'd be!

He reached down to touch his throbbing penis. His whole body ached. This was not funny. Images of Laura continued to flash through his mind. Laura licking her lips. Laura in that low cut dress. Laura in those tight jeans. Laura pressed against him, moaning into his mouth. Falling on top of him. Her hair in his face.

Then he did something he hadn't done since he was thirteen. He came. Quickly. The orgasm ripped through his body. He hadn't even started stroking himself. He hadn't done anything. Except think of her.

Damn. This meant trouble. He braced himself on the sides of the porcelain sink. His breath was coming in short bursts. There was something wrong with him. Rather than relaxing as he'd hoped it would, his cock seemed to have a mind of its own and was primed and ready for action again.

The ice cream. No. That was impossible. There was no ice cream that could make *that* happen. He didn't even want to admit to what had happened. How emasculating. He took a deep breath. He would talk to her about this tonight. Like it or not, he was keeping their appointment.

He groaned as he wiped the come from his pants and washed his hands. It wasn't supposed to happen like this. Ever. Not to a grown man. And not to a LeJeune. Hell, the stories about him may have only been stories, but when it was time to act, he knew what he was doing. And he did it at just the right time. None of that premature stuff for him. Nope.

Laura. She set him up for this. She knew there was something in his ice cream. And she knew if she came over and tried to stop him from eating it, he would do exactly the opposite. Women. They were all the same. Still, the ice cream couldn't have caused it alone. It was the heat.

Ice cream *cannot* cause a grown man to lose control. And it can't satisfy a woman. No matter what she thinks. It's all psycho something. Psychosomatic. That's it. He tried to zip his pants back. He finally had his throbbing cock packed away, but the jeans were still painfully tight. He opted for leaving them unzipped and kept his T-shirt out to cover his fly.

He'd go home and change into some sweatpants or something. And then he'd march over to Laura's house and give her a piece of his mind. His body reacted instantly to the thought of giving her a piece of something. And it wasn't his mind that he intended to share.

"Hey, Ryan." His head shot up. He hadn't expected anyone else to be here this evening. Giving himself one last glance in the mirror and taking a deep breath, he opened the bathroom door. And hoped he looked normal.

"Dusty. What brings you by?" He shoved his hands in his pockets to avoid shaking hands with his cousin.

"Aw, nothing much. Just seeing what you're up to. I heard your place is out of lights, so I thought I'd offer my couch." Dusty shot him a crooked grin.

"Oh. Thanks. They should be back on any day now." He motioned for Dusty to take a seat and then followed suit, trying to hide his discomfort at sitting while sporting a major hard-on.

"Well, the offer's open. Sorry I didn't warn you about the place and all."

"It's okay," he assured him. "I didn't realize Blake was in such a hurry to get out of here."

"Well, he wasn't till he hooked up with that model. She's a looker, but I wonder when she's gonna leave him high and dry. You haven't talked to him, have you?" Dusty seemed concerned.

"No. I haven't. To tell you the truth, I'm not sure where he's at. But I'm sure he'll call if he needs something."

"Well, the money's bound to run out. And when it does, he'll be back."

Just like me, Ryan thought. Of course, it hadn't happened quite the same way, but the truth was, both Ryan and Blake were running from the LeJeune legacy. He didn't blame his brother one bit for taking off. He did wish he had paid the light bill on the way out, though. "I'm sure Blake is fine."

"Me too. Look, it's late. I just wanted to offer the couch. So, if you change your mind…"

"No. I'll be fine. Thanks anyway."

"No prob. I'll see you around."

Ryan waited until Dusty left before locking up the office and heading home. Shooting an angry look at the refrigerator whose freezer compartment held what was left of *Fudge Ripple #9,* he groaned, all of his energy focusing on his still swollen dick. Then he smiled. Maybe tonight he'd give Laura some of her own medicine.

* * * * *

Laura wasn't expecting Ryan to show up on her doorstep. She had all but forgotten their meeting. She put it out of her mind earlier, having decided they'd both made big enough fools of themselves earlier today to call the whole thing off. And she decided she didn't need Ryan's sugar. She hoped he felt the same way.

That was the reason why she was truly surprised when she opened the door at seven o'clock to find him standing there, looking as if he'd gone a few rounds today.

"Ryan." One hand held a pint of ice cream. With the free one, she tugged on her blue bathrobe, trying to pull it closer to her body. "I wasn't expecting you."

"You and I had a meeting tonight, remember?" There was something unusual in those blue eyes tonight. All the humor she had seen earlier was gone, replaced with something deeper. Something that sent a shiver up her back.

"I, uh, didn't think you'd come." He straightened at her comment. She could have sworn she heard him let out a little groan.

"Well I did." His voice was softly seductive. That Southern drawl was the stuff of romances. Rhett Butler would be proud to have left a legacy of rogues in the South.

"I see that. You want to come in?" She moved to the side so he could enter. She tried not to think about the way he smelled as he brushed by her. He was a walking combination of sugar and musk. She closed her eyes and inhaled before looking at him again.

He practically filled up the doorway and looked largely out of place in her small entryway. She led him into the living room and watched him sink down onto her sofa. Her breath caught in her throat when she noted how at home he looked in his black sweatpants and New Orleans Saints T-shirt.

"I'm, uhm, going to go change. Then we can talk, okay?" She placed the container of ice cream on the coffee table before heading into the bedroom.

He nodded his response, and she was gone before he had a chance to do anything more. Particularly mention that kiss earlier or the disastrous results thereof.

Laura fumbled with the zipper on her jeans. She really hadn't been prepared to see him. And she especially wasn't prepared for the suddenly smoldering look he wore tonight. He was so damned sexy. She realized she'd thought about little else since meeting him again yesterday. God, he was going to turn her brain to melted mush.

This was a bad situation. Especially since she was so attracted to him. Tonight he had abandoned the cowboy get up and looked as if he were ready for bed. He wore the sweats and a pair of tennis shoes. His hair was pulled back into a decent ponytail with a couple of loose strands falling across his forehead. He looked perfectly at ease but completely dangerous.

She pulled a white tank top over her head and then considered taking her hair down from its ponytail. Afraid of giving the impression that she cared about what he thought, she did the next best thing and rearranged the ponytail.

She also considered putting on a coat of makeup, but decided against it. She didn't care what he thought, she reminded herself. Well, a little powder never hurt anyone.

When she walked back into the living room, Ryan was examining the carton of ice cream she had placed on the table. She sat in the chair near the sofa, careful to avoid him.

"This the stuff you sent over today?" he didn't meet her eyes as he asked.

"I told you I didn't send that. And no, it's not."

"Humph." He turned the plain white carton over in his hands.

"I don't care if you believe me or not." She folded her arms and then slid her legs underneath her so she was sitting on top of them.

"I didn't say that." He pulled the spoon out and looked at the melting mess on it. "So if I eat this, nothing will happen."

"That's right."

"And if you eat it, nothing will happen."

"What are you getting at?" She let out an exasperated breath. He twisted in his seat.

"I'm just asking if this is some more of the famous orgasm ice cream."

"The ice cream isn't for men," she argued.

"It isn't." He didn't ask.

"No, it isn't. Now, why are you here?"

"I'm here because of the sugar." He replaced the spoon and focused his attention on her. Those blue eyes shot through her, causing her to wrap her arms around her body.

"Okay, then. About the sugar. Are you gonna sell it to me or not?"

"You haven't had time to see if it will stabilize."

"It will. I have my first batch in the freezer as we speak. It will take about a week with testing to be sure the flavor is just what I want and to be sure it will stabilize. But I have faith in it."

"I'm sure you do. What's the new flavor?"

Heat spread across her chest. She didn't want to admit to the flavor, as it only conjured up images of those dreams she'd been having. "Banana split with fudge sauce." She tried to keep a straight face as she watched his expression change. She swore she heard him moan.

"I liked the ice cream from today. And I'm here to sample more of what you have to offer." He spoke bluntly, clenching and unclenching his fist.

"Are you okay tonight? You seem tense."

"I'm fine."

"Okay. I have a couple more flavors in the freezer, but none of them are quite like what you had today." She stood and turned toward the kitchen. She heard him behind her.

"I have no doubt about that."

She flipped on the light of her kitchen. She loved this room the most. It wasn't like her lab. The decor resembled a fifties ice cream parlor, reflecting Laura's love for her product.

"Have a seat," she directed, ducking behind the soda shop bar she'd had installed. Ryan took a seat on one of the silver bar stools.

"This is different," he commented, letting his gaze wander over the pictures of Marilyn Monroe and James Dean. A tiny tabletop jukebox sat on the bar.

"I like it," she shrugged.

"This thing work?" He flipped through the songs on the jukebox.

"Yep. Bought it on eBay. It plays CDs, though. Not as authentic as it looks."

"The ice cream parlor is, though. Right down to the glass top freezer."

"Ice cream is my passion. So, what flavor would you like?" She leaned over the counter, unaware that she gave Ryan a clear view of cleavage.

"You," he leaned forward, took her ponytail in his hands and pulled her to him.

Even though the bar separated their bodies, the heat coming from him was enough to make her breath catch in her throat. She could get used to this man's lips. And that was not a good thing. Her hands gripped the counter, and she tried to pull away, but her body resisted, forcing her to lean into the kiss even more.

"Ryan." She finally caught her breath and broke the kiss.

"I'm sorry. I'm not myself today."

"I know. And I'm the one who's sorry." She backed away from the bar and out of his arms.

"What are you sorry about?" confusion flashed across his face as he sat back down on the barstool.

"The ice cream from earlier. I should have told you the truth."

"It *was* poisoned."

"No. It wasn't poisoned. It was...well, it was different from the rest. I don't know how, but I managed to put together something that has the same effect on men as it does on women."

"Bullshit."

"I'm serious." She folded her arms. "I know you, the great Ryan LeJeune, don't believe me, but it's true. Amanda tried it out last night and said it works on men."

"Then why didn't it work on me?"

She chewed at her bottom lip. It didn't work on him? "It didn't?"

"No."

"Then how do you explain the kiss today? The one just now?"

"Who knows. But it wasn't ice cream."

She smiled. "So, you're saying you're attracted to me."

"You're a beautiful woman. And that tank top is see through."

She wrapped her arms even tighter around herself, causing her cleavage to shoot up then let out a frustrated gasp at the results before dropping her arms. "It's the ice cream."

"It's not the ice cream. Why did you kiss me back?" With him looking at her like she was on the menu, it was difficult to keep her mind on anything other than the kiss.

"Isn't that obvious?"

"No."

"Do I have to spell it out for you? It's the ice cream. You were right, okay? I eat a lot of it. And it does tend to put me on edge. So there. It had nothing to do with you." She opened the glass-topped freezer. "Now, really, what flavor do you want?"

He let a slow smile spread across his face. "What have you got?"

"Cherry chocolate fudge, Dutch chocolate, chocolate chip and mint chocolate. I have a little bit of chocolate mocha left. Enough for a taste. So, what's your poison?"

"All chocolate."

"Yes. That's where the chemical is. In the chocolate."

"The chemical?"

"The one that simulates orgasm."

"Oh. Well, I guess I'll try the cherry stuff then. Surely you have creative names for them. You know, like *Get Your Rocks off Rocky Road*?"

"Amanda wanted to have, uh, creative names. I nixed the idea. I just call 'em what they taste like."

"I bet you do," he mumbled.

"Here," she handed him a paper cup with a scoop of the cherry chocolate fudge ice cream in it and brought the ice cream scoop to her lips to lick off the excess. Before she could taste it, he stopped her hand in mid motion.

"None for you."

"Why not?"

"Because I don't believe you about this ice cream."

"You're not making any sense."

"Give me a minute." He took a spoonful of the ice cream into his mouth. "It's good."

"Damn straight."

He moaned. "Real good. In fact, I think I'm gonna come just thinking about it."

"Would you stop teasing? It doesn't work on men. The one from today was different."

"I told you nothing happened today."

"Yeah. You did. I don't believe you." She watched him continue to insert the spoon into the ice cream and then lick the frozen treat from it. His movements made her wonder how it would feel to be an ice cream cone.

"Believe what you want," he finally said with a shrug. "This is a nice set up you've got here."

"I like it." She turned to the soda fountain and fixed herself a cherry coke before sitting back down.

"You wanna know why I said no more ice cream?" He took in the last bite as he spoke.

"No."

"I said it because I want to know what happens tonight isn't ice cream induced."

"What are you talking about?"

"I'm talking about our deal. I want to know that you aren't just trying to get a hold of my sugar so you can get a hold of the cane." He waggled his eyebrows.

"You don't have to be so crude. And you're awfully cocky, aren't you?"

"Damn straight."

She flushed all the way to her ears. "I didn't mean…"

"I know what you meant, darlin'. And I am in every sense of the word. Now, about our deal."

"I'm listening."

"I want to taste the product before I agree to anything."

"Done."

"And I want to help develop new flavors."

"As long as they're within reason. And necessary."

"And I want to have wild, uninhibited sex with you."

Laura stared at him as if he'd lost his mind when the last comment slipped out. He had fought this raging hard-on the best he could all night. But it was driving him crazy. All of the blood from his brain seemed to have a direct line to his dick. That was the only explanation for such an absurd suggestion.

The plan formulated even if he had lost what little control he had to begin with tonight. And now, she licked her lips at the mention of the word sex. Those firm, full, red lips. The ones he dreamed about last night. The ones he wanted wrapped firmly around his cock.

"You're out of your mind."

"That I am. And you put me there. So how 'bout it?"

"You're out of your mind," she repeated.

"You said that already. You need to come up with a better reply than that if you plan to scare me off."

"First of all, I didn't do anything to put you in any kind of...whatever it is going on in that head of yours."

"Actually it's going on in the other head. And I'm talking about today. You coming to see me to rescue your precious ice cream. I don't believe in orgasm producing ice cream. So, here's my plan. You have sex with me for the next week. Let me prove to you that no ice cream can replace a man's touch. And if you're still convinced that it can, I'll give you exclusive rights to the sugar."

Her eyes widened and then narrowed. "You're nuts."

"Yep. I'm pretty sure I am. I think it's the heat. So, do we have a deal?"

"No. There is no deal."

"Do you have a boyfriend or something?" He raised his hand when she started to speak. "Of course you don't. If you had a real man in your life you wouldn't need the ice cream orgasm. You'd have the real thing."

"My sex life is none of your concern."

"Seems you've said that before. So, how about it?"

"You can keep your damned sugar. What are you doing?"

"I'm coming to kiss you." He cornered her behind the bar. Her hands came up against his chest as he pulled her into him.

"Get away from me."

"If you really want me to, I will," he said softly.

"Ryan."

"I've had this all damned day," he ground his hips against hers. "Now, if you don't want me to kiss you, I won't. If you don't want to sleep with me, I'll leave. But think about it. You could have something that ice cream can't give you. You could have something that few men on earth could give you. Long, lingering, honest to God orgasms."

"No wonder I never dated you in high school."

"I'm not interested in dating. I'm interested in sex. You, me, two hot, sweaty bodies sliding off each other." Ryan LeJeune. Sexy as hell, sin on a stick Ryan LeJeune just offered to give her real, honest to God orgasms. Willingly. For one week. And then she would have exclusive rights to his sugar. Without the sweet deal, it was still a *sweet* deal.

She had dreamed about Ryan for years but would never admit it to anyone. She had watched him throughout high school and wondered how it would feel to have those arms wrapped around her and those lips on her body. Now she knew. And she had turned him down. Yep, she was certifiable.

It's just sex. She bit her bottom lip as she let her eyes graze over him.

Tall. Lean. Muscular. Tanned. Blue eyes. Long, curly dark hair. Those lips. She knew how they tasted with her ice cream on his lips. He could be an ice cream model. She could create a whole new career for him. Women would pay to taste the flavors on his lips.

She gave herself a shake. Yep. She was mental. A couple of kisses and she was ready to crown him some kind of sex god. And she knew he would be. Ryan LeJeune was legendary in Oak Creek. Which was exactly why she wanted to turn him down. At least that's what she told herself. She didn't want to be just another on a long list.

Still, there was a lot to be said for that mouth.

She took in a deep breath and then crossed the few inches to where he stood, staring at her, awaiting an answer. "Okay. You wanna play that way? You've got a deal."

Chapter Five

Laura knew a hell of a lot about ice cream, but men were an eternal mystery. Ryan practically stumbled backward as she took control of the situation and shoved him back against the bar. The look in his eyes said it all. He was bluffing. And she had made a complete fool out of herself. She watched him scramble for the door, mumbling some kind of apology and then leaving her standing there like an idiot. Good riddance.

Laura managed to put off thinking about Ryan during the short commute the next morning. She didn't think about those lips on hers or the way his body had felt pressed against her. And she certainly didn't think about his proposition. Or the fact that he had her right where he wanted her and left her there.

After a restless night filled with every fantasy she could summon, she knew there was no denying the chemistry between them. And Laura knew all about chemistry. It was a reaction in the blood, the brain, the hormones that nothing to do with real emotion, and was almost as fake as her simulated orgasms. Lust could convince you that you loved someone. Just like her ice cream could con the brain into orgasmic bliss.

Just like Ryan LeJeune could make a woman believe he wanted her only to leave her high and dry ten seconds later.

She pulled her car into her regular parking space, hoping to avoid her sister and cousins and all their questions. Pushing open the door to her office, she was welcomed by her haven, which was decorated in pale ice cream colors. The cotton candy pink sofa looked like heaven set against the mint ice cream colored walls and candy blue carpet. The festive setting clashed enough to give a normal person a headache from sensory overload.

Something was off, though, and it reeked of her disastrous night. Taking a deep breath, she peeled the label from the brown box sitting innocently on her desk. Ryan LeJeune was apparently up for round two. He'd fully humiliated her last night with round one, making her ready to give up on the whole idea of doing business with him.

Ripping open the box, she saw the plastic bag lying on top of shredded newspaper, looking like an illegal drug. She picked up the attached note and, holding it between shaky fingers, hoped her heart would stop beating out of control.

Sorry. Try Again? R

She replaced the note and shoved her hands into her back pockets, rocking on her heels. Thinking. Try what again? How long had she known Ryan LeJeune? And how many times had she let him get to her? There would be no second chances. No matter what.

That decided, she grabbed the box and headed for the lab. She'd show him! The ice cream mixture came together with no problems. Ryan's conversion chart precisely detailed just how much was needed.

"Somebody's in a sour mood this morning." Amanda stood in the doorway of the lab.

"Remind me to get a lock for that door," Laura grumbled.

"Cate said she thought you were in here sulking."

"I'm not sulking."

"Then what are you up to?" Amanda eyed the mixing bowl in Laura's hands.

"Mixing."

"I can see that. What are you mixing?"

"Well, when I came in today, I had a package on my desk." She nodded toward the open box on the counter.

Amanda picked up the note. "Sorry. Try again?" She wrinkled her brows. "Try what?"

"You don't want to know."

"He wanted more money?"

Laura shot her an incredulous look. "No."

"Then what?"

"He wanted to help with the flavors."

"Is that what this is all about?" Amanda's look said she didn't believe her sister's story.

"I'm mixing up a vanilla bean concoction like what I used for *Fudge Ripple #9*. It has to be the combination of vanilla and chocolate." Anything to change the topic.

"So it worked on Ryan?"

"Not even. At least that's what he says."

"And you don't believe him?"

"Nope. Not a word of it."

"Hmmm." Amanda took one of the wooden barstools and pulled it up to the counter, examining Ryan's note again. "And he wants you to make more of it?"

"Not exactly."

"Then what does he want?"

Laura avoided Amanda's inquiring gaze. If she looked at her sister, Amanda would figure out her secret. She was hot for Ryan. "Nothing."

"Your face is flushing. What exactly did you two do last night to warrant," she looked into the box, "three pounds of sugar substitute?"

"We didn't *do* anything."

"No, but I bet you wanted to."

Laura dumped the bowl onto the counter, having beaten all the lumps out of it she possibly could. "He wants to trade sex for sugar."

"Well hell," Amanda slapped her hand on the counter, "that sounds like a pretty cheap deal."

"Cheap is right." Laura rolled her eyes.

"And he's waiting for an answer? You didn't jump his bones then and there?"

"No, I didn't. Some of us have self control." Namely, him. "But you're gonna, right?"

"You're impossible."

"No, I'm not. I just know a sweet deal when I hear one."

"I suppose you'd do it, right?"

"If I weren't married and were interested in Ryan, yep, I'd do it."

"I'm not interested in Ryan."

"So you've said about a zillion times. If you're not interested, just tell him. Screw the renegotiations. You know what I mean," she added when Laura shot her a dirty look at her word choice.

"Yeah, I know what you mean."

"Then do it. Tell him the original offer stands with the modification that he can help with flavors." Amanda dipped her finger into the new mixture. "This is good."

"It's got raw eggs in it."

"Figures," she coughed.

"Thought I'd warn you." Laura shrugged, knowing how Amanda hated raw eggs.

"You didn't use the egg substitute?"

"No. I didn't use it in the original batch, so I didn't use it in this."

"You could warn a person *in advance*."

"Consider it payback for warning me in advance about sending the ice cream to Ryan."

"We've got a bit of a crisis." Karen ran into the lab, slamming the door against the wall so hard she almost knocked the dry erase board onto the floor.

"Great. Just what I need. A crisis," Laura grumbled.

"I'll handle it," Amanda offered, standing.

"No. This one is Laura's."

"That's what I've got you guys for. To tell me I have to handle all crises." She sighed and shot a warning look at Amanda. "Don't run off with the mixture." "Wouldn't dream of it."

"What's the crisis?" Laura followed Karen down the hallway as they walked toward Laura's office.

"It's in here." Karen pushed open the door.

"The crisis is in my office. What happened?" She narrowed her eyes at her cousin.

"Something that only you can handle." Karen practically pushed her in and then closed the door on her before she could protest.

"That's why no one hires family," Laura shouted at the closed door. The lack of answer was exactly what she expected.

"I find working with family to be most useful."

Shit. She turned around to face the last person she wanted to see.

"What do you want?"

"An apology."

"Go to hell."

"Not from you. From me. I wanted to tell you in person."

"So tell me."

"Sorry." He shoved his hands into his pockets giving her a boyish grin that made her want to melt on the spot.

"Sorry I'm a little more than you can take?"

"Sorry I was such an ass. I was testing you."

"Funny, I thought you were trying to prove your manhood."

"My manhood was proven a long time ago," he stood, stretching out his long legs. Laura took in a sharp breath as he started toward her. She knew where this was heading. The same place it headed every time she and Ryan had been alone with one another.

"I'll bet." Unconsciously, she licked her lips. Boy, he looked good today. He was back in his usual cowboy wear from his jeans to his black hat. And looked good enough to eat. Or to lick chocolate ice cream from. She shivered at the thought.

"That offer isn't on the table any more."

She couldn't quite read those eyes. Was he teasing or serious? Something in her belly protested. "Oh," she tried not to sound disappointed.

"I have a new one." He stood right in front of her now, just an arm's length away. She could pull him to her if so inclined, which she wasn't.

"Oh?"

"Yes. I know I wasn't exactly eloquent and all last night. But I have a new plan. Maybe one that you'll accept."

"Okay," she said warily. "You can try."

"Don't you think you should have a seat first?"

"Yeah. Uh, sure." She managed to walk past him, ignoring the masculine scent she knew she'd never be able to get out of the carpet.

"I want to know the truth about the ice cream. I don't believe that any ice cream can do what you say it can. I've looked over your numbers and everything and apparently somebody believes it."

"We do good business."

"Yeah. I can see that. But I wonder why. I don't think it's the reason they say."

"You wouldn't."

"Why? Because I'm a man?"

"No, because you're a cocky man."

"Point taken. Still, I have to know before I get involved."

"Okay. I'm ready for this new plan any time."

"I'm getting to it. I need some of your ice cream."

Laura's stomach sank. "Okay." She waited for the catch.

"I want to do a little bit of my own experiments. Test runs. And since no one will know what I'm doing, I figured it would be the best way to test it."

"Test it? You want to test it? And no one will know? What are you talking about?" She clenched and unclenched her fists beneath the table.

"I'm talking about testing it out on a, uh, friend."

"You want me to help out your sex life by helping you trick some unknowing lover?" A thousand emotions hit her at once. He was going to replace her with someone else. All in the name of science.

"That about sums it up," he smiled.

"No way."

"Then I guess I'll have to buy my own and test it out." He stood to leave. She was right on his heels.

"You hold it right there, buster. What are you going to do with it?"

"I think you know."

"No, I don't. But I won't have my product involved in any illicit testing." She practically shouted.

"It won't be illicit. She'll be perfectly willing. She just won't know I'm using super duper ice cream," he winked.

"I won't allow it."

"You can't stop it. If I buy the stuff, I can use it however I want to."

"I won't sell it to you."

"What are you afraid of?" his voice changed back to the one that made her stomach quiver. She wished she hadn't followed so closely. Didn't stand so near him. Didn't want him so much.

"I'm not afraid of anything," she folded her arms.

"Then you're jealous."

"Of you? Hardly," she laughed.

"Then prove it."

He was too cocky for his own good. He stood there, arms folded, legs spread, inviting her in. Have a taste, Laura. She groaned. She'd like to pound him on the chest for being such an ass. But then she'd have to touch his chest. And that brought to mind all kinds of interesting thoughts. She licked her lips again.

"Fine," she sighed. "You can have the ice cream. How much do you want and what flavors?"

He laughed. "I'll never figure you out."

"I said you can have the damned ice cream."

"I know. And it's killing you to give it to me."

"Is not." She went back to her desk and pressed the button on her pager. "I need Karen," she said to the voice on the other end.

"Yeah, what do you need?"

"Mr. LeJeune needs some ice cream samples. Can you send some in," she turned to Ryan. "What flavors do you want?"

"You pick out the ones you like best." Something about his tone brought back images of him covered in ice cream. Maybe she'd put together a chocolate syrup.

"Just send something," she grumbled into the pager.

"Sure thing, boss," she heard Karen say.

"It'll be right up," she gave Ryan a mockingly sweet smile.

"Thanks. I'm sure I'll have a hell of a night."

"I'm sure you will." She turned to her computer.

"I guess I'll just wait here for the delivery then."

"We have a waiting area outside," she offered without looking up.

"Yeah, I saw it on my way in. I'd rather sit here and watch you pretend you aren't curious about my date tonight."

"I'm not curious about your date tonight."

"Suit yourself."

Ryan never dreamed it would work. The idea came to him in the middle of the night while waking from another hot dream about Laura. Kicking himself for refusing her last night, he still wasn't sure what had come over him. Yeah, he was. He wanted her, but not like that.

Now, it would appear, he was going to have several pints of orgasm ice cream and no one to try it on. He could eat it himself, but that would ruin the fun. And he didn't plan on risking another two-day hard-on. One had been enough, thank you.

And he could have remedied the situation last night if he had only given in to what he wanted more than anything right now. It wasn't over yet. He still had time to seduce her on his terms rather than have her jump on the counter, spread her legs and yell *ride 'em cowboy!*

A smile spread across his face. He knew Laura wanted him for more than just one night. It was obvious from the way she squared her shoulders while she leaned into her computer screen to the way she was carefully avoiding looking up at him.

He looked around the office, hating the color scheme. It didn't suit an ice cream CEO. It should have plush carpeting in a dark, seductive color. And the drapes should be sheer, gauzy. The screen saver he glimpsed earlier should be as mesmerizing as the woman sitting in front of it.

He thought about his own office, which had none of his personality, either. Of course, it had only been his office for a couple of days. Blake hadn't bothered adding any personal touches to it, so it pretty much looked like it had when it was his dad's. Right down to the old desk and worn out chair.

Laura reached up to rub her neck. His muscles tensed. He'd give anything to be invited over there to rub it for her. To feel that soft skin beneath his fingers. To taste her neck. His pants strained at the thought. She was still ignoring him, but he knew she was aware of his stare.

Her hair was pulled back into a ponytail like it had been last night. And her jeans clung to her body the same way they had then. Only her shirt was different. Instead of a white tank top, she wore a pink short-sleeved sweater. It outlined her breasts in a way that made him swear pink would forever be his favorite color.

His thoughts were interrupted by a knock on the door. His ice cream was ready.

"Here you go." Karen handed him the box.

"Thanks," he mumbled.

"Is that all?" Laura turned around, nodded her thanks to Karen. Karen quickly left, closing the door behind her.

"Yep. I think that'll do it." He drummed his fingers on the top of the box.

"Do you need me to dismiss you before you'll leave?"

"No. I think I can find my own way out."

He turned and strolled to the door, aware of her eyes on him all the way out. He took his time getting back to the Porsche. What the hell was he going to do with this ice cream?

Chapter Six

Wednesday nights in Oak Creek were usually quiet nights. The guys went to poker, the seniors went to bingo, and the Reynolds girls ate ice cream, a tradition ever since *I Scream* opened. Only tonight, the ringleader called in sick. Laura hadn't been in a mood to eat ice cream.

It wasn't because of Ryan LeJeune. No man could kill her urge to indulge in frozen love, as her cousin, Cate, called it. It just didn't have any appeal for her tonight. Nothing wrong with that. A girl can't live off ice cream alone.

She propped her slipper-covered feet up on her coffee table and clicked the channels on the remote. Surely something was on TV tonight. A re-run of that vampire show or something, anything, to take her mind off Ryan. She settled for a repeat of a mindless comedy that wouldn't take too much brainpower. The urge to just sit and veg out in front of the TV was too tempting.

The microwave announced that her popcorn was ready at the same time the phone began ringing. "This better be good," she called to the annoying intrusion, as if it could hear her.

"It's about time," Amanda complained as soon as Laura answered.

"I'm busy."

"Oh?"

"What do you want?" she gave up. There was no point in trying to run in circles with her sister.

"It's Ryan."

Great. She let out a long sigh. "What about him?"

"He called here tonight looking for you. He said he needs you to get over to his place right away. Something to do with the ice cream."

"Why'd he call you?"

"I don't know. I guess he didn't have your number."

Not likely. Laura couldn't help but wonder if Amanda wasn't up to another one of her tricks. Lately she seemed to be pulling one scheme after another when it came to Ryan. "What's his problem? His date run out on him?"

"I don't know. He sounded kinda weird, though. And I figured since you live right down the road…"

"I'm not going over there."

"I think he's sick."

"Maybe he should go to the hospital then."

"Come on, Laura. If your ice cream made him sick, you need to know."

Amanda was right. Damn her. If the ice cream made Ryan ill, she did need to know so she could track down the problem. "Fine. I'll go. But he sure as hell better be dying." Laura grumbled, hanging up the phone.

The last thing she wanted tonight was to go over to Ryan LeJeune's house and work out some problem he had with her ice cream. Still, if the ice cream made Ryan sick, she needed to go over there and figure out why. She couldn't have a product on the market that caused illness. Even if the patient deserved to be ill.

She changed out of her nightgown and into a pair of jeans and a T-shirt. She ran a comb through her hair and begrudgingly threw on a little makeup. It wouldn't do to show up looking like she had been sitting home alone. That's when the idea struck her. She shouldn't go over there looking like she'd just slipped on some clothes. No, this called for extra attention.

It only took ten minutes to change into a denim halter dress and more carefully apply her makeup and arrange her hair. She slicked on some cherry red lipstick and checked her reflection in the mirror. Now, this looked like a girl who had been up to something. She smiled at the thought, not wanting Ryan to think she was just wasting her time alone. She slid on her black sandals with the two-inch heels and gave a turn in the mirror. This would make his mouth go dry.

✱ ✱ ✱ ✱ ✱

At least the house was cool now. And he could take a warm shower if he wanted to. And the ice cream would stay frozen if he would put it in the freezer. Instead, Ryan found himself flipping off the lights and lighting the candles he had been using for the past couple of nights. He hit "play" on the CD player as he passed it and headed to the kitchen for a spoon.

Blake's music left much to be desired, he decided as he heard the twang of country music drift into the room. He smiled, imagining his brother racing in his Porsche listening to Garth Brooks. What a combination. He thought the car was more suited to vintage Van Halen and KISS.

He wondered about Laura's plans for the night. More appropriately, what she thought he had planned. She tried to act like she didn't care, but he could tell by her standoffishness she was putting on an act.

She wanted to know how he planned to use her ice cream. Fire practically flew from her eyes when he mentioned using it. And he only hinted he would use it on someone else. If he could figure out how to get her here tonight, he would be able to really work on the jealousy. The scene was all but set with the candles and music.

Nothing was going according to plan. Especially where Laura was concerned. From the moment that he saw her, he had thought about kissing her. But Laura was nothing like the image she sent out. Sex may be part of her business, but it wasn't part of her life, a problem he could remedy if she'd just let him. They'd both have a hell of a time and make money to boot. But Laura wasn't like that. The truly beautiful ones never were.

Ryan sank down onto his sofa and tore into the first pint of ice cream. He cheated and bought several different brands today to see which ones tasted best. And to see if Laura's was all it was cracked up to be. He had *Godiva's Chocolate Raspberry Truffle, Ben & Jerry's Chunky Monkey,* and plain ol' *Blue Bell Dutch Chocolate.* He would do a taste test later on. Right now, he wanted to taste her ice cream.

He touched the first spoonful to his tongue, letting the sensual taste, linger on his palate. It was smooth, rich, creamy. All the things an ice cream should be. All the things a woman's skin should be.

He groaned. He wasn't having an orgasm, but he was getting a hard-on. And this time, it wasn't because of the ice cream. It was because of the woman. Surely he could think of a reason to call and invite her over. He could tell her he changed his mind about everything and was ready to sign on the dotted line.

He picked up the phone and dialed her number.

"Hi. It's Laura. I'm not in right now, but if you'll leave a message, I'll get back to you."

"Hi, Laura, it's, uh, Ryan. I was wondering. Well, I was calling to see if you could come over so we could talk about this business proposition. For real. No tricks. But I guess you're not home. Oh, well. I'll try later. Bye." He hung up the phone and rested his head against the back of the sofa. No relief tonight.

The headlights coming up the driveway caught his attention. He sat up, put the ice cream down. He wished his phone call could have conjured Laura.

He went to the door and pulled it open, stepping out onto the porch. A slow smile spread across his lips. Well, hell. She had come here prepared to deal, apparently. He let his eyes roam over her denim clad body. He liked jeans, but this denim dress was a nice change. It pushed her breasts up and teased along the edges. That hard-on he had only grew worse.

"Laura," he whispered her name as she approached. She had a strictly business look on her face.

"Are you okay?"

"I am now," he smiled.

"That's not what I mean. What happened with the ice cream?"

"Come on in and I'll tell you," he said, not really sure how to answer her.

"I guess it was a success."

"I don't know if I'd go that far." He watched her take in the scene. He didn't know what she was doing here, but his romantic set up was working like a charm on her. He hadn't seen her this angry since, well, since this morning.

"How far would you go, then?"

"How far *would* I go or how far *did* I go?" He dropped his voice to a low growl and watched her wrap her arms tightly around herself, squeezing her breasts forward.

"I'm not interested in your sex life. I'm interested in the ice cream. Is everything okay with it?"

"Not exactly what I had in mind, but okay." He sank back onto the sofa and watched her carefully sit on the edge of the chair.

"Then why am I here?"

Ryan opened his mouth to speak and then closed it. Why *was* she here? His mind reeled. He called two seconds ago. There was no way she could have gotten his message and rushed over. Something else had to be at work here. And he had to be careful not to spoil it. "I needed your opinion on something."

"You asked me here because you needed my opinion?" She stood now, hands on hips. "I was in the middle of something very important."

"Now wait." He needed to think of a way to calm her down. "I didn't mean…"

"Amanda called and said you were having problems with the ice cream. You were sick or something. And you needed me to come over here. Now what kind of scam are you running?"

"I'm not running a scam." He tried to think. He could really use this if his brain would function.

"I'm leaving." She spun on her heel, but he caught her arm, causing her to stop.

"Wait."

"Let go." She pulled free.

"Wait. Please. Don't go. I do have a problem," he managed. *Think, think, think.*

"I'm waiting." She arched her eyebrow, making him feel as if he were being scolded by the teacher. That thought caused another reaction in his pants. If he didn't get a grip on the situation, he was going to lose control completely.

"Sit down. Please."

She obliged. "Spill it."

If she kept looking at him like that, he just might. "I tried the ice cream. And nothing happened." He watched her eyes darken.

"What do you mean, nothing happened?"

"I mean nothing happened. No reaction." He wasn't exactly lying. Just not being completely honest.

"I see. What did you use?"

"All the stuff you sent earlier."

"And nothing happened?"

"Nope." A satisfied grin crossed his face. Yep, she was worried. An unsatisfied customer.

"Maybe it wasn't the ice cream."

"Well, it wasn't the company," he straightened.

"Well, it wasn't the ice cream."

"I don't know. I think maybe it was. Maybe this batch wasn't any good. You didn't do something different did you?" That was it. He had her. Her whole demeanor changed when he mentioned a possible mistake. Her work was her pride.

"No, I didn't. The formulas are very precise."

"My sugar wasn't in these, was it?" He tried to sound worried, but was in truth getting all worked up watching her concern as she chewed on her bottom lip.

"No, it wasn't. I don't know what happened. Have you got any left?"

"Yeah, I do. Are you gonna take it back to the lab and test it?"

"Huh?"

"The lab. I figured you'd want to test it tonight."

"I can do that here," she argued, taking him completely off guard.

"Here?" He tried to suppress his smile.

"Yes. Unless you are otherwise occupied."

"Nope. Not occupied."

"Good."

"I'll just go get it, then."

Ryan left her in the living room. Great. She was going to try out the ice cream here. Well, he got his wish, but he felt like hell about it. He shouldn't have to trick her into this. And if she did get all turned on, what would he do? He knew what he wanted to do, but doing it was another story.

He eyed the containers he had placed in his freezer. An idea came to him, but he wasn't sure it would work. She was the ice cream goddess after all and would be able to distinguish her own product. Wouldn't she?

He peeled open her containers and then the others. They looked about the same. He gave them a quick taste. He couldn't tell much difference. But they were her creation. She would know.

His hands shook as he pulled three glass dishes from his cabinet. Maybe he could pull it off. He caught sight of his tie flung across the back of one of the kitchen chairs. A more interesting idea occurred to him.

He smiled, carrying the tie around his neck and balancing the glasses in his hands.

Chapter Seven

"What are you doing with *that*?" Laura folded her arms across her chest and eyed the tie draped around his neck. That dangerous look in his eyes was enough to send a shiver down her spine, but she tried to suppress it. She had been on edge ever since she got here. And the husky tone of his voice didn't help any.

"A taste test."

"I've tasted my ice cream before. I don't need a test. I just need to see if there's anything wrong with it." She narrowed her eyes at him.

"I know. But you know what they say? When you block out some of your senses the others are heightened." He held up the tie as if he planned to use it as a blindfold.

"You are not putting that thing on me." She pointed at the tie and tried not to react to his smile.

"Come here," his voice was a low drawl. She didn't want to obey, but her body refused to listen to her mind. She stood and moved to the sofa, giving him a wary stare with every motion.

"I won't tie it too tight, I promise," he whispered into her ear. He held the tie in front of her eyes, proving what she knew to be true. He was going to blindfold her.

"This is a bad idea," she protested. Her stomach did tiny flip-flops at both the suggestion of being blindfolded and the person doing it.

"I won't hurt you. It's just ice cream."

Laura took in a deep breath as he placed the blindfold securely against her eyes and then tied it behind her head.

"Is it too tight?"

"No," her voice caught in her throat.

"Can you see?"

"No."

"Good."

He sank down beside her, his weight causing her to almost fall into him. She licked her lips, anticipating the first taste, feeling herself grow wet from the nearness.

"Try this one."

When the spoon touched her lips, they automatically opened, allowing her to lick the flavor from the cold metal. "What flavor is this?"

"I don't know. One of yours."

"It's not one of mine," she protested. She raised her arms to take off the blindfold, but his hands steadied her, keeping her from reaching it.

"Don't," he warned softly, sending a shiver up her back.

"What flavor?"

"I don't know. I took them out of the containers. I think it's cherry something."

"It doesn't taste right."

"I told you there was something wrong with it."

His voice was so soft, so seductive, she swore she would melt if he touched her. He was already driving her insane by sitting close enough she could feel him move, but not close enough to touch her. "Try another one," she managed through her dry throat.

"Okay."

The second flavor was no better than the first. They tasted wrong. The basic flavor was right, but something was off. She tried to steady her breathing. Maybe it wasn't the ice cream. Maybe it was the company.

She recognized one of Keith Urban's love songs playing in the background. She smelled the flames from the candles, could practically hear the wax melting and dripping against the glass plate. And then there was Ryan.

Men weren't supposed to smell this good. Especially not roguish men like him. He'd slept with half of Oak Creek. And here he was playing seducer with her. And she was eating it up just like all the women before her. And heaven help her, it was all she could do not to reach out and grab him as he brought the spoon to her lips for another taste.

She froze.

"What was that?"

"I dropped a little. Let me get it."

Her breath caught in her throat. She stiffened as the liquid made its way slowly down the exposed flesh. It was replaced by his warm lips as they made contact, lapping up the ice cream. His hair brushed against her, teasing her, making her wonder how it would feel to have his hair spill across her face while they made love. She let out a tiny moan as he licked the rest of the ice cream from her chest.

"Ryan." She wasn't sure if his name sounded like a protest or a plea. In reality, it was a little of both.

"Oops. I think I dropped some more." The spoon ran along the exposed skin of her thigh, making her quiver. "Let me get that."

This time, his tongue darted out first, lapping up the cream and then tracing a trail up to the edge of her dress. She threw her head back, trying to decide if she wanted to rip off the blindfold and walk out or stay and see what would come next.

The truth was, she couldn't move if she wanted to. She may have only been blindfolded, but he may as well have her tied down. Every muscle in her body protested when her brain suggested they try to move.

"You want me to stop?" His voice was husky, his breath close to her face. She shook her head wildly, but was unable to speak. He let out a little laugh and then dripped ice cream along her chest again.

"You know, I like this dress," he licked along the trail he had made. "I like the way it laces up. I can untie it." The ties loosened as he spoke. "And explore a little at a time."

The spoon rubbed against her thigh again before being replaced with his lips. The ice cream may not have tasted right, but it apparently still had the punch. She wasn't able to resist Ryan LeJeune.

She rested against the sofa when he braced her back with his hand, lowering her. When his hand skimmed down her side, she jumped in reaction.

"I think all this ice cream needs is a little encouragement. Wouldn't you agree?" She nodded. "Someone to gently talk to it. Someone to seduce it."

Yes! She wanted to scream. Seduction. The whole scene was set for seduction. And she was falling into it as easily as she had come over here tonight. If she were to be honest with herself, she knew she had just been looking for an excuse to come over. And seduce Ryan.

"Ryan," she moaned, arching her back against him.

"Hmmm?" He moved on top of her and dropped the spoon. She heard it hit against the hardwood floor a second before he captured her lips.

Her head started spinning. What had Amanda said about using the ice cream as an enhancer? God, she had been right. His powerful mouth tasted like ice cream, and the insides were cool. She knew instinctively how he would feel if he lowered himself for another kind of kiss. His tongue would be cold, exploring, teasing. Just like it was now.

She tore the blindfold from her eyes as his head moved lower. His body pressed against her, searing her with its heat. His erection pressed into her belly, almost enough to send her over the edge. The great Ryan LeJeune was hard for her. And this time, he hadn't had any of the fudge ripple ice cream.

She reached down and pulled him back up to face her, using his long curls as leverage. When she looked into his heated eyes, she saw raw hunger. She licked her lips. It's now or never. As smoothly as she could manage, she pulled him against her and pressed her body tightly to his, wriggling her hips in invitation and glorying in his response.

"Not here," Ryan groaned and swept her into his arms, holding her gaze as he carried her up the stairs and into his bedroom. When he kicked the door open, her senses were assaulted with his scent.

Ryan gently laid her on the bed and then stripped off his shirt. Thank God for moonlight. He was incredible. She had never seen a chest so perfectly built before. A teasing amount of cinnamon hair splayed across the rippled muscles of his chest. She could cover him with whipped cream and he'd look just like a sundae. A chocolate, caramel and cinnamon sundae. A new flavor came to mind in the seconds before he lowered himself to her.

Ryan covered her mouth with his, quieting all thoughts of ice cream. "Are you ready for me, Laura?"

She nodded. "Yes."

"I don't believe you." He slid his hand down, raising her dress up around her hips. "Let me see." He burned a teasing trail along the edges of her panties.

Thank God she had worn something sexy tonight. She took in a sharp breath as his skilled fingers moved the flimsy lace to the side. At first he teased, just running his fingers along the edges of the lace, skimming the exposed flesh. She bit her lip until she tasted blood.

"Are you ready?"

She moaned, nodded her head wildly, as he dipped a finger inside.

"God, Laura," he groaned, delving further in. She arched her back to meet him as he continued his exploration, pressing against her tender outer flesh with the heel of his hand.

He pushed her dress up to her waist and ran his free hand along the waistband of her white lace panties before he slid them down her legs. "More," she managed.

She watched in awe as he removed his hand and plunged the wet finger into his mouth. "You're good enough to eat." His hoarse tone sent a shiver through her body. It started at the base of her neck and went down, down, down until her entire body quaked.

He dipped his head between her thighs and he dove in, tongue first. God, it was just as she imagined it would be. His mouth was cool from the ice cream, his tongue hard. He teased her clit before licking at her inner walls. Her body shook, and she clung to his hair.

"Where did that tie go?" he mused. His breath teased against her swollen flesh, but the comment didn't register until he moved away from her.

"Where are you going?" she half sat up.

"Shh. I'm not going far."

Laura watched as he gracefully bent over and picked up the silk tie. He wove it between his fingers and then draped it around his neck. "What are you doing?" Her breath came in short spurts, wild ideas rushing through her head, exciting her.

"Undress for me," he coaxed.

She obeyed as he sat back down on the bed and watched her loosen the laces of her dress. Her fingers were having difficulty cooperating. She finally had the dress loose enough to slip it over her head, leaving her sitting in front of him in only her bra and panties.

"You are beautiful."

Her heart beat wildly at his confession. She hadn't felt beautiful before this very moment. Ever. "What do you want?"

"I want you to take off your bra. And these," he slid his finger under her panties. They had been cutting into her soft flesh causing a sensation she couldn't describe. When he slid his finger underneath them, they tightened, causing the elastic to rub against her clit. She moaned and threw her head back before sliding them off and tossing them into the heap of clothes on the floor. She lay back on the bed, spread her legs wide for him and arched her back in invitation.

"Not yet," he teased. He moved over her, guiding her hands up above her head. "Have you ever let someone else have control of you?"

Her eyes widened at the thought. "No," she whispered.

"Why not? What are you afraid of? You know, it would be better to give control to a man instead of a dessert." The thought was ludicrous, but the sensual tone of his voice made it sound like the most inviting proposition she had ever heard.

She gasped when he took her hands into his and then wrapped them up in the headboard. His old four-poster bed was one that had been made for this kind of activity. The latticework of iron invited a little light bondage.

When he wrapped the tie around her wrists, she lost control, growing wetter from the feel of the silk against her skin. She would have passed out from the sensation, but she was too intent on finding out what he was going to do next.

"Give me control," he murmured, placing a light kiss on each wrist.

She was already too far gone to answer. Arching against him, she delighted in the way the coarse material of his jeans rubbed against her sensitive flesh. She continued to move against him, moaning, almost bringing herself to climax by that simple motion.

He remained still over her, letting her move, letting her please herself with the rough feel of his jeans. When she began to quake, he thrust himself up against her, continuing the motion, continuing the assault. She shivered with delight, her arms pulling on the tie, attempting to free herself.

She wanted him to undress. She wanted him to take her. Now. She wanted to see all of him. Naked. Above her. Inside her. *Now, Now, Now!* "Ryan, please."

"Please what?"

"Please let me go. Let me see you." She labored against her restraints. His gentle laugh only heated her movements. "You like this, don't you?"

"Yes. I do," he growled.

God, she wanted her hands in his hair. She wanted to run her fingers along his taut flesh. Wanted to explore the cinnamon hair that covered his chest. She shivered again, knowing how he would feel. He would be firm, hard. With skin like silk. "Ryan."

In one motion, he freed her wrists. Her hands instantly went into his hair, but he pulled away long enough to remove his pants.

"It won't last long," he warned.

"I don't care."

"Are you ready?"

Her nod was interrupted when he pressed against her heated flesh. He lay just outside of her wetness, begging for entry, pushing into her folds. She tried to relax, tried to let him in. Her nails dug into his back and she pressed him lower, letting his length finally slip into her. She widened, grinding her hips against him as he filled her completely. She exploded into a thousand pieces.

She arched against him, rubbing her lips against the base of his cock. His balls rested on the curve of her ass and his hair, free from its binding, fell into her face. Her flesh tightened and expanded, throbbing with him. "Oh, God," she called out. He hadn't even started moving yet, and she was already coming.

"Hold on, baby," he cooed against her ear before throwing his head back and letting out a howl. "You feel incredible," he smiled down at her. "Your pussy is so tight, so wet," he murmured.

She reached up and splayed her hands across his chest, and then ran them up and down his torso. She delighted at the shivers she caused. Her breath caught in her throat when he stopped her hands from their exploration.

He firmly gripped her wrists and held them against the soft cotton sheets, taking full control of her. She easily gave it to him, feeling completely uninhibited with him. His face twisted as his orgasm built, making him look even more beautiful. His release came quickly, as he had warned. Rather than being disappointed, Laura was spellbound. He was incredible.

Ryan collapsed on top of her, his weight only increasing the sensations as her orgasm ripped through her. She clung to him, her hands twisted in his hair, his scent all around her making her feel something she couldn't define. It had been a long damned time. And this felt so good.

"I'm sorry."

"For what?"

"I was afraid it wouldn't last long."

"It was fine, I assure you," she smiled lazily.

"A hell of a lot better than fine," he smiled back. He reached out and pushed her hair out of her eyes. When he brought his head down for a kiss, she met his lips. He gave. She took. They both felt changed.

Laura wanted to tease him about the ice cream. Tell him she knew there was nothing wrong with it. But her stomach protested. She felt ill. Maybe there was something wrong with it, after all. No, that wasn't it. She was disappointed with herself. She had given in and become a name on the list for Ryan LeJeune.

She moved his arm from around her and left the bed, careful not to wake him. He had fallen asleep with little effort, curled up against her. His hair fell across her shoulder, mixing in with her own, bringing to mind all kinds of forbidden thoughts.

She padded quietly to the bathroom and closed the door behind her. She examined herself in the mirror. Nothing on the outside had changed. But everything inside had. She had given in to her lust. And that was something she rarely ever did.

She was a modern woman, she argued. Thirty-one next month. She owned her own business. Had a nice house. Had everything she needed. Who would blame her for a one-night fling with Ryan LeJeune? No one.

No one but herself. She deserved this. She had worked hard. And he was her reward? No, that wasn't right. She splashed water onto her face. She didn't know what Ryan was. Except for a fabulous lover. Was there ever any doubt about that, though? A man with lips like that had to be incredible.

She opened the bathroom door. The light streamed into the bedroom, illuminating him as he slept. She couldn't do this again. That sinking feeling in her chest told her if she did, she'd be in danger of losing her heart to him. And she couldn't allow that. Men like Ryan ate hearts like hers for breakfast.

She may have given over control to him tonight, but it wouldn't happen again. No matter how wonderful it had felt. She gathered her clothes, careful not to wake him. And left without looking back.

Ryan knew something was wrong when he woke up. The bed felt too cold. He scrambled in the darkness for something he knew was missing. The other side of the bed was cold. He glanced at the clock by the bed. It was three A.M. Laura hadn't slept here.

He sat up, his head still reeling from what had happened. His pride was eating at him, along with his conscience. He never intended to use the ice cream as an excuse to seduce her. He only meant to tease at it. She had been so willing, though.

He groaned as he remembered her reaction to his body. She had wanted him just as much as he wanted her. He'd be willing to bet his business on it. Her lips had been soft against him, her body firm. Wet. Waiting.

He growled into his pillow. Man, she had done a number on him. She hadn't even given him a chance at round two, which he swore would last longer than round one.

And worst of all, she probably thought her reaction to him was because of the ice cream. He hadn't realized tricking her the way he had would backfire on him. He knew he was feeding her *Ben & Jerry's*, but she thought it was her ice cream. She probably thought the whole night was induced by *I Scream Ice Cream*.

His whole body ached as he made his way to the bathroom. He let out a low growl when he saw her note written across the mirror. "I told you there was nothing wrong with the ice cream." Round two was definitely in order.

Chapter Eight

Laura knew when she was being played. And she was definitely being played. Her sister had called last night telling her Ryan needed her. Not two minutes after she left her house, Ryan called wanting to talk business. Something wasn't right. She had every intention of marching into Ryan's office today to ask him exactly what kind of game he was playing.

The drive over to LeJeune's wasn't very long. The factory was just on the edge of town but was still pretty close to the houses. She fought the urge to ram her car into the back of the Porsche as she drove up. Hitting the car wouldn't do any good. And to be honest, she was angrier with herself than with Ryan. After all, she had played right into his hands last night. And loved every minute of it.

She parked her car and headed up the creaky steps to the main office. The parking lot was practically deserted, confirming her suspicions that Ryan had suspended the business until he had news about the sugar substitute.

His office was easy enough to find at the end of the small corridor right by the front door. She heard him talking on the phone as she approached.

"What I'm saying is you need you get your ass back into town." She heard his heated pitch.

"You don't understand, we're about to go under. I'm busting my nuts trying to put this deal through with the ice cream company."

There was a long pause.

"No. I think it's all a bunch of bullshit, but I've gotta do whatever since you put my ass on the line." Another bout of silence. "We're about to lose everything here, Blake. No, nobody knows."

She heard him throwing a ball against the office wall. His chair creaked beneath his weight. She tried to make sense of the conversation, but she was focused on one detail. He was scamming her. Doing whatever it takes to seal the deal. And he thought he could just charm her with a little sex, and she'd lay her business deal at his feet.

"I can handle it," he finally said. "But you better get your ass back in town so we can take care of the other details. I can only do so much by myself."

His tone relaxed now. "Fine. Yeah. I'll tell Laura you said hi."

At the mention of her name, she turned on her heels. She wouldn't let him continue this game he was playing. She wanted no part of it. She didn't expect him to step out of his office while she was making her getaway.

"Laura," he called from behind her.

She kept walking, determined to keep her head up. Determined to walk away from Ryan LeJeune and never look back.

"Laura, wait."

"What do you want?" She didn't dare turn around.

"I want to talk to you."

"Well, I don't want to talk to you."

She pulled away when his hand closed over her arm.

"Then why are you here?"

"I'm here to tell you we don't have a deal."

"What do you mean?"

"I mean our deal is off." Laura rubbed her arm when he released her. She hoped she sounded serious, hoped her eyes weren't betraying her, in spite of the tears that were building.

He folded his arms across his chest and stood there, probably trying to think of something to say. "Just like that," he started. "You got what you want and now you decide to end the deal."

"I got what *I* wanted?" She couldn't believe him.

"Yeah, you. A night with one of the legendary LeJeunes."

"You really are full of yourself. You think all this was to get you into bed?"

"Wasn't it?"

"You're the one who proposed sex for sugar in the first place."

"And you're the one who couldn't resist."

"You're out of your mind."

"Yeah, I am. I'm pretty desperate, too. And that makes me a little bit dangerous."

"Well, I think you're a little bit full of shit. I want to know what the hell is going on here."

"I don't know what's going on here." It was probably the first honest thing he'd ever said to her, but it didn't answer all her questions. She still wanted to know who he was talking to and what exactly he was planning to do to save his company.

"Who was on the phone?" She narrowed her eyes at him, her tone serious. She needed to get to the bottom of this deception. Maybe then she could figure out why being near him did nothing but stir up a serious desire to throw him against the wall and run her tongue all over his body. Even if she was mad at him.

"Blake." He let out a long sigh, his frustration obvious to her.

"So I take it you found him."

"Yeah. I found him. He wasn't really lost, just hiding."

"Then I think you should explain what the hell it is you two are planning."

"There's no plan, Laura. That's just it. Maybe I had one, and then I met you. And well, shit, everything is so mixed up now. I'm on the verge of losing my company. We got an offer this morning. I'm going to have to sell."

His words hit her hard. That sinking feeling in her chest only spread through to her arms and made her feel weak all over. He couldn't sell. Not when he'd worked so hard. She had her doubts about the sugar, though. Ryan had put the whole thing together by accident. He didn't really know a lot about the chemistry involved. He was more of a by-the-seat-of-your-pants kind of guy. And she was afraid the chemical would break down. More than afraid. She had a nagging feeling.

"I'll buy you out," she said before she could stop herself.

"Thanks, but I'll fight my own battles."

"This is about your ego again, isn't it?"

"What ego?"

"You know what ego. The one that won't allow you to let me help. Come on, Ryan, you're willing to sell me your sugar. Sell me the company."

"And what? Work for you?" The tone of his voice cut through her, making her wish she'd never suggested such a ludicrous idea.

"It's a thought." Though one she hadn't had until about ten seconds ago. He was right. It would never work. "Forget I said anything."

"Done. I'll figure a way out of this."

"Without my help, huh? I thought you and I...never mind. Good luck with whatever it is you plan to do."

She turned to walk away, this time determined to make it out of the building without making a complete fool of herself. She was falling for the guy. And that was the last thing she needed. Especially if he couldn't accept her help. What was it with men anyway? She made it two steps before he caught up with her.

He spun her around, his hand gripping her arm again, but this time there was a spark of something in his eyes that hadn't been there before. "Don't go."

"Please, don't start with me."

"I have to. I don't understand any of this, but I know I want you near me." He looked dangerous again as he lowered his head to hers. But the danger was completely of the carnal variety, making her head spin a little before his lips made contact with hers.

He completely caught her off guard with the soft invitation of his lips. It belied everything he said to her. It made her wonder if he felt something for her, too. The softness only lasted for a second, as if he'd had time to reconsider. Then, he took her hair into his hands and pulled her backward into his office, his lips still claiming hers, this time with brutal force.

Her impending tears and self-doubt were gone now, replaced with liquid fuel. She was on the edge again. All it would take to send her over would be one more move, one more advance.

He spun her around as he kicked the door closed. She gasped at the roughness he used to push her back against the desk. This wasn't a soft experience. There was nothing playful in the way he moved toward her again. This time, he took her throat into his hand and pulled her head toward him again, nipping at her lips before taking them again.

"I want you on my desk."

He lifted her onto the side of the desk before she could protest or pull down her dress, which had ridden up. Before she could do anything but oblige him whatever he wanted.

"Now, lie back, Laura. I'm going to show you exactly why you need me."

She wanted to protest. Wanted to tell him to go to hell. But no one had ever commanded her in this way before. For some reason, it seemed to be exactly what she needed. She needed someone to take control. He had started the game last night with the bondage. Today, it was different.

She gave in to the wolf-like tone of his voice and reclined back on the top of his desk. She kept her head raised, holding his eyes with hers. "What do you want from me, Ryan?"

"I want to fuck the hell out of you. But first, I'm gonna make you come all over my desk. And then I'm gonna lick it from your thighs. And then, I'm gonna make you scream out my name."

Her breath caught in her throat at his admission. This Ryan was different from the one she loved last night. This one was everything he'd said. He was desperate and dangerous. And he was making her wetter than she'd ever been.

He pulled her to the edge of the desk and slid her panties down her thighs. His hands were cold against her flesh, as if he'd been eating ice cream again. She caught a glimpse of the trashcan. Her fudge ripple container lay in there along with a heap of papers.

That was the last thought she had before his tongue started making its way up her thigh.

"I thought about you today," he crooned against her skin. "I thought about fucking you again. About having you come here and taking you just like this."

She shivered at his words. No one had ever spoken so boldly to her before.

"But I want to do something to you first."

He brought his mouth down to her pussy and licked, then sucked. Then bit. She shivered and clung to the sides of the desk. The hard edge cut into her skin, and the sensation only heightened what he was doing to her.

"You know what I want to do?"

She nodded.

"Tell me." He continued to lick, making it hard for her to think. "I'll stop if you don't tell me," he warned.

"You want to fuck me."

213

"More than that." He roughly shoved a finger into her, slid it back out and replaced it with two.

"You want to…" she couldn't think. What had he said?

"Tell me, Laura, tell me what I want to do to you."

"I don't know," she confessed, feeling the tears building up in her eyes again.

"Yes, you do. I want to make you come so hard you'll never forget it. Are you gonna come for me?"

"*Yes!*" she screamed as the waves approached. She clung to the desk, shaking her head back and forth, feeling the tears slip down her cheeks. She had never felt anything like the orgasm that ripped through her body. Never.

"That's it," he coaxed. "Be a good girl."

She whimpered and finally collapsed on the desk. She moaned when he pulled his fingers out.

"Taste yourself, Laura," he rubbed his fingers along her bottom lip. "You taste better than ice cream."

"I want you," she moaned.

"Not yet. I'm not through with you."

He moved away from her. She raised up and let her eyes follow him to the refrigerator. "What are you doing?"

"Giving you a little taste of your own medicine," he grinned.

She gasped when he pulled the fudge pops from the freezer. "What are you doing with *that*?"

"I want you to show me what you like. What you want me to do," he shrugged, as if he had just said something perfectly natural.

"What do you mean?" She sat up completely now, still a little unsure of his meaning.

"I want you to take this," he placed the fudge pop in her hand, "and make it melt."

He was insane, having her on the edge, knowing all she wanted was to have him inside of her. She eyed the chocolate stick. It wasn't one of hers.

"Well?"

"Well what?" she shot back, still not sure if she wanted to go along with this.

"Either you do it yourself or I leave you here, just like this. Without the one thing you and I both know you want."

"I don't want you," she lied.

"Yes, you do." He reached down and ran his finger along her pussy. "If you didn't, you wouldn't be so wet. Now, are you gonna make it melt?"

He stood back, arms folded, challenging her. She hadn't come here for this, but damn it, she couldn't stop herself. She couldn't think she wanted him so badly. And right now, she didn't really care if he was using her or if she was using him. None of it mattered.

"You're starting to drip," he nodded toward the fudge pop.

She held his eyes as she took the fudge pop into her mouth, catching the excess. He groaned and shifted, the outline of his cock evident against his jeans. He was hard. For her. And she had all the power.

Laura pulled her dress over her head, holding the fudge pop in her mouth as she worked. He wanted a show. She could give him a show. She removed the fudge pop and ran it down the front of her chest, just along the edges of her bra. He groaned again, not taking his eyes from her.

She used one hand to undo the front clasp on her bra and let her breasts spring forward. Having him watch her was becoming more and more liberating. She'd never felt this kind of freedom before. She ran the fudge pop down to one nipple and then to the other, delighting in the chill on her breasts and the way her nipples immediately hardened in reaction.

Ryan's eyes clouded over as he stood over her, just inches away. She could practically feel the heat radiating from his body. Still, he didn't touch her. He just stood there, his hands on either side of her. Waiting.

Laura moved back on the desk, thankful for the desk's large size. She spread her legs and placed her feet on the desk, raising herself up to his level. He leaned down so his breath covered her, teasing her, daring her.

She slowly brushed the fudge pop down her body, running it along her clit. It instantly hardened. Chills broke out at the intense sensation. Without taking a second to rethink it, she slid the fudge pop into her pussy and let out a scream. God, this thing was cold!

"You like that?"

"Do you?" she managed to find her voice.

"Yeah. You look incredible. Beautiful." He ran a hand down her thigh.

Beautiful. She felt it, too.

"You're melting," he smiled.

"Mmmmm…" was her only answer. Slowly, she began pulling the popsicle out of her pussy. When it was almost out, she shoved it back in, gasping again, feeling the chocolate drip out of her and onto the desk. She did it again and again, each time with increased intensity.

"Make yourself come, Laura," he coaxed.

She did. She moved her hand in and out, back and forth, swirling in circles. Her free hand reached down to tease her clit. When she found the right intensity, she lay there, fucking herself with the fudge pop, his breath covering her, both hands moving freely. When she came, the intensity ravaged her body, making every nerve ending stand on edge. Everything about giving up control to Ryan made her feel more alive than she ever had before. Her heart raced and her breath came in short spurts while her head reeled from the intensity of what had just happened to her. She didn't have time to recover from the sensations before he pulled the stick out of her pussy and rammed his cock deep into her.

"God, Laura," was all he said as he moved. He held onto her knees, pounding frantically, ignoring her nails digging into the flesh of his arm. His dick ached. He had never felt anything like this.

Physically, this was the best sex he'd ever had. Never had he been with a woman so eager to please or one that his body so quickly responded to. She made him hard just by being around him. Something about the way her eyes always seemed to look deep into him both teased him and made him want to please her. That's what made her different. With Laura, he wanted to make her come, wanted to make her scream out his name.

Emotionally, she scared the hell out of him, which was something he didn't want to think about. He had never shared such an intimate moment with another woman before. Sure, he'd had his share of women. Kinky women. But none this vulnerable.

His balls slapped against her ass, and he became caught up in the frenzied rhythm. The tops of his thighs made hard contact with the edge of the desk as her body moved backward from the frantic motions. He pulled her into him again, watching her breasts jiggle with his every stroke.

Her hands gripped the edges of the desk as she lay open for him, letting him take her, allowing him to drive into her over and over again. He watched her face twist into a look that resembled agony but one that he knew to be sheer pleasure. It was amazing to bring a woman like her to the edge. Every intense stroke gained a new contortion of her features. Her lips spread into a smile, then pressed together into a tight line. Her eyes opened, wild and wide and then squeezed shut again, as if looking up at him were too much for her. The force of his movements pushed her breath out of her body in a way so that her panting sounds and moans only added to his already intense need.

When she came, she opened her eyes, holding him with her intense stare. He remembered hearing once that looking deep into someone's eyes and holding the gaze could be one of the most intense emotional encounters ever. Right now, it damn near rocked his world. What sent him over the edge was not only the way she looked at him but the way she clung to him, pressing her breasts against him, pulling him down on top of her, crushing herself beneath his body.

Her walls tightened around him like a fist, milking him, forcing him to the edge, coaxing him to come inside and coat her walls with his juice. His balls reacted, tensing a second before his hot liquid shot from his body and into her. Her insides, once cold from the ice cream, were now hot, searing him, controlling his desperate need to crawl inside of her and never return. He collapsed on top of her, his breathing erratic. He didn't want to move. He wasn't sure how to move off of someone who had just changed his life.

Chapter Nine

The last thing Laura wanted to do was go on a date with Ryan. She barely managed to escape their last few encounters intact. A night alone with him was sure to do her in. Especially since she shared something so intimate with him. She wasn't sure how to face him after their last ice cream encounter. And she still didn't know what had made her say yes to the date. It was obviously a temporary bout of insanity.

She pushed aside dress after dress. Each one was a little too this or not enough of that. She finally settled on a yellow cotton sundress and a light denim jacket to ward off the night air, which was unusually chilly. Ryan told her to dress casually when he called earlier today.

She stepped into her sandals and did a twirl in front of the mirror. God, she would have given anything to date Ryan LeJeune in high school. It had been her secret fantasy. But girls like her didn't date guys like him. If they did, they only got their hearts broken. He had been a love 'em and leave 'em kind of guy even then.

At sixteen, Ryan towered above the rest of the guys. That wild look in his eyes became his trademark, and every girl in Oak Creek practically threw herself at him. It didn't hurt that he had his own car — a 1968 Camaro in electric blue. It also didn't hurt that he was captain of the football and track teams.

Laura had been a bookworm even then. She had dated, but never anyone as good looking or with the kind of reputation as Ryan. No, she dated nice guys from church camp or from the local university. No one who would be considered bad or dangerous by anyone's standards. No one in the same league with the man she was going out with tonight.

It was all she could do not to chew her fingernails to nubs as she waited on the front porch. She was anxious, but she didn't want to admit it. The plan was to wait out here until she could see his headlights coming down the street. Then she would hightail it into the house and keep him waiting. She hoped.

She sat on the porch, rocking back and forth in the old swing, letting the night air carry her hair wherever it wanted. She liked nights like this. They usually didn't come until October. Thanks to a spree of evening thunderstorms the last few days, the nights were cool and breezy. And slightly damp.

She pulled her jacket around her and watched as the lightning lit up the sky in the distance. The moon shone overhead, but the sky was cloudy further out, threatening another storm. She shivered a little. There was something about storms that both frightened her and made her want to find someone to cuddle up to.

She eyed the distant lightning again. There was a good chance the storm wouldn't hit Oak Creek tonight. They often blew around the area. She listened for the frogs to see if they were singing tonight. That usually meant rain. All she could hear was the other sounds of the night. No frogs.

She didn't hear the footfalls coming from the side of the house, either.

"Waiting for someone?"

Her heart leapt into her throat. Where had he come from? "No one in particular," she shot back without turning around.

"It's a good thing I came by then. Or you'd be out here by yourself." She heard Ryan step onto the landing and then jump over the porch railing. "These are for you," he held out a small bouquet of flowers from his garden.

Laura eyed the mixture of roses, daisies and mums. It wasn't exactly the most attractive blend she'd ever seen, but the look on his face made her flush. "Thanks," she took them, avoiding his fingers.

"So, were you waiting for someone?" The swing creaked when he sat down next to her.

"I have a date tonight." She held the flowers to her nose. The roses were sweet, but the mums smelled awful. She wrinkled her nose.

"Lucky guy," Ryan nudged her with his shoulder. "So, are you ready?"

"Do I look ready?"

"You don't want me to answer that, do you? I'd tell you what you look ready for."

"Then don't answer it," she stood and walked to the front door. "I'm going to put these in water," she announced.

"Suit yourself."

She walked into the house, aware of his eyes on her as she closed the door. Finding a vase right now was going to be all but impossible. She was too much on edge, so she settled for a drinking glass, filled it with water, and placed the flowers in there. Taking one last, deep breath, she stepped back into the hallway, grabbed her purse and then met him out on the porch. "Okay. I'm ready now. Where's your car?" she asked, looking around.

"Down the street. I thought this would be more like high school. You know, I could sneak up to your window and coax you out into the darkness to do all kinds of obscene things," he winked.

"Don't bet on it."

"Don't tell me you never snuck out?"

"No, I didn't." They walked down the porch steps together, him slowing his pace for her.

"I don't doubt that. From what I hear, you didn't do much wrong back then."

"Are you making fun of me?"

"Nope. Just telling it like I heard it."

He slipped his hand into hers as they walked and tried to find a way to tell her she had changed him. In the past week, he had managed to renegotiate parts of his deal with her. The ice cream using his sugar byproduct still wasn't ready yet. Tomorrow would be the do or die day. That was the reason why he wanted to get things out on the table tonight. He wanted her to know that what was going on had nothing to do with their business arrangement.

"It looks like rain," he said, mentally kicking himself for the generic reference.

"Yeah. You know Isis is brewing out there in the Gulf."

"Yeah." He opened the car door for her. "So, where do you want to go tonight?"

"You're the one in charge," she smiled. "I assumed you had a plan."

"You wanna just call it a night and go back to my place?" he shot her a grin and then winked at her.

"No. I want romance," she mocked.

"Oh, I see. A regular ol' roll in the hay ain't enough?"

"I have never had a roll in the hay," she teased.

"Lucky for you, I have a barn behind my house."

"Not a chance. I haven't had dinner yet."

"Fine. Romance," he shrugged and then turned the key in the ignition. The Porsche purred as it usually did, reminding him of his own engine. Just looking at her in a dress like that made him want nothing more than to take it off of her.

Laura had a plan for tonight. After what he put her through the other day, she knew the only way to get even with him was to, well, get even with him. She'd had sex before, but she had never experienced loss of control and then rebirth of control in a matter of five minutes. Ryan had given her that. He had managed to do something ice cream couldn't do. And that disturbed her on so many levels.

She could be gutsy and bold. She could make him squirm in his seat. She could make him want her, surrender control to her. She smiled as she went over everything in her head again.

"You're quiet," he commented as he pulled the Porsche into the parking lot.

"Just thinking," she mused, not meeting his eyes as she spoke.

"Oh?" She could hear the smile in his voice.

"Yeah. You gonna tell me your little secret? The one you were talking about on the phone the other day?"

"The one that had you so pissed off?" There was no mistaking his tone. He wanted to drop the subject.

"That would be the one."

"It isn't important. Just know it's not as bad as it sounded. And trust me." The last was thrown in for good measure, she was sure. After their last encounter, there should be no question of trust between them. They had done more than have sex. They had bared their souls to one another in his office.

"Fine," she shrugged. "Let's eat."

He opened the door for her and led her into the pizza joint. It was really a full scale Italian restaurant with authentic food, but everyone in town called it a pizza joint. He led her through the door, his hand on the small of her back the whole time.

He's staking his claim, she thought when she watched him shake hands with the host. He requested an out of the way booth and was, of course, obliged.

Laura was thankful he'd wanted something quiet. Otherwise, her plan would have never worked. She let him lead her to the booth, and then she slipped in first.

The booth was all the way in the back of the place and was lit by a small chandelier hanging above it. It was a place for quiet dates, a place where people with kids only came if the kids were at home.

She felt her dress rise up as she moved across the leather seat. The fabric was cold against her bare ass. She'd foregone underwear tonight in favor of revenge. She couldn't wait to see the look on Ryan's face when he realized she was open, exposed beneath the cotton material of her dress.

He ordered wine for them while she concentrated on the sensations flowing through her body. She ached for him to touch her. In a matter of two days, he had turned her into a sex fiend. Just the thought of having his cock in her was enough to make her pussy quiver with anticipation.

She tried to concentrate on the menu as she sat there, tensing and relaxing her muscles. She could make herself come this way if she thought about it long enough, concentrated enough. Imagined him there. A shudder ran through her body.

"You okay tonight?" he brushed his shoulder against hers.

"I'm fine." She was thankful he had slid in behind her. It was as if he were playing right into her plan tonight. Now we'll see who's in control here, she thought.

"What are you in the mood for?"

She licked her lips when she looked up at him. He should see the answer written right there. He smiled. He knew exactly what was on her mind. "I don't know," she shrugged, causing the smile to tease up even further on his lips.

"I know what I want. They don't serve it here, though," his voice was hoarse, low. It sent another shiver through her. She shifted again on the leather seat.

"Maybe they will tonight." She shrugged again and looked away, pretending not to be interested.

"You know something I don't?"

"No. Just a guess."

Ryan's breath caught in his throat when she reached out to stroke his thigh. They were sitting practically shoulder to shoulder, but when she initiated the contact, it sent his mind reeling. He let out a low, slow growl. If she wasn't careful, he was likely to do a little exploring of his own.

"What do you want to eat?" She emphasized the last words even as she continued to look at the menu. And creep her fingers up his thigh. When she rested her hand against his crotch, he nearly jumped out of the booth.

"You," he growled against her ear.

"Mmmm. That can be arranged."

Without batting an eye, she raised up the edge of her dress, exposing the fact that she was bare beneath. His heart stopped when she put a hand under her dress and began touching herself. His dick reacted immediately.

"How's this?" She took a wet finger and pressed it against his lips. "Is that what you wanted?" She batted her eyes innocently, but the motion was almost his undoing.

He took her finger deep into his mouth. "You're an evil woman," he licked at her fingertips then trailed his lips down to her wrist.

"You want some more?"

He nodded. This time, she moved the hem back, exposing to him her freshly shaved mound. She spread her legs wide so they pushed up against him on one side and the wall on the other. Then she moved down in her seat a little, giving him a perfect view of her swollen lips.

He'd never been with a woman who'd shaved her mound before, making the thought of sex with her later tonight one that he couldn't get out of his head. Just thinking of the feel of flesh against flesh was almost enough to make him come sitting right here staring at her.

When she shoved two fingers into her wet slit, he licked his lips. Eating her tonight was going to be top priority. He wondered how the smooth flesh would feel in his mouth, between his teeth.

This time, he took his time working at her fingers. He held them with his left hand while he let his right hand explore up her thigh. When he was almost there, seeking out her heat, she stopped him.

"You don't get to play," she scolded.

He let out an exasperated breath. This woman was going to be the death of him. Still, he took her fingers each time she dipped them into her sweetness, growing harder with each motion. She tasted like heaven. She was sweet, salty, sugary. He'd like to roll her in sugar and fuck the hell out of her. Aim for the wettest spot.

"Laura," he groaned. "I'm so hard."

"I can see that," she teased before she shifted around in the booth. She turned so that she was now sideways. Facing him. Then she leaned against the hard brick wall. The edge of her dress was well above her hips now. If the waiter were to come back, he'd get a hell of a show.

With one leg propped on the bench and one spread way out resting on the opposite bench, she began to rub her clit. He could see everything. She even raised herself up a little, letting him see her juices as they flowed out, coating her pussy.

"You know what I need?" she cooed.

"What do you need, baby?"

"I need something inside me."

God, she was bold. Sweet heaven, he was going to come sitting here watching her please herself in the restaurant.

"What do you want?" he managed between the short bursts of breath. He'd give her anything right now. All she had to do was tell him her wish and he'd give it to her and slide it up her pussy.

"Find something." Her eyes held a challenge for him. He was onto her game. She was trying to make him lose control. And hell if it wasn't working! He hadn't been this worked up since high school. He was enveloped by the sweet smell of her sweat and pussy.

The waiter came toward them now with the food. Rather than shifting like he thought she would, she simply pulled her dress back down, looking as casually as if she hadn't just been sitting there with her fingers in her cunt.

As soon as the waiter lay down the plates of food, Ryan knew exactly what he wanted to put inside of her. "Do you have a dessert menu I could see?"

The waiter eyed him warily before producing a menu. "You want to order dessert now?"

"Yeah. I thought it would be nice to go ahead and get it now," he shrugged as casually as he could. "Fruit salad."

"Yes, Sir," the waiter nodded.

Ryan learned how to eat left-handed. After the fruit salad was placed in front of him, he raised the edge of Laura's dress. Without looking, he began placing the grapes inside of her one by one. She gasped, her eyes searching his. She obviously hadn't expected this.

After the grapes were in place, Ryan started pushing the cherries in. One by one, he placed them into her opening and then let them pop on the other side. He shoved a finger in to make more room. He planned to fill her up and then slowly take each piece out when they got back home.

She wiggled in her seat with each touch. She was loving this. Her breath was ragged, tense. She was becoming wetter with each piece of fruit he shoved inside of her. And his dick was harder than it had ever been.

"I think when we get back home, I'm going to fuck you while you're still full," he commented, not looking at her as he said it. To the casual observer, they looked just like a couple having dinner. No one would suspect he was stuffing her pussy with his own special blend of dessert.

"Ryan," her hand gripped his shirt, squeezing into the flesh on his arm. "You're gonna make me come," she warned.

"No. Not here." He moved his hand. "Now, be a good girl and finish your dinner. And we'll go home for dessert."

Laura was thankful she had practiced her Kegel exercises. God, she had been so afraid the fruit would pop right out of her on the way to the car. The pressure of being filled so completely was driving her insane. It felt as if his hand were inside her, moving, pulsing, cold, hot. God, it was all she could do to walk.

She started the night wanting to control him. Wanting to be the one to make him lose it. And he had turned the tables and she was once again at his mercy. God, but she loved it! She loved the way he took control of her body. She loved the way he made her feel. *She loved.* Oh, God.

"Come here, Laura," he coaxed her into the house. "I'm ready for my dessert now."

Her heart sank. She loved him. This big, beautiful, sexual animal. She met him on the sofa and let him lay her down. His kiss was sweet, soft. It belied the completely carnal encounter they had shared in the restaurant. It also belied what was coming next.

"I'm going to eat you," he breathed against her lips. "Are you gonna let me?"

She nodded her head wildly. "Yes, I'll let you." Her heart pounded. Her pussy ached, begging for release. She hadn't come in the restaurant. Every time she had gotten close, he had stopped her. Right now, he pressed against her, the rough cotton of his jeans torturing her bare flesh.

"Don't move." He warned, pushing his cock against her one last time before moving away from her. It wasn't until he came back, spoon in hand, that she understood the extent to which he planned on eating.

The spoon was cold, as if it had been frozen. When he dipped it into her body, she felt fire sweep through her. He wiggled it around, coaxing out a come-covered grape. He popped it into his mouth, licking his lips when it disappeared.

"Incredible," he whispered, placing a kiss on her pussy before dipping his head down for another treat.

She pulled at his hair when he teased her with his chin. She was lost. She loved him; she craved him. She was out of her mind. All thought and reason had stopped. All she had was sensation.

He pulled a few more pieces of the fruit from her, teasing her with it, rubbing it along her lips before pushing it into her mouth. She could taste herself on it. God, it was the most sensual experience. The grape was warm, almost hot, and covered with a sauce even an ice cream goddess couldn't conjure without a man.

"I'm gonna leave some of it in you," he warned as he moved above her, placing himself at her opening.

"No, you can't." Could he?

"Yes, I can. I'll be careful, I promise. Trust me."

Trust him. Yes, she would trust him with her life. He slowly slipped into her, causing the remaining fruit to slide around. She was too full. God, so full she thought she wouldn't be able to take it when he fully entered her, pressing the fruit against her cervix. Carefully, he slid out all the way to the tip before easing back into her.

Their lovemaking was slow, the fruit slipping and sliding and rolling against her insides as he pulled away from her only to fill her again. Her juices ran out, coating her anus, making the cool air tease her skin.

She ran her hands up and down his chest, looking into his amazing blue eyes as he continued to take her. She would memorize this moment. Tomorrow, they may not have a business deal, may have no need for one another. But tonight, he was hers. And she loved him with everything she had.

Ryan wanted to take her with force, make her love him, make her feel every emotion that was ravaging his body as he moved so slowly it was killing him.

"I need you," he whispered against her ear.

"You've got me."

"No. I need more of you."

He pulled out of her and took the rest of the fruit from her body, flinging it to the side.

"How do you want me then? Do you want me on my knees sucking you or do you want me on my back, spread open for you? Or I could sit on the edge of the bed, bring it up to your face. Or I could bend over, ass in the air and let you lick me from behind." She twisted her nipples with her fingers as she spoke, causing the raspberry tips to harden and darken. "It's your choice."

He rolled her onto her stomach. "I want to take you from behind." In one motion, he had her in front of him, ass high in the air, her sweet little cunt glistening with the cream he had on his dick. She lowered her back and rested her head against the bed. He watched as her hands moved around to her ass, spreading her lips wide for him.

"Want me to hold it open for you?"

He watched as she slid in a finger from each hand, holding herself open even wider. Dropping to his knees, he buried his face into the folds she held open for him. Her sweet honey poured out as soon as he began to suck. He darted his tongue in and out, licking her fingers, which were still buried inside of her, holding her wide open for him.

He ran his face along her wet warmth, reveling in the feel of her juices on his nose, his chin, his tongue. She bucked against him, fucking him as he rubbed with a greater intensity.

"You want to fuck me, don't you?"

Yes, he wanted to fuck her! Wanted to bury himself up to his balls inside of her. Wanted to feel those tight muscles fist around him. He slid three fingers into her, reveling at how tight she was even though she now had both her hands and his inside of her. She squirmed against him.

"Do me like that and I'll suck you," she coaxed.

"Move your hands."

She took her hands out of her pussy and it immediately closed around him, tightening back as if she were a virgin. He felt her hand reach down to stroke her clit while she reached back with the other and grabbed his cock. She began stroking him as his hand moved in and out of her. Her juices spilled out around his fingers, her cream coating them, filling the air with her woman scent. Her cunt sang to him as he continued to fuck her with his fingers.

"I want to suck you." She pulled away from him in spite of the tight hold he had on her ass.

"Roll over," he commanded.

She did. But instead of lying flat on her back like he wanted, legs spread wide, she kneeled in front of him. "You're not in charge anymore."

He opened his mouth to protest, but when her angel tongue lapped the pearls off his dick, he lost all train of thought. She opened her mouth wide, taking him all the way in. Her hand, still wet from her juices, grabbed his balls and gave them a squeeze.

Now, her mouth and hand moved together up and down his shaft. It was almost like fucking two women at once, the way she completely covered him, leaving no piece of flesh untouched at any given moment.

Her lovely head moved back and forth, shaking her hair into her face as she coaxed him toward orgasm. He braced himself on her shoulders as his balls tightened.

The growl that ripped through his body echoed the intensity of his come shooting against the roof of her mouth then sliding down her throat. She continued to milk him, bringing him to his knees as the effects of their love play still raged through his body. When she was satisfied, she kissed his purple tip and then looked up him with a satisfied smile.

"Now, I need you to do something for me."

"Anything," he said breathlessly.

"Fuck me."

He rolled her back onto her stomach. "Raise your ass for me."

She did as he commanded. He swore her pussy winked at him when he positioned himself behind her, his hands gripping her ass. His dick was already hard in spite of his orgasm, in spite of the soreness from fucking her while she was filled with fruit. He pressed it against her opening and then filled her to the hilt, his balls resting against her swollen clit where her fingers were working frantically to bring her to release.

He slapped them against her hand, against her soft, smooth flesh while he fucked her. Her ass was begging to be filled, teasing him, the sweet rosette calling out to his fingers. He licked one finger and then positioned it at her tiny opening. She gasped when it entered her ass. Her entire back went rigid as he pressed it further in. God, she was tight around him!

When she relaxed, she began to buck against him, letting him take her pussy, her ass with the wild abandon he had wanted all night. She screamed, clawed at the sheets, twisted her ass and pussy and still he continued to fuck her. They came quickly, furiously. Two bodies shuddering in the moonlight, desperate for one another. Desperate for the feelings they hoped didn't disappear in the morning.

Ryan shuddered and held onto her as the last of his cream pulsed into her, coating her insides. When she collapsed against the bed, he cradled her in his arms and swore he'd never let her go.

Chapter Ten

Laura smiled as she dipped her finger into the banana split ice cream. She had waited all week for this. She brought her finger to her lips, trying not to think about the man who inspired this particular blend.

She closed her eyes as the ice cream hit her tongue. She gave it a second before spitting it in the sink. "Yuck!" Bitter banana was not an appealing taste. She opened the freezer and pulled out the other test batches she had used Ryan's sugar in. She peeled the lids off the remaining containers, dipping a spoon into each one and giving them all a taste. The second one was even worse, causing her to spit the mouthful of ice cream into a napkin. Her stomach sank. The ice cream didn't support whatever it was Ryan had done to the sugar. And she had to break the news to him, knowing it would damn near destroy him.

She stood there staring at the containers, her arms braced by the countertop. How was she going to tell him that this business arrangement of theirs wouldn't work?

Her heart sank. Ryan's entire future rested on his sugar substitute. He probably didn't even know it wouldn't hold up to mass production. What could he have possibly made with it?

She remembered the iced tea. It had been great there. But then again, it had only been in the mixture for a few minutes before they drank it. Maybe he could make cotton candy with it. That would be a novel idea.

She sighed. She knew he would be here any minute. He had been waiting on the results of the ice cream as eagerly as she had. Laura didn't think she could look him in the eyes and tell him his product hadn't worked.

"Laura," Amanda was on the intercom.

"Yeah, I'm here."

"Ryan is here."

"Okay. Can you let him in?"

"Sure."

Great. She took another deep breath. She had to tell him it didn't work. She braced herself, knowing that when the door opened, he would be standing there.

Ryan had been anxiously awaiting today for several reasons. The ice cream was really just an excuse to see Laura again. He hadn't been able to sleep last night with her body pressed against his. Hadn't been able to do much except focus on what had happened between them.

He was ready to see her again when Amanda led her down the hallway to the lab. When his eyes met hers, he realized he wasn't prepared for the emotions that hit him at once.

"Ryan," she looked past him to Amanda and nodded her head. Amanda smiled and left him standing there.

"Laura, you look incredible," he smiled, running his gaze up and down her jean-clad body. Her dark stare was a surprise to him. He had expected to see a tiny light in her eyes or something. Her face was practically blank.

"Ryan, I need to talk to you."

"I need to talk to you, too." This was encouraging. Sort of. She offered him one of the barstools and he sat down.

"Me first," she lowered her eyes. "Ryan, the sugar didn't work."

"What do you mean it didn't work?"

"I mean it didn't work. It broke down when it mixed with my chemicals."

"Then there's something wrong with your mixtures. Maybe you measured wrong."

"I didn't measure wrong."

"Let me see." He grabbed the container sitting in front of her and tasted it. What the hell was this stuff? "It's bitter."

"I know."

"What did you put in it?"

"The same as I always do. Here, try this one," she slid another container toward him. He scooped it up and took a bite. He tested all the samples she had, but they were all the same.

"I'm sorry," she shrugged.

"Sorry." He raked his fingers through his curly hair then narrowed his eyes at her. "Was this part of the plan?"

"What plan?"

He stalked across the room toward her, his eyes burning into her. "To get a hold of my product, my business." He gripped her arms firmly with his hands, causing her to shudder against him.

"I didn't do anything different," she insisted as she pulled away from him. He released her, trying to get a grip, trying to think.

"I think you did. Or maybe you did something wrong."

"Like what?"

"I don't know." He turned to walk away, but she stopped him, pulling him around to face her.

"Oh, no, buddy. You tell me what you think I'm doing. Do you think I'm sabotaging you?"

"I don't know," he sank down onto the barstool as he spoke. He really didn't know what he thought she was doing. All he knew was he was angry and she was there, an easy target, somebody to lash out at. He looked down at his hands then back up at her. "Who knows? I don't know how women think," he shrugged.

"I think you're being a big baby."

"Oh really?" he folded his arms.

"Yeah, really. Your background is in business, not in chemistry. How were you to know how this would react?"

"I tested it. What? You think I just decided one day that I had the formula?"

"No, I..."

"I put a lot of work into this. And if it doesn't work in your product, then I can't help it."

"What did you test it in?"

"Nothing you would understand," he stood, raked a hand through his hair. He hated himself right now. Hated that he was directing all this at her. Hated that the last thing he wanted to do was argue about sugar. But what he really despised was the fact that his entire future just crashed and burned right before his eyes.

"I have no doubt about that."

"Since you and I have no more to discuss, I'll see you around." He turned to walk away and then stopped at the door. He took the formula from his pocket, ripped it in half and threw it into the trashcan. Good riddance. He'd find another way out.

"We have a hell of a lot more to discuss." She leapt to her feet, hands on hips, but he wasn't ready to face down the challenge in her face.

She wasn't going to make this easy. What could they possibly have to discuss? He had no future, no future! Didn't she understand that? Didn't she get it? Everything he had was mixed up in that God-awful ice cream. "Laura, I can't." He softened his voice, but it didn't help the situation any. Her eyes were still focused on him, demanding something he just couldn't give her.

"Can't what?"

"Can't do this. Any of it." Even if all he wanted to do was fall into her arms and let her love away the pain.

Ryan stomped out of the lab. He would have kicked the Porsche when he got to it, but it was his only insurance policy. And he couldn't get much out of it. Maybe a hundred thousand or so. It was a vintage car, after all.

He turned the key in the ignition and listened to the engine purr. Blake had good taste in cars if nothing else. He took in a deep breath. He had to call his brother and tell him he had no choice but to sell the business.

He pulled the car out of the parking lot, trying not to think about Laura. His stomach hurt. It was the kind of dull ache he got when he had done something really bad. He remembered getting it regularly as a kid. It had been a while since he'd felt it as an adult. Seeing the look on her face when he accused her of screwing around with his formula was enough to do it to him, though. He hurt her today and he hadn't even been man enough to apologize.

That thought alone made his heart sink. Something had happened between them that he wasn't quite ready to put a name on. It was something he remembered only from dreams and wishes. Nothing he had ever truly experienced.

He loved her. He had to face it. Somewhere in the night, he swore he even whispered it to her. He loved her. God, he was an idiot!

* * * * *

A week later, Cate stood in front of Laura, hands on hips, whining, trying to convince Laura to go to the annual fireworks display that she had no interest in whatsoever. What she wanted to do was crawl back in bed and forget the fact that she'd neither seen nor heard from Ryan since he stormed out of her lab.

"Come on, Laura."

"I'm not up to it." Laura stood in the doorway, arms folded, her face a mask of determination. She wasn't leaving the house today.

"It'll be fun," Cate crooned.

"I'm not interested in fun."

"Then maybe you could tell me why. You know, cousin to cousin?"

"There's nothing to tell. Will you leave me alone already?" a smile tugged at the corners of her lips. Cate rolled her eyes.

"You want to do it. It'll be fun," she coaxed again.

"You said that already."

"Tell me, have you ever been to the fireworks display?"

"No, I haven't."

"It's for a good cause." Cate knew her cousin's weaknesses. Laura was a sucker for a good cause.

"And what's that, to help you hook up with Dusty Bayonne?"

"No. But I promise it's a good cause. And who knows, maybe Dusty will be there, too."

"I knew he had something to do with it." Cate's crush on Dusty was practically legendary. Everyone knew about it except Mr. Obvious, who seemed to have missed the fact.

"Come on. Robin and Karen are going, too. We'll meet them there. It'll be fun. A girl's night out. Besides, you owe us for skipping ice cream night."

At the mention of "ice cream night," Laura's face flushed.

She'd spent most of the day trying not to think about Ryan LeJeune. But she was right about one thing. Ryan wasn't a chemist. She had seen the formula, having fished it out of the trashcan. And had spent the last several days working on it in spite of how she knew he would feel about it. Her breakthrough had come two nights ago. But she had yet to tell Ryan about it, not knowing how he would react. She wanted him to thank her, to appreciate what she had done, but she was afraid he would be angry that she had done this behind his back. Memories from their first night together flooded her mind. He had done something to her that night. Transformed her. And now she knew the truth about him. He was a typical male.

"I didn't feel well," she reminded Cate, suddenly feeling her stomach twisting in a knot again. She would give anything if she could get Ryan out of her head. She hadn't heard from him since the day in her lab. And, to be honest, she missed him, which had nothing whatsoever to do with the fact she feared she was falling in love with him.

"I know. But you feel fine tonight. It'll do you good to get out."

"Are you gonna leave if I say yes?"

"Yeah, I'll leave. But I'll be back at seven to pick you up."

"Fine," she threw up her hands in frustration. "I'll go. But I'm taking my car."

"Great," Cate squealed. "It'll be so much fun."

No, it wouldn't. Laura turned back and went into her empty house. She had been so filled with hope before her entire world came crashing down. She didn't want to go to the fireworks display tonight. She didn't want to do anything but sit around and sulk.

Fireworks only made her think about things she knew wouldn't happen again. Ryan hadn't called, letting her know he obviously didn't care about her as much as she cared for him. So it had only been a week. That was practically a lifetime when her heart ached so badly and she feared she was falling in love—no, had already fallen in love with— someone who didn't love her in return. The last thing she wanted to do tonight was spend her time downtown watching lovers cuddled together watching the annual display of lights in the sky.

Fireworks had always reminded her of her favorite fantasy, one she knew would never come true. As the sparks went into the air, they always made her long for a romantic interlude on a secluded terrace with the man of her dreams.

The mystery lover always wore black. A mask covered his face, but she could still see his eyes. She closed her eyes, remembering the fantasy. He was standing beneath the moonlight, waiting, watching her approach. His black clothing blended into the night sky as she stepped out onto the terrace, carefully avoiding contact with him. Standing just inches from him, she always felt the heat radiating from his body, the intensity of his passion for her smoldering in eyes that were fixed on her bare shoulder. His red lips turned up in a smile, and he took her into his arms.

As she drew closer, she realized his eyes were blue. And his long hair wasn't straight as it had always been. It was dark and curly. It was the kind of hair made for tangling her fingers in and around and using it as leverage for a heart- pounding kiss.

She leaned against the front door. It had been a while since she'd had a fantasy like this. She tried to shake it from her mind, but her mystery lover—she could still pretend she didn't know who he was—was standing there beckoning her.

"Come closer, Laura," his Southern drawl echoed across the distance.

She shook her head, wanting to flee, but knowing she was trapped by his hypnotic eyes. "Who are you?"

"You know who I am. I am the monster you created." When he smiled, she caught a glimpse of his white teeth. The same teeth she wanted trailing tiny bites across her tender neck and traveling further down.

"I don't know you," she protested, her hand slipping up around her throat to protect it from his lips, which were slowly descending upon hers.

Laura shook herself. God, she needed to get out of here. Needed to get to work. Ryan may not be interested in saving his company thanks to the male pride standing in his way, but she didn't have that same handicap. And she knew she could fix his product if he'd only give her a chance.

She glanced at her watch, trying to ignore the growing dampness between her thighs. She could put sex out of her mind for a couple of hours, couldn't she? She had lived this long without it. It was already five o'clock. The day had slipped away after Ryan left the lab. She didn't have time to go back to the lab, work and come home and get ready for tonight.

She let out a curse and headed for the freezer, hoping she still had some cherry ice cream on hand.

* * * * *

Ryan hung up the phone. He couldn't do it, couldn't sell the company. Instead, he and Blake worked out a deal over the past week. Blake would come back into town, bring his inheritance with him and work side by side with his brother to bring the company back to where it needed to be. And Ryan would give this whole sugar thing another try. The first thing he had to do, though, was find Laura.

He was an ass, having left her the way he had. He felt like a damned fool, knowing he didn't deserve her forgiveness, but hoping to God she would see it in herself to allow him to apologize. He picked up the phone and waited for his cousin, Dusty, to answer.

"I was just about to call you," Dusty said when he picked up the phone.

"Is everything set for tonight?"

"Yeah, it's set, and you owe me big time."

"I know I do."

"So, the key will be in your hand in less than an hour. And Cate's taking care of bringing your girl there."

"She isn't my girl yet."

"Yeah, but she will be. Have faith, man. It'll work out."

Ryan sure as hell hoped it would work out. The townhouse on the river didn't come cheap. If it hadn't been for the loan from his cousin, Ryan would never have been able to afford the night of groveling he had planned. He had really screwed things with her. All it took was returning to his empty house to realize he needed Laura in a way he never needed anyone before.

"I can't figure out this damned tie," Ryan cursed as Dusty walked into the house an hour later.

Dusty laughed, "You look like you're getting married all dolled up."

"And you look like the king of the dead. When was the last time you slept? Help me," he raised his neck so Dusty could tie the bow tie.

"There. Don't say I never did anything for you," he teased. "I was out late last night. Had a late trip to New Orleans."

"You go there a lot." Ryan examined the results in the mirror. "Thanks, man. Where'd you learn how to tie a bow tie? Hey, I look pretty sharp."

"You clean up pretty good."

"So about this tie. Where'd you learn to tie one? They teach you that in aviation school?"

"I have my ways," Dusty leaned against the doorframe.

"Yeah well ways like that really get to women. You planning on seducing one anytime soon?"

"No, I'm not."

"You know Cate's got the hots for you."

"She's a kid."

Ryan noted how Dusty didn't look up at him as he spoke. "Well, you watch yourself. Those Reynolds girls have their ways."

"They sure do. If one of 'em could convince you to put on a monkey suit, I wonder what they'd do to the rest of us."

"Well you better watch out."

"Nothing to watch for." Dusty assured him.

"Cate's twenty-three. She's stable; she's got a good job, a hell of a business mind from what I've heard. And she's hot."

"She's a kid," he repeated, this time with much less zeal.

"She's two years younger than you. Open your eyes, buddy. You're gonna miss what's right in front of you."

"You're one to talk."

"I know. And I plan on doing something about it. Now, you got the keys?"

Dusty handed over the silver key chain. "You got until eleven tomorrow. And you owe me big time."

"I know, I know," he swung the keys on his finger and hoped Cate could track Laura down. This was going to be a night to remember.

Chapter Eleven

Laura folded the note, concentrating on placing a crease down the center. Ryan wanted to talk. The whole concept of meeting Cate at the fireworks had been a set up from the start. After she drove up and parked the car just on the outskirts of the downtown barricade, Cate met her, note in hand, and pointed her toward one of the exclusive riverfront townhouses, which was always occupied by the tourists who came into Oak Creek with the Christmas season. Since it was July, they were abandoned except for the one reserved for her for tonight.

I want to say I'm sorry, the note declared. Ryan apologizing? Her heart stirred at the thought, while her tears built in her eyes. She'd felt so many emotions lately, she really didn't want to get her hopes up. Maybe he was just after sex. They were good together in that department. But she needed more from him than sex. She wanted his heart.

Soft music played in the background as she stepped inside the townhouse, surprised by the candlelight that greeted her. Rose petals were strewn at the door, leading into the small living room and out of the French doors. She took in a deep breath, thankful Cate warned her to dress up tonight. Magic permeated the air, making her feel as if anything were possible. Her heart raced as she stepped out onto the terrace.

There he was, her fantasy lover, holding a glass of red wine and looking at her as if he had just lost his best friend. Good. She hoped he had suffered as much as she had. Hoped all this wasn't just an apology, but a fresh start. A delightful shiver ran up her back as he smiled at her.

He started walking toward her. Stalking. Mesmerizing. Okay, he looked pretty damned good, but the fantasy playing in her head really helped with the effect.

"Well, I'm here." She folded her arms, wanting him to work for the forgiveness.

"I see that." He held out the glass of wine.

"Did you want something?"

"Yeah, I did. First, I wanted to show you something."

"What's that?"

"I have arranged an elaborate fireworks display for you tonight." He used a mock British accent before sweeping an arm out over the edge of the terrace toward the lake.

"All by your little self?" She couldn't help but smile.

"Yeah, all by myself. Come stand near the edge."

"You aren't afraid I'll push you over?"

"I'll have to take that chance."

She took a long sip of her wine and then approached the edge of the terrace. Her eyes closed and she inhaled his scent when he moved to stand behind her and wrap his arms around her. Resting her head against his chest, she listened to his heartbeat and tried not to think about how perfect this felt.

"I'm sorry," he whispered against her bare shoulder. "Will you forgive me?" She turned and looked up into his soft eyes.

"We have to talk," she began, only to be interrupted when he lowered his mouth to hers.

She sucked in her breath, inhaling him as she clung to his arms. A shudder ran through her when his tongue burned a trail down her neck.

His teeth grazed against her flesh, instantly making her wet. She had never had an orgasm just by being touched on the neck. But this was no mere touch. If Ryan possessed fangs, he would have just stolen her life force. As it was, he caused a fierce orgasm to build.

She gasped for breath, trying to pull away from him. The sensation was too much. She didn't want to give him this much control over her. Especially after their last encounter. They needed to talk. The need to understand the extent of his apology burned inside her. She couldn't just fall into his arms and have everything be okay. Refusing to be one of those weak women who gave in to a sexy man, she reached up to push him away at the same time that his hand slid down the side of her throat and found her breast. All thoughts ceased when he slipped it inside her top, squeezing the edges of one breast and then moving in for the nipple. When his fingers found the already hardened bud, he pinched it, causing her to break into a series of tremors.

"Are you wet for me?" he whispered against her ear.

"Yes," she could barely make out the word.

"I don't believe you," he teased. He gathered the material of her dress, bunching it up around her hips. He dropped to his knees, pushing her legs apart as he moved.

Standing stock still, anticipating the feel of his lips on her, she braced herself by putting her hands in his hair. And holding on for dear life.

"You're beautiful," he whispered against her lace panties. Holding the dress out of his way, he put his teeth around the waistband of her underwear and pulled them down her thighs.

"Ryan," she clung to him as he let her panties slip to the floor. She stepped out of them and gasped when he brought them to his nose.

"You smell like ice cream." He smiled up at her. "I bet you taste like ice cream, too."

When he ducked his head between her thighs, she let out a moan. As his tongue began to work on her clit, she lost all logical thought. All she could do was feel. Feel him. He probed, he teased. He licked, sucked, all the while driving her insane.

"I want to fuck you," he whispered against her delicate flesh.

"Not here." Panic seized her voice. What if the people on the other side of the lake could see them? What if the people below on the streets looked up?

"Yes, here."

"No one will see us," he promised.

"But…"

"No. No buts. You are mine," he pulled her into him. "And I intend to have you."

His. She was aching, pulsing, wanting.

She closed her eyes, remembering her fantasy. Then she opened and looked into his eyes as he stared up at her.

He pulled himself back up and pushed her against the terrace railing before lifting her dress once more. The thought of being caught made her feel wicked and wild. The night breeze caught her scent carrying it up to her nose while the wind tickled her pussy, caressing it like a lover.

"Not here," she protested again, the thought of their last encounter against a railing flashing through her mind.

"Why not?"

"Your porch," she reminded him.

He laughed before sweeping her into his arms. "I had forgotten about that."

"Well I hadn't. And I don't wish to be splattered against the sidewalk."

"We'd land in the water."

"Whatever. Can we take this inside?"

"You know how to ruin a moment," he teased before kicking open the door and carrying her inside.

The bedroom was as romantic as the rest of the place. Though he had foregone the rose petals, Ryan had lit several candles, casting a beautiful glow across the antique bed. The room was nice, but her main focus was on the man whose arms were wrapped around her in a way that threatened to destroy every last bit of resistance she may have had. She needed more from him than an apology and amazing sex. She needed commitment.

When he lowered her to the bed and her skin came into contact with the soft covering, her need for him overpowered everything else. They could talk in the morning. Or later tonight. Right now, she wanted to feel him. Her fingers worked at his tie, revealing his golden skin bit by bit as she removed it and then opened his shirt buttons.

She sucked in her breath and bit her bottom lip when he rose above her, giving her access, letting her hands roam across his chest. He had the most amazing chest. The combination of his cologne and sheer maleness was enough to send her senses into overdrive, permeating her brain and her body with his intoxicating aroma. She dipped her head in for a taste of his skin, inhaling as she ran her tongue along his hardened muscles.

He visibly shook when she made contact, only delighting her even further. He didn't speak, but she heard the sharp intake of breath when her teeth captured first one nipple and then the other. Surrender. He was surrendering to her, she knew. This was all part of the apology, of the realization that there was more going on than either of them thought, wasn't it? Otherwise, a man like Ryan LeJeune wouldn't be able to give up control the way he was now.

Testing him, she pulled him into her, letting his skin rub against her dress while she slowly rolled him onto his back. She'd like to see him surrender control just as she had. Opening his shirt more fully, she began her exploration anew, first teasing his neck and then moving down to his nipples. She sat astride him, feeling the heat coming from his crotch as his cock pressed against her through his pants. It was time for him to be completely naked.

The fireworks started somewhere in the background, the first explosion causing her breath to catch in her throat and her fingers to still. She laughed, realizing it was silly to be afraid of a couple of loud noises. She ran her tongue down to his navel before unbuttoning his pants and slipping her hand inside.

His cock was more than ready for exploration, practically jumping when her hand closed around it. He groaned, causing her to smile. She dared look up at him, knowing looking into his eyes could make or break the moment. Eye to eye contact was a very intimate gesture. Would he look away? No, he didn't. His eyes held hers as she began massaging his length, running her hands slowly up and down, caressing the tip then going lower to where it connected.

She wanted to stroke him, make him come with her hand, but first she wanted him undressed. Her hand felt cold when she pulled it from his pants and moved down to remove his shoes and socks. Throwing them into a pile on the floor, she pulled his pants down and tossed them aside as well. He'd foregone underwear, a concept she found to be extremely exciting.

"Now, what should I do with you?" she teased as she climbed back up his body and trapped his legs, holding them to the bed with her weight.

"What do you want to do with me?" His voice was sexy and low, causing another delightful shiver to run through her body.

He gasped when she took him into her mouth without warning, rewarding her with the response she'd hoped for. She cupped his balls with one hand while she stroked his shaft with the other, all the while working her tongue around the head of his cock. Her new power was making her even wetter than she had been before. Moaning as she took him further into her mouth, she began grinding herself against his legs, wishing she'd had the forethought to take off her clothes before she began.

Taking him into her mouth as deep as she could, she began moving him in and out, taking him deep and then releasing all but the very tip then taking him in again. Her head bobbed up and down and her hips writhed in circles as she continued to pleasure him, and herself. Her clit stood at attention, having been rubbed against his hard legs, and her orgasm was on the brink of exploding right along with the fireworks. When she finally felt herself teetering on the edge, she released his cock and pulled her dress off over her head.

Taking control of him had been too much. Now, she wanted to give him control, wanted him on top of her, inside her. He sat up, as if he instinctually knew what she needed. She clung to him while they changed positions with him on top of her, his bare chest brushing against hers.

She opened for him when he lowered himself to her. His penis pressed against her wetness, asking for an invitation. When she arched her back, granting permission, he drove himself into her.

"Look at me," he coaxed.

When she looked into his eyes, she knew she would never be the same. He had transformed her, making her need him in a way she'd never needed anyone before. She saw her soul reflected in there and knew that the only thing she wanted was to be with him.

"I love you," she whispered against his skin as he moved slowly inside her. He didn't answer, but she knew he had to feel the same way. She felt it in his slow movements, in the way he took his time bringing her to the edge with his hands, his mouth, his cock. There was nothing rushed this time.

She held onto him, almost afraid to let go as he drove her to a place she'd never known before. She moaned, delighting in the way it sounded to moan against him. To be merged with him. To have her juices flowing all around him, whispering a seductive melody as they squeezed and flowed and slid around him.

"I'm gonna come," he grunted.

"Come inside me," she begged.

When his orgasm shot out against her inner walls, she swore she whispered her love to him again. As she arched her back into him, she thought she heard the words on the air between them. But she couldn't have said it. He may have apologized to her tonight, may have taken her beyond the edge of anywhere she'd ever gone before, but he didn't tell her he loved her back.

* * * * *

There's a saying in Louisiana. If you don't like the weather, wait. It'll be different tomorrow. Summer was thunderstorm season, and this latest one had come up during the night with practically no warning. Eight A.M. looked more like midnight by the time Ryan rolled out of bed. Laura was already in the shower if the sound of running water was any indication.

He let out a groan when his feet hit the cold, wooden floor. The real world was going to close back in on him today. Last night may have been the most amazing night of his life, but today nothing had changed. He was still on the verge of losing his business, even if Blake swore he'd be back in town before the end of the month. And his sugar deal with Laura had fallen through, thanks to a flaw in his formula. And then there was that matter of his heart.

He loved Laura. He knew he did. But something inside him protested last night when she whispered the words to him. Maybe it was fear of committing another marital mistake. Maybe it was fear of that soft look in her eyes when she said it. Whatever it was, it prevented him from returning the words, something he knew she both needed and expected.

They were more than lovers. What they shared, few people on earth had experienced. Making love to her was like coming home, in a good way, not in the coming-home-and-the-electricity-is-off way. In a way that made everything feel good and right and new. But he still couldn't say the words.

He listened as the shower turned off. He'd have to face her now and face what he couldn't say. Watching her walk into the room, knowing she expected it was one of the most difficult things he'd ever done. And she looked magnificent this morning with her hair up in a blue towel and her face freshly scrubbed.

"Good morning," she said with what he thought sounded like a hint of iciness in her tone.

"Good morning," he smiled, but he knew a smile wasn't what she wanted. Why did women have to be so needy? Why couldn't they just accept sex and all that went along with it without demanding a commitment?

"You sleep well?"

She hadn't touched him yet, hadn't moved in for a morning kiss. His first response to her question was yeah, he slept like a baby snuggled in her arms. His brain protested. Why hadn't she kissed him? "I slept fine. Did you?"

"Yeah. I had a dream last night."

Here we go. *Dreaming of you and me and babies.* Let's hear it. "Oh?"

"Yeah. And I know what's wrong with your formula. I can fix it."

"Oh? How do you know what's in the formula?"

"I saved it from the trash that day that you got so mad," she shrugged.

"And you dug it out?" He folded his arms, knowing he should be angry, but the only thing he wanted to do right now was hold her.

"Yeah. So if you don't mind," she grabbed her dress from last night, "I'm going to go to the lab today."

"It's storming outside." He tried not to protest too loudly, but none of this was how he had it played out in his mind.

"I know. It storms all the time. Besides, I'm sure you have work to do today, too."

"It's Saturday." How could she want to work all day when the only thing he wanted to do was snuggle up next to her?

"I know, but if I can get the formula fixed today and get the new ice cream into the freezer, it'll save us some time." She pulled her dress on and took her wet hair down from the towel. "Tell me you brought a brush with you."

He pointed to the dresser, trying to hide his disappointment. He felt like a rejected teenager thanks to the huge lump growing inside his chest. His eyes were on her back as she worked the brush through her mass of wet hair. He wanted his fingers there, wanted to pull her back into bed with him.. Wanted to keep her here.

"I'll come by your place later, okay?"

"Sure. I mean, I should be there." He knew he had nowhere else to go, but he wanted to leave her wondering. "Are you sure you don't want to stay just until the storm blows over?"

"I'll be fine, Ryan. I grew up here, remember? A little thunder never hurt anybody."

When she leaned in to kiss him, he wanted to pull her into him, hold onto her forever. Instead, he sat stone still as she brushed her lips against him. He didn't move until he heard the door slam.

Laura tried to put last night out of her mind and just get down to business today. The truth was, she needed to get away from Ryan as soon as she possibly could. Last night had been amazing. She walked through the rain to her car, which Ryan had moved for her last night, parking it just outside the townhouse. She sat there for a minute, just staring ahead, wondering what exactly she had expected from him.

She knew she meant something to him. She had to. If she didn't, she wasn't sure how she'd go on. Okay, so he hadn't told her he loved her. Did she really expect him to do it so soon? Guys didn't work like that, did they? They had to take time to analyze a situation, ignore their instincts and examine everything until it all but fell apart due to the scrutiny.

She took in a deep breath. The last thing she wanted to do was go to the lab today. Besides, she already had the solution to Ryan's problem. She knew the work she had done on the formula was sufficient. As for her feelings for him, there was no solution to that problem. And she didn't know what to say to him this morning. So, she decided to give him an out. She'd leave gracefully and if he came after her, she'd figure out what to do from there. If he didn't...He had to, didn't he?

Her house was cold and empty this morning, making her wish she'd stayed in the cozy townhouse with Ryan. She dropped her keys on the table by the door and made her way to her bedroom to change into something more suitable for work. Jeans and a T-shirt would do, especially since she had no idea what she'd do once she got there. A few solutions came to mind, none of which were definite. What she'd need to do was try each one and see what worked. And surely one of them would. If not, Ryan could always sell the sugar as a soft drink sweetener. It would sell like crazy in the South for iced tea.

The rain was really picking up and the thunder and lightning were increasing. When the last bolt of lightning streaked across the sky, she counted, waiting for the thunder, but she knew the answer already, knew that the worst of the storm was right overhead. Still, she didn't want to be at home alone all day. Her every instinct told her to turn back and head for Ryan's place, give him a chance to tell her he loved her, but her stubborn streak wasn't ready for a disappointment right now.

An amazing night should be enough for her. She didn't *need* a commitment. She wasn't that kind of woman, was she?

She passed the turn off to Ryan's house, a little dirt road off the side of the main dirt road, both of which were more red mud now than anything else. And fought every instinct that told her to turn off, go see if he was home. Just as she rounded the next curve, she realized she wasn't going any further.

"Great." Apparently, somebody had plans for her today that didn't involve going to the lab. A giant pine tree lay across the road, blocking access into town. This was the downfall of living down a country road on the outskirts of town with one way in and one way out.

She managed to turn the car around without getting it stuck or running into the ditch, but by the time she made it back to Ryan's turn off, the rain had picked up so much that she couldn't see in front of her face. Her windshield wipers were useless. She muttered a curse before giving in.

"Okay, okay, I'll go see if he's home."

"Laura, you're soaked." Ryan opened the screen door and pulled her into the house.

"I'm fine," she protested, allowing him to lead her into the living room.

"What the hell are you doing? I thought you were in town." He placed her by the sofa just as the lights flickered off. "Stay here. I'll find you something dry to wear."

Rummaging through Blake's clothes, he came up with a pair of

sweatpants that would be way too big and a Ragin' Cajuns T-shirt. He also grabbed a couple of towels from the bathroom.

"Here." He handed the pile to her, trying to hide his relief at seeing her. Ever since the storm picked up, he fought every urge he had to either drive out to her place or drive into town and find her. "You can just step into the kitchen to change if you want. It'll be easier than trying to maneuver the stairs in the dark. Here," he dug a flashlight from a drawer and handed it to her, avoiding skin-on-skin contact.

She nodded and obeyed. "Thanks. I didn't realize the storm had gotten so bad."

"Shit," he raked a hand through his hair, gripped with panic now that he knew she was okay. He should have gone out and checked on her earlier. "Are you sure you're okay?" he called.

"Fine," she called out just before coming back into the room. "These are nice," she held out her arms and then showed him her very well covered legs.

"They're Blake's. I figured they'd be too big. Come here, let's get you warmed up," he moved to pull her into his arms, but she ducked.

"I'm fine. Really. I came over because there's a tree in the road and I couldn't go anywhere else."

His heart sank. He wanted her to be here because she wanted to be with him, wanted him to protect her from the storm. That wasn't like Laura, though. She could protect herself. He wanted to pull her into him and tell her he loved her. He was ready now to say the words he couldn't say last night. Having her standing in front of him was all the encouragement he needed. Everything inside him had changed this morning when she left, forcing him to admit that she was the one. "You didn't have to have a tree in the way to come over."

"There was no need for you to rush to my rescue." Her sarcasm bit into him, and he flinched at her words.

"It's not like that. I just assumed…"

"Yeah, well I'm fine. Wet, but fine."

"I'm glad you're here. We need to talk." He shoved his hands into his pockets. Where to begin? There was so much he needed to tell her. So many things he needed to know. Did she really love him?

"Yeah we do."

This didn't sound good. He started toward the kitchen. "Let me get you some coffee or something."

"Do you have any tea?"

"Yeah. I do. And a gas stove, so you're in luck."

"Ryan, I need to talk to you. About your formula."

He motioned for her to sit at the table. "I don't want to talk about that. I want to talk about us."

"I lied earlier. I've been playing around with the formula since the day you left it. And I have the solution."

"Oh." Why would she lie about something like that?

"I told you that so I could leave. I wanted to have a graceful exit, so I told you I was going to the lab. The truth is…" She stopped and looked up at him. He saw the tears building in her eyes.

"Stop, Laura. You don't have to explain. I just need to know something."

"What's that?"

That ache in his chest was growing. She told him last night that she loved him. Why he was afraid of asking, he wasn't sure. "Last night. Did you, uh, mean that?"

"Mean what?"

It felt as if she were twisting a knife into his heart. He crossed the kitchen, the tea forgotten, and sank to his knees. "I'm in love with you." The words came out before he could stop himself, but the heaviness in his heart instantly lifted. It felt good to be honest with her about his feelings. Now, if she would repeat those words to him, everything would be fine.

"Are you sure?"

"Yeah, I am. And I hope you love me, too." He looked into her eyes as he spoke, searching for an answer in there somewhere, hoping the mask she wore would soften. A tear rolled down her cheek just before she slid down onto the floor next to him.

"I do love you, too. I just didn't want you to think I expected anything out of you."

"Even if you did?"

"Even if I did."

He stood and pulled her to her feet, hauling her flush against him, cupping her ass in his hands, grinding her with his cock, which had been loaded and ready practically from the second she set foot in the house.

Her mouth opened for him, allowing him to probe inside. Allowing him to fill her with the love he felt for her. She twisted her fingers into his hair, capturing him and holding him hostage with her kiss. He loved the way her hands felt in his hair, the way she deepened the kiss. Everything about her.

"Your kettle's boiling," she pulled away when the whistle sounded.

"To hell with it," he mumbled as he took her lips with his.

He had never been good at showing emotions. Especially not when they were this deep. To tell the truth, he'd never felt anything like this before. And it had scared him more than a little to have her tell him she loved him last night.

"I love you, Ryan LeJeune," she whispered against his lips.

"And I love you."

Ryan pulled her behind him as they made their way up the stairs to his bedroom. When they made it to the door, her hand ran down his arm, causing him to come undone. He turned, capturing her in his arms.

"Come here," he let out a soft grumble, pulling her even harder, more flush against him. His cock pressed against her stomach, announcing his intentions.

He lowered his lips to hers, gently at first and then with savage abandon. When he inhaled, he breathed in her. Not her scent, her essence. They stumbled back toward the bed and fell into a heap, her on top, him clawing at her clothing.

When she finally lay naked beneath him, he raised himself up so he could really look at her. She was the most amazing woman he had ever known.

"Are you ready for me?" his tone was soft, belying the savage instinct gripping him. He didn't want to make love to her. He wanted to possess her, own her. He wanted to leave his mark on her and make her his forever. But looking down into her face, he knew more than anything else that he wanted to cherish her.

He took her, moving himself slowly into her body, savoring the feel of his dick sliding deeper, deeper into her wet depths. She ran her nails up his back, causing him to stop mid motion. He wanted this to last all night.

"Laura," he begged, hoping she would heed his warning. Instead, she dug her nails deeper, urging him to take her harder.

Plunging into her body, there was no return as she spread herself open for him, holding her lips apart while he pushed himself in deeper, pulling his dick back out almost to the tip and then pushing back in. Her hands skimmed his flesh with every motion as his balls slapped against them.

She moaned, begging him to take her higher. Begging him to come inside her.

Gripping her hips, he settled in before beginning his invasion anew. This time, she was his. He crushed against her forcefully, and she met his every motion, rocking her hips, her pussy, her entire body.

"I'm gonna come," she moaned. His only response was a grunt.

His cock quivered as it shot out a release deep inside of her body. She shook and quaked, meeting his frenzied pace.

Ryan lay spent, his breath coming in slow, shallow spurts. "You're going to be the death of me."

"No, I won't," she snuggled next to him and pulled his arm around her. "I'm here to save you."

He let out a laugh. "You sure about that?"

She nodded. "Pretty sure. I can save your company, your house if you'll let me."

"How can you do that?"

"I told you. I fixed the formula."

"Oh," he smiled sheepishly. "I kind of forgot that important detail last night. I owe you so much."

"You don't owe me anything. I did it for us, for you. To save your company, like I said."

"What about the rest of me?" He turned to look at her in the candlelight and ran a hand down her cheek. "Will you save the rest of me?"

"I don't think it needs saving," she smiled.

"More than you know." He turned onto his back and pulled her fully into his arms. "Laura, I love you. I want to be with you."

She caressed the cinnamon hairs on his chest, paying close attention to his heartbeat. "I love you, too."

"Will you marry me? I mean, I don't have any money or anything. I can't even buy you a ring. But I want you to be my wife."

"Yes, I'll marry you. On one condition."

"What's that?"

"You admit the fudge ripple affected you."

He laughed. "Damn near killed me."

He pulled her closer. This was exactly where he was supposed to be.

Epilogue

Laura sat looking out of the window of her office in New Orleans. The city looked alive beneath her. Cars packed the streets and people filed along the sidewalks. She turned when Cate walked in.

"Are you sure you want to do this?" It was only the fiftieth time Cate had asked this same question.

"Yes, I'm sure. Come on, you're the business whiz kid, even if you dress more like Britney Spears than a CEO."

"Well, I'm not a CEO. And I'm not going to take your place for permanent. Just for now, okay?"

"I plan on taking leave until well after the baby is born." She patted her increasing girth and smiled. Who would have thought six months ago that she would be sitting in her own New Orleans office, married, pregnant, blissfully happy?

"Then I go back to marketing, right?"

"Yes, then you go back to marketing." Laura rolled her eyes. There had been so many changes inside her company and Ryan's in the past six months, it was hard to keep up with who was doing what. Amanda and Nick were now running the ice cream business full time, Karen and Robin were working with Jeremy at the Ryan's company and she and Ryan were basically just sitting back and watching it all unfold. She had turned marketing over to Cate, who would much rather be doing that than operating the business office in New Orleans.

Laura really wished Cate would consider using her inherent knowledge to take control of the company. She resisted, though, insisting that she didn't want to run a big company like *LeJeune Industries* had become. Laura knew that it was mostly because she missed all the free ice cream afforded her in the past. "You can still eat all the ice cream you want here, you know?"

"I know," Cate sighed, "it's just not the same. I mean, here I am in the big city, you'd think it would be every girl's dream. But there's something missing."

"I know how you feel." Laura remembered those same emotions crossing through her before she met Ryan.

"So, how is the happy husband?"

Laura smiled. "Well taken care of. Especially now that his business isn't in danger anymore. Merging the two was the second…third best thing we ever did."

"Let me guess what the first two were."

"Well, let me know if you need anything, okay? You know we're not that far away."

"I know. And Dusty flies in almost every day now, so if I need anything extra, I'll have him bring it by." Dusty had been named official delivery person and kept both companies stocked. He also occasionally carried paperwork back and forth between the two businesses and their main headquarters.

"I wish Ryan would have agreed to keep headquarters in Oak Creek."

"I know, but he's right. To be competitive right now, you need to be in the heart of business. And when you let me open my ice cream shop downtown, we'll be bringing it straight to the customers this way and via mail."

"You're right. I guess I just hate to spend my time between the two places."

"I know, but your apartment here is really nice. And you've got a big house back home. By the way, how is the *Fudge Ripple* promotion coming along?"

"Actually, I thought I'd hand it over to you. I'm due in three months and we plan to begin distribution by summer. Think you can handle it on top of keeping track with things here?"

Cate smiled, "Sure, not a problem. I can interview models during my breaks."

"Why would you interview models?"

"Don't you think we need a spokesman for the best thing since *Viagra*?"

Laura rolled her eyes, "I figured you'd see an upside to it."

"You bet."

A light knock came on the door, followed by it opening. Ryan stepped through it, the smile on his face going all the way up to his eyes. Laura had never seen him smile so much as he had since she told him about the baby. She stood and crossed the rooms, going into his open arms.

"You ready?"

"Yeah. I think we're through here." She gave him a short kiss, but the look in her eyes promised much more to come later. She turned to Cate, "It's all yours."

"I'll make you proud."

"I know you will."

"And, Laura, I'm serious about the *Fudge Ripple* promotion."

"I figured you were."

They hugged quickly before either of them could start crying. Laura knew this would be her last trip to New Orleans until well after the baby was born. She would miss Cate and her new office. But she was more than happy to stay in Oak Creek and spend time with Ryan, something they rarely got to do since the merger. All their free time had been spent either preparing the business for Laura's leave of absence or preparing for the baby.

"Blake's downstairs," Ryan said into her ear. "He says he's driving us home."

"Did you tell him we were taking a plane?"

"Yeah. Dusty's psyched about the lease of that little airplane we got him."

"Well, it's a business expense. We'll write it off."

He pulled her into the hall. "Have I told you today how much I love you?"

"No, I don't think you have."

"Come here and let me show you, then."

His lips covered hers and their bodies pressed as closely together as they could. Laura felt the baby kick, and, judging by the smile that interrupted the kiss, Ryan felt it, too. His hand slid down her body to rest on her stomach. She closed her eyes, reveling in the sensation. From now on, everything was going to be wonderful.

About the author:

Alicia's interest in romance began as a child when she used to hide out reading her mom's forbidden romance novels. She remembers very distinctly the first time she ever read *Gone with the Wind* and was instantly hooked on the concept of the Southern gentlemanly rake. She likes to think that there's a little bit of Rhett in all of her heroes, whether they be sexy cowboys or dark and brooding rock stars.

Always writing against a soundtrack, Alicia finds inspiration for her cowboys and contemporary heroes from country musicians such as Kenny Chesney. Her love for the gothadelic sounds of Type O Negative has inspired several vampire stories and stories about tragically beautiful musicians. Other inspirations include the music of Saliva, Van Halen, Santana, Blake Shelton, and Prince. (She's a Gemini. That explains the wide variety of influences!)

Alicia has completed several manuscripts ranging from comedic contemporaries to dark, sexy paranormals and fantastical futuristics.

Her favorite ice cream is Godiva's dark chocolate truffle. Eaten straight from the container, it is almost—almost—as good as reading erotica!

Alicia welcomes mail from readers. You can write to her c/o Ellora's Cave Publishing at 1337 Commerce Drive, Suite 13, Stow OH 44224.

Also by Alicia Sparks:

Dragon's Law Mace - Ellora's Cavemen: Tales from the Temple II

If you enjoyed this book you may want to check out these books coming to print soon at Ellora's Cave Publishing, Inc.
Available now in eBook format at
www.ellorascave.com

Why an electronic book?

We live in the Information Age—an exciting time in the history of human civilization in which technology rules supreme and continues to progress in leaps and bounds every minute of every hour of every day. For a multitude of reasons, more and more avid literary fans are opting to purchase e-books instead of paperbacks. The question to those not yet initiated to the world of electronic reading is simply: *why?*

1. *Price.* An electronic title at Ellora's Cave Publishing runs anywhere from 40-75% less than the cover price of the <u>exact same title</u> in paperback format. Why? Cold mathematics. It is less expensive to publish an e-book than it is to publish a paperback, so the savings are passed along to the consumer.

2. *Space.* Running out of room to house your paperback books? That is one worry you will never have with electronic novels. For a low one-time cost, you can purchase a handheld computer designed specifically for e-reading purposes. Many e-readers are larger than the average handheld, giving you plenty of screen room. Better yet, hundreds of titles can be stored within your new library—a single microchip. (Please note that Ellora's Cave does not endorse any specific brands. You can check our website at www.ellorascave.com for customer

     recommendations we make available to new consumers.)

3. *Mobility.* Because your new library now consists of only a microchip, your entire cache of books can be taken with you wherever you go.

4. *Personal preferences are accounted for.* Are the words you are currently reading too small? Too large? Too...**ANNOYING**? Paperback books cannot be modified according to personal preferences, but e-books can.

5. *Innovation.* The way you read a book is not the only advancement the Information Age has gifted the literary community with. There is also the factor of what you can read. Ellora's Cave Publishing will be introducing a new line of interactive titles that are available in e-book format only.

6. *Instant gratification.* Is it the middle of the night and all the bookstores are closed? Are you tired of waiting days—sometimes weeks—for online and offline bookstores to ship the novels you bought? Ellora's Cave Publishing sells instantaneous downloads 24 hours a day, 7 days a week, 365 days a year. Our e-book delivery system is 100% automated, meaning your order is filled as soon as you pay for it.

Those are a few of the top reasons why electronic novels are displacing paperbacks for many an avid reader. As always, Ellora's Cave Publishing welcomes your questions and comments. We invite you to email us at service@ellorascave.com or write to us directly at: 1337 Commerce Drive, Suite 13, Stow OH 44224.